Praise for C

***Carry Me Close* is wondrous!** With deft strokes of the pen, its author has created **a beautifully-layered love story** of two hurting souls set in 19th century Australia and Oregon. Though it's rare a final book in a series is the **diamond in its diadem**, moving a reader to commit precious space on her keeper shelf to it and its predecessors, Dorothy Adamek's third offering in her Blue Wren Shallows series delivers ~ **a gem that does the nearly impossible in striking an exquisitely subtle balance between fiction and poetry.**

~Tamara Leigh,
USA Today Bestselling Author of the Age of Conquest & Age of Honor Series

Once again, Dorothy Adamek's **delightful storytelling transports us** back to the enchanting Blue Wren House nestled on Phillip Island for a third captivating story set in the late 1870s. This time we fall in love with Viola and Silas in **a beautiful story of loss, heartache, forgiveness and redemption.** The visually stunning imagery and deeply resonating characters make ***Carry Me Close*** a wonderful addition to the ***Carry Me*** Series.

~ Ian Acheson
Author of *Angelguard*

Praise for Carry Me Home

In ***Carry Me Home***, Dorothy Adamek gives a familiar tale a fresh Australian twist. **With gripping characters, a playful romance, delightful writing and heart-rending moments, this novel held me tight and would not let me go.** Why, this gifted writer even makes mud romantic! A sterling debut!

~ Sarah Sundin
Award-winning Author of *Through Waters Deep*

As irresistible and winsome as a Phillip Island sunset, Dorothy Adamek's ***Carry Me Home*** is **beautifully written and a lyrical portrayal of the powers of forgiveness.**

~ Siri Mitchell
Author of *Like a Flower in Bloom*

Reading Dorothy Adamek's debut novel is a walk with friends from the cliffs to the sea. **Each word is profound – shells lovingly placed by the author to be gathered and kept.** When you reach the shore, you do it with tears in your eyes and a realization that you are changed.

~ Joanne Bischof
Award-winning Author of *This Quiet Sky*

Praise for Carry Me Away

Riveting and masterfully written, ***Carry Me Away*** will do just that, immersing you in a devastating storm, a historic shipwreck, and the idyllic hideaway of Phillip Island in Australia. These flesh and blood characters are so finely crafted they feel more like friends, each winning your heart in unique, soul-stretching ways. **A poignant, oft suspenseful and thoroughly romantic journey** through the valleys of loss and grief to the heights of healing and hope.

~ Laura Frantz
Christy Award-winning Author of *The Lacemaker*

A **gorgeously written and skillfully rendered** tale of rescue, redemption, and the courage required to love.

~ Siri Mitchell
Author of *Château of Echoes*

Gorgeous and gripping, ***Carry Me Away* is a novel you won't forget.** Ada and Tom's deep attraction and clashing needs create a poignant love story, and **Dorothy Adamek writes about grief and love in a way that is palpable and heartfelt.** But the ending – oh the ending! So sweet and triumphant and affirming that I want to tell everyone – except I want you to discover it for yourself. Let the lovely writing carry you away to picturesque Phillip Island, and be swept away by Tom and Ada's tale.

~ Sarah Sundin
Award-winning and best-selling Author of *The Sea Before Us* and *The Sky Above Us*

Carry Me Away is **another beautiful tale from the imagination and heart of Dorothy Adamek.** This Australian-born storyteller had me at the first line and secured her hold on me with a hero worth rooting for. Based on true events of a late 19th century shipwreck off the coast near Melbourne, **this lyrical, heartfelt journey of two battered souls** finding healing redemption and love will keep the pages turning – as will lush descriptions sure to make readers want to take a trip Down Under.

~ Tamara Leigh
USA Today Bestselling Author of the Age of Faith &
Age of Conquest series

Richly poetic in the tradition of Lori Benton and Laura Frantz, with the sensory prose of Joanne Bischof, ***Carry Me Away*** **masters impeccable research with a stunning love story.** The sea-swept canvas of Phillip Island offers a vibrant backdrop to Tom and Ada's unexpected adventure and resonant themes of faith and endurance amidst tragedy and loss. A beautiful companion to Adamek's fresh debut, ***Carry Me Away*** is **an intelligent treatise on the nature of rebuilding, of forgiving and of finally finding home.**

~ Rachel McMillan
Author of *Rose in Three Quarter Time*

Carry Me Close

DOROTHY ADAMEK

Carry Me Close

First printing April 2022
Print Edition

ISBN 978-0-9944572-6-4

Cover Model ~ Sophie Cutler
Cover Photography by Jason Lau Photography
Cover Design by Emilie Haney of EAH Creative

To my incredible and resilient lockdown companions,

John Adamek,

Sophie and James Cutler,

Tom Adamek and Matt Adamek.

Thank you for sharing life's adventures with me.

Acknowledgments

*We **read** to know we are not alone. C.S. Lewis*

Those of us who ***write***, do so with the same longing.

On the storyteller's road, I am blessed to look up and find beautiful souls who accompany me for short stints, each one with their own lantern of wisdom and love. Generous and kind-hearted, they have become my most reliable sources of compassion, insight, and good cheer, and, turn by turn, have walked with me, right to very last page.

My grateful thanks to Ian Acheson, Meaghan Arnold, and Kerry-Lee Harney for their early reader feedback. You tenderly held ***Carry Me Close*** when it was only a whisper and fed courage into my author heart to press on. Thank you for your precious time and careful thoughts.

Patti Jones and Katie Donovan, meticulous proofreaders and most valued early readers, I am so grateful for your bright instincts.

Tamara Leigh, fellow author, endorser, and friend, you know the road ahead and shine a beacon for me to follow. Your generous spirit equips me each day and I would be lost without you.

Matthew Collicot, thank you for your woodworking expertise and resource recommendations. Julee Schwarzburg, thank you for your expert editing. Emilie Hendryx Haney, thank you for wrapping my stories in stunning covers that I adore, and special thanks to my darling daughter, Sophie Cutler ~ beautiful cover-girl for all three books in the Blue Wren Shallows series.

Phillip Island bookseller, Lois Gaskin, thank you for the window at *Turn The Page* bookshop where you first displayed my books, and where you've introduced them to new readers, summer after summer. Locals and visitors, we are all enriched by your legacy.

Darren and Fiona Haymes, thank you for the many years of support, vision building, and the rolling green hills of our every-growing friendship. Many thanks to my brother, Con Tassios, who is the digital mastermind behind my website and directs the many ways in which I am able to deliver my stories.

Grateful thanks to Kerryn Tepe, as ever, the sister God gave me when I needed her most.

Eternal thanks to my beloved husband, John, partner of my dreams *and* dreaming partner. Nothing happens without you and I would have it no other way.

And to you, dear reader, I offer my most heartfelt gratitude. Polishing a story for you during the pandemic years of 2020 and 2021 was the greatest privilege. In a time of solitude and uncertainty, crafting Silas and Viola's romance shaped my days. Knowing you'd one day journey with them filled it with purpose.

To God be the glory.

Absence, hear thou my protestation
Against thy strength,
Distance and length;
Do what thou canst for alteration,
For hearts of truest mettle
Absence doth join and Time doth settle.

—John Donne

Star and Garter Tavern, Melbourne, Australia, August 31, 1873

There's a trail of ants on your face today, dear Clemmie. They mimic the audacity of the Star and Garter patrons whose greasy fingers stray along your gilded frame. 'Until tomorrow,' *they slur in superstitious farewell. To ensure a swift return for more of this plundered main attraction.*

You. Sweet Clementine. Aged nineteen. Standing tall in the shallows, leaning on your ledge of sea rock, dark currents rising.

This is what comes from hanging a portrait in a simple Melbourne tavern. I can just reach your smile with the duster if I climb along the outside of this staircase and lean as far as I dare before toppling below. And if you are to be restored, a woman like you needs a girl like me to defy every weak limb.

In the basement kitchen, Derry's stoking the fire. He let me in, but he's too busy to talk. There's flour to sift, and Cloda's chopping a mountain of onions. In their office, Mr. Barnes and Jasper count profits exchanged for spirits and dreams by the parched who come here. Hungry for the girl before we broke you.

Me, well, I return to study. And wonder afresh how light and mystery could embody the same painted vision.

I never tire of the way life flashes in your eyes. The spark of copper in your hair. The way an artist's brush captures the diaphanous wrap you hold loose around your plump nakedness beneath.

The ants though, they're as innocent as you. And like me, they're following crumbs that lead to nowhere. Allowed in, because Mr. Barnes needs you and tolerates me, his guilt buried where he cannot afford to dig it up.

But one day, I'll convince him to set you free. And no one will look upon your folly anymore. I'll visit every other day. Catch the cobwebs. Dust the frame.

And I shall paint my own collections. Watercolours worthy of competition First Place ribbons that will rip us from where we are now nailed, and into a kinder future.

Because second place never rescued anyone.

I

Six Years Later, March, 1879

Viola Buckley stormed home through Melbourne's hot, dusty streets. Laden with half a dozen Mariani tonic bottles, her gathering basket dug into her flesh. It may as well have been a load of bricks she carted in the crook of her arm. Still, she pounded the sun-drenched cobbles and turned into Palmer Street, Fitzroy.

As ever, her pace never outran the racing of her mind. If she were a bricklayer, perhaps their rented house would not list like a ship about to sink. She pushed past the front door that hung at odds with its frame, and if it wasn't plaster crumbling from badly laid ceilings, it was rain that pooled and dripped from the roof.

"Mother, I have your tonic," Viola called, but kept her stride until she sank onto the edge of her bed.

"*What do you see of God's creation? What makes you stop? How does it taste, and smell and feel? And the best question for you, mon Poupette, what story will it tell when you put it onto paper?*"

The counsel of Madame Nasrin, wardrobe mistress, art tutor, and dear friend pulled her in. Schooled to scavenge a world less cruel than the one her parents had brought her into, Viola had been roused each day to comb the natural world for treasures to behold with her budding artist's eye. A leaf. A feather. A gumnut.

Today, in her twenty-second year, she juggled six brown bottles from the apothecary. Slender yet potent, they dragged Mother through life with greater force than any other sedative at their disposal.

"Mother?" She slipped her painter's kit into its satchel. "Do you hear me?"

Mother did not reply, but Rosie from next door scrambled down their hallway. Dark hair plastered to her temples, a soggy apron round her middle, the woman offered Viola a predictable eyeroll.

"Aren't we both slow coaches today? I got waylaid collecting my last bundle of washing, but I'm here now, love. I won't be a minute settin' them coppers to re-boil, then I'll make your poor mum a cuppa and keep her company while she drinks it."

"Gossip wrapped in dirty laundry?" Viola teased.

"What else is there to ponder when I'm elbow deep at the troughs in that cluttered backyard we share? Not forgetting, it's tall-story-medicine I bring back for your mum. Almost as good as all that tonic she guzzles."

Viola gathered her gloves and hastened down the long hallway. Faded pomegranate reds repeated a threadbare pattern on the carpet runner that ran from the front door to the rear yard and Rosie's laundry business.

"Mother?" Viola knocked on the open bedroom door. "Rosie's starting the washing. And Madam Nasrin's waiting for me."

No one replied. In the stillness, the unmade iron bed slumped in the shadows.

"Francis Cane will be here for her lesson soon. Followed by the Sullivan sisters. You're not still napping, are you? There's time for a pot of tea first, but you'll have to hurry."

Water splashed from the pump in the lane off the backyard. And soon, the much-needed stream of girls would arrive for an hour of private piano lessons in the front room with her mother. Her absent mother. Where was she now?

Viola's seven art students, and eleven others who came for piano and singing lessons with her mother, made up the students of the Buckley Fine Arts Academy. An ambitious name. Desperate preservation drawn in bold strokes by an ageing music teacher adrift in the past, and a novice art teacher fixated on reclaiming their future.

"This is not a day for tardiness, dearest. I'm expected at the Botanic Gardens. Where are you?" The invisible war Viola always carried under her skin rioted a little louder. She could almost feel the petals in the lily pond opening, the leaves shimmering on the water.

In the pokey front room Mother called a drawing room, a grand piano, too audacious for a room so small, held a scattered mess of sheet music. Mother's pet galah, Balthazar, bobbed and shook his pink chest from his perch in a domed cage kept on a polished brass pedestal by the window.

"London Bridge is falling down,
Falling down, falling down,
London Bridge is falling down,
La la lady."

He sang in his birdy-voice, trained for performance when only a chick.

"Has ya mum done a runner on you again?" Wicker basket jammed atop her hip, Rosie stopped in the hallway. "She can't have gone far. Not with her sore ankle."

"And yet, she still seeks an audience." Viola regretted her tone almost immediately. "The poor love's breathing harder this week, isn't she? Hardly eating. Always fighting the memories."

When was the doctor due? Later, Viola would check her list named *Mother's Medical Needs.* Right now, nothing but the Amazonian lily mattered. The crowning piece in her portfolio, *The Exotics of Melbourne's Botanic Gardens.*

"Some days your mum's stronger than you think. Other days, the melancholy eats her alive. And, well," Rosie cringed, "hard as it is, love, ya still owe me for that small loan from last month."

Shame fired in Viola's cheeks. Tiny blazes. The wildfire of poverty and despair that threatened to engulf them every day.

"I'm sorry, Rosie." Viola shot her a sunken look. "The Sullivan girls will pay for another month's tuition today. And you know you can take anything from the dinner set if it's worth what I owe you."

"My eye's on the soup tureen. But I'd hate to strip away what's left. What are you painting this afternoon? Something to sell?"

"Something for my exhibition portfolio. A giant water lily. The *Victoria* amazonica." Viola checked herself in the hallway mirror, pulled her straw hat off and re-pinned some of her loose hair.

"I've painted the root tuber, the gargantuan leaves, and the flower buds, but today," she untangled her hat ribbons, "its white petals will open with the most intoxicating aroma, and one lucky beetle will nestle in its bosom overnight."

Rosie snorted but Viola continued. Her life depended on getting this right.

"Tomorrow, our lily will reopen in a breathtaking blush of pinks, release the beetle into the air, and slip herself into the pond, her skin marred by pollination in deep burgundy lashes."

"Viola!" Rosie recoiled. "My mother would scrub my mouth with wire bristles if I yammered on about plants with that kind of loose abandon." She blushed. Not unlike how Viola imagined the lily might.

But Viola would not apologize for nature. "It's a rare and recently discovered species. From the Amazon jungle. Created by God, and in no way a sordid tale. Named to honor Queen Victoria herself. Hardly loose."

She secured her hat. Thankfully, the botanical reproductive process no longer caused Viola any awkwardness. Naturally freckled skin and untamed strawberry blonde hair were trouble enough. As for reproduction, she knew about the mysterious allure of male and female plant parts with the precision of one who observed them with a glass magnifier.

"Botanical illustrators all over the world paint the lifecycle of plants. And anyone wanting to capture this rarity on paper will be there. Today. And tomorrow. After that, there's nothing left to see."

"A flower that lures stray beetles. The sordid tales continue."

Viola laughed. "I'll show you what I've sketched when I return, and then you can decide if it's scandalous. Now, have you seen my parasol?"

Rosie shook her head and turned for the courtyard. "Maybe *she* took it."

"Of course." Viola pivoted the other way.

The open front door let in the warm fragrance of wattles and the ring of industry thrown into the air by work crews from the nearby construction of the Exhibition Building. For almost two months now, raucous hammering had run down Palmer Street, rattling windows and layering them in dust that fell from the emerging structure.

Right here in Melbourne, and right on their doorstep. Which is where her sea-blue parasol normally hung, on a wrought iron hook by the door. But now that empty hook, like Mother's abandoned room, pushed Viola down the cracked tessellated pathway and into the street. She headed to the top of Palmer Street, where it intersected with the wider Nicholson Street.

Mother stood on the corner, propped by Viola's unopened parasol as if she presided over the works with a sword at her side.

"Have you forgotten your sprained ankle that isn't meant to bear any weight? Especially up a hill."

Or your students at the bottom of the hill, of whom we have desperate need?

Mother did not turn, so captivating the construction site. A vast ribcage of spaces and annexes loomed from the foundations. Already it dazzled. The scaffold of Viola's dreams. Next year it would host Melbourne's 1880 International Exhibition. Already, it hung before them with promise and filled her lungs with anticipation. One day, soon, under that domed roof, she would display her art. In a competition that would open doors and transform amateurs into winners.

A maddening kaleidoscope of butterflies beat for freedom against her ribcage. So delicate, and still enough to knock the breath from her as if it were the first time she considered it.

Winning entries went on to adorn book plates. Eclectic connoisseurs shelved them in private libraries for Natural History lovers who hungered for hidden spectacles that grew around them when no one but the artist was watching.

And winning entries elevated lives that teetered on poverty, and changed them forever.

"A twisted ankle never thwarted my ability to perform." Mother spoke without shifting her gaze from the construction.

Viola exhaled. Mother's old and often greedy dreams sucked the air from her every time. How could a woman once so elegant and poised, so adored, slip into this unraveled confusion?

Viola knew. And she winced at the reminder. Mother's daily application of Otto of Roses skin cream collided with the familiar smell of the Mariani Tonic prescribed for her nerves, the concoction that kept her enslaved in a miasma of wine and cocaine. Her linen-bound ankle added to the uneven steps that belonged to those who sought remedy for their deepest aches with a shot of lightning that only came in a glass.

"It is, in fact, a grand hall. Not a theatre. An exhibition building. And next year it will showcase famous artwork and display the newest most eye-popping discoveries you or I could imagine."

"And once the spectacle is dismantled, what will fill a domed cavern so majestic?" Mother tapped the parasol on the cobbled street and faced Viola. "I'll tell you what should. Music and performance. Theatre people, like us, and their eager audiences."

She caressed Viola's cheek. "Such rushing to sit still and paint. If only this beautiful, exotic, unforgettable face desired to draw a real audience, we could have…" She tapped Viola's freckled cheeks in various spots to emphasize each word.

Beautiful. Exotic. Unforgettable.

Viola straightened. There was no 'we' anymore. Mother's mind had tripped as sure as her foot had.

"Come now, your music students will be upon us any minute."

Mother's shoulders slumped and the weary face of the once-loved vaudeville actress shifted into the shadows of an abandoned, now injured, piano teacher. Groomed like a showbird thanks to her favorite hairpiece, she no longer needed her trademark wigs, but she never strayed too far from what she'd lost. She wore this one, this last golden piece of her old, costumed self, like a shield.

"Promise me it's only flowers. No portraits. No sinking into people's souls through their eyes."

"You know it's botanicals, dearest. You have my word."

Construction clanged with the urgency of hammers nailing fortune into time, and Viola turned them homeward.

To a singing galah and a house full of irreplaceable, fast disappearing treasures, in the shadow of a building that rang with Mother's misplaced longings and Viola's petal-thin dreams.

On the corner of Williams and Bourke, the Menzies Hotel rose into a three-story Italianate-style building. It boasted a coffeehouse, and Silas Swift was not one to ignore a fresh cup. What they'd served on board the *Clara* was a poor imitation.

From his seat at the public dining room table, he drank in the Melbourne sky from the generous hotel windows like a parched man stepping into a shimmering mirage. Six months of gray skies and rainy days each year was what he knew. But here in Australia, sun-bleached boulevards radiated in ways the streets of his hometown of Portland, Oregon, never did.

Not like this.

No sir. Not in March, and never in the fall. This upside-down country he'd sailed into courted him with light and warmth that bore into his cold bones.

The Melbourne newspaper wrote of a cricket match. And a traveling circus on its last night in town, and how it would be prudent not to miss the spectacle. But Silas had not sailed the Pacific for acrobats or elephants. He could read about showmen like P. T. Barnum without leaving home.

He folded the newspaper and mashed hard on the crease with his thumbnail. He needed to move fast through his business and forge ahead to Phillip Island. He was not a man for waiting. But today, as the day had unraveled yesterday, and the day before, waiting was all he had. He rubbed the bristles on his chin.

"Can I get you anything else, Mr. Swift?" The same girl who'd served his luncheon the last two days smiled and took his empty plate. She held an envelope in her other hand. "We have figs on the buffet table. Perhaps you overlooked them yesterday."

Her voice, like molasses, made it sound like she was the morsel on offer. He looked away from the willingness of her dark eyes. Sugary, like hers, pulled a man into old regrets. He of all people needed to keep his mind on the future. He rubbed at the fading dog bite scar on his arm.

It's healed. Forget it.

"I'm all done here." He heard the clipped rebuff in his reply. Cold. Like the unfinished coffee in his cup. Bitter for sure. Right to the last drop. He sounded just like the old man he was fast becoming.

Old and grumpy. A widower at thirty-five, he may as well be ninety-five. Hadn't Mr. Hinkle told him his eyes were like a wet dungeon? That he'd better find out how to live or he was as good as a walking dead man? But none of that was this girl's fault. Why should she pay for it?

The letter of introduction in his breast pocket burned with reproach. Kind words, all about him and once, probably true. They dared him to live up to the script he kept near his heart.

"You could point me in the direction of a reputable barber." He let the old man in him look up at her.

"Turn left at the hotel entrance and walk a block or two." Her answer carried a musical tone. Irish perhaps. She lingered. "There's many to choose from."

He nodded his thanks. Starved of more than sunshine.

"I'm supervising a delivery of logging equipment." Words escaped him before he could stop them. "For next year's exhibition. I'm handing it over to a curator for part of the American Industry display. Can't turn up looking like a bristly brush monkey."

Can't head into what comes after looking like this, either.

An inviting blush rose in her cheeks.

Feathers and Guts! Why was he babbling? Why was heat scurrying along the back of his neck? He didn't owe her a conversation.

You owe her kindness. You owe everyone kindness.

"You don't strike me as a logger. Too refined." Her smile widened.

"Normally, I… I work with wood. Furniture, staircases." He swallowed all the reasons why he'd ridden alongside a shipload of ironworks and engineering marvels. That alone clanged with the weight of a thousand debts in the corner of his breast pocket, with another thousand in the lining of his heart.

"Oh… and this is for you." The serving girl placed the envelope on the table, took her tray, and left him with a backward glance that said more than her words.

Silas tore into the missive. This had better be his summons to the dockyards.

Dear Mr. Swift,

We continue to await replacement parts for the restoration of the crane most needed for the delicate work required for your shipment relocation. Word from our supplier indicates this will be another week…

He skimmed over the sender's name and office. How hard was it to repair shipyard equipment in this bustling new town? He crumpled the letter into a wad. He needed to get moving onto real business. Onto repairs so old and so deep he barely knew where to start.

He pushed away from the table and from the girl who reminded him of all the dark-eyed trouble he'd dodged in Portland. Past the gleaming double doors of the hotel, along roads that rattled with polished carriages and open wagons. He bumped his way through unwashed crowds that mingled and loitered on street corners, and others, purpose-dressed and purpose-driven, who bustled from appointment to appointment.

Melbourne would soon collect all manner of fresh discoveries and well-preserved antiquities for an exhibition that would thrill every eye that beheld it. But he would not be here to see it.

A small corner of his heart sorrowed at this. No, sir. He'd be long gone before they mortared the last brick into the Exhibition Building. He was too busy chasing time. Watching it run over the sky in stars and lights, as he had aboard the *Clara,* wondering how his life would look if he could wind back the clock and do it all a different way.

He stood still among the rushing crowds and let sun and wind and desperation pummel him in the chest.

The way men did when they chased a second chance.

2

Unlike the disarray of home, the Botanic Gardens were laid into sweeping lawns, meandering pathways, and gleaming ornamental lakes. New vistas emerged around every corner, marked by summer houses and the Rose Pavilion where bands played on sunny days. The sacred ground where botanical artists came to hone their skills and where Nasrin fed Viola's creativity. She hated to know who she may have become without Nasrin's kindness.

"What did you smell? How did the air taste?"

"Pineapples. And crushed sugar." They exited under the ornate iron gates. But the perfume of the Lily House followed them home.

"Yes. Good." Madam Nasrin's brown eyes sparkled. Hers was the prettiest smile Viola knew. It spilled from the olive delicacy of her face, past chestnut curls, and reached from her slender frame like the sky. Wide enough to always be there. "What else?"

"Ripe summer fruit. Ready to be devoured. And if a beetle is responsible for the transformation of this lily, he too will feature on my page. Oh, I cannot wait for what tomorrow will reveal."

"Never be afraid of painting what you truly see. Ordinary diligence may sketch the page, but courage will get you noticed." Nasrin slipped her arm through Viola's, and they walked home, winnowing all they'd seen and making plans for how a good artist would fix it to their page. "Today, so many beetles hovering, but the lily only needs one to transform from creamy white to fiery red. That is what it means to capture a man's affections, too, no?" Madame Nasrin's French lilt intensified when she spoke about matters of the heart. "Only one..."

Viola stopped. Frenzied piano music trickled up Palmer Street. "I wouldn't know." She held up her artist's kit, as if romance, love, and marriage were well secured in some other valise well out of reach. "But the world is coming to us. Fortunes will be brokered in our Exhibition Building. And I'm going to make sure I am among them."

"But do you not wish for someone to peer into your heart? And you to capture his?"

"Claim first place in someone's heart?" They surveyed one another. Years of unspoken hurts screamed in mute voice and pulled at their world in ways only Nasrin and Viola understood. "For now, I will pour myself into my Exotics until—"

"Shh, shh..." Nasrin frowned. Loud arguing erased the piano music. Then a door slammed. The Sullivan girls marched onto the street, and their grandmother pulled the gate shut behind them as if it had wronged her.

"Mrs. Sullivan? Why all the racket?" Viola waved her down.

"Ask your mother. She's the one making it. Along with that insufferable bird. I was willing to put up with the madness of the Buckley household because of your affordable tuition, but no longer. My girls are terrified of what might fly at them."

One of the Sullivan sisters fought back tears. The other rubbed her elbow as if she'd knocked it and wanted Viola to know it still hurt. Neither held sheet music.

Viola's hopes sank. She did not know these music students well. And now they were leaving for good.

"When I arrived, I found my granddaughters whimpering on the settee, your mother lost in her own piano playing, uncaring or unknowing, probably both, that her bird was throwing pieces of apple at her students. And I won't pay good money for that. Good-day and good luck to you, Miss Buckley." All three departed in a fresh huff, and in their wake, a desperate voice cried into the street.

"Balthazar, come back! Balthazar, dearest…"

Viola hurried in, Nasrin close behind. But Balthazar, always his mistress's weakness, had flown out the open back door and now perched on a line of fresh washing. Mother hobbled down the back step and around a simmering tub of dirty wash water, her hand held high.

"Come to Mama. Come now."

"Good grief, those Sullivan girls can shriek." Rosie pushed the hair off her sweaty face. "I was gone all of five minutes, Viola, I swear. When I got back, them girls were in a fit because plaster pieces fell into Balthazar's cage, and that bird was in a state. Flappin' and cursin' and nothing your mother said worked to settle him 'til she grabbed him from his cage. And those girls just kept cryin' as if the apple in their hair had turned into a snake."

Balthazar hopped from one leg to the other, as if in two minds about whether he'd taunt them a little longer for the disrespect he'd suffered.

Mother made a kissing sound and beckoned with her hand.

Viola squeezed past Nasrin and Rosie. "Let me get Balthazar." She lowered her voice. "The prima donna."

Mother did not turn, but Viola was used to being ignored when Balthazar demanded his share of the attention. He'd always bowed properly when her parents had needed him to. Unlike Viola, who'd curtsied in her own fashion and always done what they asked, in her own way. Well, those days were well past them. Almost as sure as Balthazar's winged escape.

Go on, do it. Viola wished it before she could stop herself. If Marshall, her father, could glory in a reinvented version of himself, a man with a new name, new wife, and reconstructed stage career in London, why shouldn't a pink galah find his way back to the bush where it suited him best?

But Mother fought the shadows of all she'd lost. And it was Balthazar who soothed much of what ailed her. The ghosts of another life, where gaslights blinded Viola and sent her crying into the nest Madame Nasrin made for her in the wardrobe room.

Think of the lily. Rhizome, Leaf, and now *Bud*, and the two she would add in time. Tomorrow's *Bloom* and the spongy underwater berry that would become the *Fruit*. If her Exotics series bought her freedom, nonsense like this crazed bird stepping all over the washing would fade into nothing. The sooner she sorted this mess, the sooner she'd return to her sketches.

"Come, Balthazar."

"This way, good boy."

They all called to him, around laundry cauldrons that no longer bubbled. Almost extinguished, the fire smoldered. Even on a good day, the lines, heavy with washing, presented a confusing labyrinth for Mother. But with Balthazar at the heart of trouble, they posed the worst entanglement.

"Mama has a treat for you. Come…" Eyes on her bird, Mother took another step. Her slipper turned and she floundered and swayed. She grabbed for the clothesline, but the limp sleeve of a shirt offered nothing more than a button on a cuff. It caught on Mother's wig and tore it off her head. Pins scattered like parts coming undone, and the hair beneath, the graying locks of a woman past her prime, came loose.

The afternoon sun lit Mother from behind. There was no sweet smile, no innocence in her eyes. Her panic, angular and taut. Her skin pale, eyes rimmed in red.

But something about this bewilderment mirrored the innocence of her younger self.

For six years she had patted her blond wig and insisted. *"I am not the naked girl in your painting."* She still insisted. And no matter how delicately Freddy Barnes had informed them of the discovery in his tavern attic, all it had taken was one look at Viola's hair and he had his proof.

"As is the mother, so is the daughter."

Hadn't Marshall spat the same words in disgust?

And now, with the sun slipping behind her, what remained of Sweet Clementine's locks fired into sparks.

"Come, Sweet Clemmie." Viola borrowed from Mother's memories and offered the pet name that always soothed. "Lean on me."

But Mother's footing gave way, and she fell onto the cobbles of the courtyard.

The golden wig tumbled and rolled into the fire. The burning smell of human hair wafted over the yard with the sickening crackle of Mother's favorite hairpiece, snapping and twisting into ashes.

"No! That was my last wig. I have no other." Mother doubled over, and her sobbing blended with Balthazar's screeching. He rose from his perch and landed in Clemmie's crumpled lap. She pulled him close and dropped her head onto his.

Viola had seen her mother without her wig many times. And she'd seen her reach for Balthazar for comfort when no one else would do. But she had never caught a glimpse of Sweet Clementine until now. Not until the sun wrapped itself around her. In that venerability, Viola recognized some of the girl in the painting. The young woman she longed to see restored.

Rosie gathered Mother up and ushered her and Balthazar back inside. Mother wailed for the embers of her costume.

"I'll fetch Dr. Murdoch. I do not like the look of this," Madame Nasrin whispered.

In Mother's room, Viola yanked gowns and accessories off the bed. She swapped the ash-stained clothes for a nightdress and tucked her into bed.

"Poor Balthazar." Clemmie trembled. Her elbow bled and her cheek bore an angry gash. "Don't let plaster fall into his cage. He's such a good boy to me. Such a good boy…"

"You rest now, Sweet Clemmie. Balthazar is fine." Viola pressed her forehead to her mother's, where the real dangers roamed in Clemmie's memory like squatters in possession of an empty land.

❧

Silas stopped at the first ruby-red awning over a doorway. Above it, a brass shingle read: *Mr. Edgar Bolt, Gentleman's Bathhouse and Barber.*

"We're the cleanest stop on the street. I could list our regular clientele, but that would breach their privacy." Dressed in an emerald vest, a man held the door open and invited Silas in with a wink. "And in here, privacy is our speciality."

"Are you Edgar Bolt?"

"His kid brother, Eddie."

Silas followed him into a cool receiving room. It contained a large fern in a brass pot and a wall-hung mirror.

"Edgar does the barbering. The bathing and whatever comes after ya do on your own."

Silas liked the sound of that.

"Everything's carbolic scrubbed. All bathtubs, large and deep. French style. Not like how the Brits do it, in half a thimble of water."

"I could do with a close shave." And his bones longed for a soak in a deep tub. "How much?"

Eddie pointed to a sign. "It's minutes you pay for. Or hours. Whatever you need. The longer you pay for, the more buckets we deliver."

Silas considered the price list. "I'll buy a half hour. And a shave."

"Right this way." Eddie took him along a corridor and into a darker paneled room, lined with all the accoutrements for a bath: the promised tub, a wicker chair, towels, various wall hooks, a mahogany dresser with a large pitcher and ewer, and a fresh bar of soap.

Two candle lamps lit the windowless room, hung from goose neck hooks that cast a flicker onto the ceiling through pressed holes in the tin. Another man, younger but sturdier and with more muscles, appeared with two steaming buckets of water. He poured them into the tub and reached outside the doorway for two more buckets, already there.

Eddie Bolt helped Silas with his jacket, and the tub filled fast. More buckets appeared, and soon, Silas stood alone in the steam-heavy room. He stripped off fast and sank into the water with a predictable slosh and deep sigh. Heat penetrated his layers. All the angst and weariness that held him upright most days loosened like soft marrow.

Light sparked off the rippling bath water, like the stars he'd followed in night skies until those who knew where to look pointed out the Southern Cross. The formation in the upside-down heavens that looked like a kite, with a smaller beauty-spot star, just visible if you knew where to look. Silas did. Crux was a constellation that beckoned like no other.

Stars and scrolls followed him everywhere. They had been a part of him since his boyhood, when he and Charlie Hinkle had found dreams in a sack of treasure. If only they'd known better. If only they'd never touched that dirty, smallpox-ridden burlap bag.

But no. The astrolabe had been worth something then. And it was worth something now. More than ever. He sank deeper and breathed harder. The water carried an earthy scent. It peppered his breathing, and his ears pumped with the sound of his own heartbeat. The *boom, boom-boom* that sounded at life's crossroads.

"Until a spade hits the ground and digs a hole on your behalf, it's never too late."

The words of Mr. Hinkle the gravedigger returned to him. Dirt in every crease of his work-sore hands, thick mud under chipped nails, thicker sentiment in his grieving voice. The burlap sack between them.

"Don't you go burying yourself now. Haven't we lost enough? Make a life out of what's left. Take it, I insist. It's yours. Let it fire your dreams."

Silas breathed in long and hard. It was one thing to have a boyhood dream. Another to chase it. Another still to hide it in a shipment to Australia and come hunting for it four years later.

The door swung open.

"Edgar Bolt, at your service." He turned his back on Silas to arrange shaving implements on the dresser.

"Now? While I'm still in the tub?" Silas gripped the metal sides.

"No better time. Pores are at their most open. Sit up." Mr. Bolt stirred a jug of lather.

"But how can you see? The light's hardly—"

"Plenty good for me. I could shave you with my eyes shut. Now, sit still." The barber worked the lather into his cheeks, jaw and neck.

"Don't you do it this way where you come from?"

"No." Silas squirmed. "Where I come from, the customer is fully dressed. And in a chair."

"If I waited for you to dry and dress, your skin would turn cold. No condition for the superior shave you'll be getting here." He swapped the lather for a strop and razor. "Trust me. None of my customers complain. But it's your woman who'll thank me. Where've you come from, anyway?"

Silas held his chin high. How was this a good idea? Crazy Australians. Didn't they shave with rusty blades by a dusty creek? Or not at all?

"Portland, Oregon."

"Thought so. You're not the first American to come through here. Married?"

"No."

"Looking?"

"No. I—"

"Shh. Watch the ceiling." He reached over and tapped the edge of a lamp.

Lights chased each other in mesmerizing patterns, and Silas let the warmth, the soothing smells, and the *kssh-kssh* of the razor rule over his senses.

Memory ran like a carousel. He wasn't sleeping, but it felt like an open-eyed dream pulling him under, even with a barber at his throat with a blade. Soon, his legs relaxed, as did his shoulders. And still the lights flickered. Over and over, they spun like the words of introduction he'd read so many times. All he had to do was close his eyes to remember it.

Dear Mr. Shadrach Jones,

You recently bought a kit home from Brown and Burrows for delivery to Phillip Island, Australia.

I write to you today as its owner, to advise our staircase manufacturer will soon visit your country and wishes to inspect his workmanship in its new location. I vouch for Mr. Silas Swift, who has supplied us with quality staircases for over five years. A trustworthy and reliable craftsman, solid in reputation and Christian faith.

Sincerely,
Mr. Luther Burrows

Craftsman. A generous description. For the simple furniture that was their bread and butter. Functional staircases, everyday tables, and forgettable but sturdy tallboys. An unfed hankering grumbled within him.

The elaborate. The intricate. That's what true craftsmen created. They captured ideas and transformed them into something you wanted to hold in your hand. Behold with your eye. The way the ancients looked into the skies and turned them into maps.

"And… you're done." The barber applied a fresh smelling balm of sandalwood. "You won't disappoint her now."

"I'm not married." It stung to say it again, and Silas ran his fingers over his skin. Smoother than it had been in many months.

"Not a wife, mate. You already told me you don't have one." He tapped on the wall with the toe of his shoe. "This bathhouse may be small, but it's connected to a pleasure house. And there's plump pigeons in there who'll thank me tomorrow for sending a fine visitor in like yourself. American to boot. They'll love you."

He hooked his finger onto the wall paneling and slid the entire piece along.

Silas sat upright. A stream of water sloshed over the side of the bath, and he peered over his knees.

Edgar Bolt had peeled back one world to reveal another. A thin curtain fluttered. Someone laughed. Soft and welcoming. As soothing as the balm on his face.

Shame, like a cold, fat stone, fell into the pit of his gut and collided with the collection of regrets he held there.

"Shut the door."

"Sure now? You're only a few steps away. And she is waiting."

"I'm a thousand steps away. From where I ought to be."

"Bashful, ay?" The barber slid the door back into place. "I'll leave you to dress."

"No, I mean, I'm recently widowed. And in no way ready for the company of women." He ran his hands over his wet hair.

"Have it your way. But it's not their hearts they sell in there. If you change your mind, this one's name is Luna." Bolt gathered his things and left Silas to ponder how fast bath waters chilled.

Aggravated wiping with the towel left him part dry and altogether stung. How could he not have known this place was a doorway to a bawdy house? All that talk of privacy and discretion. Details so small he'd not paid attention to the bigger picture hovering above him. It resembled the story of his life. He only saw what really mattered when it was too late.

He shoved his legs, still damp, into long johns, thankful his wrinkled fingertips made fast work of his shirt. The Lunas of this world deserved so much more than a life behind a sliding door.

What if he pulled her free? Then what? How could a foreigner secure her freedom when he'd yet to find his own?

A hasty rummage in his pocket procured generous payment, which he threw on the chair, and in fewer minutes than it normally required to lace up his shoes, Silas fled.

It took a few blocks to calm down. A few more for the easing of his fury. Honora had deserved more. She had lived the life of a prisoner. One of her own making, but still. Doors and curtains had kept his wife enslaved, too.

Cool fall winds blew up and around the end of a laneway, and he stopped to shuffle one arm into his coat sleeve, then the other. Smelling sweeter, feeling grubbier than he had in a long time. He buttoned up his coat and straightened the sleeve cuffs.

Mr. Silas Swift, a trustworthy and reliable craftsman.

That's not what the angry scar on his right forearm said. He patted his breast pocket where the letter of introduction always offered well tucked reassurance. Always inspired him to be what people thought he was.

Only this time, the pocket lay empty.

He tried his trouser pockets. Nothing. He patted his chest, the seat of his pants, as if it might magically appear, but no amount of frantic searching secured the letter.

No. Not this. Not now.

A hot gust of fear bellowed into his chest.

He straightened. The bathhouse! Had it fallen out while he dressed? Had someone picked his pocket on one of the teeming street corners?

He had no way of knowing. All he knew for sure was that he hunted a twist of brass. Those who navigated the skies called it an astrolabe. He and Charlie Hinkle had called it treasure. Plain and simple.

But now, Silas knew it as the only answer to his present-day problems, and it lay another boat ride away, buried deep in the house of Shadrach Jones.

He gulped for air. Short, angry breaths. The darkening sky filled with clouds of grey and steel reminiscent of Portland. He'd lost more. Much more. This might slow him down, but it would not stop him. Not now that he was this close. Silas turned for the hotel.

He would find another way to announce himself. But even if they believed him, would they let him in? Because this worker of wood, this man of solid reputation hadn't crossed an ocean to inspect his good workmanship.

He'd come to take it apart.

Clementine Buckley's bedroom hung with the remnants of a life once lived with great abandon. Hats, feathers, shoes, and shawls overflowed from boxes on a good day and lay strewn over the bed when she needed to sink deep into her old life. Jammed between frame and mirror, three faded postcards of the seaside decorated her dressing mirror.

On the bedpost, a child's red dancing shoe hung from a silk black ribbon, so worn by years of tender touching, only a few brave threads remained. Just right for the tiny ballerina who should have grown tall and stood here, tending to Mother.

Instead, it was Viola who watched the doctor administer his remedy while Nasrin collected the scattered wardrobe pieces and turned them right way around for their hangers.

"We must interrupt her chain of gloomy thoughts." Dr. Murdoch let go of Mother's wrist. "Sunshine. Restorative foods. Frictions. Gentle walks. Sea air, not this dusty, shadowy prison. Does she ever leave the house?"

Viola shook her head. "Only to stroll to the end of the street."

"Then we must break her routine."

He may as well have said break *her*. Viola fought with the worm-eaten window sash. It fell with a thud, and a small piece of wallpaper unfurled like soft applause from the wall behind Clemmie's bedhead. But this was no performance. This was Clemmie at her most fragmented. Laudanum-heavy, her eyes fluttered into dreams Viola knew would awaken her with desperate crying much later. The ever-present grasp for all things lost.

The doctor clipped shut his medical bag. "While she sleeps, you'd best make plans, my girl."

Nasrin and Viola followed him into the shambles of their front room. Browned apple pieces dotted the settee. Sheet music lay on the floor as if it were a new carpet piece. And Balthazar slept in his cage, hidden by the brown silk cover that held him in.

Viola leaned against the piano. Dr. Murdoch went on. Ointment for her elbows. A crate of Mariani Tonic.

A crate? Who had money for a full crate?

Any moment now and Viola would need a hefty dose of something herself.

He scribbled on a paper. "The grazing is minor, but her real calamity is seated in the heart. I told you months ago her condition would not improve. Wild emotions only escalate heart muscle conditions like hers. When a woman loses her emotional equilibrium the way Clementine has, there's no full recovery. But there is the option of therapy. Some call it rest cure. I am not convinced, but…" He shrugged.

"Not convinced it would work on Clemmie or that it works at all?" Viola heard the fear in her voice.

Nasrin reached for Viola's hand and squeezed hard. Her dear friend had stitched costumes and mothered young Viola under the stage while her parents trod the boards above. But what kind of mending was there when hearts failed?

Dr. Murdoch scribbled instructions on a piece of paper. "You're made of the same determined stock as your mother, so I'll not mince my words. This incident is not one easily managed with tonics. It's not her moods alone we have to temper. Your mother's deterioration requires weeks of convalescence before we can say it has worked or not. I would recommend seaside therapy in conjunction with rest cure."

"Sea… seaside?" Viola stammered. "I can't afford a seaside holiday. We barely afford the rent here."

"Think of how you can afford it. And when you've come up with a plan, write to these people." He handed her a list of medicines and an address. "My wife and I spent a week in a Phillip Island guesthouse this past summer. It's picturesque. And secluded. Just the place your mother needs. No theatrics of any kind. Full bedrest to begin with. Good foods full of fat. Milk at every meal. Frictions of the scalp and full body massage. Daily indoor baths are the crucial element of this treatment. Cold water, mind. And eventually, she may take strolls by the beach."

"But—"

"Stay in Melbourne, and Clementine will die a miserable death. I don't mean to distress you. Only outline your options. Sell something valuable. Offer to work as guesthouse maid to pay your way. It's cruel to continue pretending Sweet Clementine Buckley will ever return to her normal self. But if there's a chance you might lessen some of what plagues her, it needs to happen in a place that soothes."

He observed the various corners of the room and gathered his bag. "Get her out of here before her nerves and heart suffer a complete collapse."

Viola followed him to the door. But the good doctor had more to say.

"This can all end with you, Viola. Learn from Clementine's foolishness. You cannot overload the female anatomy. Charles Darwin says it. Science confirms it. The female brain is five ounces lighter than that of a male. And when frayed, no way equipped for the follies your mother has attempted."

He jammed his hat on. "She would have lived a happier life if she'd focused on motherhood and the dignity of domesticity. Now her body pays the price, and if you're not careful, you'll find yourself in the same predicament."

He bowed in farewell and shut the door behind him. But nothing shut out the noise. Wagons would still rumble in the morning and the ever-present unloading of building supplies would follow. *Bang, bang, thud, scrape.* And the order of life, the frailties of women, and the remedies of men would still erode them.

"Five ounces?" She held out her hand. A withered apple weighed five ounces. Surely that deficiency was not the root of her mother's ailments?

The soothing fragrance of fresh coffee pulled Viola back to Nasrin.

She took a small cup from her dear friend and sat on the tiny tapestry stool at the good woman's feet.

"Ever since I was a little girl, this has been the aroma of you, wrapping me with your protection and care."

Nasrin held out a plate of Turkish Delight. "And ever since, you've sat at my knee and waited for me to feed, or warm, or entertain you." Her brown eyes came alive with affection Viola could rely on.

"I had no choice. But you did." Viola bit into the rose scented confection.

"I did what any wardrobe mistress would have done for a lost chicken, my little Poupette, whose parents sang late into the night. I made a nest for my little chick."

"You did so much more, Nasrin. You're still doing it now, stepping into the role of *mother* because Clemmie has better parts to play."

They sipped the bitter brew, poured from an engraved brass pot that Nasrin insisted they keep in their cupboard for her visits.

"I can't afford this remedy." Viola picked at the ruffled hem of her dress. Like almost everything else she wore, it too had been sewn by Nasrin. "Nothing we own would pass for seaside ensembles because promenading has never featured on my list. We need to be tutoring to pay the bills. Not to mention my sessions in the gardens."

Her artwork, her competitions, everything that made up her ticket out of this mess resided in Melbourne. "And how would I ever get Clemmie on a boat?"

"If the doctor suggests the seaside, I'll wager your mother's given him signs she can travel. And I may have a few suitable dresses I could alter for you."

"But, Phillip Island?"

"It will take you miles away from the Botanic Gardens and me, Poupette, I know." Nasrin sipped her coffee. "Stay then. Morning will show if she's improved. This may be the melancholy, singing a song she cannot lay aside."

The setting sun hit the window ledge and sparked off the small framed mirror on the wall.

"No, Nasrin... what if the doctor is right?" Viola shivered at the way the light sprang from one surface to another. As it did in the *Sweet Clementine.*

She stood and paced the room. "Mr. Barnes has already collected the most lucrative portion of us. But… maybe…" She surveyed the wide top of the piano. A grand piano, no less. The only gift Clemmie would never relinquish, treasured as much as her costumes and memories. "He would jump at the chance to buy Clemmie's piano!"

"No, mon Poupette." Nasrin gasped. "That is cruel, to take away something so beloved. And you are tender-hearted—"

"I can't afford to be soft. I must think of a way to get Sweet Clementine Buckley into a house by the sea." She brushed the piano keys with her fingertips.

"This could be another agony for you and her."

"The agony is being told you need to do the impossible."

Nasrin sighed. "They propped her up with laudanum after your sister died. Then they told her she would rid herself of the addiction by getting pregnant." Like the best of friends, Nasrin carried many of their family sorrows. More than what Viola had seen. "Then they told her the pregnancy ruined her. That motherhood was the illness that robbed her of vitality. That working on the stage disabled her." She clenched her fists. "How many more times will a doctor blame her broken heart on what she has done instead of what has been done to her?"

Viola did not know. "I've been working on Clemmie's restoration since I was eight years old. The only time I've known her to be serene is in that painting. Standing in the shallows. A secret peace in her eyes." Viola pressed on the creases of the doctor's paper. Perhaps this was a prescription for healing after all.

This residence by the sea called *Blue Wren House.*

3

Viola had a special talent for putting her foot where it was not supposed to land. Puddles. Tree tops. And darkened, rickety staircases that beckoned Viola and terrified her mother. Most of her life she had done it anyway, not to be disobedient, but to work out if the fear carried any weight.

"Little girls have no business climbing anything, anywhere," Mother had said, over and over. But sometimes, little girls were forced to grow up and make it their business.

Viola pushed the tavern door open and slid into the *Star and Garter. Sweet Clementine* smiled down at her. The first time she'd stood here, she'd reached the cobwebs atop a ladder, overseen by Jasper and Mr. Barnes, with Derry the cook, and his wife, Cloda, peering up at the spectacle.

Since then, Viola had found a better way. One without an audience. All it required was a little bravery, a little balance, and her toes placed just so on the outside edge of the Star and Garter staircase. And she had cleaned *Sweet Clementine*, studied it, and begged Mr. Barnes for its return ever since.

Today, she took the stairs as anyone else might in a desperate hurry, from the inside, two steps at a time. Breathless, not from the exertion, but from the pounding of her heart and the urgency that drove her on.

To beg. Once more.

She set her basket on the landing floor and formed a knocking fist, but men's voices thundered from the office within, and she halted her entrance.

"No, Father, I disagree. You made her a promise."

"A temporary relocation, foolish boy. A short-lived deviation to a plan that still stands. You'd be smart to look a little further than your schoolboy crush on Viola Buckley. How many opportunities like this come along for a business like ours? Imagine the fame for the Star and Garter."

Viola clenched her fists even tighter. She expected her appearance at their door might take father and son by surprise, but it never occurred she might wade into their own heated dramas.

"But, Father, she—"

"My mind is made up, and your outrage misplaced. *Sweet Clementine* will be among the Local Artists Collection at the Melbourne International Exhibition and I will not be swayed."

The exhibition? Sweet Clementine?

She swung the door open, bypassing the knock, the invitation to enter, and any other civility required of her.

"Miss Buckley! What is the meaning of this?" Mr. Barnes pushed off from his chair, and Jasper, open-mouthed, sprang to face her. Neither of them wore coat jackets in the warm room, their shirt sleeves rolled to the elbows. Waistcoats added some vibrancy, but it was the fire in their cheeks that caught her eye.

She held up empty palms. "I meant to knock. And I would have, except you were both yelling and making plans for *Sweet Clementine* and ..." Her breath dried fast, but her temper still boiled. "... I heard my name."

"My dear." Mr. Barnes slid a lightning-fast smile onto his face.

"I'm glad you stopped by. That one spiderweb's been annoying me all week, but I kept telling myself, Viola, devoted artist she is, will pop in and dust our *Sweet Clementine*." A messy scarlet seeped into his cheeks. "And here you are."

Viola knew if she employed her best theatre voice, she could reply with enough vexation the residents of the dwelling next door would hear her arguments.

Instead, she pushed the tip of her thumbnail into the palm of her other hand. "You made me a promise when you hung *Sweet Clementine* that she was safe in your keeping and would go no further. Does your promise still stand?"

Jasper cupped Viola's elbow. "We planned on telling you."

"When it was too late for me to object?"

"Come now, Viola." He invited her to sit. He dusted the chair seat, pretending it needed a thorough clean, maybe to smooth the way, maybe to make her laugh.

But theatrical gestures never fixed broken promises. Most days, Jasper's teasing was easy to take, because he stood aside like the emerging gentleman he would become and allowed her to tease back. That had been their game from their first introduction. But some days his charms wore thin.

"I'll stand, Jasper. Thank you." She took hold of the back of the chair. "You're planning to move *Sweet Clementine*?"

Mr. Barnes sank into the seat behind his desk. "A short-term loan, for the Local Artists exhibition. You don't build a structure like that, invite the world in, and hide the wonders right under your own nose now, do you?"

Jasper's eyes begged her to agree, as they had most of their friendship. Viola stared back at him with a *you-know-better-than-this* in her frown.

"It's a Mortimer Barnes original." Mr. Barnes shook his head. "It's unthinkable for me, his brother, to neglect my duty. I imagine other works from private collections will be there. *Sweet Clementine's* a piece of history. One of Melbourne's most beloved songbirds, painted by one of Melbourne's most gifted artists. And she'll hang under the same roof with pieces of Queen Victoria's very own art collection. How's that for good company?"

He busied himself with the fat ledger where they tallied beer orders and tavern expenditure, but none of the real cost of luring in patrons with visions of *Sweet Clementine.*

"You made me a promise." Viola's thumbnail dug deeper. "Jasper. Please, won't you convince him?"

Jasper shrugged and made a tender face, but Mr. Barnes let his exasperation creep in.

"Aren't you occupied enough to let this obsession die away? How long will it take to truly drink her in? Six years now you've burst in to stare up at her. Surely your little art students, not to mention your poor mother, need your attention. And let's not forget your... *career.*" He spoke into his hand, as if he protected her from the foulest curse word.

"My mother has my full attention, as do our fine arts students. You're forgetting she is the founder of the academy I now run for us. And my portfolio..." she tried not to panic, "is none of your concern."

"Well, you throw your artistic aspirations at me like a bargaining chip every time I suffer your intrusions. Yes. I suffer them, when you act as if you're the only one who knows her true value." He straightened his shoulders. "This is my business. It's my painting. Your affection for it may keep you inspired, and I allow it out of kindness. Not long ago you begged me not to hang her there at all."

She tried not to flinch at the word *'beg.'* Wasn't that what she did best?

Petition and plead on Clemmie's behalf. For Clemmie's good. For Clemmie's welfare.

"Now I'm begging you to keep her here. Please, what about the luck she brings your patrons?"

"Luck?" He laughed. "You and I both know it's a crock of fairy tales, told by the sober and believed by the tipsy. Real fortune always favors the owner." He jerked a thumb to his chest.

"Let me buy her. I'll start weekly repayments. It will take a long time, but the more I make, the more I'll… give." Viola bit the inside of her lip, stunned at her own ability to pivot from desperate peddler to delusional buyer.

"Even if I wanted to sell, you'd need three lifetimes to pay off a debt like that."

"But if I win my category, and catch the eye of an art publisher—"

"Even if you did, you'd pay a few outstanding bills and buy a new hat. And from the looks of you, I'd say a new hat wouldn't go amiss."

She patted her hair. "Mr. Barnes, I have never hidden my aspirations from you because, well…" She pushed past the chair and stood on his side of the desk. "You told me to trust you and…"

He pointed for her to step back and stand near Jasper. "You will never make enough money to buy such a piece, no matter how much you invest in her upkeep. Which I allow at my discretion and because of our loose family history."

"But if I win my category it will propel me into—"

"Nothing, my dear." His controlled answer stemmed the rush of her words. "Acclaim and praise will fill your head, but it won't line your pockets. Why waste the potential of a perfectly good mother on the life of a mediocre painter of flowers?"

Viola winced. "What if God made me in the shape of an artist? Even a mediocre one?"

"Rubbish. God made you to bear children. How many times do you need to be told? Men are the instigators, women the reactionary beings. It's the scientific order of things, and every doctor worth his fee will tell you that. I don't make the order. I just follow it. Look around you. Who has the power to decide where *Sweet Clementine* hangs? Me. And one day it will be Jasper. You, well, you get to decide when you view her."

She inhaled a hot, angry breath. "I decide more than that, Mr. Barnes. I decide what I will paint and how it shall appear on my paper. I decide which pieces I will enter, the stories they will tell."

"And who decides the winners?"

Silence growled, and no one replied. But the words *men, men, men,* whispered from the *tick, tick, tick* of the desk clock.

Jasper frowned and tried to catch her eye. But Viola refused to be placated.

Mr. Barnes sank back into the upholstery of his desk chair. "You'll wear yourself out and spoil your children's futures with aimless pursuits that lead to nowhere and leave you so exhausted you'll deplete the vigor required for motherhood. Professions are the ruination of women. Ask your mother about that."

Viola let her hands drop to her sides and the insults rattle to her feet. "What if someone falls in love with her and offers you a handsome sum? Then you'll let her go. You'll watch her be carted away, never to return."

Panic matched the pain that crept from her poverty. It would have served her better to cry actual tears, but Viola did not borrow from the theatre if she could help it. She needed a better strategy.

"What if I worked here one day a week? I'll do whatever Derry and Cloda ask. They need someone younger. I'll sweep floors. I work fast."

"You don't want to be a scullery maid, Viola." He called her by name, and a softness skittered into his words. "Listen." He grimaced a little, as if he weighed his kinder tendencies against his business brain. "I know the hours you've poured into studying that painting. But you'd need somewhere to hang her. And you don't even own the roof above your head. Win the fame or fortune you so desperately believe attainable, and I will sell you the painting. How's that? Until that day, she goes where I say, when I say so, and you will not begin this conversation with me again."

He reached for his pen. "How is your mother, anyway?" His cheeks flamed a little, the way they did whenever he asked about the woman they argued over.

"Clemmie's taken a turn for the worse. The doctor has prescribed seaside therapy and rest cure." She filled her lungs with a deep gulp and waded in. "I hardly know what either entails, let alone how to afford it. That's why I'm here today."

For a beggar, Viola had just enough steel in her spine to hold her head high. She may have lost the first round, but she would enter the second on the front foot and already swinging.

"I'm going to sell Clemmie's grand piano. Today, and to whoever agrees to buy it first. She needs immediate care, and not in a house that's falling apart almost as fast as she is. We need to cover travel expenses, our lodging at a seaside guesthouse, and whatever it will cost me to store our household goods for the duration of our time away."

Jasper directed her to the chair. This time, she sat.

"What?" He crouched beside her. "Away?"

Viola nodded and swallowed the lump growing in her throat.

"Clemmie had a rough fall. She's tired, but nothing refreshes her. She's lost and wandering and fighting for release the doctor thinks will only come from fresh sea air and the benefits of rich foods."

"Which you can't afford, so you're selling her beloved piano." Mr. Barnes summed up the predicament with clarity, and somewhere in those few crisp words, Viola heard the soft quaver of empathy. "That's why you're here."

She nodded. "I know you have the means. And who better than the one who's dedicated his tavern to her memory?"

Freddy Barnes stood and turned to gaze out the window. It looked over the street and into the expanse of Melbourne's Botanic Gardens. Vistas and exotic botanicals she would have to leave behind. Something told her the widower, the man whose older brother had long-ago loved and painted her mother, looked over the landscape of his heart, blind to the gardens before him.

"I'll buy the piano." He pushed off the windowsill and turned back. "And there's ample storage in the attic for your household goods."

Just like that? No haggling? No lording it over her?

"I've not yet named my price."

He sat back at his desk. "I know you think I have no morals, making a profit on Clementine's near-naked image. But if I did not, who would rescue you now, in your time of need? Remember that, next time you go charging into other people's conversations about what they can and cannot do with what is theirs. Now, how much?"

He unlocked a desk drawer, pulled out a cash box, and counted out the exact amount Viola asked for. Nothing more, nothing less. Enough for a cheap, battered, second hand grand piano that would further his collection of all things Clementine Buckley.

He slid the bills across his desk to Jasper. "The attic rental is my gift."

He may as well have said *my hold on you.* "Now, stay safe and look after your mother. Jasper, see Viola out."

"Thank you, Mr. Barnes."

He nodded. "I'll send a cart around after you vacate." But already, his finger had found a line in his ledger. And so had his eye.

"Come on," Jasper whispered, and ushered her onto the landing. "It grieves me to hear about your mother. How can *I* help?" He pushed the money into her hands, and Viola wrapped her fingers around it.

She looked up into the beaming gaze of *Sweet Clementine*. Her heart longed to protect this sliver of her mother, too.

"Taking her to the exhibition is too risky, Jasper. It's inviting art buyers to compete with me when I still have no chance. Not yet. Not until—"

"You have the best chance, and you're ignoring it and breaking my heart all in one."

Years of friendship had left them easy and familiar. Years of him letting her in to sit under the finest portrait she'd ever seen. Countless times he'd called her into the kitchen with the offer of tea and biscuits, and together with Derry and Cloda had cheered her on when she'd added *drawing* and *painting* to her mother's Piano Lessons For Young Ladies.

Jasper had been there for every item she'd written on her lists. Now, he collected the basket she'd dropped on the landing.

"Heavy," he groaned.

"Mother's Mariani Tonic."

They took the stairs and stopped right where those who thought it mattered rubbed their knuckle on the *Sweet Clementine* frame. *"Good fortune, return us to Sweet Clementine,"* they'd sing and head into the night.

Viola did it to say goodbye. She had every intention of coming back.

They stepped into the tavern courtyard where Cloda kept her dusters, cleaning rags, and buckets.

"Viola, Father is still in charge, but someday, *Sweet Clementine* will be mine and, well, anything of mine I'll share with the woman who marries me."

"Adorable as you are, Jasper, you would hate that as much as I would."

"I don't know." He shook his head as if to weigh the idea. "Maybe I wouldn't. And *Sweet Clementine* would be my gift to you if we married. You know she would."

"I know." Viola watched him through the wide and easy road he'd offered her. This twenty-year-old man-child who'd always been her friend and could never, ever be more.

"Your painting is a sweet pastime. Ladylike, gentle and—"

"No, no, it's not. And neither am I. What I do isn't gentle or sweet. It's hard. It requires devotion. Something others will peer into and judge. And it pushes me and prods me to observe and become—"

"But what about marriage?"

Viola soothed the welt in her palm with the same thumb that inflicted it.

"Marriage is no longer a vehicle for the exchange of property and goods. We're not medieval and I will not marry to own a painting." There had to be a better way.

"Your art will never bear the income I can provide. Your worth is in your spark and everything I adore in you." They stood in the courtyard of the Melbourne tavern, he the owner's son and she the visitor allowed in, thanks to his father's paper-thin guilt. Guilt neither she nor Jasper ever talked about.

"Jasper." She pulled her hand away. "I am an artist. I have four merit certificates already." She ignored their wording, *Second* and *Third*. "And I may have little money to show for it right now, but I have a portfolio that's growing with exotic botanicals and that will forge a way for me. Melbourne's Exhibition Building is rising while we speak, and when it's built and the doors open, I want to be among the winning exhibitors there, too."

"Nothing is stopping you from doing all that. I would wait."

"Wait?"

"To be done with your dallying and seek a real future as someone's wife. Mine, preferably."

The cruel affront stung, but Viola had no time to let it reside. Jasper was a youth, shaped equally by what he wanted, then chiseled to a finer point by the prevailing sentiment of men like his father. Like Clemmie's Dr. Murdoch. And Dr. Murdoch's Charles Darwin.

"Tell me, Jasper. When you take yourself a wife, will you allow her to earn a living of her own?" She took the burdensome basket.

"That's ridiculous. An insult. I'd provide for her, and she'd provide for our children's needs." He stood taller now, and free of the basket, his chest rose, too. "Otherwise, what's the point in working hard to make this tavern more profitable each year?"

Viola smiled through her sadness. He meant well. But he was Freddy's son. She pressed a kiss onto his cheek. "Goodbye, my friend. Remember, you'll find her. The woman who deserves you. Half of our academy girls would vie for your lifelong company."

"But not you." He added the full stop to her rejection.

And she would add no more. "I must go. My list for today was already long. It did not include an argument with your father, but there you have it. I achieved even more than I planned."

Jasper opened a short iron gate under a jasmine arch. In the spring it had bloomed its finest. Now that autumn ripened, some of its leaves had already turned russet and bronze. Jasper, too, wore a darker shade of regret in the creases of his frown.

She hoped her parting smile let him know she appreciated his honest friendship more than she could say. He slid the bolt on the gate.

"Don't forget to add *break Jasper's heart* to that list. You can cross off that item with confidence." He pretended he'd been shot in the chest, clutching where it hurt. They both smiled. But it didn't make the sorrow of not loving him any lighter.

4

Viola didn't care if Nasrin's pot contained tea, coffee, or yesterday's cold barley water. Her parched throat and tired feet dragged her to the side stage door of the Odeon Theatre, home to Nasrin and Leo Karoly.

Her body wore exhaustion in tired muscles, and her mind screamed at the overnight unmooring that had left her and Clemmie homeless and jobless. How would they ever return to Melbourne if they forsook everything that anchored them here?

Nasrin would know. She'd known almost everything else Viola needed. How to thread a needle. How to drip a brush in the thinnest paint wash and speckle a clean white page with dots.

She had unlocked a world of imagination when Viola needed it most. The brushstrokes of safety. A reality all her own. And in keeping her busy with drawing and painting, she had taught Viola she could design her world in ways no one could touch.

She pushed hard on the theatre door and stepped into the misery of her childhood. It closed behind her with a soft thud, and she let her eyes adjust to the darkness. Cold air brushed her legs, and someone hammered from the rafters.

It had been more than a decade since she'd last performed here. Even longer since Marshall had wrenched her into the wings and torn their lives apart.

What a small stage for such a terrible, life altering finale. The memory still stung her nape with the fury of termites let loose under her skin. On that awful night, she had won the first of many battles Marshall had left for them to wage. Ongoing and always a possibility, given Clemmie's needs. Today's battle was but one of them. Breath held, she strode across the stage. This was not the friendly hall where hardworking artists won ribbons and prizes. *That* was the stage for her. No backstage surprises. No monsters waiting for her in the darkest of corners.

She hurried down a narrow flight of steps to the comfort of Madam Nasrin's wardrobe room. Her friend turned from the small pot-bellied stove in the corner.

"Poupette!"

A small teakettle bubbled with cinnamon, cardamom, and honey. A unique tea-blend, much like the costumery pinned, hung, shelved, or hooked around them. Each piece handmade by Madam Nasrin for the many performers who'd played their part in the theatre she and her husband ran together. Between them, they represented the eclectic mix of French and Persian, with a splash of Romany that rang, even now, from a corner of the theatre. A sad gypsy tune someone rehearsed from a hidden corner.

Nasrin wrapped her in a tight embrace. "Oh, those exhausted eyes."

"I've been everywhere today."

Nasrin smiled. "I am glad you found yourself here. Like old times. Come, let's drink. And you can tell me all about Freddy Barnes." She handed her a tiny steaming cup.

Viola sank into the small chair that had always been hers. Above them, wooden spools wound with haberdashery filled pigeon-holes and shelves, aligned by pigment. Ribbons and threads collided with skeins of wool beneath bolts of tapestried fabric. All of which the seamstress would stitch into vibrant costumes. If kings or nymphs or ship captains crept into the lines of Leo's scripts, it was Nasrin who dressed them.

The memory of the wardrobe mistress, pins pressed between her lips, fitting her for a costume first sewn for another, kicked hard against Viola's ribs. Her sister had not only been a child of beauty and talent, she'd been a little taller, too. Or maybe she stood taller, happy to join in the parade of actors who took their marks.

In any case, dress hems had to be taken up because, like always, she, the second born Viola, never measured up.

"Did you save any of my costumes?"

"No, Poupette. I unstitched the last of those long ago. But this morning I altered a few ensembles I think will serve you well by the seaside. Summery, and little theatrical perhaps, but if you find a pier to promenade, why not look your best?"

"You're too good to me." Viola sank into the welcoming riot of patterns and textures of Nasrin's nest. Simple slimline cottons suited her best. A small ruffle here, a modest tassel there, but nothing like the gaudy costumery worn to assume a character.

She kicked off her shoes and rubbed her heels together, but the soothing movement toppled her satchel. A wad of papers spilled out. Lists made to navigate the swift changes sweeping their lives.

Nasrin bent to pick them up. Viola knew them by heart.

Cancel Tuition

Reimburse All Students

Pack Up House

Sell Piano

"A list for everything, save one. Where do I add my lost childhood with a mother who didn't know how to pick up the pieces? How do I get those long years back?"

"Counting losses is futile. Who can catch what is long gone?" Nasrin pulled a page from the stack and held it up. Unlike the others, with items already crossed off, this one-word list held nothing else. "Portfolio?"

"Not a true list if it only contains the title." Viola shrugged. An empty page had brought her to this woman who'd shown her the way out of the darkness by making lists.

Nasrin sat back. "Was Mr. Barnes kind? Did he buy?"

"How could he resist?" Viola blew on her tea. "He's probably rearranging chairs and tables right now, ready to dump that piano right in the middle of the tavern. Roll up, roll up…"

"And your other items?"

"He offered to store them, too. He will collect them along with bed posts and mattresses. A few dressers. Chairs. A table or two. A tub." The contents of her life sounded like a cold list of auction items.

"And Clemmie?"

"Sullen. Eating like a sparrow. Empty Mariani Tonic bottles under the bed, as always."

Nasrin shook her head. "That tonic. It saved her, you know, after your father left."

Viola tried to shake the memory away. But Marshall yelled anyway. *"I have no use for you, Clementine. If you haven't passed down any of your talent to this Viola, I have no use for either of you."*

His words had pushed her mother at the apothecary's feet. And poured out the aroma of red wine, laced with Peruvian cocaine, into their home like a fast-flowing promise. The elixir that would fix everything.

Nasrin pushed out of her chair and crossed the room to a tall chest. She pulled out a drawer and fished inside. "Try these. We have them sent to us from Paris. They include what Clemmie is used to. Easier than bottles if you're going to travel." She handed Viola four identical blue tins.

Corsican Pastilles

Antiseptic Menthol, Borate, and Cocaine Lozenges

Take every four to six hours as required for fatigue of the throat.

Indispensable for singers, orators and teachers.

"All the rage in European theatre circles. Even our American acts are bringing them in. If nothing else, they'll elevate Clemmie's mood."

Viola hoped so. She spied Nasrin's rows of wigs. Without a wig, her mother would have to face her true self. In the mirror, and in the eyes of anyone she encountered.

More than ill-fitting costumes, Viola despised wigs the most. On her eight-year-old self, a wig said her hair was not how Marshall needed her to be. Not when her parents had hoped for a sunshiny-blonde replacement baby and had to endure a curly mess of strawberry blonde with a heavy splash of coppery brown.

Years of agitation spiked under her skin, and she stood to wander the room and escape her memories. But in an act of defiance, her fingers roamed to a mass of blonde ringlets on a top shelf. To a wig made for a child.

One ringlet curled around Viola's finger. It reached out to her from the long-forgotten past. The ache of her scalp when she threw this away was nothing compared to the aches that followed.

"Where did you find this? I thought I'd..." Permanently set in curls that never fell, this too first belonged to her sister.

"I found it shortly after… that night. Buried in one of my bins."

"I hid it there. Oh, how I hated this wig. How it tore at my hair."

Nasrin rested her chin on Viola's shoulder. "Your head was too big for this one. It fit your sister because they made it for her measurements. I tried to tell your father but…" Nasrin shrugged. "Did he ever listen to anyone?" She patted the wig, and Viola knew Nasrin touched the memory of her elder sister, too.

The first and truest Viola Buckley. The child they'd all loved and lost too soon.

"Only a memory now, Poupette."

Still, tears pricked her eyes. "Caring for Clemmie means the memories lie on the surface. They are all she craves. Her world up there," she pointed to the stage above the ceiling, "with her First Viola."

"You will make new memories with Clemmie. By the seaside."

"And how do I finish the Botanic Gardens Exotics if I am not in Melbourne? It's April now. My submission is due in September, and if time were not my most pressing issue, now it's location. Dr. Murdoch can't tell me how long this therapy will take. Two weeks of strict bedrest to begin with, and then what? He says it depends on Clemmie's recovery. I've requested six weeks' accommodation, with the possibility of more. But how much more? Two months? Three?"

"Perhaps you finish your Exotics another time, but you must keep creating."

"How, when Mother will need settling in and looking after? You should see Dr. Murdoch's instructions. An entire manual of healing. Baths, massages, specific meals. A fixed daily schedule. My life is about to shrink to the size of an island guesthouse."

"Then you narrow your focus. To whatever there is on Phillip

Island." Nasrin gathered a folded cloth bundle from a basket beside the stove. "I wish I could be there to cheer you, dear one, but this will have to do. My gift to you. For the days ahead."

She unfurled a large piece of alabaster silk, embroidered with far-reaching tree limbs that turned over themselves like ivy into every corner of the fabric. And over each branch, endless flowers, some small, others in full bloom, threaded in purples and blues among silver-green leaves.

"For your brave journey." Nasrin draped it over Viola's shoulders. "My suzani shawl always caught your eye. So, I think for this next season, it should cover you."

"But… this is from the foot of your marital bed. This one is not for giving. It's for keeping your marriage covered. You've told me so yourself. I couldn't possibly take this."

She caressed the suzani's embroidered panels, the seams a little misaligned. A slight but deliberate imperfection to remind each bride that beauty also springs from imperfection. And that only the Almighty Himself is truly perfect.

It smelled of coffee. And rosewater. Against Viola's skin, it pressed like a soft kiss. She wanted to hide there forever, but she handed it over with a solemn shake of her head.

Nasrin pushed it back. "You are as priceless to me as any daughter. What better place for it than on your shoulders? Remember that your life is made up of everything people have stitched around you. The good and the imperfect."

She draped the shawl over Viola's shoulder and blinked away her tears. "I wish I could have done more. Clothed you in what fitted best, right from the start. I begged your parents not to name you Viola. That was their first mistake, although not the worst."

They sat, knee to knee, Nasrin in her comfortable old chair, and

Viola in the little seat beside the stove.

"How cruel for a baby to carry the burden of such expectation. And foolish Marshall." She made a tsk sound with her tongue. "Thinking he could replace a dead child with another. He thought it would be easy to fill the bleeding gash in their lives. Viola is not a name that sounds good to the French ear to begin with. I never called her that, you know, the first one. Mon Cherie for her, and, always, my little Poupette for you."

She ran her hand over Viola's hair with affection. "But naming you after your dead sister, while cruel, turned you into a fighter. To prove you are your own Viola. So, if you must go, keep fighting." She tied two of the suzani ends under Viola's chin.

"Look for inspiration under every leaf. In every gully. Look in the creek beds, in every brush stroke. Evidence of the Almighty is in all of His creation. Ask Him to lead you to what you must capture. And what you must let go." She pulled her hand away as if she, too, were meant to let go today. "And one day, like me, you can drape this over your marriage bed."

"Me?" Viola shook her head. "What are the chances a man will care for a marital bed with a professional botanical artist?"

"The little girl who triumphed over the callous ways of her father, and sometimes her mother, fought hard to become the Viola I see today. The right man will find her no threat."

Viola took in the room, its rich smells and playful vibrancy, but nothing in here came as close as the fuel of Nasrin's love for her.

And for the first time in many days, Viola let hope into her small smile.

5

Late April winds whisked them away from Melbourne and into a brighter blue bay. Sun splashed and bounced off the water with a buoyancy that Viola prayed would lift and carry her mother to a happier place. Already, warmth from the sun played on their velveteen traveling cloaks, and if they survived the weeks of bedrest, perhaps they would walk the beach together.

Phillip Island came into view in swathes of eucalyptus blues and greens, but Viola could tell from the way her mother leaned on her parasol, ears hardly protected by organdy bonnet trim, eyes closed against the buffeting wind, that her mind settled elsewhere.

Whatever they sailed into was less than what they'd left behind. Viola felt the same. Everything that propped them up had been packed, sold, or let go.

The schooner delivered them to the pier where their host, Mr. Shadrach Jones, awaited. Tall and dark, some kind of storm brewed in his blue-eyed countenance. He loaded their trunks onto his wagon with a strained smile.

"Tie Balthazar on well. I don't want him falling onto the road," Mother said.

"Balthazar?" Shadrach slid Viola's art valise into a corner of his wagon bed. "Who's he?"

"He's my companion."

"We're only expecting two guests."

"Then you are mistaken. Balthazar makes three."

Viola forced a smile of her own. "Mother and her pet bird, Balthazar, are inseparable." She pointed to the covered birdcage and pedestal on a trolley that brought heavier items off the schooner to the village end of the pier.

"No one told me about a bird."

"I'm sorry. I…" Viola thought fast. Had she mentioned Balthazar in her letter? "I thought I wrote but, perhaps, oh dear." Heat ran into her cheeks.

Shadrach pulled up some of the birdcage cover and faced the pink and gray feathered commotion within.

Balthazar spotted Clemmie and swayed. "Give us a kiss. Give us a kiss."

Clemmie made a kissing noise for her bird. "Balthazar has been in our lives for years. He's considered a family member."

Mr. Jones grabbed the cage and carefully laid it on the wagon bed. "Unless we're expecting other family members, we're set to go." He didn't wait for anyone's reply.

But he did assist them onto the wagon seat, and in less time than it took for Viola to wonder if she'd made a huge mistake requesting lodging from this grumpy man, they were sitting high, watching sandy tracks darken into red dirt bush roads.

Their host eyed a broken sapling fence between road and fields. Indecipherable frustration rumbled under his breath.

Clemmie surveyed the widening vistas, too. "My daughter is a botanical illustrator, Mr. Jones. While I undertake my rest, she will, hopefully, find subjects to fix to her page."

"A painter?" Mr. Jones kept his eye on the road. "Do you paint people and places, too?"

"The occasional landscape," Viola offered.

"But no portraits. We agreed years ago—"

"Clemmie, dear. We don't need to bother Mr. Jones now. Look, do you see the beach through the trees?"

Her mother breathed in a lungful of air. In truth, Viola preferred botanicals to any other subject. What else could be beautifully ruined or imperfectly stunning?

They made the rest of the journey in silence until they pulled into a property.

A generous hydrangea hedge skirted the verandah of *Blue Wren House*, a double-story white dwelling. Tidy paths pointed to fields and mulberry trees, threaded with the first cords of autumn. Bright yellows deepened into amber and fluttered from an orchard, and a grapevine grew from the side of the house, a burgundy canopy over an arbor that led to a kitchen garden.

"Let me escort you to the house." Mr. Jones paid special attention to her mother, which made Viola glad, but he exchanged an exaggerated look with a woman who waved to them from the front door.

And now, they're all yours, he seemed to say.

She felt the sting in the pit of her stomach. It was one thing for Clemmie herself to make demands. Viola could weather those storms. But when someone else bristled at her mother, it tore a hole into her heart.

You don't know why she needs her bird, she wanted to protest. *You don't know her.*

Thankfully, the woman with a sleepy tot called to them with a generous smile.

"Welcome to Blue Wren House, Mrs. Buckley. Miss Buckley.

I'm Mrs. Jones. But I'd be pleased for you to call me Finella. And Shadrach would offer the same informality, if he weren't already back at the wagon." She ushered them in. "Your rooms are ready. Molly and I will show you up."

What Finella Jones lacked in height, she added in brown-eyed warmth and well-practiced cheerfulness. Quite likely the same age as Viola, this woman was married. And a mother. And a guesthouse keeper.

Her manner soothed the rasp left by her husband, and they followed her into a friendly foyer, a welcoming receiving room to their left, and a staircase to their right that trickled with sunshine from a large window somewhere further up.

"We're most grateful you've taken us in. I know the holiday season is over for the year."

"Sometimes, it's more than a holiday that our guests need." Finella rubbed the little girl's back, a miniature dark-haired version of herself, and Viola knew she'd read her letter carefully and was ready to assist with Clemmie's therapy.

"Now, you have purchased full occupancy. The two upstairs bedrooms, as well as this one here on the ground floor. My husband and I share another room down here too, with our daughter." Molly kept her slumber-pink face buried in her mother's shoulder. "But Blue Wren House is all yours." Finella led them up.

Mother made it as far as the first short landing, sniffed, and stopped. "Smoke!"

They all sniffed.

"Oh, it's only a garden fire," Finella said. "Shadrach lit one earlier, behind the barn. And with the front door open just now, the wind has carried the smoke into the house. It's perfectly safe, Mrs. Buckley. I would not allow guests into my home if it were not so."

She reached for Clemmie's hand. "Come, I promise there's nothing to fear."

But Clemmie would not go. She shook her head, terror in her eyes. Viola saw the confusion. The memory of her first Viola, only five, and lost in a fire Clemmie had not been there to extinguish.

Shadrach returned with two more cases. Face drawn, eyes darker, he didn't linger. The distant smoke caught in Viola's breath, now a puff hardly worth noticing. On any other day, no one here would have remarked, but any day with Clemmie was never ordinary.

"It's nothing, dearest. Remember, this is a farm, too. Mr. Jones knows about the fire. He lit it. Come on, up we go."

But Clemmie would not. She hobbled down the stairs and would have reached the verandah if the doorway were not blocked by their host, who dropped the birdcage like an oversized lantern.

"The wind must have blown the cover off when we weren't watching. Where does this fella go? The barn?"

"The barn?" Clemmie cried.

"Bird?" Finella said at the same time.

Balthazar bobbed as if he too waited their answer.

Viola looked from her hostess to her host. "We were hoping we could keep him inside. With us."

Shadrach held up a scratched hand. "This was his greeting when my knuckles came too close. I'm not sure I want those claws in my house, so close to my wife and baby. What if he gets loose?"

As if he knew this was about him, Balthazar splayed his wings and let out a screech.

"He's more frightened than you. I promise, he won't get to any mischief, and Mother's trained him to go to bed peaceably."

"Don't start with me. Don't start with me." Balthazar swayed and grabbed tight to the rail of his cage with one foot.

"Balthazar, where are your manners?" Viola imitated Clemmie's voice. "Arriving with such commotion. Say hello to Little Molly."

"Peek a Boo, I see you. Peek a Boo. Peek a Boo."

Balthazar obliged and Molly and Finella giggled.

Even Shadrach the Sullen looked a tad impressed. "Charming. So, where do we take him?"

Host and hostess looked at each other, and the wordless communication of two hearts crossed between them in ways only they understood. Viola looked away, curious to observe more, aware with unexpected emptiness that her heart cried for the same intimacy.

Clemmie pressed kisses into the air for her pet.

"Could we leave him on the landing outside our rooms?" Viola offered. "I clean his cage every day, and he's well behaved unless provoked. Otherwise, he's your typical galah. Craves all the attention you have to give and then some. Once I unpack, I'll find another cover for his cage. He knows to stay quiet under there."

"The top landing it is, I guess." Finella shrugged.

Shadrach shook his head and carried him up.

"Viola, Viola, Viola." Balthazar cooed, and Clemmie followed, fixed by the only assurance she ever needed, her bird.

"Wish I could cage up that roaming deer. Nothing provokes a man more than the willful damage of everything he's worked hard to build…" Shadrach muttered all the way up, down, and out again.

"Don't mind Shad. You may find him a little distracted. There's a deer on the loose, damaging all our fences and crops."

"Birdy." Molly reached out her chubby baby fingers, but Finella held her tight.

Viola let out a long sigh. People and animals had a way of toppling each other into, or out of, their messes. "Balthazar is a large part of my mother's equilibrium. If I'm going to put her into her bed for the next fortnight, we'll all be glad Balthazar is nearby."

And to bed is exactly where Clemmie went. Into her bedclothes and under sweet smelling covers until Dr. Murdoch's timetable said otherwise.

"I still smell smoke." A fresh pastille rattled around her teeth.

"Smoke is a part of farm life and fully under the control of the farmer. Don't fret. You are here to convalesce."

"Convalesce is such a pretty word. And you're using it the way all performers do. As a pretty prop."

"It's neither prop nor performance, Mother. You're here for treatment. Now, are your feet sore? Shall I rub them for you?"

Clemmie ignored her and peered out the window beside her bed. "The bush is a fortunate place. A firestorm rages through, and everything remains charred for only so long. Then, the rains come, and seeds open with fresh life. Life returns to the bush without the manipulation of anyone."

Viola nodded. Only God himself seeded the future in all the fire consumed. Mother closed her eyes and let her shoulders slump against the fresh pillow.

"How long are we here for, Viola? How… long… will they let us stay?"

Viola steeled herself, but when she turned to reply, Clemmie had succumbed to sleep.

And Viola did not have to dig into uncharted depths for an answer.

Instead, she kissed Clemmie's forehead.

How long?

"As long as it takes for you to become beautiful again."

6

It took only two days of soldier-like attendance for Viola to turn Dr. Murdoch's manual on seaside therapy into a routine they could all follow. A horrible mix of indulgence and torture that left both mother and daughter exhausted.

Each morning, their hosts carted up buckets of cold water for an all-over cold-water bath. A deliberate shock that left Clemmie sobbing for release and Viola ready to run. Cold water therapy was meant to ease the melancholy. Instead, it tore them all to shreds.

Still, it was on Viola's list, so she faithfully wrapped her mother in bed sheets and poured cold water over her while she screamed protest and shivered in the hip bath that was delivered to her room and would not depart until they would.

And while Viola followed Dr. Murdoch's instructions, with Finella's brave assistance, she wondered how this could help, when it inflicted so much terror and discomfort and set Clemmie's teeth to chattering for hours thereafter.

Their first attempt had lasted all of three minutes before Viola pulled her mother free of the freezing shrouds. On the second, not wanting to deprive Clemmie of all her benefits, Viola kept her there one minute longer.

This morning, on their third attempt, Clemmie had wailed so

loudly at the five-minute mark that Viola pulled her up from the bath so fast, she knocked over the bedroom chair where she'd placed Mother's towels and fresh nightdress.

"Isn't this supposed to get easier?" Viola mumbled.

Clemmie's chin quivered. Her startled face, blue-lipped and tear-stained, stared up at Viola, who rubbed with great vigor to bring heat and rejuvenation back into her mother's body.

"It's a sin to do this to any person. Sick or well."

Viola agreed. But her instructions did not allow for cowardice. They directed the patient back to bed and into rich breakfast foods, oozing with fat to lay a healing thickness over Clemmie's gaunt frame.

"Please, Sweet Clemmie. One more spoonful. Finella's made such a delicious bone broth. Please..." Viola pressed the spoon to her mother's closed lips. "And after breakfast, I'll massage your arms and back and then we'll read some more."

"I care for none of those things." Clemmie turned to the window. "All I asked for was to die in a house by the sea. Not be killed in one."

Viola laid the spoon back onto the small table for two. Fatty bone broth cooled into a coagulated mass. Bread and butter remained in their dishes beside fried eggs, yolks disturbed but not fully consumed. And cream-soaked porridge set like a pot of old glue.

Each day, Viola's cheeks flamed when their hostess came to collect their trays. So little consumed by either of them, enough for an entire guesthouse of hungry holiday makers.

"I know, dearest. It's awful. But we're on our third morning already. In time this too shall end."

Clemmie did not answer. And Viola knew it would be like this until the delivery of their luncheon, when her mother would eat a morsel before more massages, more naps, more tears, and more sighs.

Viola's frozen fingers ached. Her head throbbed from her mother's piercing cries. Her temper already frayed with the constant cajoling it took to settle Clemmie. These were the hooks upon which their day hung. And the endless routine loomed before them like a spreading frost.

"Come now." She picked at a piece of toast. "What if I wander into the bush this afternoon and bring back something fragrant for you? Something fresh. A sprig of—"

"I thought you were not meant to stimulate the prisoner."

"You're not a prisoner. You're receiving treatment. And *gentle* stimulation is allowed. That's why I read to you."

Clemmie closed her eyes. Hair damp, bones even more protruding between the ribbons of her morning wrapper.

"When will you go out to sketch? To paint?" Clemmie said. "You should not have to spend your days in here. It's misfortune enough that I am stuck in this bed."

The invitation to explore roared like the sound of a distant waterfall. If she could only roam, breathe in the sea spray, and bring in some of the flora she'd seen on the drive in from the jetty.

Clemmie turned her back to Viola. An offended posture she'd adopted the first time cold water therapy broke into their day with vengeance. But when the sun found Clemmie's window each afternoon, Viola knew she would turn around.

It was then Viola brought Balthazar to Clemmie's door.

A small wooden gate led to the beach. Three days of rain had fed into the rivulets that ran from the farmlet, past low dunes that grew the hardiest of grasses, and into the shallows. Viola closed her eyes and let the wind topple her senses.

What do you feel, Poupette?

Salt air lashed her cheeks, followed by a kiss of eucalyptus and smoke from a nearby farm. Bustle-free, without the small padded accessory that should have elevated her simple soft-wheat shirting dress into something more elegant, she clambered upon a shelf of beach rock. She didn't need to impress dunes and fields. If the mood took her, she would even lie on her back and watch the sky. But she did need Madame Nasrin's shawl, for it fluttered from her outstretched arms like dreams being rattled from her bones.

She followed sand that spilled into a tea tree gully. Over small, purple succulents, into tall reeds and spinifex grass that narrowed onto a tiny foot-worn trail. Under a canopy of gumtree branches, a wild rose climbed along a fence rail and post. Well past flowering, all that remained of summer's show was a rich covering of blood-red rosehips.

The abandon spoke right into her heart. Wild roses past their bloom. She set her valise down and opened its compartments of brushes and pencils. From a tiny corked bottle, she poured water into a porcelain dish and set her small kingdom of paints right where she'd need them.

She made a quick sketch. Tenacious fronds reaching for what they wanted when no one told them where they could or could not go. Or for how long. Or when to return.

Higher up, a larger bunch of rosehips caught her eye. Jewels, at the end of a bent reed. Clemmie would like to see this. There was drama to this cluster, almost too heavy for the plant to hold.

She set her drawing board on the grass and knotted the ends of her shawl behind her back. And her hair, which she'd let fly loose, she braided in the fashion of a schoolgirl.

She climbed the fence, and like a ballerina, balanced along the top with care.

What do you see of God's creation? What story will it tell?

From her pocket, she pulled a tiny botanical sickle and snagged the edge of the branch, one arm raised, the other held out behind her for balance.

"Careful there … um… Little Miss." A voice of disapproval rattled into her efforts. "That fence top's not made for the foolishness you're attempting."

She gasped at the intrusion. She had not expected anyone to come this way, let alone find her in such a delicate predicament. And with an American accent, no less.

A sickening slip in the knot at her back unravelled into a loose betrayal of all that girded her. Well, her shawl might give up, but she would not.

Buckled at the knees and with nowhere to go but down, she jumped, hoping to land in one easy step. Instead, her left heel landed on a fallen branch hidden in the long grass. And in defiance of a lifelong promise to never, ever, let her body yield that way again, Viola folded into a perfect curtsy.

But no, this was far from perfect. The other end of the small log rose to life, clipped her kit, and knocked it sideways. Like a mirror breaking, the sound of all her precious supplies, everything she used to fashion her artist dreams, fell around her.

Scarlet humiliation toppled her fast, but red-hot fury surged in her rising.

From the other side of the fence, a man glared at her, a round felted hat in one of his out-stretched hands, his shoulders held back, as if she'd fly at him next.

Well, he was lucky she hadn't.

"Why would you scare me so? Do you not recognize someone already balancing for dear life?"

Her breath raced to catch up with her raging heartbeat. She skirted around the disarray at her feet. Her kit lay scattered like a game of checkers flung away by an ill-mannered child.

The man dropped his large traveling case in the middle of the road and a slow weariness crept into his face, like he'd set down the weight of all his troubles to pick up this inconvenience.

"You were about to step onto a worm-eaten fence top."

Tall. Cropped hair, raw umber. Clean-shaven, with no ability to disguise his disgust, though everything wrong about this moment was his doing.

She turned away before the urge to look at his eyes took hold. Enough for her were the small creases of his face. Old man creases that appeared years before their time, because they frowned at all the dangers around every corner.

"Well, you spooked me. And now my kit is overturned."

"If I hadn't spoken, you'd be hanging by the ankles. Where I come from, Little Miss, that's called chivalry."

"Where I come from, we mind our own business." She crouched and patted the grass for her lost bits and pieces. Including her dignity, which had abandoned her when she'd dismounted from the fence.

You will curtsy, full and deep, with a bright smile for your audience. And you'll stop smiling when I say so.

Marshall had never let her on stage without reminding her how she was to exit. Well, she'd done it her way then, too. With great trouble for her reward. And now she had *that* memory to contend with, prodded by this stranger.

Her hand sifted the grass. Brushes popped up like pick-up sticks.

And an old rose thorn, long dead, lodged firmly in her tip of her thumb. Like curtsying, she hadn't sucked her thumb in years. But she sure felt like doing it now. The pinprick puncture mark filled with blood, and she pressed it to her mouth.

"Look, I'm sorry I spooked you." The American leaned onto the fence. "Let me help with your things and you can return home to your parents in one piece."

She stared at his scuffed boots and dusty moleskin trousers.

He must think her a child. Well, she guessed from afar, she may have looked like a child at play. Almost up a tree.

My mother is the one in pieces, she would have liked to cry out. Instead, she rummaged for composure and gathered her sketching paper from under a wet patch of grass.

"I can manage my own *foolishness.*"

"Hey, I said I was sorry. Let me help—"

"Thank you, no need." She tried a milder tone and concentrated on assessing her kit. Paints tubes, all here. Paint cakes, three missing.

He jumped the fence. "I'm not a fan of debts. The faster we pack you up, the sooner you can be on your way. With more rain clouds coming in, your mother and father must be looking out for you." He retrieved her small porcelain water dish, bottom up in a puddle of water. She felt a little like that dish right now.

He handed it over. "Are we done?"

She let herself look at him. And hoped his full-faced stare caught all her displeasure.

Under a sturdy coat jacket and woolen vest stood a broad-shouldered man, probably accustomed to hard work and with a face somehow chiseled, like the bones had been intensified by his encounter with her in a permanent tooth grind.

Good. She hoped his jaw ached all night and into tomorrow. He had no business assuming she needed sending back to a mother or father. No business sending her into a curtsy, either.

He stared back, and her nerves sizzled under his gaze. She held on to her aggravation as if it were a priority on Dr. Murdoch's list.

Blue eyes flashed at her. Maybe not as old as she first thought. They weren't young, either. But they were mad. And for however long he stared at her, she would stare back.

Like the curtsy that had fallen from her mistakable past, staring was another one of her skills. It was all about focusing the eye on something small. She'd mastered the art in childhood. Former stage performers could always look into a sea of nameless faces for however long they needed.

He stepped back, hands splayed in surrender.

"I don't fancy watching accidents happen. I'm sorry I interrupted your reckless game."

He cleared the fence and collected his case. And with a short nod of farewell, shot off down the road with a step that crunched the grit under his shoe as if it were the last thread of her pride.

He wasn't young, but he was agile.

Good. Get going, old man.

"I'll show you reckless." She climbed the fence once more. "And foolish."

She took another step, cut the very display she'd aimed for, and dropped it into her gathering basket.

"Clemmie might get away with telling me what to do. There's nothing to be done about that." She plucked a second cluster, because it felt good to doubly do what he'd warned her to avoid.

"But I don't curtsy. For anyone."

Silas followed the dirt road away from the crazy girl as fast as his legs knew how.

What a performance. He'd encountered no trouble taking the ferry to Phillip Island. No trouble hitching a ride to the end of the road. But right on the doorstep of his destination, after almost ten thousand miles, he'd run into trouble of the worst kind.

A girl in braids, if he dared look back over his shoulder, but *no thank you*, he'd not go poking into that wasp's nest again. No, sir, not even if the astrolabe were in her pocket.

He'd stood by and let the ones he loved take all kinds of wrong steps. He'd made a good too many of his own. But it still confounded him that a man could not warn someone of the peril at their feet. Some people didn't want to be told. So, let her step into a rotten fence post and crack her ankle. That misfortune was all hers.

He grabbed a handful of eucalyptus leaves from a low branch and crushed them in his hand. Menthol and honey smells caught in his throat. They'd told him Australia reared poisonous critters and venomous snakes, right under your nose. Even now, the same deadly bushland grew around him with alluring plants crowned by tender flower spikes, others as fat as your head and so full of nectar they drew wildlife into their syrupy core.

But no one told him to look out for a blistering terror in skirts.

Would've been smarter to whistle a tune from a few paces back and warn her gently. But he didn't have the luxury of turning the hands of time. If he could, he wouldn't be tramping down an Australian bush track now, would he?

He swung open the gate. It was as they'd told him in the little fishing village. A pretty white house on a hill. Mulberry trees, an orchard, and rows and rows of fields. A neat garden and a few outbuildings and, from the sound of it, a chicken enclosure beyond that.

Someone grumbled from deep inside the open barn. Tools clanged and then quiet. Sounded like his brother Patrick on a bad day. All temper and fire. He wondered if there would be another brother, a Eugene perhaps, to calm the mood.

He shook the dust off his coat sleeves and cleared his throat. No use spooking a second person in as many hours.

"Hello," he called. "I'm looking for Mr. Shadrach Jones."

A dark-haired man emerged into the light, squinted a little, and looked Silas over.

"I'm Shadrach."

Shadrach Jones didn't look like a man in any mood to take in a guest. He wound a length of rope into a coil as if it were a noose and he the hangman.

Silas lamented afresh the lost letter of introduction. He'd have to cross that rickety bridge without it now.

"I'm Silas Swift. Sailed in from San Francisco with a shipment of logging equipment for next year's International Exhibition. But the truth is, I signed up for the job because I have a personal interest in this part of the world."

"Oh yeah. What's that?"

"My brother and I, we run a small woodworking factory in Portland, Oregon. We supply *Brown and Burrows*, and I believe one of my staircases was part of a kit home delivered to you."

"My house?"

Silas nodded and weighed up how much of the truth he'd share. It was more than something that had brought him here. It was everything. He needed this man to trust him, and that would take all the truth he could afford.

"I'm recently widowed and clearing my head." He took another long breath. "Working out the best way to rummage through that kind of grief. Figured if I came as far as Melbourne, I should make the journey to Phillip Island and see my handiwork for myself. See how it's coping in your climate."

Shadrach stared. "You're the maker of my staircase?"

"At your service." Silas tapped his hat. "We've made dozens exactly like the one in your house, but as far as I know, yours is the only one that's come this far."

The guesthouse owner shook his head. "Never expected you'd turn up on my doorstep. Can't accommodate you with lodging, but I'd not object to showing you inside. Let's go in and you can see it for yourself."

"Oh, but I've come so far. I know it's out of season, but I'd not require much. A bed, simple meals. Somewhere to think while the last few months make some kind of sense."

Shadrach blew out a sharp sigh. "I wish I could help you, chum. There is one vacant downstairs bedroom, but that would be for our guest, Miss Buckley, to decide. She's secured the entire house for an extended stay. She's not using every room, but she's already paid for them all." He waved to someone, and Silas turned.

"Here she comes now. The one you need to ask."

The spit and grit creature from the rambling rose hurried towards them.

Feathers and Guts. A sick dread climbed into his chest. Her basket overflowed with green leaves, and her painting kit bumped her leg with every angry step. She'd taken out her braids, but she still wore that overlong shawl.

"Miss Buckley, this is Mr. Silas Swift. From Portland, America. Mr. Swift, this is our guest, botanical artist, Miss Viola Buckley."

Artist? He knew her as the chit who'd flamed into trouble. His mouth felt like a pit of dust. And his hopes crumbled fast.

"I've already wasted enough of my day meeting Mr. Swift." Her pace did not slacken. "I have him to thank for my wasted afternoon, my wet shoes, two lost pencils, and my ruined sketches picked out of a puddle."

Something about her walking past, nose in the air, kicked him in the shins.

"Without my warning, you'd be limping back. Or worse."

She froze, as if she'd been slapped, then retraced her steps and stood so close, he wondered if their toes might touch. She stared up at him, as if taking stock of his eyes up close this time.

Tavern girls had fallen into Swift brothers' eyes and gladly told them so. Patrick had tales of his own. Eugene, Patrick's twin, didn't receive those compliments, but he also wore the Swift brother eyes. He just kept them guarded. Unlike Silas, who couldn't look away from this girl if he tried.

Hair like cornbread and rust, and light brown eyes that sparked and drew him back into their quarrel.

"You would not have held your tongue, because you're an old killjoy," she said.

"Old?"

"Ancient. Which is why it probably offends you to see a woman reach for anything beyond her. Am I right?" She steamed on. "I don't know why Shadrach called me over here. I don't have time to listen to you beg my forgiveness."

"Now, Miss Buckley." Shadrach grimaced. "Perhaps you and Mr. Swift need to start over, because, well, turns out he's here for begging of some kind. He's a stair-maker, here to appraise his handiwork which, as it turns out, is in my house. He's asking for a week's room and board, but I already explained, you've secured full occupancy."

Miss Buckley stepped back and transferred her heavy basket from one hand to the other, impatience etched on her face and in the fast blinking of her eyes.

"Why are you telling me all this? Why not tell Mr. Swift so he can leave now?"

"I wanted to give you the chance. Unless, of course, you have it in you to say yes and allow him to stay."

"Stay?" She looked from one man to the other. "Here?"

The laughter of kookaburras rolled over them. Distorted cackles and hoots and trills that might as well have been the entire bush, mocking him for this desperate bid for all he'd lost. Was this where his mission failed?

Not today. He'd wouldn't give up until they booted him off the property.

"Look, I'd not get in your way, miss. I promise. And I'd reimburse some costs you've already paid. All I'm asking for is a week to admire the location and view something I crafted with my own hands a long time ago when life was a little different to what… it is right now."

At this admission, her eyes lost a little of their steel, and she tilted her head to peer at him afresh. Something in his appeal had caught her attention.

"Miss?"

"Miss, is it, now? Not *Little* Miss?"

"Forgive me. I thought you were younger."

Good grief, the freckle-faced tempest still looked young. Her shawl dragged like a tablecloth, flung over her shoulders pantomime-style, the way Honora and Mary, his sister, had played when they were children.

"Mr. Swift…" Miss Buckley set the basket down and propped her hands on her hips. She paced a little, as if considering how to string her words. "My mother is convalescing from a recent fall and other ailments."

She wagged a finger at him, like a metronome, counting time, measuring her words in her own head before she set them free. "If you want the unoccupied room downstairs, it will be on one condition."

"Anything." He almost slipped his hands into a prayer like pose. "I'll keep well away from your mother and not make a sound. You won't even know I'm here."

"On the contrary, Mr. Swift." She faced him with a look of pure assessment, hands back on her hips, spine ramrod straight. As if something new lodged there. "An American visitor would do my mother the world of good. If you agree to keep her company each afternoon, I'll agree to your week's accommodation."

He glared at her, the dusty driveway beneath him a little less secure than when he'd stepped on it. And for the second time in as many hours, he found himself in a staring competition with her.

"Company?" He could barely say it. "In a sickroom?"

"Every afternoon, at one. During the hours when the doctor has prescribed reading and light conversation. You do read, sir?"

The swill of sickness and the rooms in which it roamed rose hot and sour in his gullet. They'd not let him into Honora's room, and he'd not fought to enter. He swallowed hard.

"Is your mother contagious?"

"No."

"Even so… I don't know if I'm the right—"

"You are. Trust me. *She's* fond of Americans." She said that with a tone that left him in no doubt she herself was not. To prove it, she concentrated on picking up her basket. Threading her arm through the wide handle. Propping up a rose cane, ribbed in thorns and tipped with a cluster of rosehips.

A man would be a first-class fool to commit to this kind of entrapment without first meeting the woman in the sickroom. And from the tiniest corner of her mouth where a smug twitch flickered, Miss Buckley knew it too.

Of all the obstructions, *this girl* stood between him and his mission. Although, now that he cared to assess her in return, she was no girl. Not really. She was a young woman, inviting him into her trouble.

She waited, daring him to agree, clutching her basket as well as all the ammunition, all the aces, and all the bargaining chips. But something about the way she waited made him think this wasn't all punishment for startling her and calling her *Little Miss*.

She needed this arrangement as much as he did.

"So, what do you say, Mr. Swift? Are you in?"

He sucked in another deep breath. God help him, this upside-down land was a maddening place. Leaves fell off trees in April, and brilliant constellations rose in hidden skies. But he'd come this far, and he would not be sent away emptyhanded by a wild wasp, barely out of girlhood.

"If it's an old killjoy you need, Miss Buckley, I'm in."

7

Early morning noises brought Blue Wren House to life. Arms behind his head, Silas listened to the day break through. He had no choice. A magpie chorus warbled right outside his window.

Last night, Shadrach Jones had shown him through the house. Not a lingering tour, but enough to get his bearings. Now, ground floor doors opened and closed, and that baby, a dark-haired little girl he'd encountered yesterday, cried for her mama.

Shushing sounds and low conversation mingled with the scrape of a chair and then a soft laugh. He figured the Jones family were used to tiptoeing around their guests. He knew precious little about children, but this one looked around two years old. Much the same age his own would have been if Honora hadn't …

He shifted in his bed and let the noises from above distract him. Humming? No, something more urgent. The voices of Miss Buckley and her mother.

"No, no… please … not again, please, Viola."

Someone begged, and whatever was offered in reply became lost in the sound of quick footsteps up the stairs, then the thud of something heavy landing on the floorboards above. A third female voice, the mistress of the house.

Silas snuck his finger behind the drape at his window and peered out. The sky held more blue in it now. He brought in the hot water left for him outside his door. Maybe now, while the inhabitants of the house were at their busiest, he might dare inspect the bottommost newel post of the staircase. He dressed and ventured into the entryway of the house.

Kitchen sounds rang louder from here. Soft light spilled from the windowpanes around the front door, but there were still enough shadows for him to slip into. And it was not what he saw that mattered, anyway. It was what he would feel. The staircase looked as solid as he knew it would be. He'd run his fingers over rails and balustrades last night, but nothing like what he'd do to it now.

Shadrach burst from his private quarters and almost bumped into him.

"Morning," he rasped and side-stepped into the front room, gathered something and quickly retreated. "Here you are, Molly. Found it."

For such a remote location, there sure were enough people milling around. He'd hardly touched the cool wood of the ground floor newel when a horrible shriek broke over the house.

He flattened himself against the nearest wall and let the blood curdling moan wash over him. Light flickered from a lamp on the landing windowsill, like desperate arms flailing for freedom, and blood stormed into his head to match the pounding of his heartbeat.

"Almost done, dear." Words collided with fresh crying and the sound of water being poured out. Lots of it. A steady stream of pouring and crying.

"Ah, Viola… please. Enough."

"Shh, now. You'll wake up Mr. Swift. Only one more bucket and then we're done with this cold water."

Cold water? Silas shivered and a sick churning picked up in his stomach. He sank onto the bottom step, against a thick polished beam cut from his own supply of Douglas Fir.

"You're not needed up here, Silas. Doctor's orders. It may sound cruel, but the screams you'll hear are exactly what we desire. If we don't break Honora's will, there's no escaping the torment of her mind. Her recovery hinges on these treatments."

"But..." Silas had offered every reasoning a husband should. *"It's cruel. It sounds like torture. She's already so fragile. What if she needs me?"* But nothing had convinced the nurse who experimented with Dr. Weir's treatments. Or Mary, who took over once they'd shown her what to do.

And Silas had walked away, to bury himself in the business of furniture making, because if he wasn't allowed to protect his wife, at least he could protect his brothers and their business.

The sound of low moaning tore him from that memory.

"This is the last sheet, and then Finella will take it all away."

Soft crying replaced the protestations. A resigned shivering and teeth-rattling whimper. *The last sheet.* That confirmed it then. The odious ice-cold wrapping of newly woken patients. The pouring of more cold water until their bodies gave up and sank into shock.

He could guess some of what would come next. He only hoped it would not end for the lady upstairs the way it had for his wife.

"Almost done, then I'll massage the warmth back into you, and Finella will bring us a lovely hot breakfast."

The angry, wild Viola from yesterday made soothing promises. Her tone was soft. He imagined an encouraging smile on her face. Nothing like the scowl she'd served him on the road nor the calculated pondering she'd displayed when she negotiated his stay. No wonder she was given to sudden outbursts, with this to contend with each morning.

"And in the afternoon, you'll meet Mr. Swift, and won't that be a treat?"

"Not without my wig, it won't."

"I shall fix your hair. And he'll be charmed by your..."

The clatter of footsteps on the landing shook him to attention. Empty buckets clanged against each other.

"I won't be long."

"Thank you, Finella."

He hurried back to his room and shut the door with a soft click.

Can't do it.

The thought struck him like a fist to the gut. He'd promised to read to a woman he thought might suffer gout or those ugly varicose veins, but this was impossible. What if she cried? What if she refused to talk, like Honora?

He paced, hands on his head. He was meant to come in, grab what he needed, and run home. Not wade into the sorrow he'd left behind.

An eerie silence settled over the house, and he cracked the door open.

Finella swept by with an enamel trough filled with sodden sheets. "Good morning, Mr. Swift. I'm so sorry about the noise from upstairs. I hope we didn't wake you." She looked like she'd fought with someone who'd pulled at her hair.

"I was already awake, but poor Mrs. Buckley. She..." He had no words for the hurt clawing inside him. "She..."

"She takes a cold water bath each morning. Today was particularly bad just when we hoped it might get easier. But who can blame her for fussing? It's the cruelest part of her day, but I hear you are to visit in the afternoon. That should cheer her up." She smiled, but Silas was not sure he had it in him to smile back.

"I'm not very good with… the infirm."

"She will be in better spirits when you arrive, and if not, I am sure she will be after she makes your acquaintance."

He wished he could agree with her.

"I'll have your breakfast on the dining table in fifteen minutes." She hurried on and left him in the hallway, where the staircase beckoned, but not for the reasons that had brought him here.

"Better, dearest?"

"Yes." The reply so soft he could have imagined it.

"There, back into bed with you now. You'll warm up in no time."

"And you…. promise he'll come, the American? I haven't… heard his voice so far this morning. What if he's gone?"

"He's here," Miss Buckley replied, but the warmth of her words now carried some kind of resignation.

"Do you suppose he's a singer?"

"I do not. But he's protective. He'll remain alert, and if you need something, he'll probably already know it." As if aware of his loitering, the bedroom door clicked shut, and all that followed were the muffled sounds of a daughter tending to her mother.

He rested his hand on the newel post Shadrach had selected from the three that came in his kit. All designed by Silas because he delighted in making objects that, where possible, served a dual purpose. With hidden compartments for the keeping of secrets.

What secrets did Mrs. Buckley keep? To discover that, he'd have to bypass the posts for now. Sit with a sick woman who needed company. Make her day a little easier. Do for her what he'd not been able to do for Honora. Find out for sure if any of this lunacy delivered what the crackpot doctors promised.

And to do all that, as well as break into Shadrach's staircase, he'd need to break a little of himself open, too.

Viola watched him from the window. The small bedroom clock in Mother's room almost stood at one and ticked with little beats that married the small tremor within her. She tapped Mother's hairbrush into her palm. What had she done?

She'd been watching him now for almost an hour. He'd followed the shell paths of the house under the little mulberry grove and into the large orchard where he'd picked something up and shined it on his coat. She'd invited a man no one could vouch for into their sickroom. And roped the stranger into reading so she could rummage through the bush for something to paint.

Her plan had sounded good when she'd wanted to throw *him* off balance. Now, that victory ate at her stomach.

"Clemmie, dearest." She tapped the brush once more. "Here's the plan. When Finella brings fresh towels to your room, should you feel uncomfortable in Mr. Swift's company, for any reason, you will plead tiredness and she will rescue you."

"What if the American needs rescuing from me? Who will help him?"

"He's not afraid to speak his mind." Viola brushed a loose end of Clemmie's hair. "I half expect him to admonish me for something that's out of place in here."

She ran one last check of the room. Medicine and water at hand. Yesterday's newspaper beside a stack of novels. Atop these, Viola had added a tiny book of prayers and Mother's favorite bookmark.

"You look beautiful." She fussed with Clemmie's pink cashmere night jacket that she now wore all day long, anxious to keep moving while they listened for him on the landing through the door she'd left ajar. *Nothing will go wrong*, she told herself, and let the lie sink back into her mouth like her own poison pastille.

"Who goes there? Here's trouble. Who goes there?" A footfall sounded on the landing, and Balthazar shrieked. For once, she was glad of his hostile ways.

"Who wants to know?" replied the American.

Balthazar let out a disgusted shriek.

Viola exchanged a boggle-eyed look with Mother. "My word!" she whispered. "A question for a question." And a bubble of laughter formed in her throat.

Normally, strangers reacted to Balthazar's aggression by backing away, and who could blame them when his outstretched wings banged against the cage as if he were trying to push you around. Some brave souls coaxed more birdy language. No one answered a question with a question.

She liked that. Clever words were the quick sketches of a curious mind.

"Who goes there? Who goes there?" Balthazar tried again.

"Are you brave enough to find out?"

Viola pressed the smirk between her lips. Old Killjoy was not instantly afraid of Balthazar. She swung the door open to let him in.

And there he stood. Flushed from his walk, a red apple in hand. He wore yesterday's coat and vest, but he'd swapped his necktie for a bright blue one.

"Miss Buckley. Good afternoon." He nodded.

"Mr. Swift. Do come in." She pointed to the general area of Mother's bed and the reading chair beside it. "May I introduce my mother, Mrs. Clementine Buckley. Mother, this is Mr. Swift, of Portland, Oregon."

"But the apple is local, ma'am. And much fresher than me." He offered his gift to Clemmie and bowed once more. "With my best wishes for a complete recovery."

The apple was for Mother. But the *fresh* jibe was for her.

A happy spark flashed from Clemmie's eyes. "Stolen?" She spoke in wide-eyed theatrics.

"The apple?" He shook his head. "It toppled right to my feet. Shame to leave it there, so I picked it up." He spoke to Clemmie, but a quick flick of his eyes met Viola's.

A small chuckle threatened the serious composure she tried to maintain. The face of someone who was not a little girl. Who didn't giggle. Even though that's exactly what her mother was about to do. Because Mr. Swift had arrived with a gift and wit, and those two combined always paved a way with Clemmie, who patted her hair and rewarded him with a broad smile.

A smile Viola had not seen on Clemmie in months.

"Now, Mr. Swift." Viola tried to remember what she'd rehearsed. "Our routine is fixed, with room for minor alterations. Right now, Mother's not permitted to read, but listening is excellent therapy. Perhaps avoid the newspaper court reports. Our doctor insists on nothing over-stimulating." She tapped the green manual on the table as reference.

"Does he?" Mr. Swift eyed the manual. "Some doctors are idiots. They wouldn't know how to properly treat the infirm if you begged them." He flattened his palm upon the books. "Mrs. Buckley, I am at your service. Anything your heart desires is what we shall read together. We can start here and make our way through these, one by one."

And like the sun coming out from behind a cloud, Clemmie beamed.

He pulled the book of prayers from the stack. "Is this one of your pieces, Miss Buckley?" He slipped the card out.

"It is."

Each year, on her sister's birthday, Viola gave Clemmie a bookmark. This one carried two viola flowers in a round glass vase. One in vibrant purples, the one behind it in subdued lavender tones.

"I like how the water swirls like that. It looks real." He laid the book aside but held on to the little painted bookmark. "How proud you must be, Mrs. Buckley. Your daughter is most talented."

Something about the way he held the card, admiring from up close, made Viola feel like she was being taken apart under a glass magnifier.

"Two competing blooms. The one at the front demands attention and gets it immediately, but if you look long enough, the one behind draws the eye with something more. It's the deeper shading in the petals. And the way it bleeds into the water."

Her checks flushed. Like a critic, he appraised her work. In one glance, he'd found what her mother had never seen, no more than two similar flowers on the same page. His fast interpretation fed into the hungry places of her heart.

"Mr. Swift, your chair." Mother pointed to where he should sit. "Viola has temporarily lost her tongue. Perhaps because all eyes can tell you're not as old as she said you were."

"Oh, I am old."

"My daughter said 'ancient.'"

Viola blushed.

"Ancient and grumpy. But her appraisal is—"

"Hush, Clemmie!" Viola had not expected the ancient grumpy one to charm her mother so fast. Already they were bantering in ways that could only spell trouble.

"Fear not. Your mother and I will find the best stories to sink into." The eyes of Mr. Swift held some kind of mischief, and he was now gaining ground in their quiet war-of-words. He picked up her supplies and held them out to her. Her art case and her gathering basket. Like he already knew her. And now he was dismissing her. This would take some thinking to remedy. She took her things and checked the room for her shawl. Draped over the back of the chair, under his hand on which he leaned while he waited for her to depart, lay her suzani.

She stood there like a lump, wanting to grab it, unable to because… up close, old Killjoy looked significantly younger.

"Pardon me." She tugged at her garment, and the shawl snapped like a cloth on a washing line. Mr. Swift twisted away to avoid a collision, but too late, the fabric sailed around him, and the white fringing smacked him in the face, skimmed the dresser, and knocked over a jug of rosehips.

"Oh dear!" Viola scrunched the shawl to her chest.

"Ow." He stepped back, wincing, blinking hard.

"Oh no. Did I…?" Heat fired in her cheeks and flooded her hairline with humiliation.

"Oh yes. You got me." Face red, he wiped his eye.

"Oh dear, oh dear." She pulled a clean handkerchief from her pocket and pushed it into his hand.

He blinked through tears. "Well, I still have the other eye."

Clemmie shifted her legs and sat up, more awake than Viola had seen her in days. She peered at Mr. Swift, head cocked sideways to take it all in. Mr. Swift, then Viola. And back to their guest. Assessing something Viola could not see. Or could not afford to.

Mr. Swift's teary eye opened a little and winked at her a few more times. "At least we're consistent. What shall we knock over tomorrow?" He looked around the room. "You could elbow that lovely painting off the wall or perhaps empty the contents of that wardrobe. Maybe we'll let that bird out of his cage." He delivered his teasing with hardly a smile, but mischief aplenty rang from his voice. "Go on. Get out of here. Go find something to paint."

"If you're certain you're well enough." Viola righted the rosehips and tried not to study his face.

"I've weathered worse." He winked at Clemmie, and Viola sorely hoped it was for the recovery of his vision.

She kissed her mother goodbye.

"No climbing," Clemmie whispered.

And Silas Swift, emboldened and now in firm control of the room, pointed to Clemmie and nodded as if he, too, would have given the same admonition.

No climbing, indeed! Viola hurried down the staircase. The old man had turned out to be younger, and given the right provocation, in possession of a spark of humor.

Oh, what had she done? He'd started well enough with that rosy apple and chivalrous entry. Viola hugged the wooden post at the bottom of the stairs. Given the right attention, Mother would take any thread and spin it into… what? Viola looked up.

Every night, on the landing windowsill, Finella kept a glowing lantern for those who searched for safety in a storm. Finella was wise. Viola, on the other hand, had lured trouble into the sickroom. She tried to calculate the damage. Whatever mischief Mother made in her absence would be but another small fire Viola would put out when it flamed.

Wouldn't she?

Besides, what harm could Clemmie weave in six or seven afternoons with Mr. Swift?

"Viola, Viola. Viola." Balthazar rocked back and forth in his cage and bid farewell to Viola the Wild. "Don't start with me. Don't start with me."

"He doesn't like you." Mrs. Buckley fussed with her bedcovers. "He doesn't like Viola, either. Don't let it vex you."

Silas wanted to ask if Viola deserved it. Had she always been full of belligerence and sass? Instead, he reached for a newspaper. "I imagine with your ill-health there's been much to occupy your daughter's mind."

"And how do you imagine such a thing, Mr. Swift? You, a young man, healthy enough to travel so far from home."

He smiled to be called young by the mother of the one who'd called him old. Most days, he felt very stuck in the middle. Old was a coat he wore because he had to. The costume of the oldest sibling, strung tight with obligations that pinched and pulled and never relented.

He looked at the woman before him. Sallow skin. Skeletal frame. Breath too short. Weary from whatever trauma life had delivered. He knew that in a person. He'd watched it feed on his own wife and eventually consume her.

"I dare imagine it, Mrs. Buckley, because like your daughter, I too have witnessed a loved one crippled into bedrest. Melancholy ravaged my wife's body and mind until..." The newspaper trembled a little in his hand, so he rested it on his knee.

"Until she died," Mrs. Buckley finished for him.

"Yes." He hadn't planned on telling her. It was a mystery to him how the words had even found their way to his tongue. Seeing Mrs. Buckley, bedridden like Honora, had pulled a hidden snag.

"I'm sorry," she said. "There is nothing worse than a loved one disappearing before you're ready to let them go." There was not much else to say that would not sound empty, and he was glad she did not try.

He scanned the newspaper headings. "Lost and Found. How about we start there?" He shook the newspaper as if it contained life to bring forth. "No wars or homicides."

Mrs. Buckley nodded and settled into her pillows.

"Lady's gold locket," he began. "Lost Friday night, Powlett Street, Fitzroy."

"I know that intersection." Mrs. Buckley opened her eyes. "It's been picked. Gone for good. What's next?"

Silas agreed. He'd lost his letter of introduction, probably to a pickpocket.

"Ten Shillings Reward. Lost on Spencer Street Omnibus, green silk umbrella, silver handle."

"Slim chance." Mrs. Buckley kept her eyes closed. "Already pawned. Next."

Silas smiled. She was not being lulled into any kind of sleep here. He was waking her up. And while he didn't mean to annoy Viola Buckley, there was something satisfying in defying her.

"Twelve shilling reward. Lost rosella parrot. Sunday morning, Victoria Parade."

Mrs. Buckley's eyes snapped open. "Whoever finds it will have to give it back. It's cruel to take someone's bird. Barbaric!" A fit of coughing wracked her slender body.

Silas helped her sit up. Offered her a glass of water. Watched her tremble and take the tiniest sip.

"An umbrella and a locket are lost items. A pet, a parrot, any bird, anything alive that you hold close, does not belong in the lost and found column."

"Mrs. Buckley, forgive me. The word parrot jumped off the page, and with your bird out there, chattering on…"

"Balthazar," she whispered. "Pass me my lozenges. My throat…"

She rubbed her neck, and he offered her a tin of eucalyptus and cocaine. If it didn't elevate her mood, at least it would put her to sleep.

"Let's read something else. Your daughter will take out my other eye if she knows I failed you. Besides, that lost parrot has probably already winged its way home."

Mrs. Buckley frowned. "I once knew a man like you. He chose which rules to keep and which ones to break. Because of that, he found…" She shook her head, as if the words were too precious to tumble from her heart. "Well, he found himself with the best of me, a long time ago."

The woman had found her own diversion. And it rose from her memories and settled around them. Miss Buckley had not invited him in for something so intimate. It could lead to trouble he'd not bargained for.

"Did you know I came here on the *Clara*?" He blurted out the distraction. "With a shipment of logging equipment for the International Exhibition. You may wish to see it—"

Mrs. Buckley dismissed the notion with a shake of her hand. "I will not live to see that exhibition. The years have battered my heart. I feel it giving up on me each day. Viola and Dr. Murdoch think I will recover with a little sea air, horrid cold baths, and fatty food. But when one has cradled a broken heart as long as I have, they know…"

Honora knew too. When she'd let him into her sickroom right at the end, she'd talked like this too.

"Are you good at keeping secrets, Mr. Swift?"

He nodded. Buried secrets had brought him this far. "I am the best at secret keeping."

Another coughing fit interrupted her, and this time she took longer to recover.

"Like you, that exhibition is driving Viola to places she's never been. She needs to find something in the bush that will become the inspiration for her entry. She's driven to make her mark in the amateur category. I only tell you because I think you'll understand. Your wife, how old was she?"

"Almost twenty-four."

"And, are there children?"

"No." Honora had lost all the babies she'd carried. None of them had lived to see the day, and she had gone to them.

"Viola wants a career in botanical illustrating. She thinks the exotics in the Botanic Gardens will set her free." Her voice dropped to a whisper. "Now that she's been forced to look elsewhere, she must discover her true talents. But when I can no longer hold on—"

"Now, now, Mrs. Buckley. Let's—"

"No, you listen. I know you've been roped into sitting here. Keeping me company, reading…"

Her eyes darted, as if they were connected to the cogs of her mind. Like her daughter, she formed a plan. And he was at the heart of it.

"You know what death looks like. Our hosts are good people and will do what is right, but Viola will need someone acquainted with grief to steer her through those early days of loss. Someone who is free from business and family commitments. Someone who will remind her she can finish what she's begun." She pointed at him.

Feathers and Guts! Surely the woman before him was not dying today or tomorrow? Was she?

"I am only here for the week. And—"

"When does your ship leave for America?"

"Early June. But I'm not on Phillip Island that long. Please, Mrs. Buckley, I know your therapy might seem intolerable, but you must await the restoration your doctor hopes for."

It hadn't worked for Honora, but that didn't mean the idiot doctors got it wrong all the time.

"Hope, Mr. Swift, rises from where it's least expected. That could be you, in this case. Viola will need a friend with your maturity. Your presence brings out a quicker wit in her. And a smile she thinks she can hide. You've become a sparring partner already, and she doesn't even know it."

She was asking for the impossible. "Mrs. Buckley, the seaside is a powerful place of healing."

"Perhaps we are all here for some kind of healing, Mr. Swift. Don't rush to take yourself out of that." She closed her eyes, and for the longest time, all she did was breathe. Softer and slower, until a little sob caught in her throat and she opened her eyes.

"Please, Mr. Swift, say you will."

He squirmed. "If I am here and your daughter needs me in a season of grief, I will not withhold what she requires."

"That is most kind." She patted his hand. "She thinks you're a killjoy, but I see what she cannot. Not yet, that is..." Her words slurred into the ramblings of one hooked on the opiates that dragged them to sleep.

"Whatever you do... don't torture Viola by telling her you've already had one... wife... if you think you'd like her to become the second. Not until you're sure... she's in love with you."

8

"So?" Viola dug her fingers into the pot of Otto of Roses and extracted a blob of massaging lotion. "Which book did Mr. Swift choose to read? Or did you do the choosing?"

Clemmie crushed a gum leaf from an arrangement Viola had brought her and pressed it to her nose. "He chose the newspaper."

"He what? After I made it clear that was the worst option?"

"Perhaps he wanted to prove you wrong."

"I bet he did." She massaged Mother's legs as if the knots beneath the skin were the quandary in her mind. Was she bothered that he'd defied her, or was she bothered that he'd played this new game of theirs in her absence, knowing Clemmie would inform her he'd won?

She let a small smile creep in. Winning was admirable in her books. It had always been so. Apples and games. Humph.

"He will leave soon. Best not get too used to his charms, Clemmie."

"Or you could pay closer attention to Mr. Swift. He's experienced in areas that might be of value to you, my girl. He's a man who won't be told what to do, and he's generous. That makes for pure adventure."

Adventure? Silas Swift looked adventure in the eye and told it to sit down and be quiet. Perhaps the aromatic collision of roses and eucalyptus played havoc with Clemmie's senses. Poor dear was more confused than ever. Or was the confusion in Viola?

She tried to ignore the flutter he'd created in her when he'd admired her bookmark. The way he'd understood what she was trying to say in one small floral tribute to the girl who'd come before her and always stood in her way.

"Generous? He traded time with you to secure his lodging. And brought you a fallen gift. Apples are cheap when they're picked off the ground."

"He brought me something that has no price, hope. That's all I'll say. The rest you'll have to discover yourself."

Herself? She had four months to unearth something wonderful, sketch it, paint it, and tie it up into a ribbon-wrapped entry. Right now, her room overflowed with narrow leaf peppermint gum and a large cluster of yellow banksias. And on the verandah, her gathering basket awaited, filled with great swathes of eucalyptus. Fragments that needed shaping. And that took time, none of which she'd waste on Clemmie's dreamy mysteries.

Viola tucked her mother's legs back under the covers. She hadn't spoken of hope in a long time. Had sea air snuck in with Mr. Swift and wrought an unexpected soothing?

Viola plumped the pillows. Clemmie already slept. Or pretended to, with a soft smile on her lips and the furrows in her brow softer still.

"Well, well, Mr. Swift." Viola whispered to the windowpane. Thick clouds ran in the twilight sky. "Haven't you delivered the unexpected?"

She tiptoed onto the landing, fed Balthazar a generous chunk of carrot, and pushed into her bedroom. The banksia beckoned. A display that deserved her artist's eye.

But it was the talents of Mr. Swift that she pondered. Adventurous? Curiosity grew like an awakening creature, unfolding and stretching with slow but deliberate pokes into the deep and vulnerable places she guarded well.

A gust of wind ran along the roof. She'd have to bring in those gum leaves before they scattered all over the verandah.

"Here's your tea, Mr. Swift." Finella's voice rang out.

Viola loitered at the top of the stairs, hoping Balthazar would not pick now to abuse her with loud insults. But his mouth and claws were busy tearing apart his treat.

She sat on the top step of the staircase made by the man who lived under her room and listened to him take the tray and thank Finella. He'd read to Clemmie and not left her worse than he'd found her. Probably enhanced by his smooth American tones. Mother loved that. Hadn't they all?

Junius Abner, the visiting ventriloquist from New York, had used his American voice to charm them, too. Audiences came for miles to hear his dummies; Philomena, Little Lazlo, and Cesar. But his authentic voice, the one he used to speak with Viola, had set her free.

"Do it," Junius had whispered into her ear after that last rehearsal. *"You're not a puppet. Show them. Your father hasn't a clue about the fine performer under that ugly wig."*

Soft footsteps sounded below. Viola peered into the staircase shaft. There, at the bottom step, Mr. Swift wrapped a piece of steaming cloth around the decorative top of the widest post.

Was he polishing the wood? A loud laugh came from the kitchen. Without letting go, he leaned in that direction and frowned. The sing song of mother and child threw something wholesome over what Viola watched, but Clemmie's new friend let out a puff of breath like a sneaky thief. He ripped the material away, and the last trace of steam disappeared into the air. This was more than an examination of woodwork. Old Killjoy inhaled like a man about to commit some crime. And she'd caught him.

She gathered her skirt close and smiled. This could be fun.

He pushed on the post as if it were a magic box that would open if pressed in the right place. It didn't. Then, just like a thief, he pulled a tool from his pocket and worked the tip into the wood.

"Come on, come on," he uttered under his breath. "That's it."

"No, Miss Molly. Not for little girls." Finella's voice sounded a little louder than before. "I'll take that, thank you."

Perhaps the door from the kitchen to the hallway had swung open, but now the sound of meal preparations rang louder, with the rattle of something being dropped onto a tabletop and the sound of protest from the child.

Clemmie was right. Silas Swift made his own rules. And whatever game this was, he played it alone. She didn't know why that appealed to her. Why seeing him like this drew her in. Eavesdropping and snooping were character flaws, imperfections not worth celebrating. Still, she watched on.

Instead of testing the post for support, its creator pried open the top piece the way she removed the head from a piece of fruit for Balthazar. He laid the wooden block at his feet, stepped onto the second riser, and thrust his hand deep into the crevice.

A secret hiding spot! A deep one. It swallowed his arm, which he pulled out, empty-handed. He let out a long sigh, and she almost felt sorry for him.

Like her, but for his own peculiar reasons, he was on some kind of hunt.

He slipped into his room and returned with a tin pot and a thin brush. As fast as he'd broken into the post, he now repaired it. Was that glue?

In a flash he pieced it together and returned the pot to his room. In his absence, Viola slid down the stairs, just a little.

When he returned, he pressed hard on the glued pieces. And that's when his gaze wandered to where her shawl fringe spilled and hung between the balustrades. Cutlery rattled from the kitchen. The gathering of items that would soon be laid for them on their respective tables.

But he blinked up at her as if he'd not heard a thing. She blinked back and bit on her smile.

"You are kidding me." He looked away, then straight back at her, as if to make sure she really sat there.

Finella hummed from the drawing room, and the snap of a tablecloth jangled Viola's nerves. She could only imagine how he fared.

"Am I in your way, Mr. Swift?"

"Not if you stay put." He hardly moved his lips, but agitation fired into his whisper. "Please," he adjusted his tone, "just… stay there." He turned his attention to the object in his hands. "Come on, stick!"

"What are you doing?"

"I'm… testing," he whispered and checked over his shoulder, "the newel post stability."

"Oooh." She joined him with her own raspy reply. Elongated and theatrical. "Is it more stable if we whisper?"

He ignored her and pushed the block hard. It didn't budge. He swallowed hard.

"So many pieces… and the, ah," he tapped the post at the base with his foot, "ground level newel always bears the brunt of… people taking the stairs in a hurry." A bead of sweat trickled down his neck.

"What about the brunt of people who secretly force it open with the tip of their knife, check within the cavity, then hastily glue it back before they're found out?"

He looked up and his eyes, a myriad of blues, rolled a little the way eyes do when people chastise themselves for their own stupidity.

"Listen, I'm..." He struggled for the right start, and at Viola's core, the girl who'd been told only days ago she was foolish for climbing a fence squirmed to be let loose.

But he'd left her mother with some kind of dreamy hope, and that small gesture made her want him to win whatever game he played here.

The front door banged open, and a gust of wind blew in, along with Shadrach Jones, who stormed into the hallway.

"That deer! A man can't sow a row of potatoes without having to watch over it!" He slammed the door, but it swung back open.

He stared at Viola, then Mr. Swift, whose hands still pressed on the post.

"What's going on here?" He frowned.

Viola stood. "Mr. Swift was explaining to me the various parts of a staircase. How it all fits together like a puzzle, starting with the..." She pointed.

"Newel post." Mr. Swift could barely utter the words. His thumb stroked the wood where the tiniest blob of glue had seeped from the pressure he still applied.

If Shadrach saw that, if he came any closer, he'd smell trouble for sure.

Viola hurried down. "Which way is your potato field? I'd like to sketch this deer." She pulled their host into the drawing room, where a settee resided in the bay window at one end and a small table set for one on the other. A pair of binoculars hung from a hook on the wall beside seaside prints and a framed flower made of seashells.

She pointed to the window. "In that direction?"

"Too dark to see now, but even during daylight hours, you will keep to the gardens or beach, miss. You will not step foot onto my fields or come anywhere near that deer. Do you hear me? Last thing I need is a guest with a bullet in them."

He stormed through the drawing room and into the kitchen.

Grinning, Viola swung back to the scene of the other raid on Shadrach's property. Mr. Swift had let go of the post and was rubbing glue off his fingers. She waited for him to look up. She had saved him. She wasn't sure from what, but he'd tell her. Hadn't her mother gushed about his generosity?

"You're welcome," she teased, not waiting for him to thank her. Although he did owe her that much.

Not properly shut, the front door rattled. He looked from it to her, grabbed her by the hand, drew her onto the verandah, and pulled the door shut behind them.

Light rain fell over the courtyard. She shivered and gathered her shawl closer, unsure if the sudden cold could compete with the rush of heat that spiked her arm. Whatever this feeling was, this shared secret, the rescuing of him from Shadrach's temper, and the way he'd seized her, was something she'd never experienced.

He stared. They were making a habit of this. She stared back.

"Quite the performer, aren't you?" he said.

The wind picked up and rustled the fringe on her shawl.

"Lucky for you I know when to improvise."

"Hmm." He crossed his arms. "Any luckier and you may not set my hair on fire."

"What are you looking for?"

He frowned at her, as if the gears in his head weighed her request with the wisdom of answering it.

"It's nothing."

"It's something, or you wouldn't be playing with your life, right under Shadrach's nose."

"The least I can do for Shadrach is quietly find what I came for, pocket *my possession,* that he knows nothing about, and get out of his way."

"But, is it—?"

"It doesn't matter." He scratched the top of his eyebrow with his thumbnail and shrugged. Viola couldn't tell if it was to sever her interest or if he truly felt his search was hopeless.

"Of course it matters. You've come all this way to retrieve *something.* This is not about how the wood has adapted to a new climate. This is a hunt, isn't it? A mission?"

"Some might call it that." He puffed his cheeks.

Was his exasperation riled by her interference or the pique of his predicament?

"I'll tell you this much, and then you will walk away and forget every word."

She wanted to nod but didn't care to commit herself to silence. The urgency and secrecy of all this was too intoxicating.

"Go on."

"My brother Eugene and I, we're in financial strife. Our business is crippled by fast-growing debt, and I've come here to retrieve our last hope that's buried in one of the newel posts. And that's that."

"*That's that*?" She repeated his baffling full stop.

"That's that."

"Who summarizes a story in so few words and lets it hang untold like that?"

"I'm not a storyteller. I'm a woodworker."

And unschooled in negotiating, if he thought he'd sweep her

aside with a *that's that.*

But ... *last hope*? That rang like the battered song that had brought her and Clemmie here, too. Last hopes, it appeared, dragged people further from home than she imagined.

Viola followed the taut lines of his face to his eyes. She let herself smile and wondered what had gotten into her. Why a fresh vein of foolishness rose now and pushed into this conversation.

"I know a little about looking for the lost and forgotten. I do it every day."

"No, Miss Buckley," he shook his head, "you—"

"I'll help you look for it."

His head shook harder.

"I can keep watch next time. It's too risky to attempt alone. There's two more big posts like that, and you've only been here long enough to break into one. Perhaps tomorrow, we could—"

"We?" He stepped back. "Oh no, I'm not dragging you or your mother under. If I'm caught, I'll be the only one sent packing."

"Shadrach would never upend a woman from her sickbed. Besides, two sets of eyes and ears are better than one."

Her offer stilled him, and some of the stiffness in his shoulders slackened.

"Let me play," she tried again.

"Play?" He closed his eyes and pressed his palms to their sockets. A betraying chuckle escaped him. "I haven't *played* anything in years." His eyes found hers, and in the growing dusk, blues that normally ran in some kind of watery swirl now swam in a deep pool of emotion she could not read.

"This is not a game, Miss Buckley. And even if it were, it's not for you."

"It's Viola." She raised her chin. "Please call me Viola, and I'll call you Silas. If we're going to—"

"We are not…Viola." The stiff reply he'd employed to send her away wilted into the tender way he spoke her name. A begging that sounded unlike anything threaded into her name before.

Humiliation flamed into her cheeks. She knew all her freckles were shooting into view against the spreading heat. She twisted the fringe of her shawl.

Rejection, even for something as foolish as a game, or whatever life altering endeavor he tried to keep from her, was an old familiar bruise and one she knew how to treat. Even when delivered with care.

"Of course." She looked away. "I'd best get back to Clemmie. Excuse me." She tried to move, but his hand cupped her elbow.

"Best you ponder your art." He grabbed her basket and handed it to her. The aromas of the scavenged bush filled the air between them. She grabbed the handle, but he held on.

"This is a job for one. No need to traipse after me."

Traipse after him? Did he think her a lost child, smitten by his American charm, wanting to follow him like a duckling? Is that what he saw? Is that what she showed him?

"I'm grateful for your offer, but what I need most is your silence. And, Viola, I promise if I find what I came for, I'll show it to you."

She nodded, once. A small bob of the head.

From within the house, lamp lights flickered, and the ringing of a bell told them the dinner hour had come. Their real world called them out from the shadows. But something lapped at her as sure as the beach only a few steps away. Words called to her but in an accent not her own.

Silas Swift swung the door open and motioned for her to enter. Was it the shadows, or did his face carry more regret than he cared to shoulder?

It only took a few steps, and she was back where she'd caught him. She rested her hand on the freshly glued newel post. The cool wood felt good, especially when belittlement simmered under her skin.

Thick skin. Tender Heart. Nasrin's reminder crashed into her thoughts. Just in time. No less easy.

"Your secret is safe with me." She extended all he needed and took the stairs to her room.

As if it were not a slippery slope he had engineered.

He watched her go until the glance that followed her up threatened to become less gentlemanly. Watching her like this would cost him more than he could afford. And he'd not leave her with that price to pay. He'd come this far to reclaim his worth as a man, not scatter it to the wind. He rubbed the stubble on his chin.

She'd gone from wild child on a fence top, to uppity negotiator, to caring daughter and accomplished artist, to whatever that was now that she'd dumped on him.

Let me play.

He shook his head.

No way. No, sir. Not on your life.

A passing nod was all they would share. His days of following solace into trouble were over. He still carried the bitter taste of his indiscretion with Olive, the tavern girl. She'd ripped her petticoat to wrap his wound at *Dead Man's Grip. "I have three others like it. Passed on to me by my sister who has no need for undergarments now that she's in the grave, beside your wife."*

Savaged up by her own grief, she had tended to more than the bite of a half-crazed mongrel that should have been tied up by the tavern keeper. Her touch had sneaked in to where he should never have let it. Anguished and ashamed, he'd pushed it all away in the middle of the night when it was already too late and the tavern too cold.

A small hand pressed his knee.

"Molly?" He sat on the bottom step and smiled at the child. She toddled closer and attempted to squeeze past, perhaps drawn up by the caged bird.

He lowered his arm and pulled her back. "Not without your mama. Not for you."

And certainly not for me, either.

"Here." He pulled a clean handkerchief from his pocket, folded it in half, and then in half again. Molly's warm body settled against his leg. Her brown baby-soft curls smelled like stewed pears.

He'd not made this amusement in years. A twisted kerchief that, when folded, tied, and turned inside out, became a miniature hammock with two swaddled babies. Mother had done this for his twin brothers. A toy that captured them, side by side. As they had always been. Two peas in a linen cloth. Until the day Patrick decided a safe nest was not for him. And everything unraveled for the Swift Brothers.

He showed Molly how the cradle swung. "Rock a bye baby…" he sang her the tune, but it was the babies that she cared for, so he flattened her hand and let her hold them.

The touch of her fingers seeped into him like a lost breath. If he'd only hunted a better remedy for Honora when there was still time, his own children may have hung on him like this. Reliant on the tricks in his pockets. The protection he would have wrapped them in. The love denied him.

But it was not too late to protect his brothers. He'd come all this way to bring back some kind of marvel, like the crumpled handkerchief that now thrilled Molly. If only it were this simple. If only Viola the Wild were not in the shadows, luring him in with games and other distractions.

Let me play.

How he envied the way she could turn everything into a game, of sorts. Even their conversations were word games she played to win.

Molly pulled at the handkerchief babies until they unraveled. "Gone?" She held the limp cloth by a corner.

"Not if I fix it." Silas refashioned the toy and, like a conjurer, handed back the twisted cloth that looked once more like two swaddled brothers in a hammock.

Wrapped in her stained painter's apron, Viola dabbed at the cobalt and, with the tip of her finest sable brush, dropped the pigment into the porcelain dish where she mixed her paints. She added a second darker dab, and to this a dot of indigo. A medley to swipe over her already washed paper.

Blue collided with the liquid beneath and spiked in all directions. She did not care to delve too deep into why she flirted with the blues. Enough were the wanton strokes that bled into hues and values she knew captured none of the botanical specimens she'd collected. No, tonight, Viola painted her mood.

A jam jar of wash water bore the evidence of her distraction. A muddy mess, it now turned gray. She pushed away from the table and rubbed her tired eyes. But what did one do for cloudy focus?

"When I find it, I'll show it to you." His words still played on her mind.

She removed her apron and slumped onto the edge of the bed littered in sketches. Others still papered the floor. A messy catalogue of her works in progress, displayed just so, with visual prompts, some pinned to the drapes, for better appraisal in the morning light. A bunch of wildflowers hung from a bedpost, and an empty easel awaited in the corner.

"I'll get to you," she lamented. "Once I've collected a little of everything and know for certain what I want."

Was all this the makings of a folio of works? She paced the room, imagining books that children would fall into like other worlds.

An Atlas of Wildflowers. An Atlas of Bush Flowers. An Atlas of Ferns.

She hooked her hands behind her head. If she were a man, would this ladder of dreams be so hard to scale?

"Don't let Viola run up there, Nasrin. She is not to climb."

Viola remembered an old conversation between Clemmie and Nasrin. When theatre roofs loomed high over their heads, and the narrow set of stairs that led to the theatre fly galley beckoned.

"She is unharmed, Clemmie. Fear not." Nasrin would hold out her hand. *"Not for you, Poupette. That's for the men who let the backdrops down and raise them back up again."*

Viola could only peer up at the slender gantry that spanned the width of the stage. Where sandbags anchored sweeping scenes until their time to drop arrived. No place for a little girl to roam. But Viola knew up there lay a smashing sea, a forest glade, a castle, and ships aplenty.

Lost in her memories, she bumped into her gathering basket. Dusty gum leaves fell into a heap, followed by gum nuts that rattled in all directions. She crouched to collect them, and from beneath the boards at her feet came the sound of muffled men's voices.

She pressed her fingertips to the floor. Had she spooked Silas enough for him to admit his real intentions to Shadrach? Would they bust open the other newel posts in the morning?

"...*Clara*."

She could just make out the words.

"Early June, they're saying... other repairs... the boiler."

"Long journey. Who's waiting on you at home? Family..."

She sank further into the billowing of her skirt and cocked her head. Silas garbled something in reply, as if he moved deeper into his room, and their voices became harder to catch.

"Bachelors... three of us, Swift Brothers."

She pushed her papers aside, stretched her body out, and pressed her ear to the floor.

"My brother, Patrick," came the rolled American accent, "... Eugene and me. Mrs. Knott is there, our housekeeper. Feeds the crew. But I've never been away this long. Or gone this far."

Viola kept her ear to the floor. So unladylike. And wrong.

So very wrong. But she could not help herself.

Did his room follow the same footprint as hers? Bed, washstand, window? She recalled the way Silas had forged into Clemmie's bedroom. Tweaking the reading rules. Finding her bookmark.

So lost in her musings, she did not hear the steps that carried someone up onto the landing until heels sounded at her door. Dread scurried around her, and she wondered if it were too late to roll under the bed with the gum nuts.

"Knock, knock. Viola? I've brought fresh towels for tomorrow morning. Oh." Finella looked down. "Lost something?" She shouldered the door open and surveyed the room.

"I know it looks disorderly in here. I'm sorry. But it isn't, not really. This is how I search my thoughts, and distractions..." Viola reached for the errant gum nuts under the bed, "and everything I knock over these days."

"What are you searching for?"

"A story, as strange as that might sound. A botanical delight that moves, even when it's fixed within a frame."

"Have you seen my blue hydrangeas? They're so faded now and brittle. Theirs is the story of summer that sank into autumn."

"Hmm." Viola juggled a cluster of gum nuts. "I like the sound of that. Oh, there's one more escapee, under the washstand." She dug under the backboard of the slender furniture piece and pulled out not one but three gum nuts. But her fingers brushed something else. Something papery.

She pulled out a thin linen-bound book. "Perhaps one of your guests dropped this here by mistake."

"May I see?" Finella held out a hand. "Goodness, look at that!"

She opened the cover and ran her fingertip down the front page. "I know who left this, but I don't know how it became wedged back there. What a treat. And by all rights," she smiled and handed it back, "it belongs to you."

"Me?"

Viola read the inscription.

When life tangles the heart,
When dark waves steal all you possess,
See here, your secret words, like ink dots appearing.
String them like lanterns in this journal.
And watch courage light freedom's road.
A.D.

"Do you remember the Black Swallow shipwreck and its two

survivors?" Finella asked.

"Tom Darley and Ada Carmichael?"

"Yes. Ada boarded with us for some months while she recovered."

"Here, in this house?"

"In this very room. She left this journal for whoever needed it next. Shortly after, it disappeared. I imagined a guest took it for their own, but here it is, preserved for you."

"For me? Oh, I prefer to use paint over words. Writing them down here would..." She shrugged.

"They would offer some kind of remedy for the questions we cannot ask aloud." Finella dropped the towels onto a chair. "Or the thoughts that swirl in our mind with little logic."

In her mind Viola saw the wash of blue eyes that wrestled remorse. Or regret. Silas was hard to read. Not like Viola, with her tempers and bookmarks. How much more humiliating would her secret musings appear if they came forth on a page?

"Words remind me of Marshall, my father. He wrote Sweet Clementine's scripts. Always scribbling ideas, entire plays, new scenes for Clemmie to memorize. Letters to London. He was obsessed with his own words and chose them with cruel accuracy. I..." She pressed on the book cover as if it might detonate right there in her room. "I would not want to fall into the same obsession."

"My aunt gave me my first journal. She called it an Everlasting. The writing itself became a comfort like no other. Soon enough I discovered courage in my hidden words."

Nasrin believed courage would set Viola apart as an artist. Would courage rise in her words, too?

"I prefer to keep my thoughts corralled into lists. No secrets. Firm plans with strategies."

"You could begin by keeping a record of your mother's progress."

Viola liked the sound of this.

"A health record is some kind of list, I suppose." Wishing to respect her hostess, Viola slipped the journal into her gathering basket. She'd break open a dozen gum nuts and see what hid within before she did that to her own messy self. But evidence of Clemmie's healing? That was a trove too precious to ignore.

April 25, 1879

This house is one of secrets kept an• secrets uncovere•. This book, once hi••en, now asks me to leave a trail of wor•s within the unmarke• pages.

I am familiar with •ots. An• specks, fine lines, broa• strokes, an• water to bring it together. But I •ust off the cover an• employ my pen here. I shall call it the Rest Therapy Journal.

The night is hushe•. All sleep. Except perhaps Killjoy, who moves aroun• beneath me. I hear the lift of a win•ow sash. A •rawer opens an• shuts. Does he pace the room an• won•er how he will unlock another newel post? Will he hi•e up here an• attempt the one closest to my be•room, or will he risk opening the one in the mi••le? Un•er the light of the win•ow an• in full view of anyone who may pass.

Silas is looking for something he aban•one• long ago. That is all he will say.

Mother runs towar•s her healing. Or perhaps I push her there. Either way, I will keep recor• here of her improvements.

An• I will sift islan• fiel•s an• pa••ocks an• bushlan• for something that will lan• on my page with the same allure as an Amazonian lily or some other un•iscovere• treasure.

9

When Silas visited with Mrs. Buckley the next afternoon, Viola the Wild had already left for her bush wanderings. He thought he saw the purple flicker of her shawl from the window, but he couldn't be sure because he told his foolish self to look for anything but her.

He'd done what he did best. He'd pushed her away.

A subdued Mrs. Buckley had listened to him read with her eyes closed, and their time together hardly matched the vibrancy of the time before. Had that all come from Viola?

And Silas, in the confounded ways of this upside-down country, found himself sorry to not encounter the force that had ushered him in that first day.

Another two days passed, and while he heard Viola come and go from the floorboards between their rooms, there had been no further glimpse of that bright shawl or its wearer.

With some disappointment, he bid the sleepy Mrs. Buckley farewell, frowned at the angry bird on the landing, and forced himself to pass the remaining two newel posts as if they were mere planks of wood rather than his hollowed out secret keepers.

"Peek-a-boo. I see you." Balthazar flapped his wings.

With that bird presiding, it was near impossible to break into either newel post.

Could he get away with it now, while the old lady snoozed?

"Don't start with me," Balthazar the Galah warned.

"I'll do what I wish," Silas whispered back.

Deep within the house, a door slammed and Shadrach's voice rose with urgency.

"Are you there, Swift? Someone's cornered that deer. One of the Callahan boys delivered a message. They're coming through with a wagon. Want to ride along?"

Now? Of all the hours. Silas quietly bemoaned his frustration, leaned on the stair rail, and looked down. "I'm up here. Let me grab my coat."

"Be careful, Shad." Finella made all the protestations a wife would make when her husband set off with a frenzied team to take down the cause of their collective grief. Still, he dashed through one door and out the other, ready to fight the forces that threatened his farm. Silas followed.

"Keep an eye out for the wagon. I need to grab my gun." Uncommonly excited, Shadrach made a hectic dash into his barn.

Lanky gum trees swayed beside the driveway, and light washed over the road in flashes of silver. Silas turned the other way to the farm buildings that hemmed in the courtyard. On the roof of the structure they called a menagerie, Viola's shawl fringe also caught the light. Of all places, on a roof. One wrong step and she'd be tumbling into a mess of bruises and broken bones.

Noises from inside the barn told him Shadrach still sifted through his gear, so Silas followed the garden path. A ladder rested against the menagerie wall, and at the top, on the shingled roof, sat Viola, drawing board in hand, her pencil flying over the page. This was the energy that had been missing from Mrs. Buckley's room. The wild courage that took a girl onto a rickety roof, to the very tips of the branches that hung before her eyes.

Delight to have found her shot through him like a misfired cartridge.

She looked down, not even startled at his appearance. "Come to join me?"

"Your mother's fallen asleep. And there's going to be a deer hunt. Shadrach and I are on our way to—"

"Deer?" She tucked her supplies under her arm and scurried down the ladder like she lived up there. He stared, amazed she descended in one piece.

"What? Did you think that was my first time on that roof? You underestimate my climbing skills."

"You overestimate the strength of an unsteady ladder and shingle roof."

If she twisted an ankle, who would step in to care for her mother? She was foolish indeed. Pretty. And spark-filled and audacious, but still foolish.

And fools rushed in… everyone knew that.

Shadrach called him from the barn door.

"Coming." Silas cocked his head toward the road. "A bunch of boys spotted the deer and think they can corner it. Shadrach's invited me to join them."

"I want to come." She begged with her eyes.

Let me play.

Silas looked at her.

She looked back.

She was crazy. But at least *he* didn't have to say no this time. He backed away. "I don't think Shadrach would—"

"I'll ask him myself." She overtook him and hardly waited for

Shadrach to sling the gun over his shoulder.

"Is there room for me, too?"

"On a deer hunt?" Shadrach's voice barely contained his disbelief. "No."

"But I—"

"No fired-up farmer's going to wait for a tourist to tiptoe out of their way before they shoot."

"How do you know I'll be in the way?"

He pointed at her shawl. "You're already a liability. From miles away. Anything that loud will wave off the deer."

He marched up the driveway and unlatched the gate.

"Please, Shadrach. I don't need to wear it." She slipped off the shawl and rolled it into a ball. Underneath, she wore a simple gray wool skirt and a shirt in duck egg blue.

"Have you any hunting experience?"

She shook her head.

"Then you're not suited for this excursion." He peered at the road.

Dismissed, but clearly not ready to give in yet, she turned searching eyes to Silas.

Let me play. But what could *he* do, other than agree with Shadrach and insist she return to the safety of… the roof?

They played their staring game for a few more heartbeats. Enough for him to consider his role here. Sending a woman away was a particular talent of his. He'd driven Honora into the depths of restlessness and anxiety, where a wife should never be sent.

His punishment? The ability to know when he was at risk of repeating it. The slap of rejection ripened in Viola's cheeks, right before his eyes.

"She won't get in the way." Silas heard his intervention before he had the good sense to quash it. "She's probably got a good eye, with all that painting and peering through trees."

A big grin tore across her face. And something equally broad took root in him.

Shadrach looked from Viola to Silas as if they were both daft.

"Absolutely not. That's the dumbest—" Horses and an open wagon thundered along the rutted road.

Silas felt the reverberations in his shoes. He should be inside breaking into the staircase, not outside petitioning for Viola to wander the bush with them.

Her pleading darted from Silas to Shadrach, while the crackle of hope fired right there for all to see.

"Ha. So that's how it is?" Shadrach's eyes narrowed. "Viola can come if *you* promise to watch out for her. You keep her from trouble and fix your eye on her at all times."

Viola whooped and strung a list of *thank yous* and *I promises* into happy babbling.

Shadrach leaned in. "Something about her's got you snagged. So, I'll allow it, but you'd better watch her as if she were your own." He waved to the wagon driver.

As if she were his own?

The hunting party stopped at Shadrach's gate.

"Sort the terms between you." Shadrach jumped up onto the wagon bed. "And be quick about it."

Viola faced Silas. "Finella said she'd keep Clemmie company after you left, if she's awake," she whispered. "And a wagon ride would take me further than I've ventured so far and—"

"You must promise. No foolishness. No sudden movements. No loud voices or climbing trees for better views." He could do this. He was already wired for it. He was so good at protecting people, most times they ended up despising him for it.

"No climbing. I promise."

"No disappearing where I can't see you."

"I'll stick to you like hot glue from a small green pot." She tucked her growing smile into submission between her lips.

Before Silas knew how he'd gone from solo indoor hunter, someone hoisted Viola onto the wagon. He jumped up beside her, and with their feet dangling, they swayed and rumbled over corrugated dirt roads, but that was nothing compared to the jostling within.

As if she were his own was as foolish as *let me play.* As crazy as tiptoeing along a slippery rooftop. And probably just as thrilling.

Viola felt each jolt in her bones, but the speed at which they stormed into the bush never slackened.

The excitement of finally catching the deer responsible for their busted fences and dug up potatoes proved a formidable bond. The men eyed the bushland and pointed. Someone had sighted the deer at Swan Lake, a fresh watering hole where birds and other wildlife gathered. The men tightened their grips on their guns and scanned the bush for their prey.

Silas and Viola were the only two on the wagon who faced the other way. To their left, she caught glimpses of the sea, with thick bushland to their right.

"What are you hoping to find out here?" Silas asked.

"I'll know it when I see it. A rare orchid, perhaps. My Botanic Gardens folio is now …" she blew out a breath, "… a little poorer than I hoped."

"Your mother says you teach art lessons. And you've had to let those girls go."

"Clemmie is not good at keeping her thoughts to herself."

"Her response to an advertisement I read out. Art teacher in a private girl's school. She said you'd be perfect for the job, but you're aiming for something else. I thought you'd be perfect, too. Thanks to your natural bossiness and desire to organize people."

She turned to stare.

He kept his eye on the road, mouth somber, yet somehow, a smile had clambered into his words.

"Some people need bossing around," she replied, with a friendly smile of her own.

He chuckled. "And is your eye on fame or fortune?"

She guzzled the crushed aromas of the bush. Pine. Eucalyptus. Lemon-scented natives. "A book deal. Something that will take my work into Australian homes and libraries. Even abroad."

"Ah, you seek fame."

"I seek financial independence as a professional botanical artist. Then I could free Clemmie from the many distractions robbing her of good health." She stopped herself. This was the intersection where gentle pastime met determined profession. A road she was not meant to cross, in the eyes of some. Dare she continue?

"There's a painting of Clemmie. Made when she was only nineteen and hidden away for decades." She blushed to say it, and that annoyed her. "It caused a sensation when found by the brother of the artist who painted it, long after Clemmie had become a much-loved performer. It draws patrons into the tavern where it was discovered because in it, she's the youthful woman they remember… and… well…" She supposed she would have to tell the story in full. "She's… not fully dressed."

He straightened. "Have you seen it?"

"I see it often. The owner, Freddy Barnes, runs the Star and Garter with his son. They let me in whenever I'm passing by. Mortimer Barnes and Clemmie were betrothed, but he died in an accident. A runaway wagon delivering beer barrels. Mother's never seen the finished piece. She refused the first time Freddy Barnes made the offer, and every time since. Says it's not her, but it is."

"And you want the painting?"

"I know she'd rest easier if it were not on public display. It's a wound I cannot heal unless I buy it back."

"How much will it cost?"

"More than I'll ever have. But I won't stop trying."

He breathed in hard. "I know a little about the unreachable. I never imagined a pink galah would stand in my way."

She smiled. "I guess Clemmie and I have brought with us a lot of commotion. With all her baths and Balthazar's constant vigilance."

"I guess if it's there, it's there. If it's not…" A shadow crept over his face. "I'll find out soon enough."

"And you've not changed your mind about taking an accomplice? Or even throwing me a crumb and telling me what you're looking for? Is it a gem? A bag of gold nuggets?"

"Tenacious, aren't you?" It was his turn to smile. "It's a… precious piece of… equipment."

Equipment? He was making all this fuss for a carpentry tool?

The wagon came to a halt at the edge of a clearing, and the men hardly waited for the driver to pull the brake before jumping down.

"You don't need to mind me, truly." She pushed off the wagon bed. "I'll find a spot to sit and sketch." A bitter wind raced over them, and she shivered.

"I do. It's the only way Shadrach would allow you to come."

From her basket, he pulled her shawl and draped it over her shoulders, wrong side up. "I do have to mind you."

The extra layer felt good. Being wrapped by him, even better. She looked up, but he was not looking back.

"Silas, you didn't have to—"

"Come on. Let's go."

He pointed to a thin bush track, already disturbed by the hunting party, their dust still in the air.

"Go where?"

"Wherever you like."

She took a backward step.

He pointed at the track. "Face forward or you'll trip."

She pressed her hand to her hip. Surely, he deserved more than being her keeper.

He blew out a frustrated breath, crossed his arms, and lowered his eyes upon her. "I agreed to keep you from wandering into the line of fire, so if you want our host to keep his attention on his troubles and not you, I suggest you accept his conditions and get moving."

"His conditions? Negotiated by you."

"Otherwise," he said through gritted teeth, "you'd be back on that roof sketching gum leaves. Isn't there something here that thrills you?"

Arms still crossed, he loomed taller now. On the wagon, he'd listened and talked with her as an equal. Now, on a lonely track with the hunting party long gone, he'd reverted to protector.

What thrilled her out here? Maybe he did.

A man who pushed her into her art. Who made a way for her to explore and stood guard while she did so. She let that hit her, right in the pit of her lungs. Where her breath had not scrambled like this before.

A dragonfly hovered over them. It buzzed and swooped and searched for a place to land. Still, Viola looked at him, while all the words in her reply fired in her mind and rattled into the rest of her. They regarded each other so long, it was Silas who ended up blushing first.

He ran his hand over his face, the way men did when they needed to hide, pretending to scrub away at something because they could not, he could not, brush her away.

A smile stole onto her lips. She had made him blush.

"Turn around and do the work, Viola." Gravel rough, his words pushed her onward to a narrow path between old tea trees bowed by sea winds. Stone-gray and weathered, they hung low, buckled by the elements and, in places, almost prostrate.

Littered with dry leaves and small branches, the ground they trod crunched and popped underfoot. Gray. Green. And brown. A thicket of wild grass opened to a swathe of ferns, delicate pointed fronds that swayed in the wind.

A spot of ruby red caught her eye, and Viola veered off the path, deeper into the bushland. Was this a sea berry saltbush? She squeezed one of the plump little berries, and a tiny drop of juice ran between her fingers.

Fruit thrilled her the most. The pressing of life, up through the veins of a plant and into something that all God's creatures stopped to notice.

She snipped some for her gathering basket. This was more like it. Deep in the bush, she'd found something at last. She would make a large painting of this small berry and pair it with a dragonfly. Relief washed over her, she imagined, much like the quick hit Clemmie's pastilles offered.

Behind the frown that never seemed to lessen, Silas kept watch.

Like a warden. Like a fed-up Sunday school superintendent.

He needed someone to drag that out of him.

She jumped onto another log, a slim stage that begged a small performance.

"Be careful." Silas pointed. "There's—"

"Yes, Mr. Swift, I know." She tiptoed backwards. "Danger at every bend. But I'm not on a roof, nor a fence. I'm on ground level today."

"No, really." He came closer. "Viola!"

She had no time to turn or look, for in the same breath as his warning, something wrapped over her face and hair. A web spun by a calculating spider had caught her.

She screamed and swiped at the assault. A cruel, dark memory she could never smother. Her father, enraged and pulling her by the wrist, dragging her to the shadows of the Odeon Theatre wings. To the ventriloquist's trunk, where Little Lazlo, the smallest dummy, usually slept.

She gulped for air and sank to the ground, eyes closed, beating at her hair, but nothing dispelled the nightmare of being shoved into that trunk. The smell of men's hair oil, tobacco, and the sound of a lid being slammed shut upon her.

It locked her in with the force of a key turning, and the stench of her own vomit pooled in her throat and trickled into the dark.

"She's useless." Her father's muffled words echoed in the memory. *"Worse than a wooden puppet! If this willfulness is what you've passed on, Clementine, neither of you are of any use to me."*

She fought the fear and the spider web that took her there. She thrashed and screamed. Panic fell over her like the innocent puppet costume that had slipped over her face in the trunk. Edged in lace. Like a spider web in the mind of a terrified child.

"Viola!" Silas grabbed her flailing arms. "You've bashed most of it away." He crouched beside her and pushed the hair off her face. Hairpins fell into her lap.

"I can't abide spider webs," she whispered, breath still caught. Memory, open and bleeding.

Silas retrieved her basket and scattered berries, and men's voices rang from the other side of the thicket. A growing storm of motion drummed the ground.

"There. I see something. That-a-way!" A shot rang out in their direction. A sharp burst that charged the air, followed by a second one, followed by the sight of the deer bolting right past them. They flinched and ducked in unison, both of them already crouched, awkward and hardly sprung to escape gunshots.

Silas dragged her to the ground, his hand on the back of her head. She toppled, and their bodies collided with the sickening crunch of her forehead on his shoulder.

"Ow," she moaned and tried to get up. But he held her against him with iron force.

"Don't move," he growled in her ear, which was now right next to his lips.

Was she lying atop him? He'd gathered her in so well, her arms were now pinned to his chest, her cheek to his shoulder.

Mortified, she closed her eyes and listened to the pounding of hooves and the equally frenzied beat of men who charged through the bushland after their prey. The roar subsided, but the intensity of his hold did not. Viola opened her eyes. Her hair lay over his face as surely as she lay over his body.

A moan escaped him, and the impact of their fall shot into her hip, her knee, followed by a throbbing ache in her head.

"Viola," he exhaled into her hair, and his breath caressed her face.

As did the hand which, until now, had remained on the small of her back.

They had dodged a bullet. Of this, she was sure. But something else had struck her. It came from the way he touched her face and spoke her name.

"If I didn't know better, I'd think you're aiming to dismantle me. One eye socket, one joint, ligament… ventricle… one at a time until I…?"

They locked eyes, and his unfinished sentence rang between them like a siren.

Until I give in.

Until you have won me.

Is that where he was headed? It was lunacy to think it, even in the deepest part of her. Perhaps she'd sustained some kind of head knock. She blinked hard.

Until you've won me.

Were they his words she imagined, or hers?

"Viola," he whispered again, and this time, the pain in his voice rang louder.

Good grief! She thought he'd been whispering indulgently into her ear. She rolled onto her back and sat up.

Silas tried to sit too, but something held him back. He half-raised himself on one elbow.

"Why can't you get up?" She leaned over him. "Silas? Are you hurt?"

"I am." He rolled onto his side and dragged himself to a sitting position. Even under his coat sleeve, his left arm hung at a peculiar angle. "My shoulder." He grimaced. "Might be dislocated. Wouldn't be the first time."

"Dislocated?"

"An old man injury. Doesn't take much to aggravate." He squirmed. "Better than being hit by a bullet."

"I'm so sorry." She didn't know what to apologise for first. Walking backwards to needle him, the commotion with the spider web, or landing on him like a log with enough force to inflict an injury.

She stood and offered her hand. "Can you stand?"

He nodded. "It's happened before, more times than I care to count. Vulnerable joint. I can fix it, but you may want to look away."

Viola could not look anywhere but the scene before her. At Silas, who clenched his jaw, leaned back, and rotated his back until the afflicted arm dangled into the position he needed. With a sharp inhalation of breath, he righted himself and let out a small cry, eyes closed against the pain that must have shot through him.

"If you fold your shawl in half, I'd appreciate some kind of sling."

Viola scrambled to untie her suzani. "What do I do?"

"Make a triangle. Lay it over my chest with the V to the ground."

Her fingers worked like thumbs, but she folded and draped the fabric over him with care.

"Throw that corner over my neck. You'll need it to tie me up. And then," he used his good arm to help her, "bring this up and it should hold."

Using her instinct and with his instructions, Viola cradled his arm in her beautiful shawl. She crossed the end pieces over his good shoulder. The skin on his neck felt hot. His hair carried a hint of cloves.

He winced and grabbed her elbow to steady himself. If he'd not collected her, perhaps she'd be wearing a bullet for her troubles. Good thing he took his warden's responsibilities seriously. But for his efforts, it was Silas who'd sustained the injury.

"Done." Folded in half, the sling was just the right size.

"Shouldn't need it for long. If I protect my shoulder, I'll recover faster."

Slowly, they returned to the horse and wagon, where hunters also measured their loss.

"She's not gonna be easy to catch." Someone made plans for 'next time.' For the way they'd lay a trap. Maybe dig a pit.

Shadrach found them. "What happened here?"

"An old injury. Happens often enough," Silas replied. A little too quick. A little too unfussed.

"It was *you* who shrieked? *You* spooked the deer?" Shadrach edged closer.

"I made a little too much noise warning Miss Viola about a spider's web."

Shadrach's brow creased. "Likely story," he muttered. "I heard a woman's scream. How does a spiderweb cause this kind of injury—"

"I fell on him. But there *was* a web. And when your guns fired, Silas tried to keep my head down, but I knocked him over. It's my fault." She would not let him take the blame for this. "My head pushed against his ..." She pointed to where she'd landed. On the shoulder of a man who'd deflected her culpability.

She'd never encountered protection like this. It had always been her job to look for trouble and plan ahead. Make up for Marshall's absence. Fill in Clemmie's neglect.

She caught a curious exchange between Silas and Shadrach.

"You took my instructions to heart, I see."

"It's not what you think—"

"It's what I'm seeing, chum." Shadrach shook his head. "Two people with a spectacular knack of bowling each other over."

IO

Silas ambled through sand drifts. Past shallows that shot with reflections off the rock pools beneath. How his brothers would laugh to see him picking his way home from the little white church in the fishing village. No hurrying. No barreling. Careful steps kept his shoulder tucked where it should be. Unlike his crazy thoughts, unleashed by the preacher.

Tall, youthful, but a fine orator, the way men are when they'd served some of their life in a crucible, Goliah Ashe hardly consulted his notes. Neither did he lose his train of thought. And those thoughts followed Silas home, quick on his heels and heavy on his heart.

"God redeems our mistakes," he had bellowed. *"He allows us to walk into a valley of shadows with plenty of time to reflect. And it's there, in days of stress and cloud, when the way out is unclear, that we are to wait. In the waiting comes the comfort and sustaining and restoration that we never imagined possible. Because God is the great Redeemer. And there is no mistake, laid before Him in repentance, that the Heavenly Father will not redeem in His own fashion."*

Silas considered his earthy father, Halvard Swift, who'd not believed in the restorative powers of God. At least, not where his twin sons were concerned. He'd cast the role of redeemer onto Silas. It was his curse for bringing the pox into their home, leaving it to scar his brothers' skins and perhaps render them so impaired, their father's hopes for them were dashed to dust.

"You did this," he'd said when they were sure the boys would recover but bear disfigurement for life. *"And now you can spend the rest of your life fixing it. Listen well. Their future is now what you'll make of it."*

He'd grabbed Silas by the back of the neck and turned him where he willed. *"Look at their faces. Life will be doubly hard on them. Where will they work if they look like freaks? Who will marry them?"*

In his rage, he'd shoved Silas, aged twelve, into a chair, dislocating his shoulder for the first time.

"Who will not look away when they walk down the street? Or worse, sink into the hideous fright they will bring onto children who will scream in terror but won't know how to look away."

Silas had not looked away, either. Perhaps that was the day he ceased being a child. He'd wept at the faces of his brothers, the mirror image of each other, pock marked and fevered. Forever scarred because he'd disobeyed their mother and played with Charlie Hinkle when she'd forbidden him from roaming streets that held infection.

By the time his shoulder mended, guilt had lodged in his heart, nailed shut with the finality of fiery brads driven in for good measure. From that day, he knew it was his to secure a home and workplace for his brothers. No matter the price, it would always be his to pay. He rubbed the knot on his shoulder, where Viola's shawl held tight.

Finella had offered him another sling, but he'd refused. This one carried the aromas of eucalyptus and roses. It still carried the caress of her fingertips against his neck.

The girl who'd bargained for his time had found another way to secure him. More womanly, and with her own brand of unexpected humor and the unmistakable dash of tenderness he'd encountered yesterday. Viola carried a lifeforce about her. She was like a shaft of sunlight. You'd never pin it down in one place, but if you basked there longer than you ought, you knew why you dreaded it moving away.

After a Sunday luncheon with Shadrach and his family, Silas prepared for his afternoon with Mrs. Buckley.

"Perhaps Viola will allow you a day of rest, given the circumstances," Shadrach said.

"We made a deal," Silas replied, not sure Viola knew for sure what she wanted from him any more than he knew what he wanted with her.

He climbed the stairs to the sickroom. Balthazar greeted him with the usual derisions, but Mrs. Buckley made up for her bird's cheap shots.

"Viola tells me you're injured. Come, let me see."

Viola sat on the edge of the bed and massaged a lotion from a porcelain pot into her mother's hands. The scent of roses embraced the room like a living vapor, as it did from the fabric of Viola's shawl. It poured over him in a fresh dose that swamped his senses, as it had all night, all through the sermon, and all the way home.

"Nothing a day in a sling won't fix, now it's back where it belongs." He meant the shoulder bone, but Mrs. Buckley watched him as if he'd said more.

"That's not a sling. That's Viola's shawl."

"That your daughter kindly fashioned for me."

"But that shawl is meant for—"

"It's all we had, Clemmie." Viola tapped the cork lid onto the pot. She topped Mrs. Buckley's near-full glass with water and knelt by her mother's bed. "Even though I believe Mr. Swift's injury warrants a bending of our agreement, he insists he is well enough to sit with you. So, you," she leaned in and squeezed her mother's hand, "must be a good listener. Do not cause any grief."

The way she pleaded made her look like a girl reciting bedside prayers. Could he keep thinking of her that way?

He wasn't sure how he'd fare with Viola today. Yesterday she'd been playful. But something else had usurped their collision. An awareness of her he could not shake back to how he'd found her.

She was not a girl. She was a woman who knew what she wanted and drafted plans to make it happen. Grand plans.

She turned to him. "How is your shoulder today?"

"Better. But…" She brought out the teasing in him in ways no one ever had. He wasn't sure who enjoyed it more. He or she? "Best you leave now before you accidentally crack someone's rib."

She smiled and turned to tuck a loose length of her mother's hair back into the pretty comb that held it all in place.

A small shiver ran down his neck and into the collar of his shirt. The memory of her fingers on his neck. Her warm breath… Was that when he'd pulled her to his chest or later… when she'd fixed the shawl for him? He looked away and chided himself.

Someone like him would not feature in the smallest sliver of her plans. And he'd do well to remember that. Would he be so charmed if one of the women in Portland bucked against their established ways with Viola's pluck, or would he be one to resort to the tut-tutting of the men who sent women to their rightful places?

"Painting is encouraged by all, when only a gentle pastime," she had said on the ride back from the deer hunt. *"It captures the beauty of God's creation and women may dabble. But they may not yearn for an independent living in the self-same pursuit. Affix any power to it, and it's seen as contrary to God's purpose for us, which is to marry and bear*

children. God himself forbid that we should want one over the other. Or both in equal measure."

Her words echoed in his mind, her longing to create so fierce he envied the energy it stoked in her.

"Now, both of you." Viola cloaked herself in a brown paisley wrap. "Please, don't let me find either one in worse condition when I return." And in a blink and a clatter of shoes on treads, she was gone.

He reached for a newspaper and took his seat.

Mrs. Buckley shook her head. "It's a wonder I didn't hear her screaming from here. There's no one who despises spider webs more than Viola. The sensation of it over her skin, on her face, stuck on her eyelashes, mixed with hot tears."

She pulled on the ribbon of a red shoe tied on her bedpost. "Put the Lost and Found aside, young man. You need to hear about my two lost daughters."

Daughters? He took his seat. *There was more than one?*

"I lost my first Viola in a theatre fire when she was five. Her father was too busy making grand plans for our fame while my baby rose, step by step, into the narrow fly galley, and…"

Mrs. Buckley shook her head in wild, tiny movements, the ugly memory too painful to utter. "And then there's the Viola you have met."

She continued through a sheen of tears. "Named for her sister and born to wear the shoes and wigs she left behind. But one can never replace the other… even if she's born for that very reason. This Viola longs to be seen for who she is, not as the one she was meant to replace. To occupy first place on a competition podium, and never again on the stage she rejected when…"

She swiped the air, as if to swat away her suffering. Tears fell onto her cheeks, and she wiped them with a handkerchief. "I failed both my girls. When they needed me to stand up to their father and keep them safe. My first Viola was killed in a theatre fire, and my second Viola was killed, one costume, one rehearsal, one performance at a time. It's too late to retrace those days, but ahead of Viola is some kind of win that only she understands."

The throbbing vein in her neck flickered, and she drew a slow breath. Mrs. Buckley was a woman depleted by her story. "After all the choices we denied her, does she not deserve to come first in what she's good at?"

He did not understand it all to give an answer. The spider web remained a gossamer-thin monster. But he understood what it meant to lose a child. More than one. And he knew the ache of watching his family struggle to find peace when life delivered strife into their midst.

No. It was not life. It was Silas himself who'd delivered the strife. That's why he sat here, in an Australian sickroom, listening to a frail woman lament her past. He played with the fringe on Viola's shawl, smoothing out the tangles.

"You shouldn't be wearing that." Mrs. Buckley shifted in her bed. "It belongs on her bed, not on your shoulder."

"This shawl?"

"It's a suzani. Given to her by a theatre friend. An Anatolian marriage bed covering, made by the women of the bride's family. Viola cherishes it. She is meant to find her groom, and one day cover his feet along with hers and secure them in a fold of love."

A trickle of dread ran over his spine. Already wrapped in Viola's cherished shawl, Silas felt the knot tighten. She could have asked for it back. But she hadn't.

Heat rose and poked into his hairline and along the back of his neck. If reserved for a sacred occasion, why was she wearing the shawl each day, all over the beach and bush?

"She may have had nothing else to purpose into a sling yesterday, but she has left it with you. Careless or deliberate? I wonder if she even knows. Perhaps, Mr. Swift," Mrs. Buckley shifted against her pillows, "you can make sense of why *you* wear it, other than your sore shoulder?"

"I should have given it back. I'm sorry to distress you. Shall I take it off?" He slid his good hand along the bent elbow held snug in the sling.

"No." She offered a weary smile. "You've both taken a small risk. But Viola is not one who will be easily loved by a man who has already lost a wife. If she cares for you enough to share the shawl, she may have tripped into something she would not otherwise allow. Be careful, Mr. Swift. You will walk away from here and all you leave behind. She will carry it with her."

Be careful? Viola was the one who'd almost walked into a bullet. But he wouldn't kid himself into thinking he'd escaped without injury. The beam of his life had been nicked as surely as if she'd chiseled out a small fleck of wood.

Could a woman as observant as Viola care for him without knowing it? He chided himself for daring to come under the covering of her shawl. What a fool.

Mrs. Buckley exhaled a soft breath of sleep. Exhausted by the memories and the drugs and the lifelong fight to bury what could not be buried.

And what of him? Through the window, the sky swam with fast-racing clouds. While the preacher said God forgave and redeemed, he didn't say it made the way for the impossible. Did he?

Beyond Shadrach's fields, the ferry came and went from the Cowes pier.

He'd have to get out fast. Untangle himself from her shawl and her smell and her smile. But he would not go without his loot. He'd get it tomorrow, with Shadrach's help. Pack his bags and leave before any more of Viola Buckley sank beneath his skin.

He wriggled out of the crazy softness and hidden promise of her shawl and draped it over the chair.

II

The outbuildings of Blue Wren House stood in an L shape, made of hewn slabs and some form of mud chinking. Silas figured Shadrach was the kind of man who'd done it all himself. Slashed the bush for timber to build the crude huts that created a courtyard with the new house on the hill.

He liked that about this Australian man. An honest, hard worker who'd welcomed a thief into his home without knowing it. In the crook of his small kingdom, Shadrach grabbed handfuls of loose sticks and corded them up.

"Come to help?" He pulled so hard on the twine it's a wonder it didn't snap.

"I figure I owe you something for what happened with the deer. I failed to keep my end of the bargain with Viola."

"In spectacular fashion."

"Shadrach." Silas pushed on before he lost his nerve. "I need to make a request."

"Too late. Viola already made it. She asked if you could stay longer so you could recuperate, and I said yes, although if I'm not mistaken, this is less about shoulders and more about hearts."

"I… she… she what?"

"She's smitten, that's for certain. And she's negotiated for you to stay until that arm is fit for proper use. Where's your sling, anyway?"

"I gave it back."

But the guilt that had brought him out this cool morning was not so easily shifted.

"Shadrach, I…"

"Can you add this to that pile?" Shadrach held out the bundle and motioned to a table just inside the door. "Finella loves this hut. Of all the fancy names, she calls it a menagerie. It's where she raises silkworms. Every autumn I bundle up tea tree twigs for her. She'll knit them into a scaffold for her silkworm babies to spin their cocoons come springtime."

Silas took the light bundle with his good hand and stepped into the dark room. A battered table stood in the centre. Atop it, an already growing stash of sticks. Sapling bed frames occupied one end of the room, with a stone fireplace on the other.

"Before I built the big house, this is where we lived." Shadrach followed him in. "Finella hated it. Too much dust and mud for her. My sister Molly shared it with her, too. This dingy, dusty room where we found each other. The cold skillion next door where I agonized over whether she'd stay or go."

He turned to survey all that was his. "And of course, the house and fields, all the tracks to the beach, every fence post, and every red clod of dirt."

He wrapped a loose end of twine back into the ball and looked Silas in the eye.

"When you build something out of nothing, you'll protect it with your life. This little farm, the guest rooms, the silk threads that get spun in here, that's how we make our living. And I fight for that each day. I fight the weather. The salt air. The locusts that feast on our crops and now a deer who thinks my potato fields are fair game.

But..." he smiled, and Silas had not seen many of those on this man.

"I figured out something today. If I bag that deer, I'll rid myself of trouble *and* catch my reward. There's meat and skin to be taken if I find it on my land. And I will."

Shadrach's chest puffed a little as if he'd already hung the carcass and cleaned his gun. "A man's not worth a bent sixpence if he stands around and lets something that valuable out of his grip."

Silas could not disagree. "I imagine farming is no easier than fine furniture making. You've got to look around every corner or—"

"Exactly." Shadrach nodded. "Especially when your wife and daughter depend on you. If that deer is nosing around, it's fair game."

Silas believed him. Wasn't he motivated to strike in defense of his family, too? What would Shadrach think of genuine treasure in his staircase? It now belonged to him. Every riser and tread. He owned it all. Every shadow in every hollow. A small sinkhole opened in his gut. Shadrach was not the man to ask for help.

The angst-riddled Australian pulled the latch on the door to the hut they called a menagerie and locked it tight. "When does the *Clara* set off?"

"Early June, I expect."

"Might as well let the seaside aid in your recovery, unless you're afraid Viola will mess with that more than you can bear." Shadrach cocked his head in the direction of the house. On her knees, Viola studied a bed of hydrangeas that skirted the house.

Silas blew out breath he did not remember holding in. "She's something I've never encountered before."

"Yours would not be the first battle of the heart to play out here. I threw these shell paths down to catch the lady who is now mistress of this house." Shadrach slapped him on the back and left for his fields.

Silas turned to watch Viola the Wild rummaging through whatever it took to find what she needed. This was the hour when her mother turned her back on everyone. Who could blame her? Cold water therapy pushed a troubled mind into deeper terrors. It had pushed Honora to the brink, then tipped her into nothing. Viola had her work cut out for her. But she made the most of her day.

How had she slipped into his awareness like this? In days, *days!*… he'd gone from the overwhelming need to find the astrolabe to waking each morning to thoughts of her. Her words poured into his lonely heart like a cool drink. And like a thirsty man, he wanted more.

But he could not forget greedy moneylenders like Chester Sweeney, who never made deals without securing their reward. Without the astrolabe, Silas would have to relinquish his factory to a man who spun fortune out of other men's miseries.

He leaned on the menagerie wall, and his fingers tapped a drumbeat on his leg. She had made a way for him to stay longer. Anticipation trickled into his chest and his fingers slipped into the old familiar pattern of short loops. Like the scrollwork on the astrolabe. Down, loop, up. Down, loop, up.

Hadn't she begged to be his accomplice? But if she was smitten, as Shadrach suggested, he'd gather her into a world of just the two of them, and that was not fair.

Not fair on the girl who bobbed around him with contagious emotion. Not fair on the woman who wrapped her shawl around him and did not shy away from his gaze.

And most unfair on the replacement child who shied away from being second in anyone's estimation.

∽

With the permission of her hostess, Viola clipped an assortment of hydrangea samples and filled her basket with what Shadrach may have burned or left to rot along with other autumnal cast offs. But not Viola. She held up a desiccated sprig. Hydrangeas wore their spotted and freckled imperfections with dignity.

She sat on the bottom step of the verandah and rubbed her aching temple with her palm. Her bruises ripened into confusion. It would have been heartless to not petition on behalf of an injured man. To deny him shelter. And the chance to find what he'd come for.

But that was before she'd found her shawl discarded over a chair.

If it was distance he craved, she would not stand in his way. Distance would allow her to sleep instead of blinking into the night, listening for his slightest movement. Viola ordered the blooms in the basket. Summer to autumn. And in her mind, ordered herself to stay alert.

A shadow appeared over her basket.

"This one is the prettiest." Silas sat beside her and tapped the head of a blue cluster, still bright in places, streaked in others, and thoroughly speckled. He stretched his legs.

How had she not heard him approach? This was why she needed a plan.

"Feeling better?"

"A little. Your head left quite a bruise."

"You dragged me down."

He looked away. "I'm wondering if you'd like to accept the position of accomplice. It may be open for applicants."

"Accomplice?" She leaned back. "Staircase Thief needs a helper now?"

"Are you in?"

She blinked hard. Was he gathering her up for mischief she could not resist? Or was it him she could not resist?

She busied herself with the basket. Of course she would agree. He knew she would. She'd made the offer herself.

Look closer, Viola. What do you see? Beyond the immediately visible, there was always a beneath. A deeper. An other side. If they were to play games that would keep her safe, she'd have to become the girl on the fence he met that first day. A little belligerent. Annoying, even.

"I'm not sure I can help you." She pressed her fingertip to the sharp end of her scissors, and a game formed on her tongue.

"What? You begged me the other day."

"And the other day, you didn't need me."

"Well, I… do… now." He had to force each word from his mouth.

She almost felt bad. *Push back, Viola. Build a boundary between you and him if you care to create without distraction.*

"I don't like the word accomplice." She raised an eyebrow and hoped she looked a little petulant. "If I am to help, I wish to be the… huntress. Equal to your hunter. Because I imagine I will have to take apart the newel post and you will have to tell me how."

"Yes." He could barely say it, and she bit back a grin.

"On one condition, then."

"You've already made one. Huntress. This would be the second."

"It would undergird all my conditions. I may have more."

He let out a sigh of mock exasperation, and she knew she had him. This pursuit would cost her. Her emotions would surface in ways she did not always understand. But maybe she wanted that, too.

"I will hunt alongside you, if you tell me what we're looking for."

Silas let out another sigh.

Much like the one he'd uttered when they'd last fallen together into a heap.

April 28, 1879

Clemmie is •istresse• tonight. Her lips move an• her wor•s flow, but neither of us knows what's being sai•. To me, it is gibberish. To her, a cruelty she cannot hol•, an• wor•s seep from her in •reamlike babble an• hisses.

Her bo•y craves the Mariani Tonic. She thrashes in •esperation, searching for whatever plagues her. I offer another pastille. A poorer substitute for the full-bo•ie• wine mixture.

I wait for restoration while the sky fills with stars an• the last of the sunset falls into secret places beyon• the horizon.

Silas, the man for whom horizons an• ti•es pull with other secrets, has tol• me it is an astrolabe he seeks. A navigational piece no bigger than my fist, use• by sailors to measure time an• space an• •istance.

A valuable treasure. Something he will sell to pay off •ebts. To secure his business. He will not say why he let it go, only that it was a huge mistake, an• one he must un•o before he can •o anything else.

An• in his lament, I remember the Sweet Clementine. I think of objects that hol• sentiment an• belong to the wrong people.

Hi••en in the wrong hollows. Hung on the wrong walls.

I stare at Clemmie. Her anxious rocking lulls her to sleep. An• in my quest for Clemmie's healing, I see some of Silas. A man who has nothing to lose.

Tomorrow, I have agree• to help him. Alrea•y I know this is more than a game.

An• I coul• no more •eny him my help than I coul• •eny Clemmie.

Because, like Clemmie, what Silas nee•s is something he has alrea•y given away.

12

It was one thing to agree to an act of theft and vandalism. Another thing altogether, in the light of day, to actually roll up her sleeves and steal. Viola collapsed in a puff of billowing skirt-folds onto the sandy beach and threw a handful of pretty shells into an old biscuit tin where she collected treasures.

"One thing to openly take riches thrown up by the sea, another to…" She blew out a puff of confusion. And the little worm of anxiety that had burrowed in her all afternoon twisted and rose to the surface. She rested her head on her bent knees. Did thievery weigh on her so, or the company of thieves?

One helpless thief. Fellow hunter. Reclaimer of the lost. Silas.

She dug her hand into the sand. Her curled fist fed the tiny grains into a coil that widened, then narrowed. As with her paints, sand did what she told it to. And playing with it corralled her wild thoughts into calmer, deeper, new perspectives. *Was it not a noble gesture to help the helpless?* She swept the sand with the heel of her palm. *Certainly. Admirable, even.* She turned over another handful and let it slip between her fingers. Clemmie would adore this, when she finally rose from her bed.

Or… Viola thrust both hands in, she could take the sand to Clemmie. Right now.

She grabbed her tin and filled it to the top with all the sand she could carry. When Clemmie combed through, not only would she find shells, but the odd piece of dry seaweed, a seagull feather, and hopefully her own sliver of calm.

A spot of rain hurried her on and, armed with her loot, Viola bid the beach farewell for one more day. "Thank you," she whispered over her shoulder. Rest cure may still be a tyrant for mother and daughter, but seaside therapy was proving a true indulgence for one of them.

"A bad idea," Silas muttered to himself. "Foolish. The workings of a desperate knothead." He slid the small pot of yellow glue into the basin of steaming water. A family recipe, the preparation had been passed down from his grandfather to his father, and now the three brothers Swift all held the formula a close-guarded secret.

Had Eugene completed the orders Silas left in his charge? Some men were not cut out to run a business. He stirred the softening glue. Some men were better off following instructions. Eugene, the twin who carried the worst disfigurement, was such a man. Timid and needing to be told what each day required, he'd nod and walk away, no objections.

Patrick was every factory owner's nightmare. Argumentative, sullen, and driven to prove Silas wrong at every turn. When mill towns had called for loggers, Patrick had not hesitated in signing up. All he'd needed, like most prodigals, was his share.

Silas owed him, he'd said, looking him right in the eye.

The glue liquefied, and the memory of his brother's demands thickened and swirled.

Across the oceans, and still the trinket from Mr. Hinkle's sack made Silas do dumb things. Like take on an accomplice. No… a fellow huntress.

He listened for her. She had a way of entering like a sea gust. Purposeful, and quick to rustle up something in him he dared not identify. This morning, he'd spied a wreath hanging against the glass of her bedroom windowpane. Something she'd twisted together from the pieces of the bush.

Something twisted in him too. A soft knock hit the door he'd left ajar.

"Ready?" Adventure-pink, her cheeks matched the shine in her eyes.

He put his finger to his lips. "Almost," he whispered. "Everyone occupied?"

"They are." She peered into the ewer, where a piece of toweling soaked. "If you're going to borrow my hands, let's begin." She wrung the towel free of water. "Now, to the post," she whispered, giddy as a schoolmarm on the last day of term.

She'd seen him do this once before. Today, she led the way.

He picked up the glue pot and followed her out. Tied in a knot at the small of her back, as ever, she'd pulled that shawl into a twist. Like his sister Mary on the days she baked bread. Swaddled and devoted to the task. Viola stopped at the midpoint of the stairs and, without haste or prompting from him, wrapped the square post in the hot towel.

He half expected her to turn and stare at him with some kind of smugness.

Instead, she asked about her mother. "Clemmie was asleep when I went to her just now. How was she for you?"

"Quiet." Melancholy was the word they'd used for Honora. It

was the same here.

An emptiness with no remedy.

Viola pressed on the towel, the same way he had done, and he overtook her to stand two steps above. The corner of her lip caught between her teeth. And it startled him that now of all times, at this grave moment, with steam rising off her fingers, his attention would fall to her.

"Who goes there? Who goes there?" Balthazar called from the landing.

"Balthazar, you shush now," Viola called back. "It's only me, silly bird."

"Viola, Viola, Viola." The galah sang.

Silas was not sure he'd call anyone who wanted more of Viola *silly.* Stricken perhaps. But not silly.

"The towel is cooling fast." She looked up at him. "Your astrolabe has to be in here, surely. I feel it in my bones, awaiting our rescue."

His heart hammered faster than his work crew on a busy shift. He reached into his pocket and pulled out the fine-tipped mortice chisel best suited to skewering wood. His hand shook, too. "When the glue lets go, you can pierce the post off, right here." He pressed his fingertip to the join. "You'll need to wriggle it. Use the smallest amount of pressure."

She nodded, her cheeks a little more flushed, her resolve more than appealing. Viola Buckley made a fine, unflustered accomplice.

And in that moment, it both puzzled and delighted him to discover she made a most excellent companion. Someone who'd chosen his side. He'd not felt that in… how long? Surely not since… Charlie?

"What makes a man throw away something so valuable?" She smiled, but her enquiry felt like she'd pressed the tip of a blade between his ribs.

Don't let Viola know you've taken one wife if you want her to become the second.

"A stupid impulse." Or if he cared to tell the unvarnished truth, a lit fuse on a stick of dynamite thrown into his future. "Foolish. Something you'd not know about." He teased, giving her something to bite on but no real answer.

She jimmied the wood pieces until the smallest crack of wood captured their attention.

"Good." He leaned closer. "Now the other side."

She worked there too, and in no time, cleaved the top panel, clear off.

"I get to dig in." She handed him the post piece, which he collected to his chest.

"But my good arm is—"

"Not as fast as mine." She sank her hand into the depth he knew would be cool, if not a little rough along the edges.

Wide and brown, her eyes mirrored the anticipation he felt. Round and searching, her naked curiosity pulled him in. And under. An endless eternity of scouring. Was it the post she dug into, or him?

She smiled. Gleeful. Broad and expectant. Then her teasing softened into something else. Awakening. A sinking. Her eyes darted over his face like it was the first time she'd seen him.

Then a frown appeared. Her knuckles sounded on wood. Still, she held his gaze, and he, foolish man, could not have looked away if he tried.

Her frown deepened. "Nothing." She drew her empty hand away and stepped aside for him to peer in.

He sank his own hand in to be sure.

"Don't trust me?"

"I do." She sounded like Patrick. "I… I just need to be sure."

And what was more convincing than the cold chasm of the empty post?

"I'm sorry," she said.

"At least we know." He swallowed the disappointment.

"What if it's not up there either? What if…" She let the end of her question float away.

"What if I've come all this way for nothing?" And all he had were these moments with her to sift through on his long voyage home.

"It has to be in the top one," she whispered with a soft burst of triumph. A big grin spread over her face. "There's no other post left. This empty one means we know for sure. Come." She squeezed his arm. "Let's bust it open, this minute."

Even through the layers of his cotton shirt and undervest, her touch scorched him.

"We need to repair what we've dismantled first." This time, even he heard the *killjoy* in his voice.

A shower of rain hit the landing window.

"Quick, now. Brush these edges with glue. In a minute, they'll be tacky enough to stick."

She'd had a front-row seat to this before and knew to work fast. With the pad of her little finger, she tested the glue, then slid the top back into place. Soon, the broken-into newel post looked like the other two.

Undisturbed on the outside. Ripped apart on the inside.

"I normally use brushes to create. Not restore," she said.

"Creating restores the soul," he replied, and she beheld him as if he'd stolen her choicest secret.

A streak of glue stuck to her hair. Like a golden thread, it floated right in front of her eyes and caught on an eyelash. He pulled it away, brushing against her cheekbone. He'd done this before, when she'd fallen on his shoulder, when he needed to numb the pain by looking into her eyes. He wanted that now, too. Because Viola both numbed his pain and roused his pleasure.

With a gust similar to the shower outside, Shadrach shouldered his way into the house, shaking off the rain.

"If it's not a downpour, it's some other deluge," he complained to no one in particular.

Silas and Viola stood still as statues. If their host grumbled his way to the kitchen and to his wife, they'd not be seen.

"Who goes there? Who goes there?" Balthazar called from the landing, and Shadrach looked up.

He frowned. "You two again?"

Brush in hand and red faced, Viola's mouth dropped into an O.

Silas winced. This is what happened when people gave in to bad, foolish, delirious ideas.

"We… um…" Viola jumped in with an uncooked answer.

"We've been talking about painting," Silas finished for her. His mind scrambled for more. "And I thought, what better souvenir than a portrait sketch by someone who will become a famous Australian artist."

"She's going to paint you?" Shadrach looked from one to the other.

"Mm-hmm." Silas nodded.

"When?"

"Right now."

"Her mother told me she doesn't do portraits." Shadrach crossed his arms over his chest.

Silas didn't know that. And his words died on his tongue.

"Well, I… I don't, normally." Viola leaned on the stair rail. "But

I am willing to bend the rules for Mr. Swift."

Shadrach sniffed. "I see. And can you work by the light in the kitchen, Miss Buckley?"

Viola opened and closed her mouth. "I can try."

"Good. Grab your equipment. I'm sure that brush alone is not all you'll need. And you, Mr. Swift, can follow me to the chair where you shall sit. Where we can all watch you."

Dread pooled in his lungs. Their host was not only suspicious, he was boxing them into a corner like naughty schoolchildren.

"Mr. Swift has asked if I would make a charcoal sketch of him, and Mr. Jones insists I do so in the kitchen." The words sounded weird and wrong. Had she really said them out loud?

"For a portrait painting?" Like an hourglass, Clemmie let the grains of sand slip from her fingers into a thin stream.

"No, only a fast sketch. I promise." She breathed in hard and hoped her nerves would not betray her.

"Portraits are trouble." Clemmie poked at the sand. "For the painter and the sitter. To show someone how you see them is a bold undertaking. Are you certain?"

Viola had no choice. She busied herself straightening Clemmie's small collection of books and nodded, hoping to convince herself as much as her mother. "Nasrin taught me portraiture using her face. But sometimes Leo would sit for me so I could practice men's faces. I'll pretend it's him."

"You cannot replace one man's face with another."

Viola pressed her fists atop the book stack. If she began untangling how it all made her feel, how would she concentrate on the task? Her mother's warning reminded her of Nasrin's.

To draw a face is to spend time considering what it is to be the one beneath. It requires becoming lost in the unmoving facade that reveals and conceals the real person within.

"Don't worry, dear. This is not like the *Sweet Clementine.*"

I am not the girl in that painting, Clemmie would normally say. Today, she played with the sand at her fingertips. "I was only nineteen. And Mortimer Barnes saw in me something that even I hadn't…"

Viola turned around so fast she almost knocked the books over.

"I was that person in the painting for the narrowest moment of time, and he," Clemmie looked away, "he caught it, because only he saw it. And in a heartbeat, he was gone, and I was never the same."

Viola rubbed her mother's arm. The lightest touch was all she had to offer for a wound so ancient, so vivid. And so denied.

"Remember this, my girl. The artist is not removed from the portrait she draws."

"Well, I'm not practiced at it, so I doubt I will produce anything as beautiful or as nuanced as the *Sweet Clementine.*"

She would have liked to stay and listen to more of what her mother remembered. Reluctantly, she kissed her on the forehead and left her sifting the sand for fragments.

13

In the farmhouse kitchen, Shadrach sat at the table and sipped on a steaming mug of tea, Molly on his knee. Finella busied herself at the other end, emptying out the contents of two long crates. Glass jars, dusty ceramic crocks, dozens of them, all sizes. Perhaps they'd been in storage somewhere, because Finella wiped them with a damp rag.

"Tea?" she offered with a look that said she was as surprised as Viola to find everyone crammed into her busy kitchen.

"Perhaps, when I'm done." Viola turned her attention to Silas.

Shirt sleeves rolled to his elbows, he straddled a chair that he'd turned the wrong way around, arms draped over the back of it like a rowdy boy who'd been told to sit there until his temper expired.

Light from a window illuminated one side of his face, leaving the other in shadows. She wished for more shadows. For fewer people. For fewer butterflies that beat hard against the cartilage of her ribs.

Silas cleared his throat, and Viola tightened the screws on the three legs of her easel. At least that was secure. She could not say the same about herself. How had she found herself in this predicament?

Because they'd been caught. And this was the only way out. That's all, she told herself, ignoring the rising tension in the warm kitchen.

Shadrach and Molly babbled happily, but their words made little sense to Viola. It was as if the hum of conversation had been replaced with a current that collected her in. Soon, when she lifted her eyes from where she sorted her charcoal sticks, he would enter her view.

She raised her head, and Silas locked eyes with hers. He frowned, as expected, and two small puckered lines split his face in equal parts between the eyes. She'd get to them later.

"My art teacher, Madame Nasrin, says human heads are never perfect circles." If they were to watch her work on an unrefined skill, perhaps she might cover some of her inexperience with the scant little she remembered. "Nor are they perfect ovals. She says to begin with an egg shape, and work from there."

She lifted her eyes from the rough ovoid shape on her page.

Silas breathed through his nostrils, discomfort a clear line in his lips. His left heel tapped a nervous beat onto the floor. His thumb ran over a pink scar on his arm.

And her eyes roamed all over his face, because unlike any other time she had looked at him in conversation or snuck a peek when he wasn't looking, this was a true, deep study.

She knew his many faces already. Frustrated, annoyed. Pained when he'd broken her fall. Now, something else barged in. Fear. White knuckled, he gripped the back of the chair as if he were about to fall into a dark hole.

A dark hole.

Of course!

Had Shadrach voiced his suspicions over their loitering on the stairs? A man on the alert for a creature that trespassed on his property would sniff out the same under his roof in a heartbeat.

This is why they were all squeezed into the kitchen. Shadrach pretending he was interested in art while Silas sat pinned to a chair.

He rocked a little, like someone trying to calm themselves, and with his finger, he marked a slow pattern on his sleeve.

With quick strokes she outlined the shape of his eyes, the bridge of his nose, and the flare of his nostrils. Next came his mouth, but it was easier to take her pencil to his ears, his eyebrows, and the outline of his hair.

Shadrach held his daughter up. "Do you see Mr. Swift on the page?"

Molly shook her head.

"Me neither." Shadrach peered from the paper to the artist's model. "Good grief, chum. You look like the guilty about to face a jury. Here, stand up."

Silas peeled his arms from the chair. He did not like being told and shot Viola a *clearly, I'm not the boss here* frown.

Shadrach turned the chair around. "Now, sit."

Silas claimed the chair again, a fist on each knee.

"Up… up." Molly scrambled into his lap.

"I don't think so." Finella intervened, but Silas shook his head.

"I don't mind. She remembers our game from the other day." With a grimace he brought his hands together to fold some kind of doll from his kerchief. With the child in his lap, the crease lines in his frown softened a little, and newer ones appeared where his mouth smiled.

Viola positioned the rough outline of his lips, the Cupid's bow, the corner of his mouth, and heat seared her neck.

He looked directly at her and she directly at his lips. And they both knew it.

A few more strokes and he came into view. Her hand wobbled. In real life he was a man who sported a few days' growth. But this was a clean-shaven version of him. Someone who welcomed the warmth of a sleepy child into his arms. He clawed his way from the page and with each mark she made, fixed himself before her. Vulnerable. His eyes pleaded with her to keep his secret.

She snuck a look around the room. Finella rummaged in her crate of jars. Shadrach's mug would be empty now. Or cold. But his interest remained hot.

She shaded and added depth. Sharpening the line of his jaw. Filling in the darkest places of his eyes and rubbing out the smudges she didn't want to leave behind. Light and dark. Shade… contour, sharp, soft… the image in her mind blended with the living one before her.

Onto the page appeared a youthful, handsome man.

She closed her eyes and let the vision come. The soft rise of the corner of his mouth when she'd gotten the best of him. The barest smile of triumph when he'd gained over her. They all belonged to a brave man who'd come far and would soon leave for good.

Did she see him as he was, or how she wanted him to be? She looked from her page to his face.

No. This would not do. She'd gone too far. He was not old. But she had judged him so. Like everyone who'd judged her unfit for an independent career as a botanical artist, she, too, had made assumptions. He was not a killjoy. Anything but.

Something trembled inside her, and she pushed a small scrap of paper under the pad of her hand to keep from blotting her work. There was life in him, and she would make sure it sparked from his eyes.

Molly nestled into his chest. Silas closed his eyes for the briefest second. As if drinking in the marvel of a child in his arms.

As if… he longed for it.

She drew a deep breath. He would return to Portland. Marry.

Father children and live a full life.

A small tear rolled down her cheek, and she brushed it away. The frenzy of her work took over, and she poured herself into him with such abandon that the sound of Finella coaxing Shadrach into another room barely put a dent in her efforts.

She blinked hard and another tear fell. She wiped it away. There was no time for distractions. She had an apology to draw.

She fashioned his lip into the start of a smile. As if she had reached to clasp his jaw and move it, just so, with her thumb.

The tapping of his foot stilled. But she continued digging him out of the recess of her mind. Or was it her heart?

It was not enough, this stoic face he'd allowed her to sketch. Nasrin had taught her that the subject of a portrait never smiles. In this, Viola chose to disobey. For there had never been a portrait that needed it more. Small smile lines beside his eyes, nothing extravagant, but wholly him.

She blew on the paper and set her pencil on the easel ledge.

"I have misjudged you," she whispered, unclipped the page and handed him the sketch. "Forgive me."

His arm had fallen asleep but his heart was fully awake. She had pushed through tears to sketch this, and he'd not been able to reach her, pinned to his chair by a sleeping tot.

She dismantled her easel, collected her things, and disappeared from the room.

Molly did not stir. Chickens cackled in their far-off roost. And when the sound of Viola's footsteps faded, he dared take in the sketch.

A smiling version of himself peered back. Not a full-blown smile, but one just about to form. The fullness of it hidden in eyes drawn crinkled with warmth. Where was the long-suffering demeanor he'd fought to maintain? The bristling in his chest at being told what to do? When had she seen this man?

In the looking glass, he was a failure. A man abandoned to working long hours, who squeezed more from the day than God intended. A man who'd lost more than he should have ever gambled. A scoundrel.

The man who held onto this paper was not the man upon it. At least in her eyes.

How did a man walk away from someone who saw him in that light?

The force of that pinned him down and tightened, as sure as if she'd taken his finest brace and fixed it, turn by turn, with every stroke of her pencil.

14

The next day, lured like the tavern ants that meandered over the image of *Sweet Clementine*, Viola found herself back in the warm kitchen in her own search for crumbs. Sugar and spices and jam making occupied Finella, who hopped from table to stove like a busy bird.

Viola returned their luncheon tray, but she'd balanced something altogether more delicate through the landings and corridors of this house. The desire to return to the scene of her own vulnerability. A greater mystery to her than whatever method Finella employed to bottle her jam.

"Can I help?" Viola ignored the vacant chair in the corner. It reminded her of all that had emptied out of her when she had seen into the heart of Silas. "Clemmie's content to watch the rain trickle down the window, and I..." A sigh consumed the tail of her thought, and she busied herself with pulling an apron from a hook on the wall.

"You're not here for the jam, I can tell." Finella ran a large wooden spoon through a bubbling pot on the stove.

"Is it that obvious?"

"After a few summers, I now recognize this kind of trouble." She blew a strand of hair away. "Guests have a way of telling you what they need, even if they don't fully know it themselves. It comes with the location. When a weary soul rests by the sea, all defenses collapse. It sends some into a frenzy. Others need to talk. The weariest fall into a sleep they've not known for years."

Viola secured the apron strings. *She* was wide awake. And all because confusion had unbuckled in her yesterday.

"Talking might open the floodgates. I'm afraid that might—"

Silas strode into their midst, hair wet from the rain. Purpose snapped in the way he took to *that chair* and shook open his newspaper.

"I hope you don't mind if I warm up in here. Got caught in a real gully washer."

Viola pressed her hands to her hips. *Him? Here? Now?* Her craziest self had come this far, knowing he might appear. But the sanest cord within her needed more of Finella's answers first.

"You've become fond of that chair."

"It's a fine corner." He wore his almost-smile like an old winter scarf. A layer she'd already unraveled. He tapped the newspaper. "And look here now, I've already found something you might care for. An advertisement by a portrait painter. You could do something similar. Hang up a shingle. Turn a sketch into a painting. See into a person's soul."

The room stilled.

"Portraiture is not for me."

"Sure now? Wouldn't hurt to try."

She stared at him. It already hurt. One day soon, he would leave. For now, he regarded her like no man ever had. That confounded her more than the last time he'd sat there.

"And what is that I spy?" He bit back a grin. "Have you been scaling fences again?"

He pointed to the table. It held an assortment of earthen

containers and cutlery. And a large pan of ....

"Rosehips?" How had she not noticed them until now? The nearest pan overflowed with the generous harvest, and three others like it sat on the floor where Molly scooped baby handfuls into a small cup. "Finella, however did you gather so many without being knocked into a puddle by Silas?" She stepped into the easy flow of their teasing.

"I had a little help from Shadrach." Finella topped and tailed the rosehips with a paring knife. "We collect them every year after the first frost. It's how we remember Molly, Shad's sister." The rhythm of her chopping slowed and then ceased. "She was only fourteen when she fell into Saltwater Creek, looking for me, and, well... she died." Whisper thin, her voice trailed into the unspeakable.

Viola gasped. "Oh, how awful. And... she was Molly, too?"

"Her real name was Matilda." Finella juggled a handful of the hips. "We named our baby in her memory, but our hearts turned to Molly in weeks. We do this to keep a promise. And we remember our precious girl who wanted nothing more than bread with jam."

Viola's heart sorrowed at their loss. And for the pocket of grief it now left. Grief that would bleed all over the innocent child who played at their feet.

In a dusty corner of her mind, her younger self stood poised to sing. Nervous and excited, she had scrubbed off some of the face paint used to hide her emerging freckles. And in a moment of clarity, as clear as it got for an eight-year-old, she had defied her father and pulled free all the hairpins that secured the ringlet wig to her battered head.

"If I had a girl like you instead of Little Lazlo, I'd leave your hair loose. Just like you have it now." From his pocket, Junius Abner had produced a tiny silver-edged mirror. *"See?"* Viola had no use for the

mirror. All she had needed was a chance to show them a pain-free way.

She had no idea it would be her last performance. That the fury of her father would be so unleashed, he would punish her for going on stage in an incomplete costume.

"Useless!" he had yelled and dragged her behind curtains so heavy and so thick they may have been a portal to another world. *"This is not a game. It's not the real you they come to see. It's your dead sister, and that wig was central to her performance. How foolish can you be?"*

She shivered and swallowed the fear and rebellion of that day.

"It's not without complexity, being born to fill another's shoes," she ventured. "I didn't have my sister's hair. Or eyes. Or frame. Or skin. And on the stage, I did not have her ways. I had my own. And they were… not enough." The dregs of old panic tripped into her words. "Marshall called her The Original Viola. I was the Other Viola. I would hate for your beautiful Molly to feel she cannot be herself. That is a cruel fate for anyone."

"Oh, no, Molly is named in loving memory—"

"But how do you look at one child without searching for the other? I know from bitter experience that could be a false cure."

One of the pots bubbled and popped. From outside, kookaburras laughed in the rain, and Molly babbled her own sweet songs. Silas lowered his newspaper. Perhaps he, too, needed to take in Finella's answer.

Their hostess pressed her lips together before replying. "Curses are lifted when we refuse to believe them. Shad and I could not have embraced one another if we believed it was beyond us. We've named our Molly in victory. She is one of the prizes of our love."

She moved to the stove, and Viola considered her words.

The *prize of love* sounded like the *price of love*. Perilous furrows and grooves.

Silas watched her, as if he possessed the ability to read her mind. She took up Finella's knife, but her hand shook. Was it the burden of old echoes or Finella's answer that made her tremble? She dropped her hand to her side.

Silas folded his shirt sleeves to the elbow and joined her. Right there. Right at her trembling side. If his movement were the lightning, his proximity rolled over her like thunder. He leaned his arm into hers, barely there. Wholly felt in the lightest touch.

"May not be customary in these parts, but I figure Viola needs an accomplice."

He sliced off the top of a rosehip, chopped off the bottom, and dropped it in the pan that contained the jeweled fruit of the rose. Or perhaps it was a seed pod. Viola wasn't sure, her mind too full of the presence of Silas to unscramble botanical intricacies.

He filled out a simple cambric shirt and dark woolen vest with work muscles she was sure had not developed at a kitchen table. Still, he did not seem to mind standing there.

Enlivened by his presence, she dug into the rosehips. He dug in right behind her. Their fingers touched, and shivers marched along her wrist and into her cotton sleeves.

She snuck a peek at him. Had it only been a week ago that she'd thought him somber? A week was enough time for Romeo and Juliet's tale to unravel. But she was no Shakespearean character. Even if Marshall insisted his daughters, and even their pet, carry names penned by the bard.

Viola chased another rosehip. Silas snatched it.

"Thief," she whispered, and tried to quell her smile.

"Are you sure?" He pressed his thumb over hers. "Perhaps you're stealing from me."

"Your hand is chasing mine."

"And… are you caught yet?"

Finella elbowed between them. "Not done with these yet?" She looked from Silas to Viola. "When you've finished playing in the rosehips, we'll strain this earlier batch through muslin. But first…" She peered under the table. "Molly? Where is that girl?"

As if in answer, a soft thud, followed by a child's wail, rang through the house. "The stairs. Oh, that rascal…" Finella hurried away, calling behind her for Viola to mind the bubbling pot. "And keep stirring."

The stirring spoon sat on a plate. Silas reached it first.

"She meant me." Viola held out a hand for the spoon.

He brought the spoon to his nose. "Smells good."

Viola poked him in the arm. "Give it to me."

He ran his finger through the small puddle in the hollow of the spoon and brought it to his mouth.

"Mmm." He licked his lips.

"Silas—"

"Ever tried rosehip jam?"

"No."

"Me neither." He plucked a teaspoon from a cutlery caddy and scraped a portion of jam from the cook pot. "Open wide."

"Silas!"

He came closer, the spoon almost hidden in his grip, almost at her lips. Some kind of delicious daring had come over him. A playful, slow torment that swept away any trace of *killjoy* right before her eyes.

He cupped her chin with one hand.

She opened her mouth.

What do you taste? How does it make you feel?

She closed her eyes. *Baked crabapples and cloves. His hand on my face.*

She pulled the spoon from her mouth. "I expected the aroma of roses. It's almost tangy. And sweet."

Silas watched her lick her lips. Jam bubbled on the stove. And they stood there, watching each other, with all that brewed between them.

"The pot will stick," she whispered. And even though he stood perfectly still, it felt like he hurtled towards her with the same intensity that had dislocated his shoulder. "Please, give me the spoon."

He handed it over and returned her to their task. Stirring.

Perhaps he'd done that all along. For Viola felt as if she'd been dragged through a sticky mess and did not know what came next. She dug into the pot. Jam splattered and begged for her rescue, but not with the focused intensity of Silas, arms crossed over his chest.

"I want to know why you cried when you sketched my face."

He waited for her reply, slowing time to the aching urgency of sugar about to burn and Viola about to combust.

"Did I cry?"

"You wiped away tears."

"That's not crying. Crying is what Clemmie does when we douse her in cold water."

For the longest time, he said nothing.

"When a man watches a woman sketch his features, he wonders what she makes of them. *Tears,*" he emphasized, "are never a good sign."

"It was four tears," she admitted. "Four stranded pieces of my emotion that had nowhere else to go."

"You said you misjudged me. I want to know how."

She bent over the jam as if her own fortunes thickened under the scalding mix. Softened rosehips rolled to the surface. Heat steamed into her hair.

"I was thinking about how you annoyed me that first day. How I failed to see you weren't as ancient as I first believed."

"That made you cry?"

"That, and a combination of other things." The jam hissed and popped.

"Tell me."

Dare she? How reckless to confess girlish things like *it struck me that you will leave soon and that I will never see you again,* or *I saw your longing for a child and let myself slide into that picture like the fool you already think I am.*

"If I've caused tears, I wish to make amends. But I'll wait…"

She looked up at him. "Wait?"

He thrust his hand into his pockets. "I could have broken into that post today if I wanted to, Viola. My arm's not perfect, but I'd have managed. But I asked myself if I wanted to go home with a pocketful of something, or maybe tuck something into my heart as well."

"Your… heart?"

"I could have kissed you right now, too." He said it like he tasted the words for the first time. Rolled them on his tongue like jam. "Right here, in this kitchen. But I…" He frowned and started again.

"Look, meet me tomorrow, on the beach. There's a driftwood log near Red Rocks, a perfect place to talk. And we might even decipher why you sketched a smile onto a face that wasn't smiling."

Her heart hammered and rang with the wildest replies. *Something to tuck into his heart? A walk? A kiss?*

Lost in his words, she did not notice the pan roll to a furious boil until jam splattered onto her wrist.

"Ow!" She cradled her hand.

He pulled the pan to a cooler part of the stovetop and plunged her hand, along with his, into a water jug on the table. "Apprentices bump into hot glue pots in our factory all the time. Cold water's their friend."

Her breath hitched. Cold water was a miserable morning therapy, reserved for shocking a patient into apathy. But not this. She tried to wriggle, but he held her down.

"Not so fast. A burn will race into the layers of skin or be held back. Depends on what you're willing to bear. Cold or hot?"

She surely endured this burn. The one on her wrist and the one on her insides that flowed like molten glass running into crevices she didn't know existed.

A commotion came from the kitchen door. Silas sent off whoever it was with a fast wink. And the molten glass that already trickled inside her solidified into brittle desire.

She'd never experienced the tending of her pain by a man. The giving of aches, yes, but not this kind of deliberate and maddening dance he'd pulled her into.

With a cloth underneath to catch the water, he drew her hand up and out. He examined her wrist, then turned it over. And in the crack of time that only he and she occupied, while the jam set in the pot and Molly hummed from beyond the kitchen walls, he pressed his lips upon her curled knuckles in a featherlight kiss.

April 30, 1879

If Silas can extinguish the flame on my skin an• light a fire within me, he is worth letting in.

I also have questions, so I make a list of them here.

Why tell a man he stirs your affections if he will soon leave your hometown, your country, an• your presence... for his own worl•? Why heap fresh grief upon myself if all I am to •o is suffer a quick loss? Then I remember how he kisse• my han•.

An• I know he also juggles quan•aries of the heart that •eserve to be unlocke•.

15

Was it always the way for a man chasing a woman that the earth beneath his feet shifted like loosened sand? Silas veered toward the harder packed shoreline, where rock-pool edges provided a sturdier footing but still lapped at his feet with ice-cold hazards.

If this were a game to arrive first, she'd beaten him already. She sat upon the log, engrossed in some pursuit. Was she probing her heart for what it might expose, the way her mother did when she revealed more of the Buckley women and their story for him to peer into?

"My daughter carries a compulsion, Mr. Swift," she had shared today. *"To own a painting of me, made when I was too young to know better. She thinks by owning it she will right all our wrongs. She writes lists marked with every road she must take to fulfill this fixation. I tell you this, because that sketch she made of you created a longing for which she has no list. And if she were to make one with your name on it, it's only fair you understand the immovable obstacles she battles. Perhaps now is the time to tell your story, and in full."*

For a sick lady, Clementine Buckley sure had determination in reserve. And nothing he read from the newspaper held as much interest to her as the chronicles of her life.

His story, in full, was not one he cared to revisit. In short, he'd once taken a wife. Loved her and lost her. Even in his thoughts, prepared as he was to turn them over like dusty planks, the words sounded warped.

Upon the cradle end of the driftwood log which protruded like the palm of a hand, Viola looked every inch the artist at work. A drawing board in her lap. Behind her, red rock cliffs presided with the wonder of mountains that rose from the sea, but she took up all of what he truly looked at.

He was not blind to the way they sparked when they played. But what lay beyond games? What would happen to that spark when she heard about Honora? Should he begin with Mr. Hinkle? Charlie? His brothers? Communication was not his best skill. His words often tumbled out like curls of wood, in the many odd and unnecessary layers that sat over what he really meant.

She looked up.

He waved a greeting. "Making progress?"

"Eucalyptus leaves. The more torn up by insects and weather, the more they appeal. Even this gnarled and knotty piece of wood is beautiful."

She tapped a spot in invitation.

He sat and took the paper she offered. Elegant, tapered, a blend of greens and silvers and blues, edged in thin red lines.

"Exquisite. I could almost pick one up."

"There are more eucalyptus specimens and gum nuts in my bedroom than clothes, books, and shoes combined."

"In my room I have a portrait." He handed back the painting. "Your mother tells me it will be worth something someday."

"She's still a little mad at me for making that sketch, but not nearly as mad as she would have been if I'd made it of someone else. She's quite the fan of *that American you found for me.*"

He laughed but the chuckle rang too shallow for where he really wanted to go.

"And you? I respect your mother's fondness. She is easy to like. But it's you I care to know."

He couldn't tell if she squirmed at his question or if the log beneath her felt uneven. Either way, she placed her drawing board on the sand. The idea of her picking it back up, looking into the face of other men to do what she'd done with him, stirred a jealousy he had no right to feel.

"It was unfair of me to rope you into the charcoal sketch," he said. "But now, it's left us with an outline that needs filling in, don't you think?"

She nodded and turned all her attention on him. A man could get lost in eyes that brown. Polished walnut never shined so bright. He could ask again about why she cried, or he could begin with what he owed her.

"In Portland, we make chess tables in our factory. Black and white wooden squares, with drawers for all the pieces. And a flip side for backgammon. And my life, right now, feels a lot like one of those game tables. Inside out, wrong side up."

She blinked.

Feathers and Guts! What was he doing, rambling about tables? His collar felt too tight. His shirt too buttoned. He freed his sleeve cuffs and rolled them up, like a man about to dig into an abandoned well.

"What I mean is, I have left a struggling furniture business in the hands of one brother, while his twin has abandoned us for something better."

The wind messed her hair, and she pulled it back to see him better.

"Eugene, the younger twin, he's bashful and not the least interested in the role of boss, where I've left him. And sullen Patrick has decided he's better off with his inheritance and a mill town job."

He carried on, building a scaffold of time and events he hoped would lead her to know him more, before Honora emerged.

"We lost a shipment of wood, paid for in full, in a dockyard fire. I refinanced in a hurry and with the harshest money lender that would take me on. And if I don't find a way out of our debts, Swift Brothers won't belong to any one of us."

A deep breath pulled him to the real reason all this mattered. She had to know him at heart or this conversation and her tears would all be for naught.

"I failed Patrick. But I owe it to Eugene to do my best. My carelessness brought smallpox into our home when they were babies. They're men now, with full beards to hide their disfigurement. But they wear anger at me on the inside. All three of us carry that ugliness."

She followed his story without a trace of fear, and the unburdening felt so good it surprised him.

"Which brings me to Mr. Hinkle, gravedigger and cemetery caretaker." He dug his heels into the sand. "His son Charlie and I ran the streets together, and one day he told me his father had found dropped treasure in a sack on the cemetery grounds. Ship's treasure. Held up to the sky, it told you where you were and how to get to anyplace you wanted. Any sea, under any sky. It measured time and distance, told you when the sun would rise and set, and calculated the position of the planets. It may have come from ancient Persia, but when you held it," he made a cup with his hand, "the world and all its heavens lay in your palm."

She smiled. "How could a young boy resist that kind of treasure?

How old were you?"

"Twelve. My mother tried to keep me at home because she knew smallpox had struck the streets where the Hinkles lived, but I snuck out anyway. I brought home the sickness that bypassed me, my sister, and my parents, but found my twin brothers." He ran his finger along the log in short loops. The calming pattern he made whenever the weight of life crushed his chest.

"My mother refused to look at me for days. But when her babies fevered and their skin puckered and blistered, she told me I would spend the rest of my life in atonement for what I had done to them."

Viola's frown deepened.

"I started paying the very next day when news arrived that Charlie Hinkle had died. Weeks later, I went to his grave. His father wept to see me. He begged me to live the bright life taken from his son."

Silas rubbed his hands together. Some memories were like chunks of ice, easy to chip apart, but each one burned, no matter how you held it.

"My parents locked me in to responsibility, but Mr. Hinkle made me promise I'd chase freedom and adventure."

"How?"

"He gave me the astrolabe. Told me there were stars to follow. But I didn't know what that meant. I was only a boy and already promised to a future in my father's business. Point is, that astrolabe became a burden. I would take it out to look at the scrollwork and dream about far-off stars. Hemispheres and foreign countries. And then, when misfortunes overtook us, when everything became too dark for us..." He rubbed the flesh around the dog bite on his arm.

Visions of Honora rose in his mind. *"Get rid of it!"* she had yelled. *"I'll never be with child if that ruinous thing is not cast from this house.*

Your mother said it brought the pox to her children. And now it's robbing me of mine. Get rid of it!"

He closed his eyes. He needed to pull Honora out of the grave, but he didn't want to. Or know how.

Viola reached for his elbow. "What happened here?" Her fingers touched the skin beside his scar. But he was not up to that part of the story. He never wanted to sink there in the first place, and he would not take her there, either. At least, not now.

"It's nothing. A dog bite. Got away from his owner and took a chunk out of me."

"I think I understand." She brushed her hand over his shirt sleeve. "When you held Molly the other day, you looked so forlorn. It must pain you to remember your brothers, when they were babies much like Molly, with her beautiful baby skin and innocent ways. I didn't want to sketch you in sorrow, though I saw it. I wanted to capture the man who can stare at me the way you do and make me feel the smile beneath."

She *had* seen sorrow in him that day, it was true. But she'd seen a poor reflection of the truth. He swallowed. "Viola, it's more than that—"

"It is. And now it makes more sense." She knotted her fingers. "In my sketch, I let myself see a man who will soon leave. Perhaps it's silly or childish, I don't know. But I wanted to replace the sadness with something good, a smile. So I added it, but not without some grief of my own."

The sun hid behind a cloud, but she kept her eye on him. "I know replacement comes at a price. It's not as easy as erasing frown lines on a page."

She swallowed hard. And he realized, with a plunge of heart, she had her words stored up too, and like him, she was desperate to lay them out.

"Every day, I chase the chance to come first. Because I won't settle for second place. I still chase whatever is left of a mother's love when Clemmie weeps into my sister's little red shoe. Every day—" Her voice cracked, and Viola the Wild stepped into uncharted waters. "I… I chase inspiration that bombards my senses here on this island."

She waved her hand over the beach. "I chase an invisible clock, for the hours I need to prepare my portfolio to enter a competition that will yield nothing unless I win. And now," she faced him, "you are chasing me. And although it terrifies me, I also want to understand it. Before it's too late."

Her emotion was too much for her, and she barely held it in. And the moment to tell her about Honora flew into the wind like a fistful of sand.

He took her hands in his. "It's not too late. There are many hours that stretch before us, unexplored. Perhaps I can help."

"You?"

He nodded. "I could dig up more time for you to work on your art."

"How?"

How indeed? With a gulp of sea air, he killed the words he should've spoken and stoked the ones he cared for more.

"You'll see. Let me play."

He started with daily trinkets and diversions for their patient. As well as his own small gifts—a piece of fruit or posy—Silas searched for additions to the sand Mrs. Buckley so enjoyed, now transferred to a larger pan.

With Viola's permission, he slipped down to the shallows where he plunged it into a rock pool at low tide.

"Your wife's low spirits are a direct result of the reproductive cycles she has failed to carry. Her grief has morphed into rebellion of the mind, and she must be broken of this, in mind and spirit, if she is to return to reproductive stability."

Sea water seeped into the sand, followed by a rush of seaweed.

"Melancholy such as hers requires serious measures. We aim to crush her will. Then, she can proceed toward good health. For this, you must step out of our way."

He'd stood out of Dr. Weir's way for his wife's own good, but crushing her will had not healed it. And he'd not sit back and watch another woman, young or old, vibrant or melancholy, crushed by the same thinking if he could help it.

Water sloshed onto his hands, and by the time he arrived at the house and up the stairs, he wore some of it on his sleeve cuffs.

"Well, now!" Mrs. Buckley dipped her finger in and brought it to her lips.

He laughed. "I thought you might like a taste of the sea, but I didn't think you'd put it in your mouth."

"There is much about me that would surprise you, Mr. Swift." Mrs. Buckley played with the seaweed. Long strands swayed in the water like green ribbons. As did a mesh of pink seaweed, eyelash thin and prettier in the water than out. When she tired, he took the pan from her lap and placed it on the floor at the foot of the bed.

"You've missed Viola today," she said.

"She's in the courtyard, but I did not want to disturb her."

"She worked until late last night. I fell asleep, and when I woke, her lamp still flickered. I asked to see her work, but she said she would show me later. But I'm impatient, Mr. Swift. And *later* is almost gone for me. So I snuck into her room before you arrived to see for myself. Here…"

From her side table, among her drugs and creams, lay a collection of papers hidden under a newspaper.

"The light in here is better most mornings. Aren't they something to behold? But wait, not these. Where's the sea urchin?"

She dropped a page entitled *Eucalyptus Macrocarpa*. A pink blossom-head tipped in yellow. She shuffled others. Lightly painted sketches of ferns, wispy sea grass, and one that looked like the red berries they'd found on the deer hunt.

"Where is it?"

She swung her legs off the bed, but her foot became tangled in the sheet. She kicked it free, and the momentum propelled her into the medicine table. Bottles flew, as did pots of lotion. Lozenges scattered and trickled under the bed, but it was the tiny unlit lamp, with shade of frosted glass, that toppled and splintered over the wooden floor.

Silas knew how fast one disaster darted into another. Houses turned to cinders. Entire streets fell into ashes. His heart clattered with relief that this lamp had not been lit, for was that not how fires started? When the innocent rose from their beds and knocked flames into blazes.

Mrs. Buckley collapsed back onto the bed with the same speed at which she'd tried to rise, and he was glad she took that course. If she'd gone the other way, she would have met with the glass-littered floor. Except for one glass piece, the largest, which had torn through frayed ribbon and skewered the soft leather of the little red dancing shoe strung to the bedpost. The threadbare keepsake fell to the floor like a rotten piece of fruit.

"Oh no! Nooo!" Mrs. Buckley cried.

"Stay where you are." Silas pressed his hand to her shoulder.

But Mrs. Buckley ignored him. She fished it up, extracted the glass shard, and gathered the shoe to her cheek as if it were the only thing in the room worth saving.

"My lost baby girl." She sobbed, and Silas wondered how Finella had not heard the commotion and why she was not running up the stairs already.

"They thought opiates would cure me. That being with child would cure the opiate addiction." She cradled the shoe, whispering the turmoil of years. "All I really needed was to cry for my baby and remember her whenever I wished. Instead, Marshall… forced me to …"

"Shh, now, Mrs. Buckley." Broken glass kept him from reaching her properly, but so did jagged memories.

Her breath kept snatching. Her hands shook and the vein in her throat throbbed.

"If you promise to not move, I'll race down and fetch Finella."

The old woman did not reply, but her soft rocking and the shoe pressed between her palms told him she'd not go far. She had already slipped into a time and place where few could reach her.

Halfway down the stairs, a chilling thought caught him like a hook. Where were Viola's paintings? They'd been on the bedcover when the lamp broke.

He took the treads, two at a time, past the pink galah on the landing, and skidded to a halt at the open bedroom door.

Mrs. Buckley must have shared his thought.

For she too had abandoned her bed and now knelt at the foot where Silas had left the pan of seawater into which the paintings had slid.

Viola pressed her spine against the menagerie wall, where she sat on a sawn-off log and held a desiccated leaf to the afternoon sun. So little remained of the skin it resembled some kind of skeleton, stretched tight, spread thin like golden lacework over a frame.

Viola knew about being stretched tight. She felt it now. The day was never long enough for all she wanted to complete.

Gulliver, the ginger house cat, sidled up to her and ran his cheek over the rim of her basket. She scratched under his chin. "Has Balthazar tormented you enough? Pay him no mind. He'll never rule the outside world the way you do."

Gulliver collapsed onto her shoes and made himself comfortable, pressing her with his warmth. Now, this was a pet. Not the screeching, attention-seeking noise in a cage that her mother adored.

Shadrach appeared from the barn with a large shovel.

"Got something for you." He rummaged in his breast pocket. "I picked up the mail from the general store this morning." He handed her a letter and hurried away into his fields. Viola broke it open and read the words in a hungry gulp.

My dearest Poupette,

I trust you're settling in well and that Clemmie is not resisting her daily treatments.

Are you painting each day? Does this island inspire you to dig into yourself and draw the courage you need? You are in my thoughts. Especially today.

I read in the newspaper a list of items already promised to the Melbourne International Exhibition. Pottery and tapestries as well as some of the local artists' collection. Mortimer Barnes is on that list, with Sweet Clementine *among the pieces.*

I tell you now so you or Clemmie do not fall upon the news by accident. Time is moving like a wind and whipping up the Exhibition Building into the grand structure it will become.

Please, please, remember she always loved you, from the start. Behind her brokenness is always a mother who held on.

Fondest regards,
Your Nasrin

Viola tucked the letter into her basket along with the leaf sketch. News from Nasrin was the best medicine and the sweetest indulgence. But if Clemmie knew Mortimer's painting would leave the small tavern for a wider audience, it was just the poison to kill her.

Silas would be drawn to reports about the exhibition. Viola imagined the bedlam it would cause and knew she would have to confiscate all newspapers, or at least forewarn him.

She hurried into the house, up the stairs, and found Finella in the sickroom doorway, a pan of broken glass in her hand, an ashen look on her face.

"Viola. I was just coming to find you."

"What's happened? Is that the little lampshade?"

"This is… nothing… and your mother is unharmed, but it's…" Finella's words faltered, and she turned to Clemmie, who whimpered. Silas stood beside her. His face grim.

The room appeared tidy. The bed freshly made and her mother in the reading chair Silas normally occupied.

"Clemmie?"

No one spoke. They didn't need to. For in an instant, her gaze fell properly onto the bed. Upon fresh towels lay her most recent paintings. Island Natives now ran like dripping candles.

The affliction hit her in the chest with the force of a dozen

Marshalls. How had the paintings she'd left in her room found their way in here? And why were they wet?

"Viola." Silas tried to fix her attention. But she could not look away from the wreck on the bed.

"Your mother knocked the lamp over, and we didn't notice the paintings had fallen into…" He stopped as if he couldn't say the next words.

"Into…?"

He swallowed hard. "A pan of seawater I left there."

Viola's breath escaped sharp and raspy. "You ruined my paintings?"

"Not him." Clemmie sobbed. "Me." She clung to the red dancing shoe and ran the ragged, dirty ribbon through her fingers as if it were the finest Oriental silk. "I wanted to see what you'd painted, so I carried them to the light of my window."

"But I said I would show them to you."

"I meant no harm. But when the lamp shattered so close to her little shoe…"

Viola turned away, but the madness followed. It anchored in her heart, ripping her open with the strength of a barbed claw. She would need to start from the beginning. Rework what she'd lost from a place that didn't hold the rage that swept her now.

"You've had that useless shoe at your fingertips for years." The roar in her voice took her by surprise. "You've never once let it out of your keeping. You sleep with it and tend to it like it's going to bring her back. But my work," she pounded her chest, "the pieces that I need to keep us from whatever poverty awaits us, are in your grip one moment and you let them slip into ruin."

Balthazar let out a shriek that matched Viola's words. Did she sound like that? She didn't care. Red and hot, she wrapped her arms around her middle, wishing for protection from what she'd walked into.

"The hours this took. The days of wandering, searching, waiting for the light to be just so." Withered versions still adorned her room, but the bright originals that she'd painted wept into Finella's towels, much like her mother did each morning.

Had Clemmie's neglect been willful vengeance? Had Dr. Murdoch's therapies pushed her beyond reason?

"Mr. Swift?" Shadrach's voice came from the top of the stairs. "I'm wondering if I might trouble you for a moment."

Silas dragged his gaze to her. "Viola…" He tried to speak, but she shook her head.

"I don't blame you." She spoke over Clemmie's soft sobbing. "Go. I need to be with her now." This was no time for visitors.

It was time for Viola to pick through the pieces, as she'd always done.

16

Shadrach pounded the narrow path along his fields like a major general. Silas followed.

"Accidents happen, chum. It's not your fault. Breakages are common in a guesthouse."

"It's not the lampshade. It's Viola's paintings. If I'd returned them to her room instead of…" *Instead of laying them out as if I were looking into her heart…*

"I know little about her art or how she'll replace it," Shadrach walked only a fraction faster than he talked, "but I do know when my wife needs me to remove one guest from the presence of another. Physical activity is how to hook a man from within the womenfolk." Edged in mud, Shadrach's trousers were as filthy as his hands.

"Where are we going?"

"Dugout. Just beyond an old clay pit of mine."

They made their way past fields and into a clearing.

"When you watch someone a certain way and they know it, you need to switch your viewpoint. Know what I mean?"

"I guess." Silas wondered if his host alluded to him and his nefarious ways around the newel posts.

"If a man can't catch a thief eye to eye, sometimes he needs to crawl on his belly." They stopped at a large, deep hole. "I've been digging this for days now. I've seen hoof prints nearby, and I just know that deer is sniffing around."

"You're laying a trap?"

"Exactly." Shadrach produced a hatchet from a cluster of tools on the ground. "I know your shoulder's almost mended, and I don't want to slow down your recovery, but if you can help, I'd be most grateful." He hacked low branches off tea tree bushes and tossed them into a pile.

Silas yanked the limbs to the dugout, where he followed instructions to cover the ground but not throw any in. It felt good to stretch and work the way he did in his normal world. The way he loved to move among the sweet-smelling supplies of his small factory, lugging timber to where they turned it into furniture.

The planks he worked came already stripped of their skin and cut straight. But here on the edge of Shadrach's clay pit, the raw, spindly pieces they carted smelled just as good. Pungent camphor. Salt-laden sea-gusts. And freshly turned soil mixed with the sweat of the men who toiled over it. Soon, the dugout disappeared from view beneath a mound of discarded tree branches. From under an oilcloth, Shadrach produced a gun.

"Get in."

"What?"

"Get in."

"In… there?" A tremor of fear spiked in his gut. Shadrach wasn't going to shoot him and toss his body in this pit, was he?

"There's crouching room for us both. We're going to hide and wait. Let's see what crawls our way."

Relief trickled through his insides, the way sweat tripped and soaked down the back of his shirt. It was one thing to be the hunter with a pretty accomplice. It was another to have the barrel of a gun at your neck, even if he only imagined it brushing against him on their way down.

The dugout held them in, shoulder to shoulder. Cool and dark, there was a crude earthen ledge to perch on, and just enough room for their knees to bend. They adjusted their rooftop and sat under it, a helmet of green through which they peered onto a muddy mess of footprints and leaf litter.

"Kind of feel sorry for you, chum. You come all this way and you're left minding an elderly lady in her sickroom most afternoons. I hope this serves as a diversion."

"Today, especially."

"I was wondering, while I dug this pit," Shadrach kept his voice low, "if you hadn't made that deal with Miss Buckley and I'd let you in for the night, would you have left the next morning? I mean, how long does it take to examine a staircase? And then I wondered whether you'd still be here with us if you'd not injured your shoulder."

"That's a lot of questions." Silas sifted through them for the easiest one to answer. "I, ah, sure didn't expect to have to negotiate my stay with Viola. But I'm glad she was willing."

"After making you squirm." Shadrach laughed. "She did enjoy that. But she didn't figure you'd injure yourself. Or fall for you. These things, they have a funny way of contorting over themselves, don't they?"

Was it too late to climb out and leave behind the man intent on skewering him from all sides?

"I didn't know if you'd let me in at all. I had a letter of introduction from Luther Burrows, of Brown and Burrows, but I think someone pickpocketed it in Melbourne."

"You didn't tell me about a letter."

"I wasn't sure how. I thought it sounded all too neat to say I had it and then lost it. I hoped you'd judge me fairly when you saw me."

"Hmm." Shadrach let this information hang between them for the longest time. The surrounding bush ticked and creaked, and birds that they'd scared away returned to twitter and squawk.

"Don't know how a man can afford to leave any business as long as you have. I wouldn't take my eye off this farm or my house for one second." Shadrach swiped at something at his temple.

"I couldn't afford not to leave."

"And why is that?" Shadrach sounded like he'd cornered him in a court of law and waited on evidence to turn the gun on him, there and then.

If he ever found out about the astrolabe on his property and it wasn't now, Silas would pay for it big time.

Shadrach moved the nose of the gun along ground level a few inches to their right. "Look! Up ahead," he whispered. "There's our little beauty."

Not far off, the red deer nudged the ground with her nose. She was beautiful. Sleek, young, curious.

"And she's drinking from the waterhole I dug for her." Without a second thought, Shadrach cocked and fired his gun.

The sound took Silas by such surprise he almost collapsed, except there was nowhere for a body to fall. But twigs and dust and leaves spilled over them like a rain shower.

The deer stumbled but remained upright, took another step, and darted into the bush.

Shadrach let out a long breath. "So close. I almost had her." He reloaded the gun. "How did I miss? That was a clear shot."

Graceful and unaware of her own beauty, the deer reminded him of Viola. A peril for him as much as this deer was to Shadrach.

If he set his sights on her, would she suffer the same fate as Honora? Would he love her as she deserved? Because God knew he hadn't protected Honora as he ought. He brushed that away with the same false hope that one could brush away the evidence of gunfire.

Shadrach slapped his neck. "Some creature's taken a bite out of me." He leaned his gun on the rim of the dugout and used both hands to flick whatever had fallen into his collar.

And in that moment, the deer limped back into view. Grazed and bleeding, she avoided the waterhole, and stumbled over two fallen logs.

Could he let such a beautiful creature suffer a moment longer than she deserved?

"I'm sorry," Silas whispered, grabbed Shadrach's gun, aimed, and fired.

A length of twine ran across Viola's room from a nail on the doorway frame to a hook atop the windowsill. Close to ruin, she'd hung her artwork like a row of washing. A crude exhibition of something salvaged but still lost.

Clemmie whimpered on Viola's bed, the little red shoe cradled to her chest.

"Could you trace over the paintings?"

Viola settled onto the bed, wedged behind her mother and the bedhead. She drew Clemmie into her arms and held her tight.

"No, dearest. That wouldn't work in this case."

Nasrin had taught her to draw by tracing, but the imprint of another was not how she'd wanted to learn. Even as a child, she knew the perilous road of imitating someone else's style. She would do it her own way. Viola had bristled then. And she bristled now. And like always, it was up to her to make amends.

"I'm sorry I snapped at you, Sweet Clemmie. I let the shock speak words I didn't mean," she whispered into her mother's hair. Clemmie rested her head on Viola's shoulder. She weighed so little now, she reminded Viola of a brittle egg.

"How will you replace them, your lost paintings?"

The unhappiness of decades rang over the room. For all the ways Viola had been chipped at and held up for scrutiny and never measured up, Clemmie failed to grasp that replacement was not always the answer.

"I won't replace them. I will let them dry. In the morning, I will file them away and start over."

The preacher at Nasrin's little church had shared the lesson of the Israelites on their way to the Promised Land. God had visited them with daily manna. All they needed lay in the freshness of a new day. Tomorrow, she would rise and gather.

"But time is running out, isn't it?"

Viola reached for the hairbrush and tended to Clemmie's hair. At day's end, this normally soothed them both. Tonight, she could only untangle the easiest of knots.

"Yes, Clemmie. My portfolio must be submitted by the first of September if I am to make it past the first round of judges."

Clemmie hung her head and remained that way for the longest time while Viola massaged her scalp with the soft brush. Then, just when she appeared to be dozing, a new agitation roused her.

"Mortimer took three weeks to complete my portrait." She cleared her throat. "He said it was the fastest portrait he'd ever painted, because it was the first he'd made of someone he loved."

Not wanting to break into her mother's memories, Viola

continued brushing.

"I only saw an early version, and he was so excited. Something fueled that period of his work in ways I did not understand. I was so young. So delirious with love for him, I could not see what he saw. For all I looked at was him."

Had Clemmie forgotten where she was? She had always kept a well-cinched lid on her memories of Mortimer Barnes.

"My strict parents did not approve of a poor artist who lived with his family above their tavern. But he first laid eyes on me at an Easter Sunday piano recital and never looked away. He was everything they did not want for me. And perhaps that's what drew me to him. He painted me in secret. And we became engaged in secret. And all our secrets, he laid bare in that painting."

Hair once golden-bright and tinged in copper sparks, the luster of the girl Mortimer Barnes had adored now lay in Viola's palm in sickly yellow and silver strands.

"Freddy knew we hid away in that attic. I think he thought he loved me too, but it was a boyish diversion. I knew it would fade. But what I had with Mortimer should have lasted a lifetime."

Clemmie nodded, the way people did when sorrow whispered from the soul and would not let go. "He knew. He knew before I did, and he weaved her in for me to see when he pulled away the dirty cloth he'd used to hide us from view. And there we were, wrapped in the light of all his love for us."

"Us?" Viola stilled her brush. "Who is *us*, dearest?"

Clemmie swayed, a marionette pulled by time-worn strings.

"My first Viola. Already in my belly. It was Mortimer who saw it and rejoiced. His child. So he painted the swell and the glow in my skin because it shone from within."

His child?

Viola stared at her mother's back. At the bones that protruded from her bent neck. Her delicate skin.

"My sister was ... *Mortimer's child*?" The unthinkable pressed against Viola's chest, coiling and crushing her breath like a python that had always lived there and now constricted anew.

"My sister...?"

Clemmie swayed, almost folded in two. As if her secrets weighed more than her frailty could hold. "She was Mortimer's," she whispered.

Viola shook her head, the disbelief too heavy for her, too. "My sister wasn't Marshall's?"

"Oh, she was. At least, she became his too. He made sure of that. He'd followed me from recital to recital, like Mortimer. Only he didn't want me for myself as much as he had an idea for a theatre act. A songbird, he said. After Mortimer died, I had to act fast. I let Marshall talk me into marriage knowing it was the only way to keep my child. My parents would have given her away."

Her fingers slipped into the shoe, digging in perhaps for all the hidden pieces of her story.

"By marrying Marshall, I kept Viola. And he turned us both into performers. I learned to sink into Sweet Clementine, the woman on the stage, because I always sang for Mortimer. And I would whisper into her ear, *sing for Papa*. She didn't know. She adored what it meant to sing and dance. She would have done it for anyone."

Pride pushed her upright.

"It was Mortimer who first called me Sweet Clementine. When Marshall pondered a stage name, I suggested it."

Viola held her tight, barely able to string the sorry details in her mind.

"Viola was my half-sister? And I am Marshall's, but she was not?"

Clemmie nodded. "But both of you are mine."

Tenderness shone from her eyes and pricked Viola's heart with an unfamiliar balm.

"And Marshall knew, all along?"

"He knew, but he convinced himself it wouldn't matter. He gathered us both in. And I was blind in my grief to look for anything but a way to hold her."

All this time Viola had wrestled with Marshall's preference of one daughter over the other, and even as his true-born child, she had not measured up to the one he'd chosen to adopt.

Like a cold monster, he continued to deride her, right there in this room, along with the night shadows. She pulled her shawl from the bedhead and wrapped herself in it.

Guilt and loss patched her room in the shadowy remnants, which never, ever matched up. The reflections of her hanging art flickered off the wall. And the reflections of Clemmie littered their landscape now, thicker than ever.

"I am so tired, Viola. So very tired…" Clemmie's voice trailed off, and she roused herself from the bed.

They'd come here to shake off the melancholy that had an even deeper root than Viola knew. And all along, Clemmie had been telling the truth. She no longer was the girl in that painting. Marshall had let the golden touches Mortimer discovered burn into an ash heap.

Viola tucked her mother into bed with soothing words. Chosen carefully to lull her into sleep, which she prayed would revive her by morning.

For secrets released from their cage did not always absolve the teller.

May 1, 1879

Rest an• therapy are sisters at war.

Ill-bre• shrews competing to bring upon us the un•oing they keep like stones in their pockets inten•e• for the greatest blow.

How can healing look like this? Clemmie, curle•, shivering back turne• to me in •eepest humiliation of the col• water cure we seek. She refuses any more than a spoonful of nourishment. An• I gir• myself •aily for a morning of stubborn lip pressing an• hea• shaking.

What I am charge• to bring her is neither rest nor cure. An• this will wear us both •own. Her true rest arrives when Silas brings himself an• small gifts to cheer her on an• Clemmie takes him •own the rabbit holes of her min•.

Do I count that as healing? This slight brightening of her cheeks when he arrives?

Then again, mine brighten, too. An• my chest tightens, an• my mouth feels like it's full of berries an• syrup.

This afternoon, Silas an• Clemmie allowe• the collision of my paintings with a simple pan of seawater brought in for her amusement. Even in her illness, Clemmie will •o as she wills, even when she knows it is wrong.

How it vexes me. An• how I will pay for it. I am as impoverishe• as the •ay we arrive•. The •amage• pieces relegate• to the inspiration pile along with quick sketches an• a collection of plants, shells, an• other islan• specimens.

But it is Clemmie's secret I wrestle with now. Her first Viola was the chil• of Mortimer Barnes.

"Why can't you be like your sister?" *Marshall's voice crackles into my ears, as if he's stan•ing right here.*

"You know why," *I want to scream back.* "How dare you ask

a little girl to become someone she will never be, then demand explanations of why she cannot, when you of all people can."

He took my mother, then my sister, as his own gree•y possessions. Converte• them into the greatest prizes with the same calculate• efficiency he employe• to aban•on me when I prove• unconvertible.

My fingers tremble to write it.

An• a tiny selfish part of me is gla• my sister was not his. She belongs to me an• Clemmie, now. Only us.

This piece of Sweet Clementine, unearthe• at great price, is part of why I am here in this quaint house by the sea. But how •i• I see the light in my mother's eyes on a tavern wall, an• not guess the reason?

Among the •ebris of this •ay, I hear voices. Silas an• Sha•rach in the courtyar•, lumbering with a wagon loa• I cannot properly see. An• as if this •ay coul• not have stolen more, my eyes a•just to the sha•ows where they •rag that poor, hunte• •eer.

They tell Finella about a shot that inflicte• injury, then another that foun• its mark. Brought •own in the light of •ay, they will hang the •eer by lamplight in the barn.

"You will do as I say. Or you and your mother will suffer the consequences."

Marshall knew how to point a loa•e• gun at me, too. He only ha• one bullet.

The wor• useless.

But unlike this beautiful creature Silas an• Sha•rach now heave between them through open barn •oors, I live.

An• I will prove Marshall wrong.

17

"Who goes there? Who goes there?" Balthazar squawked.

"The quill maker," a low voice rumbled in reply. "What have you to offer?"

Viola rose from the chair to roll Balthazar's cage out of the way.

Silas appeared in the doorway, bearing a tray of food. "Good afternoon, ladies. I trust appetites are strong today."

"Mr. Swift? Where is our hostess?" Clemmie answered first.

"I thought you'd be pleased to see me." He set the tray on their table. Steaming oyster soup, lamb chops with cauliflower and potatoes, bread and butter, and a generous dish of rice pudding glazed in melted butter and cinnamon. "I shall be taking my luncheon here with you today."

"With us?" The crisp unbelief in Viola's voice sounded less welcoming than she intended. Why did her confusion always wrangle its way out like this? Perhaps because a fight had always reclined in her.

"Your mother and I will eat up here. *You* will march on out like a good girl."

Good *girl?*

That stung a little, but she ignored it.

"Your lunch basket is on the verandah." He leaned in and

whispered in her ear. "Take it and run."

"Run?" She pulled back. "To… where?

"Wherever your roaming takes you. I've made arrangements with Finella to relieve you of your lunch duties. Every day this week. We'll see you again at the evening meal. Oh, and when you return, I expect to see the work you've made in the hours I am here."

Viola opened her mouth and closed it again.

"I am banished?"

"And do not return without significant progress." He busied himself with the table setting. Forks, spoons. He fiddled with a saltshaker as if it were his sole responsibility.

He was making up for yesterday's loss. Gratitude danced over her heart like a rice-paper kite.

"You don't have to, Silas. It's very good of you—"

"I'm not being good. I'm being smart. So should you."

"But Clemmie's medicine. I administer that after lunch…"

"I'll do that, too."

"But dosage—"

"I measure and cut wood into staircases, Viola. You think 'dosage' will be a problem?"

Just to be sure, she produced Dr. Murdoch's timetable pamphlet.

"Dosage is here, under *Midday Medications*." He took it without looking.

"Go." He stared at her, and her insides frayed. "Bring us something amazing. You, on the page. We expect nothing less."

The notion that someone other than Nasrin charged her to do her best thickened around her like fast-growing ivy. Silas was not simply indulging her. He was making a way for her with his own time and energy. Had he plotted this all night?

"Thank you." She dragged her shawl over her shoulders, wishing she had better command of her words and emotions.

"Oh, and um, at four, we're taking a walk through Finella's garden. Your mother and me."

"A walk? You can't. This afternoon is not the right time."

"It is the best time."

"It's not on the list." Heat rose in her temper. "The list says rest for good reason."

He ran his finger along the instructions Viola had followed faithfully every day since they'd arrived.

"Here?" He read the words as if she hadn't been saying them over and over. "Afternoon Nap. 4 p.m.?"

"Yes!"

He ripped the page out of the manual. "I don't see it." He shrugged.

"You… you can't tear that out!"

He ripped the paper into four and let the pieces fall to their feet.

"Silas, you can't do that!"

"Who says?"

"Dr. Murdoch. And me."

"I don't see Dr. Murdoch. I shouldn't be seeing you, either."

But he did see her. He stared. She stared back.

Perhaps fortified by her stunned silence, he forged on. "And since the day seems bright enough and your mother has ample wraps and I am here to help her to the hammock, I have asked Finella to serve our afternoon tea outside. Won't that be fun?"

He consulted Clemmie, who betrayed Viola with a small clap of her hands even though her wide eyes matched Viola's.

"The hammock!" Viola pressed a hand to her hip. "Are you out of your mind?"

"Maybe. Are you?" He whispered but held her gaze. "Call me a lunatic, but I want your submission in that exhibition on time. It won't happen if you stand here with your mouth open. I figure if you push yourself hard, your accomplice should push you, too."

He reached for Clemmie's hand and helped her to the table. Like a waiter, he laid her napkin across her knees, filled her water glass, and stood behind her chair. At attention. Ready to serve. All afternoon.

"Get out of here. Before I change my mind and make you want to stay more than you want to paint." He ran his thumb along the top of his eyebrow, pleased with himself. He'd thought of everything. Even a quick command that weakened her knees.

Make you want to stay...

Mischief spilled from Clemmie's eyes, and she pointed to the door.

Viola smiled. Was it only last night that she'd whimpered over a battlefield of unthinkable memories? And Silas? He stood there with an aura of belonging that made her insides ache.

"I appreciate you giving up your luncheon hour—"

He grabbed her by the shoulders and turned her around. Every poke and prod pushed her away.

His efforts bounced her out of the house and into the world she needed to reinhabit. The bush and its canopy. The seashore and its shallows. And that generous gesture pulled her in, as sure as if he still held her by the fingertips.

Finella waited for her on the verandah with the basket and a picnic blanket.

"Before you get cross, let me explain how your American sweet-talked me into all this."

"My American also ripped up Clemmie's timetable."

"He thinks you're at risk of fatigue."

"Fatigue?"

"One of his relatives, a sister I think, cared for a family member who followed a similar schedule. Silas said it's exhausting and debilitating on the one who acts as nurse, and he feels responsible for yesterday's mess. This is his way of redeeming your time."

"How does he know he won't suffer the same exhaustion?"

"Because your mother is more likely to take advantage of you in ways she won't with him. Plus, it's a task divided between the three of us now. And you can explore and sketch and refresh. Out there." She motioned to the track which led to the beach.

Viola pressed the basket to her stomach. Divided in two, one part held her lunch, the other carried a slim water bottle with swing top lid and porcelain stopper. The weight of the basket tipped whatever internal hope-scale tottered within her. Depending on the day, on the hour, on the task even, they had become each other's co-conspirators.

"This is a lot more than a helping hand, though. Isn't it?"

"It might be." Finella pressed her lips into a knowing smile.

"I don't know if this is helping or messing with the impossible."

"The impossible? No, your two hearts are not the first I've watched knit together under this roof. On these very shell paths, sand in your shoes, prayers in your breath. Neither are you the first to come here looking for the elixir of the sea for one ailment, only to discover an altogether deeper healing."

"I don't think I can tell the difference between healing and an unraveling."

"The two often look the same."

In her heart, she tucked Finella's wisdom and carried it like a delicate piece of glass all the way to the beach. By the time she spread the blanket over a soft patch of dry sand, her stomach rumbled.

Under the wicker lid, she discovered a jar of soup, two red apples, and two thick slices of brown buttered bread. Another smaller jar held a serving of rosehip jam, and alongside it, Finella's large wooden spoon.

She smiled at the wooden spoon. A reminder of their sweet encounter.

When he'd kissed her wrist. When he'd wanted more and said so, aloud.

Tied to the spoon, she found a note.

Dear Miss Viola,

Try not to fall off a roof.

Or out of a tree while I'm not there to pick you up.

And come back with something of yourself on the page for me.

Words like that were bound to make anyone swoon. *Yourself. For me.* With a note like that in her pocket, how was she meant to even remember why she found herself outdoors? She relished every mouthful of soup. And when had bread and apples ever tasted this good? She marveled at the racing moon-white clouds. They tousled and tangled and shared a full-blown world.

Like the sky, the hours stretched before her, but nothing ever stayed the same. She pulled out her sketch pad. She would not squander this precious gift. But his note distracted her again, and she lay back on the blanket to read it once more.

Yourself. For me.

He waited for her on the verandah, a piece of beach driftwood in one hand, his favorite whittling knife in the other. Thin shavings curled where they fell. The shaping of wood, both comfort and spark. A habit that always began with his need to ponder one complication that often revealed the real and sometimes unexpected dilemma beneath.

That's how the mind rumbled along back roads and forgotten laneways just when you needed it to stay put. Like the flames of '73 that raged over the foot of Yamhill Street where they'd lived and worked.

The Swift family had suffered no deaths in the fire. Theirs had come in the days after, when a fire-weakened beam crashed onto Hal Swift, who inspected the ruins of their factory. Much like their father, it had held up the business for twenty years, but now it was up to Silas to sift through the embers and make a future for his brothers. If his mother hadn't drummed it into him from a young age, his father's last will and testament was about to condemn him to his fate without reprieve.

Silas dug a little deeper than he meant to on the driftwood stick. An ill-placed gouge nicked his skin. He rubbed the sore spot and wondered why was he thinking of *that week,* now, with Viola about to return?

Like now, he'd been carving a pattern into a block of slap wood late one night when his mother had told him he'd better lift his head a little towards Honora Ackerman.

It wasn't what he needed to hear. The Ackermans had lived and worked their small beveled glass business beside his father's carpentry shop for as long as he could remember. Honora and his sister were firm friends. But Honora's parents had died in the fire, and overnight she had become a homeless orphan.

"It's the Christian thing to do, Silas. Marry her and your good deed will blossom into love with the passage of time. Build over the vacant lot

that Honora will bring into the marriage. Think of it as dowry. Of saving a poor orphan girl already loved by us all. Secure a better future for your brothers. They need you to be thinking sharp, now. We all do. You're thirty. Honora's eighteen. It would mark you as a man of honor. Stand tall."

Stand tall?

She'd been the one who'd almost daily reminded him of the deformity on his brothers' faces. What it would cost them. How Silas would be wise to ease their burden. Enough to bend a man in half and keep him from looking anyone in the eye.

Now, Minnie Swift, his widowed mother, gathered her wits and strength and made plans out of the dust left to them. And he could not have told her to leave him be any more than he could have abandoned the pretty fair-haired Honora to her fate. Perhaps he should have. Perhaps her fate without him would have been better than the short and miserable future beside him.

Guilt had watered responsibility over him since his boyhood, and it was now as deep-rooted as a century-old red cedar, intended to shade them all. Deaths, debts, or delinquent brothers, it didn't matter. Silas had to stand tall.

Viola, on the other hand, marched toward the house a little stooped at the neck. She trudged up the verandah steps, dumped her belongings at the front door, and lowered herself into the empty wicker seat beside him with a sigh.

"You first." She closed her eyes. "Then me."

He smiled at the way she slipped in beside him. She had taken her hair out of its pins, maybe hours ago, and it framed her face in the delicious messy mix of strawberry blonde, kissed by a day in the sun. Lucky sun.

Her chin carried a smudge of charcoal, as did her forehead. When had he ever sat with this kind of ease beside Honora? He rubbed the back of his neck. He could not remember much of the happiness they'd shared, but there had been some. Before the days when the loss of babies hung between them like a chasm. When he'd taken her in, given her a home and his name.

"Well, I guess my report is favorable enough," he said. "Mrs. Buckley managed some of her lunch. I read, she listened, eager for that walk I promised, but taking the stairs exhausted her enough for us to sit right here instead. And now she's sleeping."

Viola opened her eyes. "I want to say *I told you so*, but I'm more grateful than I am in need of proving you wrong." She extended her legs and raised her feet off the ground in a pointed-toe stretch.

"The walk. The hammock. Maybe some of that was to tease you a little. Turns out a half hour outside was all your mother cared for."

"You fed her imagination, and Clemmie could not resist the dream."

Silence rose between them. The kind where the last few words spoken aloud reverberate upon themselves in a chamber of echoes.

"And your day?"

"Much walking." Viola let another long breath escape. "I thought having all those hours to myself…" She shrugged, and for the first time, he observed the tint of humiliation in her cheeks.

"I fairly ran out of the house," she continued, "but after I ate my lunch, for which I owe you humble thanks, I walked along the beach, then along Saltwater Creek, and the task suddenly sucked me under. I have so much to gather, Silas, so much to collate. For so long, I thought this submission would be the extravagant, the exotic. My tribute to the Botanic Gardens. Now it has become a study of all that flourishes on this island, but will it be enough?"

"Enough for what exactly?"

Frustration shaped her frown. A reaching for something she couldn't identify.

"I knew you'd be waiting to see what I sketched today. I'm sorry. I could show you," she pointed to her satchel, "but I don't like it. And I'm not sure why. It's similar to what Clemmie took from my room, but it's…" She crossed her arms, scrunched her face, and looked adorable.

"I think the pressure to come home with something extraordinary got in my way today." She rubbed her eyes. "I'll do better tomorrow. Maybe my mind was on you… and Clemmie. I have always fought for time, not focus. But today, it felt like I was being pushed onto a stage and there were hot gaslights blazing and people…" She shook her head. "Oh, it's silly. I'm sorry. How foolish it sounds." She made another befuddled face and gathered her loose hair into a twist at her neck.

The chunk of coal that sat in his gut flared like a guilty ember. Had he done this to her? Set her up to fail? The memory of Patrick yelling at him forced its way in.

"How hard is it for you to let us choose our way? When will you let us decide for ourselves?"

"What do you want?" He dug the words out of a place he seldom ventured. "When your art is complete, what do you need it to do?"

"It needs to storm the senses," she began in a small whisper. "Transport people to a world they know little or nothing about and sink there. And I need a publisher to see my work as it might appear in a book. Something they will want to bind up and send beyond the exhibition. Far and wide."

Her dream, so beautifully explained, danced from her words and into their midst.

"And whose eyes will these publishers see through? Yours or theirs?"

"Theirs, I guess."

"Use mine, then."

"Yours?"

"I already know what's caught my attention in a world that is not my own. I am your audience, from the far off, wide world." His voice trembled, and he wondered if she heard it.

"How?"

How indeed? Would someone like Viola consent for her most precious works to be viewed through his eyes?

"You've beheld Australian bush flora a thousand times, but I see something exotic. I can tell you what stops a man in his tracks."

The sun slipped to the edge of the day, and the sky burned in pink and orange flames. She did not reply, but he could see her lips had parted. She was listening. Considering his offer.

"I know a little about wanting to fix a pattern to something. For me, it's wood. For you, it's paint and petals."

"Hmm." She shifted in her chair and looked into the ever-changing sky. "So, you become my eyes."

He nodded. "Shadrach's arranged for a deer butchering next week. He seems to think I should be there. But until then, I'm here for you."

"And the astrolabe?"

It was a good question.

"That deer is no longer a threat. Could you not tell Shadrach about it? He would be more reasonable about your plight."

Nightbirds called from the other side of Shadrach's fields, where curious species spread their branches and sent new leaves and shoots into the night.

"He might. But I prefer my original accomplice."

May 10, 1879

Clemmie falls into a deep sleep fast, but wakes often with murmurs and fits, and I brush her hand with mine until she finds an even breath.

Lamplight is not the best for creating art, but I discovered today that neither is the light of day, when distractions rule the heart.

From my window, I watch the last glimmer of sun slip into the sea with all the force of a celestial orb. But within me, something rises. I know it is what I feel for the man who sleeps beneath the floorboards of my room.

And we dance around the little circle drawn for us. Too afraid of what it might contain to step within. Too afraid of what it means to step away.

He... in my world of drawings. And me... in his quest for the astrolabe.

We know, without saying so, when these two objects of our respective desires are met, the hours we share will cease.

I wonder how he knows about Rest Therapy. If the one his sister nursed recovered well. I want to ask, but the story, passed to me by another, is not mine to dig into. Finella was right. I have this journal to utter the unutterable.

How has he become a driving force in what I need for my future?

He is in the effort. In the inspiration. Whatever this crippling is, it was never on my list.

18

Silas threw a piece of driftwood on the rough table in the menagerie. His morning walks along the beach now ended in here, sorting pieces he could not leave behind.

Long sticks, suitable for a frame. Smaller ones that fit together for walls or a door, and others perfect for shingling. He would make a driftwood house with a perch and a tiny round opening for small birds to nest in.

Footsteps crunched across the gritty paths, and from the open doorway, he spied five youths sneak into the barn. He followed them at a distance.

"I could have shot her, easy," one of them bragged. "Pure luck that American was there."

"I heard he fought Shadrach for the gun."

"I heard the shot put out his shoulder."

"Oi, Simon! What's wrong with you?"

"Nothing." One boy kept back from his company.

"He's scared. Can't even look at a skinned hare without losing his breakfast."

"Am not." The boy scraped a groove into the dirt with his shoe. "I just don't want to stick my nose up its rear, like you."

They laughed and circled the animal, strung up by the heels to rest for the twenty days required before slaughter.

Rest. Silas grimaced and allowed the boys their gawking. No one in their right mind called this rest. But these curious fuzz-faces were too young to know any better. A natural mix of innocence and bravado would push them on, but in time, real love and real losses would cord them by the heels, too.

“I pulled the trigger,” he said.

The boys snapped to attention.

“Just looking, that’s all.”

“Shad knows us. Our farm’s next door.”

“No harm meant.”

“We’re leaving, anyway.”

They drifted out, all except Simon, who clutched his stomach and ran behind the barn.

His friends laughed and hollered. “Wipe your gob on your apron when you’re done.”

Silas kept his own smile in check and followed the boy to a grassy patch where old barrels, a rusted iron wheel, and other farm equipment sank under dusty oilskins. Doubled over, young Simon emptied his stomach into the long grass.

Silas remembered a day when he, too, had lost his breakfast. When his mother had pulled him aside to tell him Charlie had died, he’d run from the house and vomited in the gutter. Would his baby brothers be next? The fear that bore into him that day had never truly quit.

“A spoonful of applesauce might settle your stomach.”

The boy nodded, wiped his mouth on his sleeve, and leaned on a tarpaulin. A corner slipped away to reveal a small blue boat.

“They said you’ve shot bears and you skin buffalo and—”

“I’m a woodworker. Only skinning I do is of my own knuckles if

I'm not careful. And I've been careful longer than I can remember."

"How did you catch the deer?"

"Waited until she came to me."

"That's lucky. Never came to any of us." Simon's friends edged closer.

"Who gets to keep it? You or Shad?"

"It's Shadrach's land. His gun. His dugout. His deer," Silas replied.

"Maybe he'll give you something. Like a hoof."

"What's he gonna do with a hoof?"

They spoke the universal language of boys. Of conquering and owning and taking plunder in memory of battles won at great price. "He could put it under one of those glass domes. Like a trophy."

Beyond the barn, a door banged, and Silas caught sight of Viola. She crossed the courtyard with little Molly on her hip. Had he seen her with the child in her arms before? His mind spun. Here was a glimpse of who she would become someday when she let a man into her life for good. Someone for whom she would carry a child. It made him want to discard every ounce of *careful.* To grab her now and suffer the consequences later.

"I don't need a hoof," he replied, but the boys already made their way through the bush, yelling their goodbyes. "I need her."

She skirted along the shell pathways. Molly giggled and hung on while Viola tipped her from side to side. Her skirt billowed with every twist and turn.

"London Bridge is falling down, my fair baby."

He leaned against the barn and clapped.

"Oh, there you are." She pulled herself up. "I've come looking for you."

"Me?" He drank her in. Her hair reminded him of the spiced tea his mother steeped every Christmas. Honey and ginger. And the sight of her was just as refreshing.

His time with Mrs. Buckley had swept Viola into the depths of industry. She'd worked hard, often away from the house, and he'd guarded her hours as best he could. But now she'd come looking for him.

"I need to borrow your eyes."

Molly wriggled, and Viola swapped her to the other hip. But she held his gaze and locked him in with a raised brow. For someone who disliked showmanship, she commanded the stage of life with a unique brand of theatrics.

"I like what I see. I could look all day long and not grow weary." He pushed off the barn wall.

She blushed. "Silas, I meant my paintings. I've been showing them to Molly while Finella visits with Clemmie. But it's not her opinion I need as much as yours."

"You need me." He said the words out loud as a statement, and it felt good in his heart to hear them.

"And right now, if you don't mind and if you're free."

If she were not holding that darling child he could easily reach for her. At least, in his mind it was easy. It was near impossible not to, when she breezed into his thoughts looking like she did now. Bright and filled with hope. Needing him. Inviting him in.

Stay away from your wife's recovery if you wish to see her improved.

Mary had clicked the door shut and not opened it for him until Honora gasped her second-to-last breath.

But Viola, she breathed in and took him with her. A man would do nearly anything for that kind of trust. He reached for Molly, gathered her in his arms, and followed Viola to the house before her smile lured him into greater trouble.

His thievery of Shadrach Jones knew no bounds. He climbed the stairs, carried by the fanciful allure that, in another life, Viola and this giggly child were his. The longing for a family of his own, so heavy, so deep it drove him to steal images of another man's daughter, along with a woman he knew committed herself elsewhere.

He brushed the guilt away. This was about Viola's happiness, and the more she had to show him, the happier she became.

Across the landing, pinned between the doorframes, a length of crisscrossed twine held up her work. She took Molly back and gestured to the string of papers with her free hand.

"Imagine this is a book and the readers are voyagers stepping into a quest. What will they discover?" Eyes bright, she was a sight to behold.

Above them hung four pages of various shells and seaweeds. Sketches, some of them partly painted. Others already brimmed with the fullness of life.

"After the shoreline, we've sandy tracks to meander, with swathes of purple noon flowers, sea grasses, and then, into the bush." She followed the string that returned on itself like a maze. He followed her.

"I'll heighten the reds of the bottlebrush when I paint the final version. And the yellow wattles and silvery green eucalyptus." She looked every inch the painter, guiding him through a gallery of her work. And every inch a mother, with Molly's fingers threaded in the cord of her apron. "Then, of course, ferns, and imagine we're walking into the depths of the bush now. And the canopy is thick and dark, and we stumble upon lemon myrtle, fluffy and white and…"

Molly squirmed for her mother in Mrs. Buckley's room, and

Viola set her down.

Gooseflesh spiked along his collar, the way it did when, aged nine, he'd stood upon a crate to reach the top of his father's workbench and used a plane for the first time.

"To plane a piece of wood the wrong way is like brushing a cat's hair backwards. A wise woodworker respects the minute markings that denote the run of the grain," his father had taught him. And Silas had never forgotten. True art always bowed to a certain flow. And Viola had collated her ideas into that kind of natural order.

Sunlight hit the pins she'd used to clip paper to string. They flickered like stars. "It's brilliant. If you're waiting on my suggestions, it's near perf—"

"No." She crossed her arms over her chest and smiled. "I wanted to observe your face. Finella was taken by the book idea, but I made these sketches with you in mind. You and the people of your hometown. I expect they'll ask about your Australian travels when you return, and you will tell them. But imagine if they saw the printed plates."

"I was on your mind when you created all this?"

She nodded. "Wasn't that our plan?" She crushed both hands into little balls of hope.

He surveyed a painting of pink sea urchins. Some whole. Some broken open. All of them delicate and beautiful. And his breath, which he'd never lost in all the times he'd run up to this crazy landing where the Buckley women resided with their secrets and eccentricities, where an aggrieved galah defended them, and where dreams hid in plain sight, left his lungs in one puff.

Viola's art was a hopeful bonfire. She held the match. Strengthening her only sent her faster into the world that would separate them. "This is a wondrous crossing for the luckiest wanderer."

Her eyes brimmed with delight. Watching him watching her from where he leaned upon his own newel post like the rod it was to his back.

Imagine if they lived by a compass and not the clock. If time were not the cruel master about to break them apart. The post dug into him.

What if he started a woodworking business? Here, in this new world where buildings rose from their foundations faster than anywhere. Melbourne embraced craftsmen and laborers. He could become one of them. Viola at his side. Their future straight ahead.

"Why are you looking at me like that?" she whispered.

"I'm wondering if…"

But no, this string of dreams, as fragile as Chinese lanterns in the wind, was hers alone. He'd come for something he could easily kick open right now, grab and run. And probably should.

"Silas?" she whispered, this time with more urgency.

"I'm sorry. I don't know how to look away." He pointed to her paintings, hoping to ease the awakening they both felt. "When all this brings what you want, you'll have to become accustomed to being noticed by many eyes. Not just mine."

In the dim-lit kitchen, Viola sliced red apple pieces into the chamomile tea pot. Tonight, Clemmie's distress had required their last tonic of morphine, and Viola envied her mother's fast escape into a world of dreams. Unlike Clemmie, Viola remained wide awake, bone tired, thoughts racing.

She'd heard Silas leave, as he had every evening this week, for a night walk along the shallows. His quest for the astrolabe had brought him so close, but now he sidestepped and picked his way down another path. Impatience unsettled her nerves, this waiting for him to break into the staircase one last time. Because no matter what they found up there, it would alter everything they'd fallen into down here.

The silence of the house hemmed her in. But thoughts of him stirred her up.

She carried the pot to the drawing room. On a sideboard, a tray of clean glasses and cups awaited service. She filled two with the steaming elixir and followed him into the night.

It was easy to tell herself she returned the goodwill he lavished on her each day, with this one cup of tea. To admit that she searched for something deeper may have sent her back to her room.

She found him on the hard-packed sand, in a wide span of silver that reflected the last light of day. With a long stick, he fossicked and poked and raked up the shore.

Viola's shoes hissed in the dry sand, and he straightened at her arrival.

"Chamomile tea." She passed him a cup. "What were you doing?"

"Nothing." He tossed the stick and shepherded her away from the water. "Let's sit on our log."

"Wait. I want to see." She turned back.

"Nothing to see." He steered her by the elbow. "Let's sit—"

"I don't think so." She pivoted. "Show me."

He considered this a moment, then let her go. Already the tide encroached. And now Viola did the same. She crouched and peered at a pattern in the sand.

"It's an arabesque scroll. A pattern I make when I'm thinking."

"Arabesque?" She foraged her mind for what that looked like.

"An uncut line. Like a vine that keeps wrapping, around, and around."

"Like the pattern of my suzani?"

"It's in your shawl, yes. On walls, tiles, ceramics, carpets." He swallowed hard. "Once it mesmerizes you, you see it everywhere. I found it on the astrolabe first."

"An astrolabe has scrollwork?"

"Not always. Mine does." The tide crept closer and foamed over the top of their shoes. "Scrollwork symbolizes the unbroken flow of nature. Sweeping and gentle. No hard corners. Undulating. Like the sea."

The beach rose in a short wave and slapped the sand as if to say, *yes, like that.*

It was hard to tell, but she made out the letter V. "This is no idle scratching in the sand. Silas, this is beautiful. It's..."

After the V came an I. And an O. Further along, the letters. L, A.

Her name, not once, but over and over until she could see nothing else.

"You wrote my name in the sand."

"Is that what you see?" He sipped his drink. His chest rose and dipped.

"It says so, right there."

"It does."

And those two words pulled so hard at her resolve, she understood what it meant for the earth to respond to the forces of the moon. For sea currents to race into sandy crevices and fill them in. For a woman's heart to be drawn into the stream of a man's affections.

"Why keep it hidden?"

He shrugged. "It's still... incomplete."

"What else does it need?"

"More of you."

He crossed the space between them, took her drink, flung the last mouthful into the shallows, and dug their two empty cups into dry sand.

She willed the crazy beat of her pulse to calm. But night winds and waves rustled between them. He pulled her hand into his.

"That astrolabe was never meant to be mine. But once I had it, I would look through the arabesque scrollwork into the night sky. It looks like this."

He pressed his finger to her palm. "Diagonal line, from top to bottom. A small loop, another diagonal line, back up in the opposite direction. Like a copperplate V."

He drew into her hand and up over the fabric of her sleeve. A long shiver ran over her. Scalp. Neck. Arms. All of her tingled with the sensation of him on her skin.

"When I was a boy, I thought I saw something of my future when I held it up to the stars, like a mariner, but I had no inkling. Properly read, an astrolabe shows how all things celestial fit with everything earthbound."

His fingertip retraced its steps, the loop of the V now easy for her to imagine.

Overhead, stars twinkled from high places.

"And what did young Silas see of his future?"

"Maybe I saw your shawl."

She would have liked to gather that shawl right now, for it had slipped and hung limp in the crook of her arms.

"What I hoped to see one day was the Southern Cross."

"And have you?"

He nodded. "First time, on board the *Clara*. But I'm looking at it right now, too." He turned her by the shoulder so they faced away from the beach. "See?"

A myriad of lights twinkled above them, none of them known to her by name.

"Stargazing isn't one of my skills. But I admire them for their brilliance," she said.

"Stars are more than brilliant. They're signposts." He pointed to a brighter mass. "Those two, side by side. They're called The Pointers. Higher up you'll find Crux, see? Looks like a kite." His finger outlined another shape, this time in the sky. The other hand of this foreigner, who navigated into her hemisphere in ways she did not know herself, rested on her shoulder.

"I see it."

"Follow a line from Crux to the horizon, and you stand where we are now."

She blinked hard to stay focused on the stars, the warmth of his cheek so close to her own.

"Terra Australis. The Great South Land, which means…" He turned her 180 degrees and cradled her face. "True North is in the opposite direction."

Their bearings, polar apart, could not be any clearer.

Not to be ignored any longer, waves pushed in with a greedy pounding. Not the gentle lapping or soothing splash that had surrounded them until now.

A sudden crash grabbed them around the ankles and splashed over them, into her hair, off her chin, and into her eyes. Viola shrieked, and an awkward series of watery, tangled steps pushed her backwards.

Silas stumbled too and shook himself clear of the worst, but a second wave toppled Viola so fast her footing, much like her heart, slid into places she could not properly see.

"My shawl," she cried and fell to her knees, water flooding her from all sides. "I tripped over it but…" She slapped at the receding puddles. "I don't see it."

Silas hunted with her. This time, the stars told them nothing. Under a darkening sky, every movement of the water, gentle or urgent, looked like it could be fabric. But it wasn't. They reached and came up with dripping grabs of nothing.

"I can't lose it." She stood, dripping herself, ice-cold and stunned, her eyes on the inky waters. She pressed her hands to the top of her head. Willing the sea to give back what it had stolen.

Another powerful wave crashed over them. Then two more. The night sea no longer crept. It stormed and mocked and did as it pleased. Cumbersome and cold, her drenched skirt dragged, but Viola refused to give up. Each time a wave turned its back on her, she scoured what it left behind.

Long buried in deeper waters now, Silas' pattern in the sand would never come back. But she could not walk away from Nasrin's precious gift.

Silas kicked up whatever sloshed around his shoes, seaweed mainly. And then he lifted his foot.

"Here!" He fished into the ankle-deep waters. "Viola, it's here!" He squeezed some of the water away.

Relief pounded in her gasp, and she pressed her hands to her chest.

They clambered out of the shallows, and he draped the suzani over one end of the log.

"You're almost as wet as your shawl."

Viola shook her wet cuffs against her sodden skirt. "You're no better."

He settled her beside him. "Catch your breath. Then it's straight back to the house with you."

She ran her hands along the wet ends of her hair. "I don't know what I would have told Nasrin if I'd lost it." She shivered. "Thank you."

He rubbed warmth into her hands. "Lucky find."

Lucky indeed. They'd dodged a bullet together, and now, under the distraction of a starry canopy, they'd rescued a floating shawl in the dark. And they were back to where it had all started. His fingers, writing dreams into her palm.

"I've seen you draw this pattern before."

"It's how I think, how I distract myself. Lately I've come out here when I…"

His fingers stopped, as if the movement contained a secret he'd write on her skin.

"When you…?" She laced her fingers with his.

"When I need to forget about kissing you."

She let the words wash over her. Isn't that why she'd crept out here with flowery herbs in their tea and so much more in her heart?

She leaned her forehead onto his.

"Is it working?"

He shook his head.

"Wanting you is inescapable."

He let her fingers go, cupped her face with both hands, and fell into her eyes with more questions than she had capacity to decipher. Between that glance and whatever came next, Viola's world stopped as sure as if the waves had ceased their rise, mid crest.

He pulled her closer and drew her in with a slow, honey-scented kiss. It ran over her like unhurried beach breezes.

Then, ignoring the trickling tide at their feet and the aching cold of soaked clothes, he pressed his other hand to her back and wrapped her in himself. His kiss lifted her into raw, undreamed of places and deepened into the best kind of collision. A grab for all the combined losses they'd brought with them to this beach.

19

The Swift family had carried their identity with them into America from Sweden in the 1840s. Together with his brothers, Silas had learned the art of woodcraft passed down from father to son for generations. If it wasn't in the blood, it was deep in the skin of every sawdust-covered one of them.

Their father had taught them how to drive a nail home without leaving the indent on the face of the wood, and the importance of keeping the left hand out of the danger zone when using a chisel, away from any slip that might occur. Neglect of this precaution often left a man with a nasty cut and a stiff finger joint for life.

Now, so many miles from where he'd learned his trade, Silas dragged a little wooden boat onto the shoreline and fashioned it for courting.

"When making a drawer, add a secret partition. People will be glad for somewhere to hide their valuable documents. When making a lady's writing bureau, insert hollows for a safe place to hide jewels or love letters. Give your customers something they didn't know they needed."

Like a staircase with deep pockets.

Perhaps that's why he festooned this boat with grapevine leaves, in a loose arabesque design. A vessel he never intended to use for fishing or sailing. No sir, he intended on using it to sweep Viola away in plain sight.

It would take more than a boat ride to dispel her fears of being anyone's *second* anything, but perhaps it was the start that would convince her to listen, for while he did not know if she could properly love him, he knew she cared enough to want to know what that might look like.

And so, he added borrowed blankets and cushions inside the boat, and some on the sand, with a chair against a hard-packed dune for Mrs. Buckley. Marooned by the water's edge, *Miss Molly* awaited her passengers. On the blanket, a tray of buttered scones and rosehip jam and a steaming teapot awaited his guests.

He paced, sand the impediment in his shoes and trepidation the lead in his boots.

They arrived with the wind at their back, whipping and rustling their hems. Under a fluttering parasol held by Viola, Mrs. Buckley took slow steps, her head wrapped in a hat and violet scarf.

Viola wore a dress of spearmint stripes, trimmed in white. Until now, she'd wandered the bush in more serviceable attire, practical and sturdier, but this unseen outfit had been stitched for promenading, and it put her on display.

It was at the lathe he'd first observed the charm of line, of curves and contours that flow continuously, diminishing and enlarging. He'd seen it in the astrolabe. And he saw it in her.

He forced his attention on her mother.

"What a day for celebration. Look how far you've come, Mrs. Buckley." He helped her into the chair. "Next you'll want to row the boat."

"If I were younger and in better health, I'd be in it already."

While Silas and Viola made friendly conversation, Mrs. Buckley sipped her tea.

"How good is a scone with jam?" Viola asked between happy bites. "Clemmie?"

Mrs. Buckley nodded but only managed a mouthful.

When they'd licked the last of their jam-sticky fingers, Silas stood and brushed the sand off his trousers.

"Wind's died down, Mrs. Buckley. Perfect for a short row along the shore." He offered his hand.

"You go where you must, Mr. Swift. It shall be without me." She reposed in the low chair that already sank a little in the sand. "But I'll remind you, Viola has never allowed others to steer her course if she can help it. If she's not holding the paddle, she'll—"

"Grab it and club me in the chest with it," he teased. "I know."

Mrs. Buckley grinned. Maybe this half hour in the sun *had* done some good already.

" 'All other doubts, by time let them be cleared.' "

Mrs. Buckley spoke into the wind.

" 'Fortune brings some boats that are not steered.' "

"Thank you, Shakespeare. Thank you, Sweet Clementine." Viola secured the end of her lap blanket. "Ready?"

She turned to him, and before he could reply, yelled, "Go!"

She made a dash for the boat and he chased, as had been his plan all along, if not perhaps this real kind of running. Buoyed by her enthusiasm, he grabbed her around the waist and hoisted her up, happy screams and all into the boat, which he pushed deeper into the shallows, and hopped in behind her.

Miss Molly held two shipmates comfortably. Mercifully, the decorations he'd trimmed her with stayed in place.

Eyes closed, Viola drank in the breeze and let the sun kiss her face.

"You outdid yourself, Mr. Swift. These adornments are the finest." She reclined into the blanket and cushions and sunshine. "And have you noticed? Clemmie hasn't asked to return to the house." On the shore, Mrs. Buckley's parasol marked their picnic like a faraway mast.

"Why do you call her Clemmie?" He pulled on the oars. It was not what he meant to begin with, but it had been on his mind since the day he'd heard Viola use her mother's name.

Her soft smile hardened into whatever memory he'd netted.

"Marshall tried to teach me to say *mama,* the way my sister had. But Clemmie's mind could not fathom that she would never again hear her little girl's voice, and mine was not enough to draw her from that grief."

"You called her *mama* and she didn't hear you?"

"She didn't respond. And Marshall would snap his finger at her and say 'Clemmie, Clemmie!' She would turn to him when he called her like that, so I learned fast if I wanted her attention," she closed her eyes, "I had to call her Clemmie."

He rowed a little slower. "Did that grieve you?"

"Among the many sorrows, I think it was one of the least." She opened her eyes. "There was more missing from our lives than calling her mama. *Clemmie* holds its own sweetness."

"But how are you not mad at her for that?"

"Because I know Marshall stripped away her worth. He loved her for the performance, not who she was. I know how that wounds a soul. It's not my fault I was born to replace my sister, and it's not Clemmie's fault she was broken by her loss."

"And your father?"

"He will always be *Marshall.* He has done nothing to deserve the name *father,* which I stopped using the day he left us."

The oars splashed and gurgled, dipped and rose.

"When Marshall abandoned us, it became my duty to decide what we did and how to make it happen. At first, I would ask the questions, and Clemmie seemed to know the answers.

Where will you work now, dear Clemmie? And me, shall I go to lessons now, Clemmie? Has that theatre paid you for that show? What's left in the cupboard, dear Clemmie? Shall I run to the shop and get more of what we need?

Within a year, the questions became more urgent. *Is there enough of your medicine? Is the doctor going to bring more? Shall I run to the apothecary, dear Clemmie?*"

Viola knotted her fingers.

"It was Nasrin who told me Clemmie had become addicted to laudanum in the weeks after my sister's death. And it was the doctor who recommended another pregnancy, reason to sober up. She did, long enough to give birth, but her delight only lasted until the melancholy of new mothers took hold and... never left her. That, and all the other aches, is why I don't hold it against Clemmie. She has cared for me as best she can, and I have done the same for her."

Silas had never heard of a mother not responding to the cry of her child. It broke him to hear Viola had learned a new way to grab her mother's attention when she deserved to be bathed in it. His own mother, strictly devoted to the good of her family, had never abandoned her post. He wished that for Viola, and more. Unconditional love and attention.

"Want to know a secret?" Viola picked a vine leaf and tore it into small pieces.

"I want to know them all."

"My sister was not Marshall's. Her real father was the man my mother would have married if he hadn't been killed, the artist who created the *Sweet Clementine.* The painting I will buy back one day."

"When you win a prize?"

"When I win *first* prize. Other prizes are for those who are happy enough to disappear. No one remembers second or third."

She played with the broken leaf. "I know Clemmie will die soon. I see signs of her decline, her shallow breathing, her growing anxiety. But each afternoon you arrive and her countenance changes." She smiled, this wild creature who'd found a way to survive an absent mother.

"I saw another advertisement, Viola. Something I think you should consider."

"You're determined to find the right job for me, aren't you? Is a boarding school looking for an art teacher this time?"

"Better, a competition."

She leaned closer. "Do tell."

"A Christmas postcard competition, open to all artists."

"Hmm. I suppose I could consider it."

But her reply, and the way she stared at Silas, didn't sound like she considered anything but him. Their knees touched. The way their lives did. No longer by accident.

"I wish I could take you away from all the striving and troubles on the shore," he said.

"Where would we go?"

He wondered, too. Where was there for the two of them?

"I have limited resources. Even this borrowed boat needs to be returned. What I have is a tangle of debt. It would be unfair to you, right now, to even suggest..."

"We're two streams, aren't we, Silas? Converged for a moment, on our way to fortune neither of us can see yet."

"Fortune?"

"Your astrolabe. Isn't that the fortune you seek?"

"If it's there. Hopefully, some collector will pay handsomely for it."

"But it's the icon of your inspiration. Isn't there some way to keep it?"

"I have no choice. Inspiration doesn't pay the money-lenders."

She made a sad face. "Meanwhile, what are we to do, you and I?"

Was this the right time to tell her about Honora? Maybe this boat ride had been for her to admit her mother had less time left than she'd hoped. That was a preparation not easily made when a loved one languished.

He let the oars slide to a stop and snapped the locks.

"What are you doing?"

"Making us a place."

"In the middle of nowhere?"

"For now. If the middle of nowhere is all we have, then shouldn't we occupy it with abandon? Make it our own?"

Viola leaned forward and met him where he leaned in. Forehead to forehead.

Grand foolishness like this on a small boat was never a good idea. But this, the rosy smell of her hair.

She cupped his face. "Stay."

He groaned. "I wish…"

"Then I need to know you will return."

He swallowed hard.

"Silas, please tell me you'll come back."

"You have much to wade. Soon, and in the coming year. But if you care enough for me—"

"I care, in whatever measure comes after enough. And then you can double that, or triple it, or… just take it all."

They stared at each other for the longest time. Maybe they committed each other to memory.

"Well, aren't we in the same boat, then?" he said. "Because I care more than enough for you." He pulled her in and kissed her. This moment deserved to be kept unsullied. The exchange of affections. Promises for future days. How he'd ever return to Australia remained a mystery. As did many other things. He pushed them all aside as if they were a scrap of seaweed on the tip of an oar. Now was not the time to walk her through a graveyard.

Balthazar rocked on his perch. Viola pulled the newspaper sheet from the tray of his cage and rolled up his mess. Most days she did not see eye to eye with that galah, but today Viola understood the restlessness of being caged up. Of knowing there were obstacles, whichever way you turned.

She dumped the soiled paper into a bucket and relined the cage with a fresh sheet.

"There you are, Balthazar. Attended to as if your mistress herself swept away the troubles of your little world."

But Clemmie sat in her reading chair under a blanket of listlessness. She had loved and lost Mortimer Barnes. She had loved and lost her first Viola. She had loved her stage roles and lost those, too. Clementine Buckley had lost all she'd wanted, and this is what it looked like.

Viola felt the deepening of wants, too. She wanted to win. To restore her mother to good health. To restore *Sweet Clementine* to a place of dignity. This three-stranded cord frayed within her like a ribbon. Had she braided her life with the impossible? Would she too, one day, peer from a window and wonder what might have been?

She grabbed the litter bucket and made her way to the menagerie where she knew her hostess had taken Molly. Finella dipped an old hairbrush into a pan of water and sprinkled three flowerpots with water.

"Winter-blooming hyacinth bulbs." She dipped her brush again, and Molly, like her mother, dunked her full hand into the water. "My Aunt Sarah loved hyacinths. I'm sure it's an inherited fondness."

"A most fragrant plant to nurture." Viola contemplated her hostess, happy in her motherhood. Happy to repeat the occupations of the women who'd come before her.

What about Viola? She'd been happy to abandon the theatre in preference for her own kind of performance. But would she escape the inherited melancholy of women like her mother?

"Silas Swift kissed me," she blurted, not to brag, but because she hoped Finella would help her make sense of this new list she kept in her heart.

Finella's head snapped up. "Kissed you?"

"Twice. Well, I should also count a kiss on the hand, so that would make three kisses, so far."

Finella smiled and gave the brush to Molly. "Does that thrill you or terrify you?"

The question alone pulled most of the air from her lungs. Viola breathed in more, but it was never enough when she thought of him.

"He will leave soon. And three kisses, while lavish in themselves, is a meager number and terrifying when I consider how glorious it would be to… add more."

"Mr. Swift has become more than a friend. It's never easy to consider a parting," Finella said.

"I have the makings of a truly good portfolio up there on your landing. Like a treasure map, laid out to follow and paint into giant, eye-catching paintings." Viola paced the menagerie. "I have chased this for years. I know what I am to do with charcoal and paints and brushes, but I am not competent in matters of the heart, and I fear I will take mine back to Melbourne in poorer condition than when I arrived."

"See these shell paths?" Finella pushed her back into the courtyard. "Shadrach made them for me. He worked himself into delirium to show he wanted me to stay when I had made up my mind to leave. But when love appears, there's nothing that time or distance can do to hold it back."

She ran her fingers along the crude doorframe. "This menagerie was my first home. His sister and I slept right there to begin with." She pointed to two sapling frames. "Recent winds have damaged the roof, and it's always going to be dusty thanks to the dirt floor, but I often come here to potter with my bulbs. I raise silkworms in here in the spring. But what I really do is slip back into time and let the memories in. I was on a boat, about to leave for good, when my heart told me to return. To Molly, and to Shadrach. To these four walls."

Finella's eyes filled with tears. "Shadrach offered to take me to Melbourne for a honeymoon in a real seaside hotel, but I only wanted this one room where his affections first drew me in. It's here I encountered love with a man who dragged a load of shells in the rain and spread them out for me like a magic carpet. I chose dirt. Mud. Shells. And memories."

"Memories," Viola repeated. "How will Silas and I make them beyond this island?"

"If you want a future with him, you must fight for it as hard as you fight for your art."

"How?"

"Discover what there is for him when he returns. Is there a way, a place, for you to walk life together? You owe it to yourself to know what it will cost you to embrace him. And what it will cost him."

Finella looked like she held a secret. One she coaxed Viola to uncover.

"Cost?"

"The pursuit of love is a courageous act unlike any other. It will alter you from within if you let it."

"I wish I knew where to begin."

"How about in this unremarkable hut, complete with its own history of love-matches?" Finella stepped back into the menagerie. "The island butcher's been called to Melbourne for a family funeral. Shadrach and Silas will slaughter that deer tomorrow. In here. That's why Molly and I are moving the hyacinth pots out of harm's way. I imagine the job will be a little less delicate than jam making but, if you could weather it—"

"Ew." The mere thought churned Viola's stomach. "A butchering?"

"I made mud bricks, to find Shadrach. I wanted him to know I fit in his world."

"Silas is a woodworker. Not a butcher."

"It's not the occupation that matters. It's how you fit beside him. It's where you learn who the other one was, in the days before you met. The world they come from shows who they are and what they carry in their heart. If what you discover works for you both, neither of you will want a future without the other. No matter what."

Finella delivered *no matter what* in three slow beats.

It sounded more like a warning. A call to battle. And in the cool breeze of that May afternoon, Viola shivered as if a freshly woven spider's web had dropped into her hair.

May 18, 1879

Finella talks in riddles. She pushes me to hunt for the real Silas the way I search for my botanicals. The flaws. The imperfections I so adore in nature.

My mind's eye sneaks him into the Exhibition Building. I want him to behold my art when it is on a wall. And I draw him, stroke by stroke, like the finest of sketches, into the world that awaits me when I return to Melbourne.

But where is that?

Our rented house is no longer ours. By now, our girls have found new tutors.

I have paid for another month here, and then what? Clemmie slips deeper into her thoughts, demands less of me. If ever there was a sign, the absence of her neediness is it. She is distant. Withdrawn. Contemplative. Drunk on regret.

A candle in her final hours.

She has had enough of newspaper and book reading. Silas has taken a sack of driftwood in and amuses Clemmie with how they fit together. A round birdhouse made of twisted sticks and twigs.

Unlike Balthazar's cage, this house has no door for locking and unlocking.

But it has a small opening where Silas says blue wrens can peek in and stay if they choose. If only I had a way to keep him here. If only it were as easy as collecting sticks and pressing them into a nest. But no bird ever flew into a nest against its will.

It is easy to promise to return. It is the right thing to say. But what if he finds his world, his brother, his business, all need him more when he returns than when he left?

What if there's no astrolabe in that last newel post? What will become of his debts?

And what will become of me? I have learned to borrow from him every day.

I have learned to love just when it requires of me to lay it down.

If he is to return to me, I must give him goo• reason.

I •on't •are start an actual paper list with his name on it, but somewhere... the name Silas is being inscribe•.

An• I am not sorry.

20

From the menagerie doorway, Viola watched Silas run the butchering knives along a sharpening stone. The *ksshh-ksshh* made an ominous sound. Soon, these blades would sever a carcass, but disquiet already chipped at her knot-tight nerves.

Still, she faced them, the hunters and their deer, nose down, long dead.

"Shh." Shadrach raised his arm. "What's that?"

A squawk, then another high-pitched protest, cackled from the chicken yard.

"Your hens might be thinking the knives have come out for them, too." Silas grimaced.

"Might be a snake. Wouldn't be the first." Shadrach squeezed past them, leaving Silas in charge and Viola his accomplice once again.

She fastened the strings on her borrowed apron. On the beaten-up table, a salt crock and various pans awaited whatever pieces of meat would emerge from the slaughter. Some would be cooked today, some would be salted, while others would end up in the mince bucket for sausage making.

"Will this sicken you?" Silas peered at her. "If Shadrach's held up, I may need you for more than carting pans and buckets of meat into the house."

She replied with a tepid smile. "All I know is Finella handed me this apron with a look that said, 'you can do this,' and now here I am."

"And… here you are." He parroted her words, the way Balthazar might, but Silas was no mimic in a cage. He added his own meaning to *here you are.* His words a pure caress. "To be honest, I think Shadrach was glad to step out. The prospect of catching a thief is more alluring than taking one apart."

Viola knew the feeling. Her stomach rolled with a storm of desperate butterflies, the giant moth variety, banging to be let out.

She would have been more comfortable bringing in a refreshment tray for when this was all over. The raisin dough she knew rose in a yeasty loaf under a clean cloth in Finella's kitchen. Here in the menagerie, the smell of raw animal flesh, of hide and hoofs and coagulated blood, drove a flood of gall into her throat.

She needed a distraction. Did he prefer to work in silence or was conversation welcomed here? But Silas already sized up the deer, like a wanderer with an old map.

"How does a woodworker find himself roped into slaughtering a deer?" she asked. "Is it a privilege reserved for the one who shot it?"

He shook his head. "It's Shadrach's good fortune I'm here for this. Woodcraft, I learned at my father's workbench. But my mother's father, my Grandpa John, was a butcher."

He pressed the tip of the knife where she figured the heart might be.

"My father came from four generations of Swedish woodworkers. There was no doubt in his mind that wood was in our blood. But Grandpa John wanted to test if there was any butcher's blood, so he took us boys in for a summer. We felt the knife in our hands, the skin of a carcass, the meat underneath, all the different muscles. None of that put us off, but it was the butchery smells that convinced all three of us there would only be sweet smelling sawdust and fresh curled shavings at our feet."

"And glue," she added.

"Plenty of glue, my able accomplice."

Nearby, another chorus of squawking chickens rang out, followed by the sound of Shadrach's angry voice and the thwack of his shovel.

Silas held a knife in each hand, like a juggler. "When you work with wood, something comes to life. My father always said even the restoration of derelict pieces was an act of noble charity. Meat-works?" He shook his head. "The draining of lifeblood, skins being stripped, animals quartered. It took little convincing. Wood was our mistress. And we returned to her, our first and only love."

He snapped his head up, and she felt her heart rip like a piece of old leather. She nodded and busied herself with the knot of her apron, suddenly way too tangled.

First loves, like her sister, always inhabited the tales of the heart. And there was very little left for whoever came next. Silas turned away, and Viola was left to the spike of calamity she fought when *first loves* appeared, even if only a man's dedication to his woodwork.

Preoccupied by keeping the small barb under wraps, she missed whatever Silas did to begin the butchering, but soon enough she raised her head and found him holding the deerskin in his left hand, while his knife ripped at the carcass, inch by inch, keeping the skin intact. The disrobing revealed streaks of fat that ran like marble underneath, alongside veins and sinew.

"My sister," he pulled at the skin the way he might pull off his socks at day's end, "married a baker."

Hands behind her back, Viola gripped the doorframe for support.

"Mary married well, my mother used to say. She'll never go

hungry. Whereas Swift Brothers might go bust and all our empty chests, caddies, dressers, and well-turned spindle chairs won't fill hungry bellies."

Viola looked away. Where was Shadrach? Her stomach heaved at the *deesh, deesh, deesh,* of shredding skin.

Think, Viola. Talk with him as if you're on the beach log. Look anywhere but the deer.

"Have you missed your siblings while you've been here?"

He nodded. "I was already missing Patrick. He's angry at what life's dealt him and needs to kick into the wind awhile to show he doesn't need me."

The deerskin hung by one last inch. Silas sliced it clear off and gathered it in a bundle to his chest like an old mantle. *This happens all the time,* she told herself. *It's the way of the hunter and his prey. It's the way of a farmer and his chickens.* How else did they sip on bone broth?

"What happens to the skin?"

"I reckon there's a few pairs of gloves in this." He passed it to her. Soft and suede-like, it weighed more than Molly on her hip.

"Can you dunk it in the saltwater next to the mincing bucket?" He pointed to a filled wooden barrel on the dirt floor. "I need to tell you about something, but I don't know where to start. And I'm babbling about woodwork and butchers and bakers, which is far from where I need to take you."

She pressed the skin under the waterline with a washing paddle and turned to face him.

He stood, legs apart, staring at the deer, his chest rising and falling as if he were about to carve out his own heart.

"Silas, what is it?" The surge of bile she'd kept at bay lapped her throat. She wiped both hands on her apron. "You can tell me anything."

"Well, it's two things. Newspaper shipping notices have announced the *Clara* sails on May 31. That's only eleven days away."

"Eleven days?" A cold breeze snuck into the menagerie.

He stuck the largest of the knives into the shoulder area of the carcass. "Eleven days to gather what's mine and return home."

The knife slid with ease, and she knew from the way he turned his back to her that whatever he would add to the departure date of the *Clara* would hurt more.

"A staircase is the crucial test of a joiner's ability. Treads too narrow and risers too high make for a hazardous climb and dangerous descent. I decided that one day, people would come to me for the best staircases their money could buy."

He swallowed hard. "Because when you owe someone who looks to you as my brothers did, you don't give up. But I also owe my sister." He dissected a portion of flesh and threw it in one of the pans. "Mary stepped in and did her part for our family, too. She …"

He disappeared behind the beast to reach in between bones she could not properly see. Like a man severed in two, one of him butchered the deer, the other butchered into his past.

"My mother died a year after we lost my father, so Mary did what I could not for our family until… she left us."

He looked at her, his words a mix of easy to understand and murky as mud. He threw a leg piece onto the table, and Viola ignored the finality of its fate. Instead, she conjured images of Mary cooking their meals and setting a place for each of her bachelor brothers at a table they'd made for the home they shared.

He dropped other pieces into the mincing bucket. The deer, once covered in a fine red coat, now lay in pieces. But Silas looked like a man whose battles were only beginning.

He skewered the tip of the knife into the wood of the table, wiped his wet brow on the arm of his shirt, and turned to face her.

"Mary helped us with our own Rest Therapy." He swallowed hard. "And Mary almost fell into the same melancholy she tried to remedy with… on … my…"

His throat thickened with a twisted fishbone of words.

"On?" Viola repeated.

"No." He shook his head. "With my—"

"You in there, Mr. Swift?"

A deep voice rang over the courtyard, and before Silas could finish his sentence, a tall, fair-haired man knocked on the menagerie window.

"Goliah Ashe," he announced himself to Viola with a deep nod and tip of his hat. "Village preacher, here to visit Mrs. Buckley."

The preacher? Viola stepped outside. "Mr. Ashe, I'm Miss Buckley. Silas has shared some of your sermons with my mother."

"Well, I'm not here to deliver one, if that's what you think. Silas has passed on her request to see me."

"She has?" Viola wiped her hands on her apron and threw one last look at Silas, who leaned over the menagerie table, one arm on each end, head bowed over all he'd severed.

She was meant to help him take it all inside to Finella, who had clamped a mincer to the kitchen table, where herbs and salts and barrels awaited the fresh meat.

She longed to point toward the verandah and front door.

Up there. Top of the stairs.

But she bid the preacher follow her away from the menagerie where one kind of butchery had taken place before her eyes, and another, one she failed to comprehend, within the cavity of her soul.

As far as preachers went, Goliah Ashe was probably the most ill-suited in looks. Viola imagined most young girls, and perhaps their mothers, would have spent hours listening to his sermons and returned home with little of what he'd said. Her mother would say a beautiful man like he was more suited to the stage. He towered over her, and his voice resonated in ways she'd known theater folk worked years to perfect.

Flocks needed a shepherd with a powerful voice, yes, but broad shoulders and fine blue eyes that held mischief were not of any use from a pulpit, surely.

He followed her up the stairs.

"Please excuse our landing. It's part bird enclosure, part botanical catalogue."

He ducked under her paintings.

"Who goes there?" Balthazar quizzed.

"Goliah Ashe, at your service," the preacher replied without hesitation and looked like he would gladly wait for conversation from the silly bird. Viola showed him into Clemmie's room and made introductions.

"Mr. Ashe. Mr. Swift has delivered some of your lessons, but he neglected to tell me of your stature and presence. Come, sit." Clemmie welcomed her guest.

No stranger to polite conversation, Mr. Ashe eased himself into the sickroom with all the right questions of Clemmie, inquiring in general terms about her health and letting her share as much as she cared to, with a warm smile or understanding nod of his head. After a few minutes of this, Clemmie turned to Viola.

"I'd like to speak with Mr. Ashe in confidence."

Confidence? Viola looked from sheep to shepherd, and only when the preacher nodded *we'll be fine* did she back away.

Of course Clemmie would want a private audience. That was no surprise. What bothered Viola most was missing out, again, on another important conversation.

At the newel post that remained for her and Silas to break open, she lingered and ran her palm over the rounded top. Like his arabesque pattern, this too had no start or finish. A well-shaped wooden ball turned and fixed onto a square collar of wood.

"... you see." Her mother's voice caught Viola's attention. "I need to make arrangements for a funeral."

Viola clutched the post. The living did not arrange funerals for themselves. They left that to the ones who would stand by open graves. Unless they were Clementine Buckley and wished for the perfect finale.

That dreadful thought followed her through the house and into the courtyard.

She needed Silas. And whatever he tried to tell her about Mary and their poor Rest Therapy patient. Hoping he'd collected himself now, she hurried back to where men's voices escaped the open menagerie door.

"I don't envy you this kind of entanglement." Shadrach had returned. "There's a deep chasm between you."

"I'll try again when the preacher leaves."

She pressed her back to the menagerie wall. Was everyone whispering behind her back today?

"She had this look about her. I don't know if it was the knife, the meat. I kept throwing her pieces of my story like some youth who doesn't know how to talk with the girl he likes, but none of what I truly wanted to say."

She stepped away. Silas deserved to talk with another man about the struggle of their feelings in private. Hadn't she done the same with Finella? She pressed her hands to her stomach, but it failed to calm her.

Weariness fell over her, and nightfall sped into the disappearing day. She turned away, but in her haste, kicked something. It clanged, then rattled at her feet. An empty watering can. The ring bayonetted her in the chest.

"Viola?" Silas appeared at the menagerie doorway. "Was that you? Did you trip?"

She shook her head and backed away.

"Wait, Viola."

She held up a hand. She had tripped, all right. Into something she knew little about.

"When you're ready, Silas. Finish what you and Shadrach started."

She hurried to the kitchen-end of the house. Through a side window she spotted Finella running meat through her mincer. Fat and gristle and all the odd bits of the deer fell into the blades.

Nausea agitated her insides like the mincing crank. She dashed back to the front of the house, and another window caught her eye. The landing window, where Finella kept her lantern. All of a sudden, she needed that light. She needed to peer into it, like a woman lost at sea, over perilous rocks and sea ravines.

Shadrach and Silas made their way through the courtyard too, meat buckets in hand. Viola waited for them to disappear from view before she scrunched across the shell path, lantern in hand.

She longed to be away from people. Alone with her thoughts and aches. She remembered the ladder at the back of the menagerie. So she climbed. Into the shadows of dusk and the core of her thoughts.

Last time she'd perched here, Silas had agreed to watch over her on the deer hunt. Now only salted pieces and a pelt of loose skin remained.

Lantern light flickered, and to keep her hand from tiring, she hung the metal loop on the end of a gum branch. Light spilled over her. Like the promise of guidance Finella hoped this would be.

Whatever Silas needed to say, could it be as bad as what she'd already suffered? Her father had called her *useless,* and she had proven him wrong. There had never been anything as hurtful, as damaging, or as cruel. And she had used that to carve herself a future. One she now wanted with Silas.

The thought struck her with renewed force. Eleven days, then he'd been gone.

But women waited years for the men they loved. Some watched them sail into wars and never lost hope. She would wait. If his financial predicament meant he would be poor all his life, that would not extinguish her affections.

Was that what he struggled to articulate? The fear of poverty? Everything he owed his family?

A plan lit in her heart, and her mind wrote it out like a list.

She would wait. And she would tell him. If they looked hard enough together, wouldn't there be a hopeful glimmer for them? More stars appeared. The longer she sat, the more she counted. In the stillness, they pointed like a chorus of answers.

Follow the stars to the horizon. Find South. Find North. Find home.

She pressed one foot, then another on the rungs of the ladder and descended with a small flourish.

I'll wait for you, Silas. Come, watch the stars with me.

From Finella's kitchen came the mouth-watering aromas of fried onions and meat sizzling in a pan, but an altogether different hunger rose in Viola. The fierce longing for Silas.

She would do for him what he had done for her. She would push him on to find his solutions. To walk back into Portland and all that meant to him. If he lost it all, she would still be here.

She knocked on his door and it swung open like an empty yawn. His belongings were all here, clothes on hooks, a jacket on the back of a chair. A stack of papers littered a small table. Everything in this room said Silas lived here, but the steaming ewer said Silas had been here only moments ago.

Confusion simmered and a new thought, like the worst of all trickery, clogged her throat. Surely Silas was not softening the glue? Not without her. He wouldn't. He'd promised.

She peeked, and in the ewer sat the glue pot. She dug her hands into the deep pockets of her apron. There had to be an explanation. But nothing about this day had unraveled with much order, and this was no different. The leather pouch where Silas kept his woodworking gear sat on the bed.

She tilted the glue pot. It swayed like melted wax. And something swayed within her, too. Anger and rejection and the feeling of being overlooked. It was as if an underground force had broken at her feet, and all reason swept her away.

She grabbed the steaming cloth, the glue pot, the chisel and brush, and let the befuddlement of this day carry her to the top of the stairs.

"Viola, Viola." Balthazar greeted her.

"Hello to you, my feathered friend," she whispered back. "Where is everyone?"

Other than a stray pink feather that fluttered around the top of his cage, he had nothing for her. Clemmie had farewelled her visitor. Mouth open, she slept, hands folded in a prayer-like pose.

Viola draped the steaming cloth over the post and waited. An eerie hush covered the house, like the lifting of a velvet curtain on a ready stage.

Heart beating, nerves coiling, she held her breath and counted to ten. Then twenty. How long for the steam to work its way into the wood? She counted to twenty again but could not risk another second. With the foolhardy courage of someone who'd trod this road once before, she applied pressure to the newel post.

Up and down, she pressed the chisel. All day long, she'd struggled not to eavesdrop on conversations, but this break-in was something she would not abandon.

"Come on," she spoke over the post in the same whisper Silas had employed. For all her prodding, nothing budged. She pressed again, this time on the other side.

And then she heard a beautiful crack. The splintering of wood. A few more twists, and the post top let go of its mooring. She set it on the landing.

Heart pounding, she lowered her hand into the hollow.

Nothing.

Leaning in to extend her reach, she searched the dark for treasure. Smooth and polished on the outside, Silas, or someone in his factory, had left the guts of the post unfinished, and splinters snagged at her wrist. Then her fingertips grazed something. She dug deeper. Soft. Some kind of cloth? She pressed the slippery fabric to the rough wood until her fist emerged with Silas' treasure.

She weighed it in her hand. Metal wrapped in something silken turned inside out.

It's here, Silas. You can pay your debts. It's here.

She listened for him. He'd be here soon enough, would he not? Her heart pealed at her audacity to swoop in and take over where he'd thought he might go without her. No longer accomplice. She was in every way his equal. Thief.

All that remained was to turn this bundle right side out and peer through the arabesque scroll for herself. Viola tiptoed into her room and set it down on the bed like a newfound chick fallen from its nest.

She should wait. Repair the post. But something feminine pulled at her. It radiated from the cloth. As if to say,

Study properly, while you can.

While you are truly able to look at me.

21

The astrolabe was as beautiful as he'd promised. A round clock-like face atop other dials and letters in a circular script she could not read, with only one decipherable number, *1564.* It weighed no more than a smooth beach stone.

She did not know how a sailor came upon navigational answers with this. But she knew she held a priceless piece of Silas in her hand.

When turned the right way around, she discovered the twisted wrapping was a pair of a lady's elbow-length gloves. Made of leather and silk and yellowed with age, one contained the astrolabe. The other glove held it all together.

Dare she slip them on? She'd never seen a pair so delicate, not even in Madame Nasrin's wardrobe room. She wriggled into the silk and down into the slender parts where her fingers barely fit into the tight leather.

A row of tiny stitches on the elbow ribbons caught her eye. She looked closer. And blinked hard.

August 22, 1873 – Silas and Honora

She shook her arms, as if embers from a fire attacked her.

Silas and Honora?

Horror scuttled from her chest into the back of her throat.

These were no ordinary gloves. They were bridal gloves, commemorating a wedding date. *Silas and Honora?* The words burned into her flesh. She peeled them off and picked up the astrolabe.

Silas has a wife. She clutched her stomach. *Oh, God, please let it be his father. Or an uncle in whose memory he was named.* But no…

Her heart screamed the ugly truth in words she did not want to let in.

Silas has a wife.

She pressed her hands to her mouth, the astrolabe between them, and prayed for answers.

Perhaps her excitement to find the treasure had caused her to misread. She dropped the astrolabe in her pocket and with her eyes, with the tip of a finger, and with every bleeding beat of her heart, read the words on the ribbon once more.

Silas and Honora.

"Viola?"

Silas called her from somewhere. She did not turn, so fixed was her gaze on the mess she'd brought out of the dark and into their world.

"Viola?" His footfall hit the landing. "Viola!" This time he whispered. "You found it?"

She pressed the gloves to her chest in a crunched-up ball of nothing. Oh, how she wished it were nothing. Mere cobwebs to be swatted away.

"I was warming up the glue, to fix the bottom newel post," he said, eyes wide breath short. "Shadrach thought he detected a wobble, but I didn't expect you'd swoop in and…."

Viola shook her head, and he stopped to take in the panic bleeding over her.

She let the gloves roll from her fingers. No longer ribbonlike, they hung from her trembling fists like bloody bandages.

Honora's bridal gloves. The sound of his own gasp emptied over them.

Honora had stitched them, among other pieces of her wedding attire, her trousseau, and all the dreams of motherhood that she'd never tasted. No matter how well dressed, there was always a mantle she never wore. Motherhood.

And that was the fault of the astrolabe, but… where was it now?

Get rid of it. Honora had screamed through hot tears. And now, the face of another woman he loved held accusations and questions.

"Viola, listen to me." He stepped closer, and she dropped the gloves into his hands like rags. "I forgot I'd bundled the astrolabe in these. I… we'd… been arguing for days and exasperated, I grabbed the nearest thing from our dresser, and stuffed the astrolabe in there, tied it in a bundle, slammed every door between our room and the factory below…"

She stared at him, eyes brimming with tears.

"Whose house, Silas? Whose dresser?" She choked on the words and shook her head. "Whose gloves?"

He looked through his own tears into the twisted mess between his fingers. He could not wring the truth from himself without wringing something in her, but he had no choice.

"The house I shared with my wife, Honora."

"Hon… ora." She whispered the broken-up name. Her eyes half closed to whatever vision swam before her. "Honora, your wife. Your…. *wife?*"

"Please, Viola, let me—"

"Unmarried. You and your brothers. You said that."

"Eugene and Patrick are the bachelors. I am a widower."

She stared. "Widower?"

"Honora died a little over a year ago. After the loss of three babies in four years. After a battle with melancholy and the anguish that left her undernourished. She hardly ate. She hardly spoke. And no amount of bedrest, foolish therapies, or cold water baths restored her."

He rubbed his hands over his face. The air in Viola's room thickened. The smell of dried eucalyptus leaves clogged his throat. He wanted to run. To take the ugliness of his marriage and the pain it still caused, and flee as he had that day, blind with fury, into his factory and to the first hollowed post he could reach. One he knew would go farther than he ever would.

How wrong he'd been.

How wrong he still was.

Viola's hands covered her mouth like the only support left to lean on. "Why would you not say?" she whispered. "Your wife, her own Rest Therapy. You've been a man in mourning this whole time and not shared it with me?"

"If I had told you, would you have shared my grief?"

"I … would have."

"From afar, or from up close?" He shortened the space between them, desperate to reach her and let her know she had deserved to discover this much earlier and from him directly.

"I'm not proud of the husband I was to Honora." He dug for the truth, like a man grabbing on barbed wire to keep from falling. "I spent too many hours building our business. And I didn't see how she suffered. I neglected her, and in her grief, she rejected me."

Viola said nothing. She just looked at him as if he'd clocked her on the head and she waited for the room to stop spinning.

"You had a wife. And you loved her." Trance-like the words rolled around in her mouth and off her tongue. "A wife…"

"I *had* a wife, Viola. She's dead and I am not proud of keeping that from you. I'm not proud of other things, too. The way I reach for you when I know I can't have you."

He stopped and started again.

"After Honora died, I thought the comfort of another woman would kill the emptiness, but I learned the hard way that you can't replace one wreck with another. This dog bite you saw, I got it when I was at the wrong place at the wrong time, with the wrong woman. I regret that, too. I wanted this to be different with you. I wanted to build the right layers of emotion and affection. I needed to tread carefully. I've put my foot wrong too many times, and your mother warned—"

"Viola! Hurry. Where are you?" Mrs. Buckley stumbled across the landing and rattled the latch on Balthazar's cage. "Come here, sweet boy."

"Clemmie?" Viola pushed past him. "For goodness' sake. You are not allowed to take him out."

"Fire!" Mrs. Buckley whispered and drew the bird into her embrace.

"What fire, Clemmie?"

"Don't you smell smoke? Something nearby is aflame."

They raised their heads. They sniffed and listened.

And from the yard came the terrified voice of Finella.

"Where's Molly? The menagerie's on fire!"

22

Smoke filled the courtyard. It was the heart of chaos, and it roared in Viola's ears like an open-mouthed dragon.

Please, God, let this fire not be my fault.

"Molly!" Finella screamed.

"She's here." Shadrach appeared from behind the skillion door, half-hidden by fresh smoke that billowed in wide swathes over house and garden. Molly clutched the handle of a small brush but lunged for the arms of her mother.

Viola did not blame her. Fear and blazing wood crackled over them. And mother and child quivered, terror-struck at the sight of smoke that barreled from the menagerie roof.

Shadrach dunked buckets into the rain barrel and tossed water onto the roof from ground level. "Find the ladder!" he screamed at Silas. "If we climb higher, we attack from the top."

Viola wanted to double over. Her insides twisted, and her throat filled with the acrid bite of sickening guilt.

Not Finella's menagerie! What if the fire ran along the roofline and into the other outbuildings? What if this razed the entire L-shaped configuration of barn and skillion, too?

What if sparks flew onto the guesthouse?

She had done this. The caustic realization pushed her down, and if she let herself, she could have folded into a crouching position on the shell pathway.

But she stood upright, wanting to help, knowing she may have done more than enough already.

Molly cried and buried her smoke-slapped face in her mother's embrace.

"Should I run for more water?" Viola thought of the well. Of the water barrels all over the property. The animal troughs. The puddles …

Finella didn't answer. She fought her own tears. And Viola could only imagine the anguish. Finella's first home with Shadrach ran with flames. Valiant, yet so feeble, the men's efforts diminished against the growing blaze.

"Sun-baked wattle. It's all tinder now," Shadrach yelled.

Viola ran to Shadrach, her arm over her mouth to keep the worst of the smoke away.

"What can I do? Please." She tried to catch his attention. "Let me help." She coughed into her sleeve.

"Move back!" Shadrach yelled. "Stand with Finella or get inside the house." He shoved her with his elbow and threw another bucketful of water through the open doorframe.

But all the frenzied attempts, man against fire, could not stop the shingled roof from collapsing. In what felt like minutes, as well as an age of agonies, it crumbled inward with a crash and hiss of roof and beams and thundering dust, rising from a cloud of ashes to consume more.

Finella gasped. Shadrach continued the assault with water from another rain barrel. But it was too late. The menagerie had lost its roof, and now the walls billowed with smoke. The sapling beds and weathered table would not stand a chance. The hyacinth pots.

Viola remembered the saltwater, where she'd dunked the deer skin. Was that still there, or had they taken it in with the meat?

"The deerskin!" She spotted Silas, who emerged from the smoke. "The other water barrel."

Covered in soot, he too pushed her aside, but he'd heard what she said, for he bypassed Shadrach and braved the blazing doorway.

"Wait, no!" she yelled, hardly able to raise her voice over the noise of the fire. "Silas!" She coughed and tried again.

"Silas!" Shadrach called, too. "Too dangerous. Stay outside."

But Silas ignored them and slipped in anyway.

The seconds passed. They ticked like hours, measured by the screaming of her heart. Shadrach continued to douse the flames. And Silas? She could not tell. *Please, God. How can this be happening? Where is he?*

Silas burst out, his back to them, the wet skin of the deer draped over him like a costume.

And while they'd beaten the fire away from the other outbuildings, the menagerie was lost. Silas crumpled to the ground, heaving for air.

Shadrach did not stop until the barrels ran dry. By then, all that remained were smoldering beams and the small stone fireplace. The charred menagerie smoked and wept in steam that raced over the courtyard and into their nostrils and hair and settled deep into their hearts like cinders.

Finella sobbed into Molly's shoulder. Sweaty and begrimed, Shadrach comforted his wife and child. Even with the worst of the smoke no longer spilling from the menagerie, Viola knew a clear breath of air would not be drawn here for hours.

In similar disarray and equally filthy, Silas appeared from behind the menagerie. He'd thrown the deerskin off, but he carried Finella's blackened lantern.

Hours ago, Viola had looked into it for clarity and direction. Now, her stomach heaved, and this time she knelt on the ground. Delirium threatened and she knew some of what her mother battled when life's tragedies condemned.

This was all her fault. She had done this.

"How'd that lantern get there?" Shadrach roared.

She would have to speak, but none of what she had to say would make any sense to them. It hardly made sense to her.

"Shadrach…" She stood to face him. "I put it there, earlier. I…."

He stared hard, rage flaring in his nostrils. "You what?"

"I, I—"

"Why?" He looked at her for answers, as did Finella.

How could she tell them, now that putting the lantern there proved naïve and empty?

"I wanted a moment." Feeble, her voice hardly carried what she owed them. "With Silas. A glimmer of something I thought we might share. But I was foolish and misguided." Her fingers braced the side of her head.

Shadrach turned away with a face that told her he didn't care for her reasons. The menagerie now let out the heartbroken sigh of crackling timbers that came after this kind of trouble. And he had nothing in him for her right now.

Silas stared at her. He did not look the same. It was not the grime of the fire. It was a worse kind of blemish. Something neither of them would wash off in a hurry.

"I doused from one of the water barrels already in there. I saw the damage from inside," Silas spoke to Shadrach. "We caught it before it reached the barn. The menagerie's gone, but that fireplace is rock solid." He rubbed his eye. "Don't blame Viola. I let her go, halfway through a conversation we should have finished. It's my fault, too."

Viola wanted to object, but her throat burned with tears.

"I've lived through a fire that destroyed most of my hometown," Silas continued. "I know it doesn't help to say it right this minute, but I can help you rebuild. The main thing is we're all safe and you didn't lose your barn. Or house."

Even though he spoke to Shadrach, Silas let his gaze fall on her.

"I can fix this. Please, let me...."

He pleaded, this man who'd put out her mess. A man who'd kept his mourning from her and the loss of someone he'd once loved. Long after the smoke had cleared, his betrayal would cling to her, as sure as her guilt would.

He had loved someone else. And not told her.

He'd married, shared a life with someone he called wife. And not told her.

Because he knew Viola would not bear the notion of him loving her *next.*

Second.

Never first.

As she loved him now. Carelessly.

She backed away terrified of what he'd cracked open in her. Like a bushfire, Silas fired her every emotion. And threw water on it.

"Let me fix it," he said again.

"Viola!" Clemmie called from the house, followed by pounding on a windowpane.

Viola brushed at her tears with her sleeve.

"Forgive me, Shadrach, Finella." She hoped they would hear

through the brittle shame to the heart of her regret. "Somehow, I'll find a way to pay for my damages."

She could hardly speak the words.

For this, like all damage sustained this day, would cost her dearly.

If Silas knew anything, it was that Mrs. Buckley would need soothing. Smoke would have snuck inside, and now Viola would have to choose how much of this day's misery she would share with the woman who hated smoke and fire with good reason.

Shadrach pulled Finella close. Whatever he'd lost would never be as precious as the family he gathered up.

Silas backed away. His offer of help would serve his hosts well, but that was for another time. He turned for the house, the ash of this day still in his mouth. But Shadrach and Finella were not the only ones who'd suffered loss.

So had Viola. So had he.

His affections for her were no more diminished because he'd loved once before. But how did a man convince a woman she would not replace his dead wife, when all he had to offer was Honora's empty side of the bed? When his rooms above the factory remained unchanged. He'd given Honora's best clothes to his sister. But he knew his dead wife's aprons lay deep in a drawer somewhere. There was a sewing box too, with Honora's unfinished baby things. He'd not had the heart to deal with that. Nor the cradle that he'd made but never varnished.

And in his heart, hidden in his deepest secrets, the longing for someone to replace the one who would have stood beside him for a lifetime was real.

He was a man who wanted a wife, the truth of that longing as clear now as when a cool breeze blows the smoke from a fellow's eyes.

There *was* a place in his life for a wife. Not any wife. Viola.

He stepped into the guesthouse foyer. Loud sobbing sounded from the landing. Mrs. Buckley sniffed and must have pressed a handkerchief to her mouth, because her words came to him in muffled gasps.

"I thought the fire would reach us. The open door and the suffocating smell..."

"The fire's been put out, dear. Molly and Finella are safe. But, Clemmie, I am to blame."

Silas held the doorknob in his hand. Had they heard him come in? They would if he shut the door. It would not do to listen. He'd already broken her trust. He should tiptoe to his room. But there was not a bone in his body prepared to do that.

"I wanted him, Clemmie, whatever Silas and I were. Something I couldn't properly envision. And I would have waited for him, but now, there's something I *can* imagine. Honora. His first bride. His first wife. The one whose impression is left on him forever."

He sucked in his breath. She wrestled with *him*. That was a good sign, was it not?

"There are worse things than being someone's second love, Viola."

"Are there, Clemmie? I wouldn't know. I only know being the second is the worst."

"I wish I had known how to show you that you are more than... second..." A sob caught in Mrs. Buckley's voice. "How much you are... the only..."

She gasped, and the sound of a bird squawking pierced their conversation.

"Clemmie, what's troubling you? Your heart?"

"Ahh… oh… Viola!" Mrs. Buckley whispered.

Balthazar squawked and flapped his feathers. *Fwoop. Fwoop.*

"Aarrrghh," he screeched, perhaps to ward off whatever plagued his mistress. Under the cover of their commotion, Silas shut the door and crossed to the foot of the stairs.

Balthazar shrieked again. "Bricks and mortar, will not stay, will not stay, will not stay…"

"Hush now," Viola tried to subdue him. "Oh, Sweet Clemmie! Again?"

Silas took the stairs two by two. He found them as he imagined. Viola on her feet, her mother slumped against the newel post.

Viola held the bird, whose mood did not improve when he saw Silas.

"Who goes there? Who goes there?"

He didn't answer. It was Mrs. Buckley who commanded his attention. She clutched her left arm, eyes rolling, closing.

"I heard Mrs. Buckley cry out."

Viola struggled to get the bird back into his cage. "Don't pinch. Ow. Get in."

But Balthazar the Galah had a mind of his own, and he must have pinched her again, because Viola let him go and swatted him away. He landed on Silas's shoulder, dug in his claws, and flapped his wings for good measure.

"… will not stay… will not stay…" Panic driven, the bird gripped harder.

Pain came in waves. A sharp stab and then the deeper ache of awareness and wonder at how this would end. He shrugged hard and prayed the bird would find another perch.

Viola tried to collect him, but he would not let go.

"Easy, boy." Silas groaned. "Go to Viola."

Balthazar flapped his wings, then with one last dig, launched in the opposite direction. He flew into walls, collided with Viola's artwork, knocked string and papers to the floor with a hefty dusting of his own pink and gray feathers. Unleashed into his own confusion, Balthazar flailed and spun for safety that never appeared.

Mrs. Buckley withered. "Balthazar!"

Viola and Silas both called, but he swooped to the ground floor newel post. Silas followed him down and into the hallway of the house. The last of the setting sun bled through the windows over the door.

Balthazar flew into the glass and bounced back. Frantic, he beat his wings and tried again. Each attempt only frustrated him more. More feathers flew. As did curse words.

"He'll kill himself," Viola whispered.

Before the bird could injure himself further, Silas reached for the door handle and pulled it open. Smoke-laden air smacked him in the face and welcomed Balthazar into the real world.

"No!" Mrs. Buckley screamed. "Don't open the door! Balthazar!"

But her bird flew into the evening sky and disappeared into the treetops.

Once, Patrick had dared him to leave his thumb in a vice while he counted how many times he could screw it before Silas begged for mercy. He remembered how it felt to be let free, but in his chest he felt that same tight crush right now. He prayed Balthazar, the bird who knew how to sing, was smart enough to fly back.

"He's gone!" Mrs. Buckley cried.

"Try not to fret, Clemmie. I'm sure we'll see him on the verandah tomorrow, waiting for his breakfast." Viola tried to soothe.

"He doesn't know how to sleep outside his cage." Mrs. Buckley inhaled a quick gasp. "Oh, my poor baby."

Silas grimaced. Should he go into the courtyard and call for the bird? Would he even come to him? He hurried up the stairs instead, slipped his arms under the ailing woman, and carried her to her bed.

Viola pressed two pastilles into her mother's mouth. She held a cup of water to her lips. But neither water nor medicine found its way into the woman who refused anything but the comfort of her bird.

Viola lay beside her and stroked her cheek.

There was something wrong about the way he and Viola tried to coexist. Collisions found them at every turn. And as he had done before, he backed away from a sickroom, knowing more now than he had then, about the ache that would follow him.

And those around him.

May 20, 1879

At first, I thought it was my hea•. The ache that fin•s a broken heart the morning after crying oneself to sleep. But it's more than sorrow. It's actual poun•ing.

Sha•rach an• Silas work on •ismantling what's left of the menagerie.

I •on't know how much it will cost me, but Sha•rach has kin•ly sai• I am to keep my attention on Clemmie an• we will come to an agreement later.

I sit besi•e her an• watch her life •rain away. Her skin clammy. Her breath short.

Neither of us has eaten breakfast, an• my stomach wrestles with the pungent smells of meat cooking •ownstairs. There are women here, too. Finella's frien•s help with the •eer meat. Insi•e, outsi•e, all han•s occupie•, an• there will be much to show for their efforts.

In Clemmie's sickroom, all is quiet. She trembles in her sleep. In her blind distress, her hands seek something, and I slip her the little red dancing shoe. Balthazar is gone. Perhaps kept from returning to us by the constant work on the menagerie. Or perhaps he's found his freedom. His cage stands empty. Door open. I cannot bear to look at it. I have disliked him with a passion, but now, a new melancholy creeps upon me. I unpeg my paintings from the string and admit that Balthazar was the song of the past.

Now that is gone too.

And with it, I have lost the voice of my sister. Writing it here makes me long for her.

The girl I never knew.

Clemmie stirs again. But no amount of whispering in her ear brings her to me. I tell her I am here. Viola. I care not which one she thinks breathes against the ashen skin of her cheek. I only wish she would open her eyes so I can see the light within one more time.

Finella brings us a luncheon tray, but I cannot eat. Clemmie is not roused by smells or the soft talk around her. She inhabits a world of her own. A place between here and wherever her heart will take her.

I stretch my legs and return the tray to the kitchen. On my way, I see Silas. Words fail us. For where would we begin? He enquires of Clemmie. I shake my head and say I fear there is nothing left of her except her will to die in a house by the sea.

He steps closer, and I dig my hands into my pocket.

They do not belong to him, my screaming head reminds me. But the astrolabe does. And it's in my grip, so I relinquish it. Like an ember that might combust and set us alight.

His breath is not easy. Something is caught in his chest. I see the longing in him to speak, like the thrashing of some winge• creature caught in a net.

He wants more than I can offer, an• he has less than I can accept.

I bi• him goo• •ay an• return to Clemmie. Where I sit. An• wait.

The •usk of night was always her favorite. When gaslight lit her up.

Gol•en wigs, opulent costumes, an• a•oring au•iences. She rule• her worl• an• knew how to share it with a bir• an• her baby girl. But most of all, she knew how to remain the heart of that performance.

Now her booken•s are gone. The crooke•ness a little balance•. Only she remains.

Lamplight flickers like a weak breath. It bounces off the mirror.

Her eyeli•s flicker too, an• there's an urgency now. Disquiet rises, an• she exhales as if each breath •rags something she will never reclaim.

This long •ay has hel• nothing but waiting. A waiting so heavy it •rains the life of those who watch, as well as those whose eyes remain forever close•.

Sweet Clementine calls for Viola, an• I assure her...

Your Viola is here. She never left you.

23

Balthazar's cage stood at the end of the verandah. Cleaned and set deep into the lonely corner, it reminded Silas of an empty tomb. He ignored it and listened instead to Shadrach, who talked in low tones. Death and burials had dominated much of his thinking these last few days. The entire house had slowed to mark the passing of Clementine Buckley and lend their grief to Viola.

All but him.

Finella had swept in and tended her that first day and night, her soft voice bracing and calm in the sickening silence.

He'd waited to hear Viola sob or whimper, imaging how he would bound up the stairs to comfort her as he'd promised, but what came after death in this house was a thick hush. The glimpses he snatched were of her dry-eyed, staring at the sky through the bay window of the sitting room, Finella and Molly her company.

Shadrach had fetched others. Women who laid out the body. Men who carted it away.

Even Molly played her part. New companion to Viola. She babbled into the silence as if nothing of great solemnity had occurred around them with songs and childish gibberish which Viola clung to, tighter than his best tongue and groove joint, because that little girl had become her shield.

Whenever he approached, Finella or Shadrach would ease him away. "Not yet, Silas. When she's ready."

No one understood that Viola's predicament was one he'd promised to attend.

Steer her through the grief.

And so they'd buried Mrs. Buckley. A small gathering. With words of comfort spoken over them by Goliah Ashe under a shower of rain that pushed them away from the little island cemetery before anyone truly felt ready to leave.

Too late for the funeral, but right on time, her friend Madame Nasrin arrived to collect Viola up and entomb her in their shared grief. The two walked and talked, wrapped in the impenetrable bond of two sorrowing friends.

"The season of mourning is sacred, Mr. Swift," Madame Nasrin had said with a kind but firm smile. "When a woman loses her mother, it is other women who tend to her. She needs to rebuild herself around this loss, and then…."

And with that vague kindness, she had sent him away. The ache of that rustled over him like the withered hydrangea leaves that carpeted the verandah. They pooled in the corners, a reminder that while he'd seen tears in the eyes of many, he'd not seen Viola cry for her mother. Not once.

"And you trusted her?"

Shadrach pulled Silas from his thoughts.

"Who?"

"Viola. You trusted her to dig with you for this," he examined the astrolabe, "and you didn't tell *me*?"

"I thought you'd say it was yours, technically, and that I should push off before you turned that gun on me."

"I may have." Shadrach shook his head in amazement. "I knew

you two were up to something. Whispering on the stairs. Guilty faces. But then you put out a fire that could have taken down my entire barn. That's not the heart of a thief." Shadrach handed it back.

At their feet, Molly played with the finished birdhouse. Finella had twisted a ball of yarn into a family of birds, and Molly flew the trio in and out.

"If only her mother hadn't warned me to keep my wife a secret. If I had only told her from the start—"

"She may have pushed you away."

"She's done it anyway. When I promised Mrs. Buckley I'd be here for her when Viola needed a friend."

"Friends she has aplenty."

Female voices rang from the kitchen, and Molly skittered her birds from her father's right shoe to his left. "Cheep, cheep."

"Have you seen her cry?"

Shadrach frowned. "Can't say I have. She may, behind closed doors."

"Eyes puff up and stay red for hours, even when the crying's done in private. My guess is she's holding on, like the little girl who stood on a stage and swallowed all her tears thinking it made her strong."

"And you think she should cry?"

"I should be able to ask her how she is and draw out of her anything she wants to tell me. If she needs to cry, then she should do that, too."

Silas stood. He needed to pace. But people and furniture cluttered the verandah, along with a life-size birdcage and miniature driftwood birdhouse. He needed a wide beach. A brisk wind. And Viola, on their driftwood log.

"Maybe you could speak on my behalf, Shad. Please?"

"What would I say?"

"That it's her mother's request, made to me the day we met, that I should speak to her now."

The sound of something tumbling down the stairs clattered and thumped. Silas turned and found the front door open. When they both checked the verandah, Molly and her birds were nowhere to be found.

"Molly!" Shadrach hobbled over the wooden birdhouse.

But Silas was ahead of him and reached her first, at the bottom of the stairs, where she lay flat on her back, wide eyed and gasping for breath.

"She's winded." Silas pulled her into his lap. "Breathe through your mouth, little missy. Nice and slow..."

She did as she was told, but her eyes remained wide and fixed on her father.

"She must have fallen from the stairs. Did you Molly?"

Her shoulders rose and fell. And then a little nod, with shallow breaths and a sob that caught before it could fly.

"Miss Buck-a-ly," she whimpered, and scrambled into her father's arms. "Birdy."

Finella hurried into the drawing room, spied the scene, and slid to a complete stop.

"What happened?" She stroked the sweaty brow of her child. "Another fall?"

"Tumbled down the stairs. Probably looking for Viola." Shadrach rubbed Molly's back. "Silas helped her catch her breath."

Viola and Madame Nasrin stepped out of the kitchen, too.

"Molly, my darling." Viola patted the little girl's arm.

Finella extracted the child from her father, her eye on Shadrach, and silent words of thankfulness exchanged between them.

"Viola." Silas joined them. Perhaps with near misses and gallant saves, now was a good time to reach for her, too. "May I have a word, please?"

Fitted in somber mourning clothes, she turned to him. Her cheeks wore the peppery-red of someone who'd bent over a washtub all morning. A mishmash of hues. Shadows and flames.

"We're... in the middle of cooking..."

Nasrin pressed her hand into the small of Viola's back, and Silas could not tell if the older woman pushed Viola to him or ushered her away. But he caught the frustration in Viola's eyes and her slight indecision before she made her way back into the kitchen. He folded his arms and let the closing door shut him out once more.

Viola sagged into the kitchen chair. Before them, on the table, beside a pot of mint and cardamom tea, a large mound of seasoned meat awaited the meal preparation Nasrin had offered to make.

Black sleeves folded up, she rolled spiced venison into pea-sized balls for an Anatolian dish she declared Storyteller Soup.

"This soup takes no time to cook but hours to prepare. When so much meat must be rolled this way, we must also find something to talk about. And so, we make stories to pass the time. In days gone by, the village storyteller would come to this soup-making with new tales so young girls did not stir from their tasks."

Grateful for the thought Nasrin put into all she did, Viola smiled at her friend. The preparation of today's food was an easy place to hide, when the questions about her future loomed like a storm in the wind.

Now that Nasrin had come to collect her, she could leave, as early as tomorrow, if she wished. Viola pinched a small piece of meat and rolled it in her palm. The aromas of crushed cumin seeds, parsley, and onion warmed against her skin, and tears pricked her nose.

The onions were not to blame. It was the way Silas had refused to look away from her just now. How many days had passed since the fire? Five? Six? He too would leave in the next day or so.

"Do you have a story for us, Nasrin?"

"Not an old one, but perhaps you are ready for something new? Is it time to come and live with me, Poupette?"

"The theater is not my home, dearest." Viola rested her head on her friend's shoulder. "I know your offer is genuine. I need to secure employment and somewhere to spread my work and complete my portfolio. I can't do that in your theater. There's no room."

"Could you apply for a teaching job in a school?" Finella asked.

"I could, after I obtain a teaching certificate." She thought of the teaching position Silas had shared with her. "Clemmie and I secured our students on the back of her fame. And our lower fees. Now…"

Now there was only Viola herself. And what was she worth? Freddy Barnes would have said she was *perfectly good mother material,* squandering her days on dreams and fancies she'd never chase down. She pushed thoughts of him and Jasper away.

It was confounding enough to fathom life in a theater. It would be like living with the specter of Marshall, but what about life in the shadow of *Sweet Clementine?*

She pressed another glob of meat between her palms.

"Although…." An idea formed. "All our possessions are in the attic at the Star and Garter. And Mr. Barnes is in the business of collecting goods that carry the Buckley name. Why not me, as a boarder?"

"And how would you pay for your room?" Nasrin studied her.

In her mind, Viola saw the tavern. Derry's flour-covered table and Cloda's sweet treats. Jasper would be all smiles, and she would have to deal with his misplaced affections, but that was not the only thing misplaced within the Star and Garter.

"I shall offer to work with Derry and Cloda. They're often troubled by some of the heavier jobs."

"And Mr. Swift?" Finella's words threw a rock into her thinking. "Is he that easy to discard?" She exchanged a look with Nasrin, as if they'd been waiting to broach the subject all day.

"Discard is a harsh word, and I could no more discard Silas than I could discard my heart. But I don't know how to…" *Stand in second place.*

Viola remembered the way he'd looked at her. Full of pleading, reaching for her. Tender enough to turn any girl's head. Until a girl's next thought became, *Is this how he looked at Honora when he courted her?*

Had Honora run into his arms, full of bright hope for their future? Had he pressed his forehead to Honora's, the way he'd done with her?

She shook her head. "I will never replace another woman in the affections of her husband. Never." She added another tiny meatball, like a full stop, to the pan where hundreds more awaited the fragrant soup broth.

"Perhaps you are discovering the road to love requires work. As does art." Nasrin scraped more minced meat into her hands. "What have you truly ever aspired to that did not demand some kind of sacrifice?"

Viola wiped her hands on a wet cloth. "To willfully walk into what is left of another person's life is not sacrifice, Nasrin. You, of all people, know what that looks like. Why would I choose that slow poison for myself again?"

Nasrin shrugged. "Only you can say, Poupette. All I have to add is that I see a man desperate to make his case. And you must be bold enough to listen, if he has served you and your mother, as you say he has."

"I won't wear the wig of another," Viola whispered, knowing Nasrin would not press her for more. She leaned her elbows on the table with renewed determination. She had been diverted, but not derailed.

"I shall write to Mr. Barnes today for scullery work and lodgings."

Weighed down by Molly, Finella lowered herself into the chair Silas preferred. "What if you're wrong? You think you know how you would like to be loved and already judge a man for his inability without affording him the chance to prove himself."

Silently, the rocking of mother and child pushed to and fro in Viola's mind.

I have misjudged you.

She'd done it once and had been moved enough to admit it. But this…

She looked from Finella to Nasrin, and then away from their gentle persuasions. To be loved as the first in someone's heart was no cheap desire. She knew what she had to do.

"Long ago, I was someone's second chance, and he walked away when I failed him. I won't watch another man wish I was *'like her'* ever again."

May 25, 1879

Finella remin•s me that writing here is the sifting of murky streams that overbur•en the min•. She insists that not all catastrophes appear so, when committe• to the page.

So I let my thoughts tumble aroun• me, as fast as my han• can write them.

Courageous wor•s, penne• to•ay in a letter to Mr. Barnes

requesting lodging in his attic. I know he won't deny me this on account of all he's gained from Sweet Clementine.

I have slipped all my sketches between the sturdy covers of my satchel. My brushes are washed and dried. My collection of botanicals pressed between the vellum pages of scrapbooks I brought here naked.

I return to Melbourne with dried rosehips, gum nuts, shells, and driftwood. A small pot of sand and dried, brittle seaweed. Ideas. Inspiration. A book outline. Dreams that have shimmered on far horizons now captured in vibrant strokes.

I leave richer than when I arrived.

But oh so poorer.

I know Silas packs his bags, too. Tomorrow, he leaves.

He has spent much of his time rebuilding the menagerie. Then he sharpened all of Shadrach's tools and hung the pretty birdhouse on one of the mulberry trees.

Finella steps between me and Silas.

"I have known the impulse to flee the man who snuck into my heart," *she says.* "Because I thought it was the only way. I was wrong. And I pay for that mistake every day. Please, don't be wrong, Viola. Not if there's another way."

She has pressed a letter from Silas into my hands. She says if I can leave it unopened, I should walk away and never look back.

But if I open it, if I tear off the tiniest scrap, I am obligated to do what it asks. The clock ticks. The bags are corded. The lamps are lit, and under the cover of night, I dare let him in one more time.

Dearest Viola,

You are in my every thought. In every affection.

If I occupy even the smallest corner of either your heart

or mind, please allow me one more hour of your time. At our log on the beach at first light tomorrow.

Affectionately,
Silas

24

One week after the fire tore through Portland in 1873, Silas had picked through the ruins with his mother. In their temporary lodging rooms, Mary cared for Eugene and Patrick, not yet twenty, who drowned under summer colds.

Silas wrestled with a cold too, but he had become the provider now. There was no time to wallow abed. The unexpected burial of their father had slowed down the recovery of the Swift family business, but this day, it would rise again.

Thanks to his mother's quick thinking, and Honora Ackerman's tear-stained smile, Silas had been thrown into a match everyone thought "*for the best, all things considered.*"

They'd married two weeks later, he, unsure of himself and knowing precious little about his bride other than she had skipped rope better than Mary when they were children.

"She's still a child," he'd told his mother. *"She should go to an aunt or grandparent."*

"There's no one to take her in, and she's not a child. At eighteen I was already mother to you."

Minnie Swift had mourned the sudden death of her husband the only way she knew how. By counting what was left and putting it to work. And she coaxed Silas to do the same.

"Affection will come later. I'll ask you how you feel about her when she's given you a son or two, and you'll marvel at the love that will have taken root by then."

Silas knew now that children were not the root of love between a man and wife. They were the product and the reward, but not the root.

Honora's dowry had bolstered them financially, but every plank that went up in the construction of their new dwelling felt like another barrier between them. She had watched them cart away her old home. Barrows of glass, twisted timbers and ash, replaced by the scaffold upon which they would expand Swift Brothers, Fine Furniture Makers. None of Honora Ackerman remained. And even when he tried to find her with the tenderness she needed, she sank further into her loneliness.

And no one, not even Mary, saw the melancholy take hold until it slept between Silas and his bride like a boulder in their bed.

She ached for her lost family. And she ran into the mist that came with her illness for comfort. At first, no appetite. Then the purging. And no matter how many times God allowed a new life to form in her belly, the child never appeared to glue them together as Minnie Swift had promised.

No, it was not children that rooted a man in love.

It was more.

Silas walked along the Ventnor beach where the sun caught hold of the day and dragged it up into a granite-blue sky, heavy with clouds more suited to the rain-soaked heavens above Yamhill Street, Portland, than this Australian beach.

He loved Viola. He let that sink over him. He loved and admired her, something he'd told himself he would never attempt with any woman. Ever again. No matter what.

He searched for her over the empty beach where gulls cawed and flew high. What if she did not want to hear what he had to say? No, her curiosity was a powerful force.

From his pocket he pulled a thin-edged chisel and dug the tool into the log, the way he wished he could wind himself into her heart.

A spot of rain fell from the sky and landed on the sun-bleached log. Then another, and another. Rain clouds pooled together.

He peered along the bush track. Nothing.

The wind picked up a fine layer of sand and scoured the beach. A drop of rain landed on his cheek. Then, laden and moving fast, heavy clouds let down a full-blown shower. He could only stand here so long, in his travel clothes, before becoming wet through.

Come on, Viola. He ran his fingers through his hair. A bent gum tree offered some shelter, so he crouched under its low branches. Rain beaded on his coat sleeve, and the frustration that pooled in his chest overflowed and sank into the deepest part of him where he felt it the worst.

The bruising a man fought to ignore when he called, and she did not reply.

In the courtyard, Shadrach's horse and wagon waited patiently amid the rain. A slick tarp covered his traveling bags.

"About time." Shadrach crossed the barn floor. "Day's run away from us, so we'd best leave now if you want to make that schooner."

They were all in here. Finella, Molly, Madame Nasrin, and Viola.

Silas stared at her, and the pink in her cheeks deepened. Her hair, like his, was slick with rain. But heat crackled and charged between them.

He wanted her to argue with Shadrach. To beg him for a few more minutes. To put herself between all else and claw her way to him. But she stood there, dripping into her shoes. And the rain continued to pelt the barn roof.

Finella was the first to say goodbye. Like a good hostess, she said all the right things, but the crease in her forehead told him she knew this was not the way to depart.

Madame Nasrin offered her best wishes for his journey home and thanks for the kindness shown Mrs. Buckley.

Viola stood still.

His chest threatened to cave in, and Shadrach called him from where he waited in the rain as if they were only heading out for a morning drive instead of forever.

Finella ushered Madame Nasrin and Molly out of the rain and onto the verandah, where they huddled and waited for Viola. An occupation he knew well.

"I waited for you," he said.

"I was on my way, but Molly vanished and Finella was frantic, so I ran outside to look for her."

He nodded. "You did the right thing."

"Swift!" Shadrach yelled into the pounding rain.

Silas ached to bring her close. He rummaged through everything he wanted to tell her on the beach. It weighed a ton, and he hardly knew where to pick it up.

"I need you to know that I thought of you first thing when I woke up, every day." He breathed hard. "I stared at that ceiling and knew an entire sky and sea and every starry dream would come between us. I told myself not to fall, that it would do neither of us any good. But I fell anyway. Hard." He swallowed the panic that strangled his words. "And I will still be thinking of you last thing before I fall asleep, knowing you're angry at me for keeping my widowhood from you."

"Silas!" Shadrach roared.

"Silas," Viola whispered. Her breath came in gasps. Other than his name, she had little else. He didn't care. Today's words had to come from him.

"I wanted our affections to have no other influence. No debris from the past for you to have to hold."

Tears pooled in her eyes, and her shoulders trembled. "If I'd known from the start about Honora, I would have had the choice to protect my heart."

"From me?"

"I don't know…" She ran her fingers through her wet hair. "I don't know how to be loved in the hollow left by someone else."

"I would never love you like that!"

"You would not mean to, but you would."

"I'm not your mother or your father."

"Your affections are as genuine as mine. Of that I have no doubt. But it's not enough, and I have nothing in me to fight the memory of a dead wife. And before you say more, I know from bitter experience, she would always live between us."

He caught her by the arm. It was a gentle hold, barely there, but it was still a hold.

"*Not enough*? Isn't that everything you've fought against your whole life? You were *not enough* for Marshall and now you tar me with the same brush?"

She stared at him in recognition of the awful truth. Her chest rose and fell, lips pressed tight, eyes wet with unshed tears, and her heart, if anything like his, was battered and exhausted.

They faced each other in the gutter of defeat. Both of them, the loser. Both of them, lost. In the shadow of the house where her mother had died, Silas saw some of the fatigue that Clemmie had left her daughter. The legacy of melancholy he did not want this wild creature to embrace.

He'd made a promise, and if nothing else, he would keep his word.

He would not leave her in the puddle where he'd found her.

"There's a bright future ahead of you. Beautiful and of your making. I have seen it strung like stars, and I know it's good. More than anyone, I want your success. And you'd better do everything in your power to make that exhibition entry what it needs to be." With a gentle caress, before he lost his nerve or she pulled away, he brought that sugar-wrist to his lips, kissed it, and stepped back into the rain.

Each step tore into him with all he'd left out. Because there was more. And having started, he would leave nothing unsaid.

He stopped mid-stride. He had nothing to lose now. Further away, Shadrach hunkered under an oilcloth on his wagon seat. On the verandah, the others waited, obscured by misty sheets that soaked the courtyard.

When he turned, she was still at the barn door. He would have to shout, but he'd already won her attention, because she'd either stepped face first into the rain or she was crying.

"From the very first moment you fell into my world, it was never about who *you thought* you were or might be." He blinked hard. "You occupy a place in my heart because only you knew how to carve it out. Only you."

On the verandah, Finella ran a towel over Viola's hair.

"I won't condemn you, dear Viola. You know what your heart can endure. There's enough to weather in the loss of your mother. More than enough." She scrubbed, a little harder than Viola cared for. "But the man sure did pour his heart out."

Indeed, he had. Viola blinked tears away. Now that they'd fallen, they refused to abate.

"Watching him drive away like that, felt like," she swallowed, "another coffin being lowered in the ground." A soft hiccup accompanied her crying. And the flow of tears, the way they knocked and lashed their way out of her, fast eroded whatever remained of her endurance.

"He held me together," she whispered into her clenched hands. "I wanted to think it was all me, my strength, my ability to face another loss and stare it in the eyes. But this..."

She cried some more. Not only for the man she'd let walk away, but for the sentiment in his farewell and his heart, wide enough to understand she would never be the right one for him. How that hurt. More than all the other losses piled together.

And she continued to cry, because in crying, she beat the invisible layers down. Marshall was a distant, bitter memory. Clemmie, Balthazar... They had both fled their cages, too.

And now, Silas. Gone. She buckled at the waist and succumbed to the sobbing.

Finella hung the towel on the verandah rail, and Nasrin untangled the fringe of the suzani shawl.

"I hear another wagon." Finella pointed to the driveway. "Someone's coming down the road."

"Coming back?" Viola stood.

"No, but someone else is making a trip into Cowes." Finella looked at Nasrin. And Nasrin, always the mistress of the wardrobe, shook the shawl and ushered Viola down the steps.

"You wave that wagon down." She draped the suzani, still damp, over Viola's shoulders. "That was no way to farewell a man whom you love on a journey of weeks over deep seas. You send him off with your best wishes and give him a reason to find his way back."

"But Nasrin—"

"Have I ever defrauded you of my love? Have I not shown you my best affection, trust, and confidence? And did I not know your sister and adore her in her own right? Do I not stand here as proof that I knew you both and loved you as you deserved?"

"That is not the love of a man and woman," Viola argued. "You love me like a mother."

"Because you allowed me to replace Clemmie when you needed me. And you did not love either of us less for the love of the other."

Viola's heart screamed with the puzzlement. Years of reckoning that refused to twist straight.

"At the very least, you owe him a decent farewell. And if you don't run onto the road this very second, your only chance will disappear into the bush. Now go."

Viola looked to Finella, who nodded. "Run!" She pointed to the road.

And so, Viola ran. Mud collected on the hem of skirt, and her chest emptied fast of any proper breath. Nasrin and Finella were right. She had offered Silas a weak farewell. She, of all people, who prided herself on only the best and who demanded that from those around her.

On the pier, a small group huddled close to the gangway near a moored vessel. Viola had not been here since the day she'd arrived with Clemmie and Balthazar. Under a sunless sky, she searched, the wind blustering and blowing right through her. And there, beside Shadrach, she spotted him.

"Silas!" she called, and he turned, bemused, then delighted.

"How did you get here?"

"I hitched a ride."

"Have you come to run away with me?" Teasing puckered his sad smile.

"I've come to say a proper goodbye. You deserve better than what I managed in the barn."

Tears, she discovered, got in the way, but she carried on, the way Clemmie would have wanted her to. On this stage, this wooden pier, atop fast currents that pulled them apart.

Viola Buckley summoned her best voice, posture, diction, and after blinking hard, her focus.

"I didn't thank you for all you brought into Clemmie's last dark days. Your presence filled her room with something she adored."

He closed his eyes and nodded.

"And I didn't thank you for letting me share in your astrolabe hunt. We had fun, didn't we?"

"We had fun."

"And I didn't thank you for being my eyes, when I needed them."

When I needed you. Like now. Because now, crying was all she had. She brushed her tears away, but it did nothing for the pain that blinded her from the inside.

The schooner whistle blew.

"And I have a parting gift." She bundled her shawl into a sodden mess. "In case you ever need bandaging."

He took it without properly looking at it. For his tear-filled eyes were on her lips.

"You can't give me this." His voice cracked.

"How else will you carry me close?"

With the shawl between them, he pulled her in and kissed her in answer to her question, the way she imagined all kisses felt when they were to be the last. Urgent and greedy and way too short. He cradled her face between both hands.

"You're infuriatingly willful. And headstrong, and way too driven for me to ask you to change any of that. But when you've conquered the world of botanicals and have found the Viola who has already won first place in my heart, you come find me, too."

He gathered his traveling trunks and bags and held her shawl to his chest, all the way across the gangplank onto the boat and into the deep divide that would carry him away. He raised his hand in farewell, and only when the boat pulled away did Silas call to her one last time.

"My parting gift to you is on the beach."

25

Saltwater Creek overflowed, so she stripped off her shoes and stockings and let the icy waters rush over her naked feet. The cleansing power of nature in full force. The medicine of this island. Saltwater and fresh air. She wriggled her freezing toes, and the sand shifted beneath her, just a little. Enough to let her know she could not afford to stand still. She stepped onto the hard sand on the other side. Someday, their log would be swallowed by sand, too.

But more than the wooden seat they'd shared, it now bore …

Her name?

Recognition ran through her blood like quicksilver. She knelt on the sand. Were her eyes mocking her? She ran her fingers over an arabesque design. Flowers and leaves and scrolls wrapped around *ViolaViolaViola.*

His parting gift was a piece of art. No small trinket. An intricate carving. Had he longed to show her the way she'd shown him her book idea? She pressed her cheek to it and let the tears flow. She could not walk away from this love letter. But how could she take it home? She ran both hands over the grooves. This was him. And it was her. In one piece.

"This is some mean trickery, Silas. You hear me?" she called over the waters. "You can't leave this here and not expect me to take it for my own. That's not fair." Her fingers fell back into his design, a replica of what he'd started on the sand.

A slow shiver ran over her.

A replica.

She could lay down a thin paper sheet, rub charcoal over it, and transfer it to her page.

She waited for the revulsion to rise. Oh, how she detested making copies. But revulsion did not come, and a tiny wave of gladness pressed into her smile.

"A portrait and now this." She shook her head. "No man has ever made me break my own rules. Not once. Now twice."

She ran back along the beach, leaving footprints behind her like place makers, dodging seaweed blown into drifts, all the way back to her belongings already tucked deep into cases and trunks. She dug and found what she needed.

Tissue papers and a stick of charcoal.

Back at the beach, she used two flat rocks to secure the paper and, with the greatest of care, rubbed charcoal over his work until it appeared before her eyes.

Not the original, but just as precious.

When done, she held the paper to the wind. Like a white flag in surrender. Then she rolled the replica up for safekeeping, for she knew the sea and the sand would conspire to bury the original for good.

Viola's last morning on Phillip Island dawned a little brighter than the day Silas had left. The sun swept over the well-watered orchard where apple trees spread their leafless limbs and sank into their season of rest.

Viola leaned on the windowsill of Clemmie's room and rubbed the arch of her back, as if the burden of leaving were right there. But it was not. Leaving was no burden. Not with Silas already gone. The guest rooms already echoed with abandonment.

Downstairs, Nasrin taught Molly a French tune. Later, Finella would run her brooms and dusting rags and furniture polish up here, and her family would settle into winter, a huddle of three, until fresh guests arrived for their summer holidays.

One last time, Viola peered into the courtyard. Shadrach had strapped her belongings to the wagon and now stood in the menagerie doorway, his arm around Finella. Together, they examined the new roof.

Viola turned away from the intimate gesture before she needed to add envy to the worm of loneliness that sat in her heart like a newfound tenant. She'd left making amends over the menagerie to last.

On the landing, where Balthazar had annoyed them all, she took another big gulp, grateful for the space where she'd strung up her dreams like all the trinkets and fancies on the back of a peddler's cart.

I want to die in a room by the sea.

And hadn't this house fulfilled Clemmie's wishes?

She smiled at Nasrin and Molly on her way out. "One last errand."

Fashioned in the same wattle and daub style, this time the menagerie had been rebuilt with two windows instead of one. The dirt floor had been raked clean, the fireplace scrubbed, and fresh shingles covered everything like a new hat.

"It's not the same, is it?" Viola ran her hand along the new door.

"It's better," Shadrach said. "I can slam this door and it will actually latch shut."

"But, the memories…"

"Are untouched," Finella replied. "I am sad we lost the table more than anything. It was the perfect place to make damper, and," she smiled, "I will still raise silkworms here, in the spring."

"Thank you." Few words matched Finella's grace. "I'm glad you're both here. I want to fulfill my payment and anything owing. And I have this gift. It's a sampler of everything I have loved most about this island."

She presented them with a parcel and took great delight in watching Finella tear it open.

"Oh. A beautiful painting."

A vine covered skiff against a dune, with wisps of blue sea. And up on a hill stood a pretty white house. Finella and Shadrach admired it together. "It's a treasure. To be cherished. Thank you."

"It is you I must thank. Without your help I could not have followed Dr. Murdoch's instructions. We threw your home into disarray and our stay here cost you more than you bargained for. Here, especially." She looked into the rawness of the wood around her. "As promised, I want to pay for the menagerie repair."

Shadrach exchanged a look with Finella.

"Silas took care of it all."

"But I saw others working here."

"The Callahan lads from the farm next door. Silas paid their wages. There was no talking him out of it. Said it was his to do."

Viola reached for the ends of her shawl and felt the emptiness in her fingers. She wore a traveling jacket now, one of her mother's, but it did not comfort her like the silky fringe of the suzani.

"I've not met anyone as generous as Silas. He… continues to give and give…"

"He would have loved you, Viola, if you'd let him. Don't let yourself think otherwise." Finella's words cut to the core of Viola's heartache.

"He would have, I know. Along with all that's swept up by the undercurrent of our lives. And that's no way to live. I don't want that for him, or me."

Shadrach pulled a paper from his pocket. "His Portland address."

Viola knotted her fingers behind her back.

"He said leaving it with us would save him the ache of watching you agonize over taking it or not." He slipped it onto the menagerie shelf.

"We'll let you decide without an audience," Finella said. And they left her in the solitude of this tiny room of memories that would forever hold their deepest, most indelible, beautiful scars.

Viola stared at the shelf. Silas had not only left her a piece of art.

He'd left her an open door.

June 1, 1879

Nasrin makes me a cosy be• in her war•robe room.

It's not forever. It is a place to breathe, as it always has been.

She has forgiven me for giving away the suzani. She looke• me in the eye for the longest time.

"Did he deserve such a gift?"

"The shawl and everything that should have accompanied it," *I replie•.*

Ma•ame Nasrin is one who can see through artifice better than anyone. She can spin a costume out of nothing an• turn the poorest man into an emperor with a paper crown. She tucks me into her nest. Whispers a prayer into my ear an• calls me Poupette.

She watches to see if my heart will yiel• or if it will restore. I watch with her. For I •o not know where to put my affections for

Silas. They were as much a part of me as my shawl.

Now the col• seeps in. I have much work ahea• of me, an• that cannot happen in this theater. When the lights •im, I know nightmares will pro• me with cruel jabs. Marshall an• his rage. His angry re• face, furious at my mother for somehow not creating a performer in me when perhaps the missing element was Mortimer Barnes. A man of talent, whereas my father was a man of vain ambition.

An• am I not also his •aughter?

Ambitious. Wanting to win, wanting to prove myself to whatever sha•ow is left of him.

I watch the flame flicker in the can•le Nasrin has left for me an• think of Silas. I think of him returning home to where he will lie at night an• look at the ceiling of another room.

Does he still sleep in the same be• he share• with Honora? I write that here, an• the scal•ing races to my very fingertips. How easy for whoever came first to pop from memory or imagination.

In my min•, she is a beauty. Fair haire•, like the First Viola. Elegant an• poise•. Will Silas return to his home an• look for her sha•ow?

Oh, be gone from me, Honora. Rest in peace.

An• I shall search for my own.

26

Already she missed the easy slip her shoes made on Ventnor beach. Urgent or ambling, her walks always delivered deep, bolstering draughts of sea air.

Now, Viola's heels clattered along the cobbled Melbourne streets. Dressed once more in her mother's walking jacket and wrapped at the neck in Clemmie's violet scarf, Viola let the urgency push her on. Better to face the consequences than stew for hours over what awaited her.

She'd learned that lesson before she knew how to read. How to throw her gaze upward, blinking at the opera boxes, tilting her head backwards, sending her tears where they would not enrage Marshall. Hidden from him and denied by her, crying became a secret luxury, then a forgotten response. If she could not cry when she needed to, why bother later?

It was this strength which pulled her up and into the life she and Clemmie lived together. But letting her tears flow on Phillip Island had let some of her real self out, too.

She stood at the corner of Leopold and Domain Roads, where Mortimer Barnes had been killed, and peered up at the three small attic windows of the Star and Garter.

"You can do this," she exhaled. "Yes, you can."

Derry and Cloda sat in the same chairs they always occupied, sipping strong tea and letting morning creep upon them. But the sight of her sent them into full flight.

"Viola!" Cloda pulled her into a thick embrace. Viola laughed and dropped her things onto the floor at their feet.

"Let me look at you." Cloda pulled her away and examined her face, her hair, and looked deep into her eyes. "Mr. Barnes told us about your mother. We're awful sorry for your loss."

"Thank you."

"Come, sit here." Derry pulled out a chair for her. "Are you really moving into the attic?"

"Seems so." She smiled into their well-creased faces. How she'd missed them.

Cloda poured her a cup of tea, and Derry pushed a plate of shortcakes at her. "Have you eaten?"

"I have, but who cooks better than my dearest Irishman?" She tore into a piece of currant cake, cooked with bacon lard and smothered in butter. "So good." She spoke through a mouthful and grinned at them. Nothing had changed in here. Heat from the stove and genuine care from these two souls never failed to boost her spirits.

"Was it awful?" Cloda ran right into the heart of what Viola had brought to their kitchen.

"It's what Clemmie wanted. To die in a house by the sea, and… it was awful." Viola exhaled from the weariest hollow. "Rest Therapy depletes everyone. I think it hastened her death."

"I'm mighty grieved you had to endure that all by yourself. But you're back with us now, and we'll fatten you up in no time. You're thinner than a sycamore twig."

Before she could reply, the door flew open.

"Viola!" Jasper bounded in. His hug rivaled Cloda's. "Finally. I can't believe you're here. I'm so *glad* you're here. And…" His grip lessened, but his intensity fired into something deeper. "Your mother. I'm so sorry."

"Thank you." Her throat thickened with emotion. Along with Nasrin, these people were now her closest family. A mishmash of humanity, not the blood relatives that had shunned her mother for marrying a theater man.

Jasper drank her in, and she elbowed him away with a playful poke. So he leaned on the table and drank her in from there.

"You didn't write to me."

"My days were full with Clemmie and…"

"I know. But I thought, perhaps—"

"I brought you a gift." From one of her bags, she produced two small boxes folded out of stiff cardboard and lined with tissue paper. Along the bottom, she'd sprinkled a layer of sand, and atop that, a sampler of seashells. One box for Jasper, the other for Cloda and Derry. She'd also painted a tiny beach vista of sea grass, sand dune, and rock pool blues onto a small tag with the words, *Greetings from Phillip Island.*

"Oh, what a treasure." Cloda showed Derry, and Jasper grinned so hard it pained her. That fondness she could never reciprocate. Not when he'd first declared it, and certainly not now. Especially now that Silas had sailed away and taken all her endearments with him.

"Did you look after *Sweet Clementine* for me?"

"If you mean did I climb the stairs backwards and nearly kill myself dusting, no. But she's still there. Want to see?"

"Soon." Viola did not want to look up into those bright eyes for the first time since she'd lost Clemmie with Jasper looking on.

But all three of them stared at *her*. Jasper in wide open glares.

Derry and Cloda in more polite appraisal. Perhaps they measured her for change. Could they see her longing for Silas that tightened inside her?

"Viola Buckley, my dear girl." Mr. Barnes joined them and clasped her hand between his palms. "My condolences." True sadness spilled from his eyes. "Cloda has freshened up the attic room, and we want you well rested before you begin working. Tomorrow, next day. No matter."

"I'm most grateful, to all of you. In the end, Clemmie chose where she died. And all thanks to you, Mr. Barnes, for buying the piano that paid for our time on Phillip Island."

He nodded, mouth pinched tight.

"We're all still here for you," Jasper added.

"Oh, and there's one more of us for you to meet later. Little Tess, my niece, our new scullery maid, and she's learning fast." Cloda poured herself another cup of tea. "Her smarts are from my side of the family."

"Scullery maid?" Viola appealed to Mr. Barnes. If he'd taken her in for pity's sake, she'd be so mad. "Is there enough work for two of us?"

"There's plenty of scullery maid work for one. And Tess is the right girl for that. You, my dear, will eventually work the taproom. That job pays more than scullery maid." He pointed to her as if she'd won a prize.

"Taproom? Pouring beer?"

"Collecting tankards and glasses to begin with. And delivering plates of food. I'd be wasting you at a scullery sink. Your spirited nature and quick wit are not to be squandered."

"You want to parade me in the tap room for your—"

"*Parade* is harsh—"

"You would have me stand," she tried again, while cold misgivings multiplied around her, "in the same room as my mother's painting and listen to the lewd remarks made by men who come to gawk at her each night?"

He had the grace to look a little embarrassed. He brushed at his lip with the back of his hand. "I don't need another scullery maid. Tess came to us weeks before your letter arrived. I need someone to work with me and Jasper during our busiest serving hours. The job and attic room come as one. Decide if you want them."

Cloda and Derry examined the tabletop as if it held all the secrets they'd never bothered to look for in all the days they'd worked there. And Jasper's cheeks ripened into beet-red spots.

"Take it as a compliment." Mr. Barnes slid a small chuckle into his voice. "Your mother is admired by many. If you should hear the idle chatter of men who forget there's a lady in their midst, it's easily forgiven."

"How?" She stared at him, lost in the horrors of being looked over by men. "How does one forgive the idle chatter of men, Mr. Barnes?"

"You just do. You tie on your apron and do the job."

Visions of Marshall stormed her senses. *"Just put it on!"* he whispered into her wig.

She could leave now. Take her things back to the Odeon Theater and sleep there, but she'd earn nothing.

Cloda rose and brought a basket of onions to the table. She picked up a knife and proceeded to make a pile of peeled, pungent slices. Derry pushed his tea away and hobbled outside, muttering something about the woodpile.

"This time next week you'll be so used to it you'll wonder why you made any fuss at all." Mr. Barnes left them too, and only Jasper remained at her side.

He offered a quarter smile. "Come on, let me take you up. I'll be there to make sure it all goes well. We'll be working together. We'll make a game of it."

A game? Viola wanted to cry. Serving men who looked up at her mother's near nakedness was no game. Making Silas smile was a game.

"Let me play." She wanted what she'd had on Phillip Island. The power to make her own decisions. To negotiate. To make a fair exchange.

What would Silas have done in her predicament? She'd roped him into a job once, too. He'd played along with good humor because there was something he wanted more. His astrolabe.

She dug deep and found a smile. Some of it was real. "You're right, Jasper. I will do my very best. Let's have a look at the attic. Nasrin will be along soon with the rest of my things."

He collected her bags while her throat collected all the bitterness she could not swallow. Her bones ached and her head throbbed. They took the narrow stairs to the landing outside the room they used as an office.

Sweet Clementine smiled, as always. Viola looked up through the fresh awareness of what that painting showed. What only Mortimer had seen. Now she knew, too.

"I screwed one of the beds together. Cloda made it up for you." Jasper set her bags down. "Most of your belongings are in that corner, under dust covers, but we thought you'd like a sitting arrangement too, so we made this."

He swept his hand over an armchair and cheval mirror, atop one of their well-worn carpet pieces. She tried not to think of Jasper rummaging through her things.

"Thank you." She dropped her satchel onto the chair. "I wonder where I might find our old kitchen table."

"Why would you need that? You'll be taking your meals in our dining room, with me and Father."

"Because," she rummaged in the corner, "we can slide it under that window so I have somewhere to spread my artwork. Oh, here." Crates that contained their odd mix of kitchenware covered the tabletop. She passed him a box of cutlery. He held it like a crock of rotting sardines.

"What's the matter?" She grabbed the next box and found a spot for it on the floor.

"I didn't think you'd be throwing yourself into art before you unpacked." He sounded like a petulant child, and his bottom lip drooped.

"I am arranging this space so I can work on my submission that you have known about for months. Don't go making that face."

"I was hoping you may have reassessed your priorities."

Together they moved the table. He was still her friend, and she hated this big lump of misery between them.

"Look." She rummaged in her valise and pulled out the string she'd used in the guesthouse. "See this ball of twine?" She handed him a tack and the end of the string. "Secure it to the top of the doorframe and I will do the same over here." She unraveled the ball until she reached one of the attic windows.

Her mind let in the image of Silas peeking at her from behind the string line.

"For your washing?"

"No." She laughed. "My sketches and the outline. Jasper, are you listening? I'm—"

"We took the door off the frame," he blurted out.

"Pardon?"

"The door. To bring in your things. This table you so desperately need would not clear the doorway until we unscrewed the hinges and removed the door. I told myself it was all worth it because it meant you'd come back. That you'd miss me."

"I did miss you."

"Not how I needed you to."

"No." She took the lead he offered. "I missed you the way I missed Nasrin. The way one misses—"

"A friend. I know."

"And as my friend, you're the first to see," she pulled open her satchel, "the grand plan for my exhibition entry. A book idea. From Sea to Shore. All the beauty that surrounded us on Phillip Island." She rummaged through the sheets and laid some on the newly arranged table.

"I'm sure it's beautiful."

"You haven't even looked."

"I don't want to look, Viola. I've waited all this time for you, not your botanicals."

"I am my botanicals," she spoke softly.

"Not forever. Once that exhibition is no longer your only thought, you'll have to find *someone*. And you might not be so blind then."

He stormed down the stairs, so seared and gravelly that he rattled clear to the ground floor like a spilled sack of stones.

"Ah, Jasper. There you are. Help Madame Nasrin carry this trunk to the attic, would you?" Mr. Barnes ordered him back up, and Viola ached for her friend. He did not wear sorrow well. With much bumping and heaving, her trunk arrived between a frowning Jasper and bemused Nasrin.

He nodded a sour goodbye.

"Now there's a foul mood," Nasrin said.

"He's angry at me for not abandoning my painting to become a wife."

"Poor Jasper."

Viola shook her head. "I don't know how to help him."

"Living under this roof won't help." Nasrin surveyed Viola's new living arrangement. "But it's roomier than I imagined."

"And I am to wait tables with Jasper and Mr. Barnes."

Nasrin winced. "No scullery maid work?"

"They have someone already, but I will have all day up here to paint."

Together they unpacked and hung some of Viola's clothes on pegs in the wall. Had Clemmie hung her coat there, too? They popped lids off her possessions and placed the most needed items within reach.

"Mortimer Barnes painted *Sweet Clementine* up here." Viola said.

"Clemmie told you that?"

Viola nodded. "She also told me my sister is part of the *Sweet Clementine* painting. Did you know?"

Nasrin gasped and shook her head. "When Leo and I met your mother, she was already Marshall's wife. We never had reason to doubt…" Nasrin sat on the edge of the bed. "Well, I …"

Viola touched a wall. "This is the room where Clemmie and Mortimer spent most of their time. She told me they would have eloped by the end of that fateful week. Instead…"

Nasrin's eyes closed. "She rushed into a marriage with Marshall because he promised to take care of her, but he really only wanted her for what she could bring him." She looked up at Viola. "That much, Leo and I discovered."

"Mortimer saw his future in her smile and painted all his hopes and dreams into it. And I never saw it in Clemmie for good reason."

Nasrin gathered a paper that had slipped onto the floor. "And what is this?"

Viola examined the scrap and a sharp flame kicked in her stomach. "Silas told me about a Christmas postcard competition. I didn't know he'd cut it out of the newspaper."

She read the conditions. "Unique Australian submissions. Nothing wintery. No snow." Pin holes studded the clipping. "He must have fixed it to the string. I don't remember taking this down, but then I don't remember much about the days after the fire. After Clemmie died. They're all such a blur."

But this was a clear invitation from Silas to never forget he expected great things from her.

"The deadline is next week," Nasrin said.

Viola pondered Jasper, who thought she would hang washing on this line. And knew for sure she would enter the contest. If she were to be an independent botanical artist, she would work on more than one project. More than one competition. Even a little postcard competition. She would enter them all.

She worked the push pins into all the corners of the attic until two taut string lines divided the room. And then, before she added anything of her own, she pinned the newspaper clipping in the brightest shaft of light.

27

On the first day in the attic, Viola watched the winter sun slow-waltz past smoky clouds and slip in through the attic windows to wash the floor in three square patches of light.

On the second day, she arranged, then rearranged her room to best capture this light. Her sketches and book ideas hung on their strings like dancing marionettes. Much like the swirling water jars on her table that churned with paints and dreams.

From Sea to Shore – Australia's Phillip Island.

And while big ideas danced in morning light, Viola worked on her entry for the Christmas postcard competition. A small effort, it was still a piece of the future she had chosen. An independent botanical illustrator needed a body of work to build upon.

A replica of what she'd made for Shadrach and Finella. A beach guesthouse and all that surrounded it. She fashioned the top of her card into a scallop that resembled an unfurling wing, painted it pink, and set it to dry on the windowsill.

"Now, for my other self." She brushed the tangles out of her hair and wondered where Balthazar alighted. Wings outspread, she hoped, chatting with Molly from the roof of Finella's menagerie.

And Silas? How close to home would the fathoms have carried him by now? How many days before he sold the astrolabe and forged out of debt?

She secured her hair into place with all the barbs and prodding needed to keep her presentable for her first evening of work. Then she added a few more for good measure.

The pain of a dozen hairpins distracted her from the bite of loneliness. Her mornings and afternoons would be for art. But from tonight, her evenings would belong to the Star and Garter and all who drank there. And that was the loneliest thought of all.

"Splendid." Mr. Barnes appraised her like a newly acquired canvas. Crisp, crossed and knotted at her back, she wore a long white apron over a clean shirt and skirt atop a flurry of nerves that crackled like a short fuse.

"Nails?" He motioned for her to show her hands. "No ink or charcoal residue on the hands of the server." Satisfied, he smiled. "Now that we have the piano, the mood often becomes rowdy. But the regulars are satisfied with hot food, a warm fire, and a healthy stream of drinks. And they will be delighted with you."

He cocked his head. "So smile and entertain them."

"Entertain?" The notion made her want to crush the apron between her fingers. "I thought I was to deliver food and drinks."

"In your most beguiling way, Miss Buckley. Every instinct of your mother runs through your veins. Why not visit that upon our guests who come to pay her homage."

"Because I am not an entertainer." She pressed on the imaginary creases of her apron and pushed her head high, her voice steady. But inside, the little girl who'd fought to pull the wig from her head shook herself awake.

The tavern door swung open, and the first patrons dribbled in.

Mr. Barnes pulled her aside.

"In this establishment, you will encounter men who sit here for a few hours to unwind after their busy days. Some will spend their last coins tonight to take their mind off the poverty that awaits them back home. Others will puff their chests and buy three times over what those on another table cannot. And there's a man for every station in between. All united by the one thing we offer. *Sweet Clementine.*"

He smiled at a party of men who squeezed past them.

"I didn't expect we'd collect Clemmie's many fans but," he shrugged, "she lures them in. Now, imagine how they'd react if they knew her daughter worked among them. Bring a sullen face to their table and you'll have much to answer for. Bring a sweet smile and leave them with their drinks. That," he tapped a finger to her cheek, "is what I mean by entertainment. A smile like your mother's."

Piano music jangled alongside the ever-growing hum of patrons. They greeted one other with good cheer and found their seats at long tables. Some of them looked at her with interest. A new face, she imagined, would stick out like a newly smashed thumb tonight.

Jasper swooped down the stairs, pulled her away from his father, and into the kitchen. "Ready?" He strung an apron around his middle.

Cloda stirred a large pot of stew on the stove. "You've not burned those pies, have ya?"

"Never." Derry examined the pie bottoms.

Viola turned to Jasper. "You serve too?"

"Father insists I am familiar with all aspects of this business. Serving is key to understanding our patrons."

"And have you been instructed to smile at them?"

"No. Why would they want my smile? Now, listen." He raced through the simple instructions. Trays. Drinks. In this door. Out that one. "Let me know if someone's bothering you. They mean no harm, but I'll wager some fool will try to impress his mates with antics you won't like. Just ignore it."

"Ignore the fools, smile at the rest." She followed Jasper into the largest of the tavern's rooms, where the piano-man played a lively tune.

"Gentlemen." Jasper welcomed the nearest huddle. "What are you in the mood for this evening? We're serving Scotch pies or Irish stew. All for sixpence, with a tankard of ale and all the music your ears can take in."

"What about all that our eye can take in?"

They peered at Viola as if she were a menu item in a foreign language.

"This is Miss Viola. Be nice to her or I'll instruct her to serve your table last."

"We'll be ever so gentlemanly," one of them replied. The others roared with laughter and continued to stare right at her, as if gentlemanly and lecherous meant the same thing.

"The five of us will have a pie and ale to begin with," interjected a portly man, bald and bespectacled with finer looking clothes than his friends. "Let the girl attend to us." He tore off his glasses, polished, and returned them to his well-fed, overheated face.

Viola turned on her heels for the kitchen.

Five pies. Five tankards. And five minutes into the job, Viola knew she could grow to hate it, in this one sitting. It wasn't the way she'd been dismissed that poked at her pride. Or the unguarded way some had looked at her. What had she expected in a tavern?

Neither was it the smug, overprotective stance of Jasper or the patronizing ways of Mr. Barnes. It was the genuine fear that her future might look like this, if her art failed to provide. That weighed heavier than her overladen tray.

Whispers reached her when she returned to the table. Pockets of the large room dropped their chatter. And questioning eyes settled on her.

She ignored them and passed out the refreshments.

"I see it," a younger man whispered. "It's the hair."

They all stared. The pianist played on.

"I see it in her eyes."

"It's her, all right. Oi, Miss," a man with a crooked nose called to her. "Tavern gossip says you're the daughter of our Sweet Clementine. Is that true or is Freddy Barnes pullin' our leg?"

Viola froze, the empty tray at her side like a broken wing. And in her chest, a beat picked up, like Balthazar's frightened rocking when he savaged himself against the cage door.

"Maybe she could sing us a song. Come on, darlin'."

A low whistle rang over the room, followed by hands that slapped the tables in anticipation. Where was Jasper? She scanned the room, but Mr. Barnes shushed them with a sly smile.

"That's enough, you lot." He climbed onto a chair. "There's no point keeping it from you any longer. You'll be pleased to discover that, yes, Miss Viola Buckley *is* among us now, and she'll be serving you ale and tucker if you'll behave."

The room exploded with cheers. Mr. Barnes raised his hand. "You'll do well to remember Miss Buckley has only recently lost her mother. And in this establishment, we hold Sweet Clementine in the greatest of respect, and I know you'll regard Miss Viola the same way."

All eyes turned to her. Some took her in with greedy interest. Others offered an awkward smile. Mention of the recent death of Clemmie served Mr. Barnes well.

"She's the spitting image of our Sweet Clementine. A salute for Miss Viola Buckley." All tankards rose in unison.

"Sing us a tune, little songbird," another voice pleaded. "You know how."

You know how.

The tremor grew from her heels and stormed upward. It pulled like a flood and lashed the ground at her feet where Marshall's words boiled and rolled up into her memory.

"You know how," he had yelled and yanked the wig back over her hair. "*They've paid good money to see you sing and dance and you will do it, and you'll do it with a smile on your face."* His voice had dropped to a whisper in her ear. He'd pasted a theater smile onto his face, and she had trembled then, as much as she trembled now.

You know how.

Along the ceiling, pipe smoke curled and lantern light shone over the room. Two quick breaths were all she needed, but she took a third because it was always on the third breath she dropped a curtsy.

This time, she offered a quick nod of acknowledgement and retreated to the kitchen. Derry worked fast to replenish the stew and pie dishes. Cloda added a splash of peas into the thick gravy that oozed onto the plate.

Viola fumbled with her apron strings, knotted harder than she knew how to undo them. Jasper followed her in and stilled her hands.

"There's nothing to fear. They don't even know you and they already love you."

"I can't do this, Jasper. I don't mind leaving a plate at someone's table, but I will not leave a piece of myself."

Cold and numb, she shook with fear.

He cracked the door open for her to peek into the room. "See that man there? A respectable post office master. He comes in all quiet and reserved. By closing you'd think he was here from Italy for a debut concert. His name is John Robbins, and he sings opera.

"That man..." he pointed to another table, "... runs a small boot-making business. Lost his eldest, a son, last year in a gun accident. Comes here to forget his losses. Name, Jimmy Collins."

Jasper scanned the room. "That's Ned Sully and his cousin Oscar Brown. They run a butchery down on Blackwood Street. One of their wives ran away days before Christmas and never returned. The other is raising their combined children, eight of them, all by herself in rooms above the shop.

After that you've got Jeremiah Hall. Respectable cheese monger. Going blind, fast. Married. One daughter. Fragile wife. He's been coming here a few weeks now. Sits with Billy Croft, who's got the worst limp you'll ever see but will out-sing any other patron."

Jasper let the door swing shut.

"They're all wounded in their own ways. Afraid and lonely, but they forget that in here. Once you know their stories and griefs, you'll be able to smile for real. It will take some time, but I know you can do this."

He looked at her with the same pleading she'd offered when he'd promised she could have the *Sweet Clementine* if they married. This would be all his one day. And she saw his desire to share it with her. All of it. All of them out there. All of him.

"Unless you have another job." Jasper shrugged. "One that offers room and board and a place to play with your paints and there's a Jasper there who will look out for you."

How would Clemmie have done this? She would have worn her best golden wig and held her shoulders high. But she loved an audience. Viola did not.

She would have to find another way to stand tall.

"Until your smile is real, pretend they're me." Jasper juggled another laden tray. "Reject them with a sweet dose of kindness."

28

Portland, Oregon,
August 21, 1879

For years Portland had carried a reputation as the Unheavenly City. With street crime on the rise, and secret underground trapdoors and deadfalls, people often disappeared soon after wandering into seedy taverns.

Still, he wished he'd brought Viola back with him. What would she make of all this? She would see beauty in the rivers and mountains beyond, but her eyes were fixed on the botanicals of another continent.

Silas let himself into Nicholas Taylor, Curios and Collectibles, Dealer of Antiquities and Fine Arts. Display cabinets winked silver, gold, and crystal salutations. A large tapestry of victory-bound horsemen stormed into battle, and he stepped back before the cavalry knocked him over.

Steady, he told himself. *You're travel weary, that's all. The Pacific Ocean's still rolling in your blood and messing with your head.*

"How can I help?" A young man rose from behind the counter where he'd been crouching. He cradled a bucket full of ink-stained rags. "We're about to close up."

"I'm looking for the owner."

"Good thing for me he's not here. I've made a mess of his books, and when he finds out, he will kill me."

"Your father?" Silas asked.

"No, my boss. I'm the new apprentice. Mr. Taylor's away. Don't expect him back for another few days."

"I have a brass and silver astrolabe. I'd like an appraisal."

"An astrolabe?" The apprentice wiped his smudged hands. "Collectors wolf them up. He'll want to see it. Leave it with me—"

"No." Silas pocketed his treasure. "I want to know when I can speak with Taylor directly."

"End of this week, I imagine."

Silas left his name, thanked him, and took up his bags, no richer than when he'd walked into this shop.

Out on the street, people hurried past on their way home to family meals and end of day rituals. Silas dragged himself down old familiar streets, past Madame Drouilhat's Restaurant, the Empire Bakery, the Portland Soda Works, until the Swift Brothers sign appeared at the foot of Yamhill Street. Would he walk into a mess like the one in the curio shop? It only took a moment for the boss to look away and anything could happen.

"Silas Swift, the man himself!" Someone bumped him with a rock-hard thump. There was only one man who threw around his physical strength as a greeting. Chester Sweeney. Broad, with lanky blond hair and cannon ball eyes that shifted from steely grey to winter fog.

Years of school-yard taunting meant *Sweeney the Meany* had forged a path for Chester, the boy. He'd inherited his father's money-lending business and adopted the insults of his childhood in earnest.

"Back from the other side of the world. Took you long enough."

Chester's smile was as wide as it was menacing.

"Ship came in yesterday, from San Francisco."

"But you've been gone months."

"Ship was delayed. Diverted to Sydney for repairs."

"Grew yourself a sailor's beard, I see. I trust your endeavors proved fruitful. We have much unfinished business."

Silas cleared his throat. "I'll know in a week or two."

Chester leaned in and whispered. "If you can't make repayments, that fine building becomes mine. But where are my manners?" He raised an arm in triumph. "There's happier news to celebrate. Let me be first to offer congratulations. You must be proud of that Eugene. Who knew…?"

He made a face Silas could not decipher, all raised eyebrows and fake grin. Was he mocking? Was this open delight at some catastrophe that awaited him?

"I shall expect a meeting with you, Silas. Perhaps after the festivities?" He sauntered off without waiting on a reply, and Silas trudged homeward with a barrage of freshly muddied dread and confusion.

Festivities?

His instructions to Eugene had been firm.

"Don't overstretch. If there's something new or you're not sure, leave it until I return."

What had Eugene done now?

Swift Brothers – Fine Furniture Makers stood tall. The rebuilt, three-story building faced the winding Willamette River with views of the Cascade Mountains in the distance.

Someone had propped the shop door open with a chunky wooden stopper. That was new. He hoped it ended there, but his gut told him the front stoop was only the beginning.

Inside and to his left, in front of a wide window, they normally advertised their goods. Chests on one side, chairs on the other, tables in the middle. Still there, he was glad to see, but someone had rearranged them.

Various carpet pieces had been brought in, and it looked like he'd stepped into someone's dining room. Or bedroom. Here and there, flower-filled vases on wooden plinths added cheer.

A chess table held court in the window. He'd sold enough to know it was an item well worth making and required little advertising. But now, it beckoned people from the street. Pawns and queens and bishops lined up for battle.

Like the Curios & Collectibles shop, this display swayed under his feet. There was a strategy here he'd not thought of before.

This could not be the spark of Eugene, could it?

A little grudge of irritation pinched him around the collar. He checked his pocket watch. It was almost time for the small team of workers to head home. He'd peek into the workroom first and seek answers later.

He spotted four regular woodworkers. Two new faces worked among them. Young, twelve or thirteen at most. One swept sawdust into a tin pail. The other applied a coat of lacquer to the frame of a chest of drawers.

He should have announced himself, but the familiar sound of wood being shaped by expert hands and razor-sharp tools pegged him to the floor. This space back here, not the shop in front, was the equivalent of Viola's box of paints and brushes and water pots. And the ache of her not here with him kicked him in the guts, harder than he anticipated.

"Silas!" Joe Harper, the eldest employee, barreled into him with an exuberant punch to the arm. "Son of a gun. We thought you'd left us for good. Look what the wind blew our way."

All heads turned, tools set aside, and benches abandoned with fast brushing of hands over aprons. The welcome filled his heart with gladness. The small but faithful crew gathered around, faces full, chests puffed. Something deepened in his own chest. A sinking feeling that didn't match the mood his men exuded. Eager faces looked up at him, the newly arrived boss. Home at last. He'd never seen so many smiles in the one workroom.

"And where's Eugene?"

"Oh, he's in the office, I expect," Joe offered. "There have been a few changes around here, Silas. For the better, mind you. I think you'll be pleased. I mean, why would you not…?"

His voice petered out, and Silas caught the soft snort of suppressed laughter from one of his crew.

He made his way to the glassed-in office. Behind the simple desk sat Eugene. Head down, he worked on a ledger with meticulous attention. Dressed in attire Silas had not seen on him before—a new vest, and with sleeves rolled to the elbow—he tapped one of his heels against the wheeled castor of his chair. Was that a new pair of shoes as well?

His beard was fuller, but his brown hair had been cut shorter than he normally wore it. Eugene looked more like a man than Silas had ever seen him.

He cleared his throat, and his brother raised his head.

"What?" He beamed and pushed off the chair. "Silas!"

They'd never been a family that showed much of their fondness. That was always implied. In hard work. In diligence and focus. That was how Silas imagined they knew he cared. But relief kicked in, and he wrapped Eugene in a bear hug.

Nothing looked out of place. Quite the opposite. It looked like someone had come in and elevated his business a notch or two, the way a mother might remake her son's bed after he'd done his best.

"You're looking fine, Eugene. All business. Look at you." Twenty-five and now as tall as Silas, Eugene's slim build had filled with new muscles. "All is well, I trust."

"More than well. I can't believe you're here. And I can't wait to hear all about Australia." Even under his well-groomed beard, Eugene's pock-marked face reddened, and he fiddled with his sleeve cuff. Was that new, too? "But I have much to tell you. Come sit."

Eugene pulled out a chair reserved for visitors. Silas ignored the unfamiliar sensation of being on the other side of the desk. His brother swiveled and bounced against the tufted leather of the owner's chair until he found a comfortable position.

"Well, out with it." Silas leaned back. "Tell me how we came to look like a merry widow's front rooms out there and why people on the street are congratulating me because of you."

Eugene exhaled a long, soft whistle. Then he bit down on a smile that refused to be tamed. "Promise to listen to the end."

Silas gestured with both palms for him to carry on.

"I experimented with the shop, Silas. I wanted to create a new weekly display, bring something into view that had been overlooked in the past. And soon we had more customers peering in, discovering large and small pieces they needed. Or wanted.

"I hang a drape on a Saturday morning, arrange the new window, and then drop the curtain on Sunday. When people walk by, they've learned to stop."

He smiled. "It started off as a game, I guess, but soon brought in new and returning customers. We not only advertise what's for purchase, we show them how it might look in their home alongside their other pieces. I have added nothing new to what we make. I only displayed it differently."

Silas heard the delight in his brother's voice and perhaps a small insecurity as well.

"I'm impressed. You've done well."

"Really?" Eugene lit up like a firecracker. "I'm so glad. But there's more." His eyes shimmered with something Silas had never seen before.

"I am to be married." He ran his hands along the desk edge, then gripped the corners.

"Married?" His baby brother? The one in Patrick's shadow, the one who'd always followed and done what he'd been told?

"Indeed." Eugene's big blue eyes widened as if it were almost too hard for him to believe it, too. "I never thought a face like this would appeal to anyone, but she's not just anyone, Silas. She's the one who suggested we adorn the room with flowers. She's…" He looked behind Silas and let out a short, happy laugh. "There you are, my love."

They both stood.

"May I introduce my fiancée, Miss Olive, soon to become Olive Swift."

Olive?

The office shrank and caved in. Too hot, too dark, too full of people. Silas ground his teeth and hoped the fatigue of travel played with his mind.

But no, he knew this dark-eyed girl. He shooed her away from his most regretful thoughts. Thoughts of a night spent in the company of a woman who was neither his wife nor someone he'd ever thought to wed. Now his brother wrapped his arm around her and presented her with all the gentility and respect Silas had not.

Warm and sugar-sweet, she smiled. "I'm most pleased to meet you. Please, call me Olive."

She spoke the way one might if they welcomed you into their home and wished to settle you in. His mind spun so hard he could not yet tell if this woman remembered him or not. If she were here with real affection for her brother, or not.

He offered his warmest congratulations, hoping the fear running through him did not temper the news he was meant to be celebrating.

"You'll have to tell me everything. After I have eaten. I'm starving."

"We will. And there is so much more, but to begin with, Silas…" Eugene's eye shone. "You could not have arrived home at a better time. The wedding is the day after tomorrow."

Silas felt the blood drain from his face as sure as he saw the blush rise in Eugene's.

Olive remained composed and smiling.

And nothing about that made him feel any better.

29

His bags felt heavier in the short distance up to his third-floor bedroom than they had through all the ports and platforms between here and Melbourne.

Had their weight grown heavier, or had his shoulder lost some of its brawn?

Sleep in his own bed would cure most of what ailed him, if sleep itself didn't deliver the dreams he could not escape. Of rosehip jam and gum leaves and a girl who'd accidentally burned down a farm building because she thought he'd like to look into upside-down Australian skies with her.

Silas pulled the astrolabe from his case. When he strolled the *Clara's* decks, it had remained hidden in his breast pocket. When he'd forged his way through crowded gateways thick with pick pocketers, it had remained deep in his bags where only his hand knew where to find it.

Now, he unwrapped it and slid out the topmost drawer of his dresser and dumped it onto his bed. Shallow enough for socks alone, it was the hidden tray underneath that he reached for. He pulled a wooden pin to reveal a secret compartment the same length as the drawer.

In it, he kept the deed to the Swift building and his father's will.

He slid the astrolabe on top of the documents, returned the drawer with a satisfying bang, and stared out the window at the Willamette River. It wound to the east, like a thread of quicksilver.

"So…" Eugene leaned on the doorframe. "Was it all worth it?"

Silas returned to his bags. "It was there." He nodded. "Charlie Hinkle's astrolabe."

"I thought it was yours."

Silas shrugged. "Maybe I call it that to keep Charlie alive in my memory."

"So, you'll sell it?"

"For a good price."

"Silas." Eugene came nearer and cleared his throat. "I know the display probably took you by surprise, but I didn't mean to defy you."

Silas threw dirty clothes into a pile for Mrs. Knott, and Eugene unpacked the past few months in the same fashion, discarding details into piles, letting his words fall around them in odd clusters.

"The window started as a test. Then one day I walked past the flower sellers and wondered, what would happen if I added something fresh. You know, for the ladies to catch their eye."

He screwed his lips together in a sheepish smile. "But it was my eye that was caught, when I saw Olive outside the shop next to the flower seller. She'd gone to see her father, the antique dealer, Nicholas Taylor."

Silas stopped his rummaging and peered at Eugene. "Taylor?"

Eugene nodded. "When the flowers wilted, I went back for more, and there she was again. It was Olive who suggested we rearrange the window to look like the inside of a home. It all started there."

Olive. The daughter of Nicholas Taylor. Soon-to-be wife of his brother.

Panic surged in his chest.

Between them, Eugene and Olive had enough cause to knock him into the tail end of next month. But his brother was not talking like a man who had the slightest inkling that his beloved was any more or any less than what he thought of her.

But Silas knew otherwise. Olive, the tavern Girl. He closed his eyes, but the scorching regret of that night never stopped wafting like a thin line of smoke that filled his nostrils with shame. And now fear. He needed to gather his wits. Eugene was talking business.

"These improvements meant I could comfortably put on the new boys. And with more workers, we can take on more orders."

Silas threw everything left in his bag onto his bed, among them, Viola's portrait sketch.

"Olive came to see the display each week. We soon became friends. We went on walks. I know it's hard to believe. Me, and someone like her. But she doesn't care how I look. She's become as much a part of the new display as the flowers themselves."

"And you asked her to marry you."

Eugene nodded and breathed in hard. "I did. And she said yes, straight away."

"Are you sure you know enough about her?"

He heard the stupidity of his question. If Eugene knew *enough,* he'd not be smiling like a goose. He'd be yanking Silas around the room and sending him into the walls by the shoulder. Silas himself had fallen hard for Viola. And in less time, probably. It happened. Time was not the problem.

Eugene smiled. "Maybe it's been a fast courtship, but it's been so for a reason. She saw the man beneath the face and wants *him.* How could I let that go in a hurry?" He dug his hands deep into his pockets. "And there's one more thing. I wrote to Patrick. He's coming on tomorrow's train. We will all be here for my wedding."

Silas heard the desperate cry for peace from the brother who only ever sought harmony.

"And it would mean so much to me if we could stand together, three brothers with nothing but celebrating my future to bind us. Please?"

The wild dog that crouched deep in Silas's wounded chest gnarled so hard it felt like claws now twisted for blood.

"Patrick," he could hardly utter the name, "who raced into the world without a backward glance?" Silas dragged the wild dog by the collar into a darker corner and fought in vain to compose himself. Patrick, who'd taken a third of his business. His jaw would hurt as bad as all his aching muscles in the morning, but he had nothing left to unclench it.

"I know you blame him for crippling us, but I couldn't imagine him not being here, so I wrote to him."

Silas looked at Eugene with fresh eyes. Was it possible his youngest brother was even taller? He certainly held his head high. In his absence, he'd shown initiative and ingenuity. He'd taken risks, small ones at that, but he'd not sat still. And he'd reached out to Patrick, their prodigal.

"I told you not to change a thing, and you tipped everything into some kind of new order."

"And there's no catastrophe to show for it."

Silas juggled his rage for Patrick that never really disappeared. Now Olive, too? His past had been dug up and littered his mind with the stench of whatever any dead man ever gripped.

"Let's see how we fare tomorrow with Patrick." Silas rested a knee on his bed and tried to remember how he'd felt on the eve of his wedding to Honora. Had it look like this? Innocent and hopeful? A little giddy?

Viola's sketch rolled from the bed and bounced to the floor. Eugene picked it up and rolled it out. He made another whistling sound.

"This is good. Where'd you have it done? Melbourne?"

"Phillip Island. Blue Wren House. The artist who made that..." the breath in him slowed and he tried again. "The artist who made that was another guest, and she practiced some of her portrait sketching on me."

"She?" Eugene examined the charcoal sketch. "Well, *she* saw right into your soul."

"It's nothing. Give it back." He held out his hand, wanting the paper in his possession more than anything right now.

Eugene raised an eyebrow. "I know this look. It's the one you make when you're trying not to smile. Why were you looking at her with this face and not the scowl you reserve for everyone else?"

"Eugene, don't toy with me. I'm tired and I have the newfound notion of you getting married to absorb, our business to assess in the morning, and now Patrick's coming home, and I am in no mood for games."

Eugene handed it over. "Fine. Sleep your journey off and we can talk more in the morning about this *she* who's made you all prickly and grumpier than usual."

He left Silas to the silent stampede of fear that stormed underfoot. In two days Silas would stand, probably with Patrick beside him, and watch Eugene marry Olive Taylor. He rubbed at his overgrown beard. Did she really love Eugene for himself, or was this some sick revenge on him?

While he'd tried to forget their encounter, he knew this much. They'd promised each other nothing, and the true fruit of their encounter had been the bitter, hollow reproach that pushed them into the cold dawn and divergent pathways home, cobbled in regret, weighed down by a shame deeper than he'd ever carried.

Could this get any worse? He knew the answer to that. He sank onto the bed and cradled his head. How did you tell a groom about your indiscretion with his bride-to-be on the eve of their nuptials? He leaned back and his hand fell into the fringe of Viola's shawl.

Let me play.

Walking away from her was his biggest regret, but he'd walked back into some of his finest culpabilities. He paced the room. Kicked his bags out of the way. Leaned on the closed bedroom door with both hands and begged God for answers to questions he had no business asking.

Forgiveness and redemption were like a pair of messy twins. Having Patrick here would make life a thousand times harder. He'd bring his arguments in and his stir-mongering and he'd…Silas pressed off the door and stood bolt straight.

Patrick! If anyone was able to see through this hasty wedding it would be Eugene's twin. Nothing else had brought him home in the two years he'd been away.

Tomorrow he would observe Olive. And he'd watch Patrick with her, too. Silas nodded to himself and picked up Viola's shawl. He'd arrived just in time.

It took a month for Viola to adapt to working evenings in the tavern. At first, her feet ached, and her head pounded every time she laced up her apron and heard the first patrons enter the tavern. Her body slipped into the routine long before her heart followed. But by mid-August, Viola had become tavern girl by night, artist by day.

With Jasper's encouragement, she considered each man someone who carried with him an anguish or misery, or simple desire for escape among friends. In time, she learned to slide her smile from toothy and forced into something less stiff. And in a few short weeks her smile contained genuine sentiment.

Jasper shouldered her away from situations he deemed rocky, and soon enough, Viola herself learned to judge between drunken behavior that would end in a scene she could command and ones she could not.

The men who tried to drag her to the piano for a sing-along soon learned they'd be sent back to their chairs by Freddy or Jasper. The unconvinced heard from Viola herself she preferred watercolours to music. That gave them reason to pause. But only long enough to pivot.

"How about you paint our portrait, then? Life size, like *Sweet Clementine*?"

This was the latest cajoling. Whose portrait would she paint first, with the accompanying insults of who was the ugliest and who would need lots of 'artistic adaptation.'

"But you're not a botanical, Mr. Robbins." She would smile and leave a simmering plate of stew for consolation.

In the attic, under morning light, Viola's portfolio took shape. Paintings she discarded as *not right* for her submission, she sold to quieter patrons who approached her with respect, wishing to acquire a handmade gift for a loved one. A small piece to pretty up their wall.

"Viola?" Mr. Barnes called up to her attic from the landing outside his office.

She set down her brush and viewed her work. Rust-edged leaves and gum nuts.

All she had to do was close her eyes and the scented memory

drifted over her. And with it, always the memory of Silas. He raided her dreams and demanded more of her each day.

"Coming." The stairs from her attic room were narrower and steeper than the other flights and among the many skills she'd learned was the good sense to not race up or down.

"Yes, Mr. Barnes?" She knocked on the door that was already ajar.

"Come. Sit." He pressed a curled blotter over one of his fat ledgers. "I have a proposition for you."

Dread pooled in her throat. If *he* asked her to sing, she would pack her bags.

"Mr. Jeremiah Hall. Know him?"

She nodded.

"Man's like a dog with a bone. Asked me a week ago about a portrait he's willing to commission. Wants you to do it and won't stop yappin' about it."

"I don't do portraiture." She wasn't sure if that was a lie, but she hoped her answer did not require qualification.

"You've not studied how?"

"I have some knowledge but very little experience and nothing that someone would want to commission."

"Well, he does. And of course, it's not your experience that he cares to buy here, but your name."

"I am already engaged in a large project. And I could not promise to apply myself—"

"It's a portrait of his daughter, a gift for his wife. There are many who boast and throw their bravado around the tavern, but very few who can pay for it. Real money, Viola. Haven't you been telling me for years something like this was in your future? As much as I hate to admit it, perhaps this," he shrugged, "is what you meant."

She shook her head at his mistake. "I'm a botanical artist."

"Consider this request. Your work could hang in his house. Mrs. Hall's friends could become envious and want the same. You'd be foolish to reject him."

"Viola's an expert at rejecting men." Jasper leaned in the doorway. "She's going to be an independent botanical rejecter of men."

"Thank you, Sir Jasper Barnes, Lord Sarcasm," Viola whispered under her breath.

"Hush now, you two." Mr. Barnes swiped at the air with his hand. "Viola? What do you say?"

She moved to the window. From there, she could see the Botanic Gardens. The pathways, the gates, and beyond to the glass roof of the Lily House. It had always been botanicals. They told a story.

Faces did too, but she did not want to look into them. Not now that she'd peered into the eyes of Silas and could not easily forget them. Somehow, she held onto the intimacy of that and did not want to sully it with other faces. Other stories.

"Botanicals, yes. People, no." She spoke to herself.

"How will you fill your days when your exhibition entry is complete? Why scoff at portrait painting when it could position you among those who can afford your work? Think of it as Clementine's gift to you. Her legacy will open doors, but who knows for how long? Doors you cannot afford to slam shut."

"She can afford to." Jasper's energy spiked the air around them. "Why are you encouraging her to do this? You've agreed with me for years." Jasper pointed from Viola to his father with both hands, gesturing as if his words were not enough. "You know it only keeps her enslaved in dreams she cannot attain."

"Perhaps I have seen for myself the level of her dedication and the growing interest in Viola's work from those willing to pay for it. And I," Mr. Barnes shrugged, "may be among them someday." He shut the ledger with a loud thump. "Perhaps the unattainable dreams are yours, dear boy."

Jasper's face darkened. He turned on his heels and dug them on every stair tread until all that remained of his anger was the echo of doors slamming.

"I don't mean to reject him. He's a good friend, but I—"

"I know." Mr. Barnes sighed. "You are, each day, more and more every inch your mother when I fell in love with her. Only in my case, I was besotted and had no business thinking she had anything for me. She didn't even know I was there."

"She knew. But… you were still a boy. And…"

"And her heart belonged to someone else. As did mine in the end. By the time I gave it to my late wife, I had found a way to love the right person. And so will Jasper. But you…" He pressed his hands into a perch and rested his chin upon it. "You must find a way to love portraiture. It's the freedom you chase, is it not?"

Viola was not so sure. Mr. Barnes, of all people, pushed her toward freedom.

Well, freedom had many faces, but did it look like the daughter of Jeremiah Hall?

There was only one way to find out.

Mrs. Knott laid a heavy breakfast table most days, but this was something else. Hearty eggs and hash welcomed Silas to the long table where he and Eugene would start the day. Later, the woman would feed the carpentry crew a hot luncheon and leave the brothers a cold supper.

"Now, tell me more about Australia. What do they breakfast on there? Did you see some of their weird animals?" Eugene asked. "Did you eat any?"

Memories of the breakfast hour at the guesthouse were not among the first to share. Not today.

"Slippery Bob is cooked kangaroo brains, but they did not make it to my plate, thankfully. I shot a deer, though."

"What?" Eugene looked up, and Silas could not tell if his brother's lip curled in disgust at the kangaroo or the deer.

"The deer ran wild. Someone dug a pit and I was there at the right time, grabbed the gun and…" He made an explosive noise and Eugene replied with an impressed face.

"You hunted down a deer *and* the astrolabe. You snagged more than you set out to find." Eugene took a large gulp of coffee. "Not forgetting the artist that made you go all red."

Silas ignored the jibe. "There's plenty of time for my travel stories. But today, I want to know what needs doing before this wedding tomorrow."

"It's a small gathering, at the Hoyt Street chapel at eleven. Olive's parents are hosting a dinner afterward in their home. Olive's sister died in childbirth, and they've had a few years of heartache. The celebrations won't be too elaborate."

"You've got your groom's coat? You're—"

"Yes, Silas. My wedding clothes are hanging upstairs. We have a room booked at the Occidental Hotel in Seattle for three nights for our honeymoon. And then, we'll return here."

Silas pondered the ease with which his brother's life had slipped into this well-oiled program without his interference.

"And Olive, will she stop here today?"

"The next time I'll see Olive is when we exchange vows. She and her mother have much to do today. Olive's…" He paused. "She didn't cope well when her sister died. The baby died too, and the entire family has struggled in their own way. When I told her some of Honora's story, how we watched her slip away and how that shook us, she understood."

Eugene stirred sugar into his coffee. "She says lost people often take wrong turns during times of grief, and even the best of souls often turn inside out." He shrugged. "She's run around town a little, Silas, she's admitted so. Looking for comfort from the wrong kind of men, at Dead Man's Grip, a tavern down by the cemetery. They often sent there to fetch her mother, who would sit by the graves. Sometimes, Olive would go into the tavern to talk with one of her friends who works there."

He shook his head as if to scatter the past and smiled. "She's mine now, and that's all that matters."

The fork in Silas's hand felt like a log he'd been holding up way too long. He set it down. So, Olive was not a 'tavern girl.' She was a girl who'd been at the tavern when that dog had lunged at him. Either way, she was that Olive.

"She confessed all that to you?"

Eugene nodded. "I don't want to know the details of those tough days. I'm glad to know I'll be there for all the ones that come next. She's chosen me, and that makes me the luckiest."

Wide and innocent, his smile beamed across the table at Silas. It was not the smile of a man who even suspected his brother may have featured, even for one second, in the past of his beloved.

And telling him now, what good would that do if he didn't want to know? Would it matter *who* if Eugene didn't care to know any of the *whats* or *wheres*? Who was Silas to blot their happiness with his guilt? Wasn't it enough he carted it around?

The front door of the factory burst open. And there stood Patrick, with a grin and all the brass of those who carried zero guilt.

"Greetings, brothers!" Hat in hand, he bowed.

Like Eugene, Patrick had filled in his lanky boyhood frame with muscle. Not surprising given his choice of work. Last seen, he'd stuffed all he could into his two bags, and with a stilted farewell had left them to explore Oregon's logging fields.

"Patrick!" Eugene flew from his seat. "You're early."

"But I'm here." He slapped Eugene on the back, and for a moment Silas almost saw the brothers as the same person. Bearded, broader, somehow taller, both beamed to see the other. "And I've brought someone you will just adore."

He made way for a blond companion.

"This is Fern, my wife."

Wife? Silas stood. But his legs felt heavy, like they weren't meant for the shift they undertook.

Short, pretty, and plump, the rosy-cheeked woman stepped in with careful movements. Silas heard Eugene gasp, and he wasn't sure if some of that came from him, too.

For Patrick had not only arrived with a wife. He'd arrived with a wife who would soon bear a child.

"I'm so pleased to meet you both." She smiled at Eugene, and Silas joined them.

Anyone returning home deserved to step into the warmth of family. Even if it scalded Silas to embrace his brother.

"You can stop staring like that, chops open wide, and show your new sister to a chair," Patrick teased, but he didn't wait for them to move. He ushered his wife to the display that pretended to be a sitting room with two chairs and a side table.

Fern seated herself as if they'd shown her to a private drawing room. “Oh, that’s better.”

“Married?” The disbelief in Eugene’s voice matched the questions Silas bit down.

Patrick swept his hand over the vision of his wife and thrust out his chest. Always proud, always a little too loud, and almost always sullen, Patrick’s edges had been worn down, and here stood a man with a family of his own. He held onto his wife’s hand and stroked the back of her glove.

“Tied the knot last Christmas.”

Eugene and Patrick exchanged details of how they’d found their brides.

Silas ran his fingers through his hair. He’d need to submit to the barber today if there was going to be a family wedding tomorrow. But from the way his brothers’ chests puffed, Silas had no doubt the little control he’d once had over what they did or with whom was probably lost.

But to turn up like this, as if nothing had ever happened, as if leaving had not almost decimated him…

He mashed his lips so tight it was a miracle they did not bleed. There would be time enough to corner young Patrick. Now was not the moment to throw the last two years and all their suffering into his face.

The twins before him were no longer boys. They were men, and away from him they’d worked out how to choose for themselves. A small weight clattered from his chest. It didn’t go far, but it hung there. Enough for him to wonder what would happen if he stepped right back.

What if he let life unfold around him instead of beating it into shape? Would these two need rescuing from their hasty marriages? Would their regrets become his troubles, too?

Fern looked up into the eyes of Patrick and laughed at something he said. Silas knew that look. Viola had smiled at him that way on their boat ride. Her laugher had spilled into his heart that day like music. Like fresh water. Like everything Silas wanted and did not have.

He retreated to allow Eugene and Patrick their reunion. His brothers had secured the start of everything he'd ever wished for them. A future filled with love and purpose.

And what did he have?

A burning bundle of anger slung over his back, and a vibrant shawl draped over his bedroom chair that should have been spread over a marriage bed.

August 23, 1879

Yesterday I tied up my exhibition entry. I used the same string that I employed to display it for Silas. From Sea to Shore – The Beauty of Phillip Island.

The submission office was quieter than I expected. A small room for the quick handover of all I have fashioned. No ceremony, save an attendant with very little interest.

I stepped onto the street, and these assailing thoughts hurried on after me.

Would my entry become buried under those that will come in after it?

How many will I compete against?

How many do I need to climb over to be first*?*

There is a desolation that comes with handing over my art. Silas goes with it. How is that possible? I ask foolish questions, for I know how it is possible.

So, I ask a wiser one.

How do I forget him?

To begin with, I welcomed Helena Hall into my attic, delivered by her father, a strange man whose eye I could not properly catch behind the glasses he wears. I tried to tell him there were better portrait painters to be found, but he said he wanted an original, signed by me.

Mr. Barnes is right. It is the hint of Clemmie that captivates. Not my art at all. Not yet. But I cannot afford to ignore the opportunity, and so Helena and I took tea first so I could watch her.

She is a natural beauty, about to burst into full-blown elegance. Golden-haired with deep blue eyes and lashes that don't belong on a twelve-year-old but will send her marching into womanhood with enviable allure. I can see why her father wants her likeness painted. He says his daughter is the image of her mother and this gift will mark a wonderful occasion. Perhaps it is her birthday.

When he left us, Helena told me she arrived in Australia three years ago from London. Her Australian father imports fine cheeses from all over Europe, and her English mother is very much a homebody.

Their only child, she does not appear spoiled or lazy. I don't know how I would hide either of those qualities on my canvas. Laziness is one of the ugliest faces.

I made several fast sketches. Helena looking away, looking up, looking at me.

My hands shook when I let memories of Silas trip in. His misery in the bubbling guesthouse kitchen.

It doesn't matter what I sketch or paint now. It can be Helena Hall or the new leaves on a plum tree. I could paint a patch of weeds and still think of Silas Swift.

Because each time I start something new or look over a painting half done, it is his words that ring in my heart. "There's a bright future ahead of you, Viola Buckley. Beautiful and of your making."

And when Helena Hall has been collected by her father and I have tidied up my attic room, when the sun has set on another day and I prepare to wait tables, a small treacherous thought digs in, and I brush it away like a tick.

But it returns, nonetheless, and taunts me with a notion that turns my stomach in upon itself.

What if I had fought against the terror of being loved second with the same determination I fight to come first in my painting?

30

The Taylor family drawing room gleamed with candlelight. Dahlias that stood on plinths and created adornments along the staircase also decorated the table where servers laid a wedding feast.

Silas balanced an ache in his chest the way he did the glass in his hand, with a worn smile and a tighter pinch in his chest that had started early and now rose into a crescendo.

Against a trio of musicians who provided the undercurrent of lively tunes, the food appeared on a long buffet table, enough to lull a man into a deep sleep if that man were free to let himself go.

Silas was not. No, sir. Not today. His job, as it had been for as long as he remembered, was to watch out for his brothers. He did so from the other side of the room, even though a gangly man, who introduced himself as Ruben Lockwood and wore his mustache as thick as he could grow it, roped him into a conversation.

"I hear you've only this week returned from Australia. Is it as savage as they say?"

"Savage?" Silas shook his head. Only on the heart, if you offered it. "Australia's a country of mysteries. Modern, yet still undiscovered. Young. Raw. And unforgettable. Any traveler fortunate to visit will come home a changed man."

Mr. Lockwood showed suitable interest. They talked of animals and bushland, but Silas twisted his attention back to the bride and groom. Eugene and Olive bathed in the glory of their day with smiles that carried a language only the two of them knew.

Their sister Mary mingled with them. While her visit from Salem would only last a week, she always brought a calm to the chaos of her brothers.

Across the room, Patrick and Fern also smiled and ate and threw themselves into the festivities. Now was not the time to delve into the hand Patrick forced. Today was for celebrating.

But how did one undo years of protection and worry for the boys that he'd been told would not amount to anything? Sunny days like this did not always follow a groom or his bride. Didn't Silas know that well?

"... then the board wishes for..." Mr. Lockwood droned on about a boarding school. Or perhaps it was a school board. Silas nodded and took a sip of water, for in the pit of his stomach, a knot formed and twisted hard.

Today, a radiance rightfully hers spilled from Olive's dark eyes. But underneath, tucked behind a smile, panic flashed over her face when she glanced at him across the room.

Gone as fast as it appeared, only Silas saw what her quick laugh and cheerfulness hid. Guilt and fear and the desperation to keep the memory of that night buried in the darkness where it had occurred.

Silas caught the eye of Nicholas Taylor, who made his way to them through the crowded room. The father of the bride hosted this occasion like a man who'd reached into his own heart to fix the aches of his wife. He made speeches and encouraged more eating, more drinking, and more merrymaking.

Perhaps he too knew that Olive had wandered far from home and now breathed a sigh of relief to see her married and happy.

"A word with you, Mr. Swift?" Nicholas Taylor leaned between him and his constantly talking companion. "If you don't mind, Ruben."

"Not at all, cousin. The wedding feast is dictated by the father of the bride. Command as you desire."

Taylor led Silas outside to a small garden under a sky already losing its glow.

"I'm sorry I was not in the shop when you visited. With all our preparations, and then learning you are to be brother to our dear Olive, I hoped we might speak tonight."

"I hoped the same, sir." Silas ran his fingers over the astrolabe tucked in his breast pocket. Nothing about this day felt good. But the weight of the astrolabe calmed him. Perhaps Honora had been right all along. Maybe he did treat it like a lucky charm. "I'm grateful for your time," he continued, "especially on a night like this. Eugene and Olive make a fine couple. I don't mean for you to—"

"I needed some air, but my wife will spy me gone all too soon and I will have to return. But, you have an astrolabe for me, yes?"

Silas nodded. "Months ago, Mr. Hinkle suggested I show it to you."

"A good man. My wife spent many heartbroken hours at the cemetery weeping over our daughter's grave. Hinkle often sent someone to fetch Olive to bring her mother home." He polished a pair of glasses and slid them on. "All in the dim past, I'm glad to say."

Silas pulled the astrolabe from his pocket and handed it over.

Mr. Taylor turned it this way, then the other. He weighed it in his hand as one might a gold ingot. "Where did you find it?"

"Mr. Hinkle found it. Many years ago, when his boy Charlie was still alive. Dropped, he thinks, by sailors who ran through the cemetery one night. He gave it to me shortly after Charlie died. Mr. Hinkle wanted it to lend purpose, inspire the life his son would never enjoy."

"And did it inspire you?"

"For a long time, yes."

"And now?"

"Now I carry too many business debts and I wish to sell it."

"Hmm…" Mr. Taylor surveyed it some more. He breathed in through his nose and exhaled through loose lips, the way one might when uncertain.

"Let me consult with an expert on metalwork." An over-bright smile sprouted on his face. "For now, let's not fuss too much over business. We have a wedding to enjoy."

He ushered them back to the chatter and heat of the room. But Silas felt a chill slide up his spine. Mr. Taylor knew something he did not want to admit. Not here, at least. Because this was a party, and Taylor owed it to his daughter that all her guests, Silas included, remained buoyant and happy.

Silas returned to sample the cream-filled meringue nests. He would have to wait. After all the miles he'd journeyed and all the time he'd lost, and with the astrolabe in the right hands, the answers he sought were as shadowy as ever.

"Having fun?" Patrick sidled up to him. The brash, indulgent youth who'd left them two years ago no longer bristled at the slightest provocation. Something had sweetened him, too. Probably Fern. But there would be time tomorrow to dig into Patrick's true condition.

"I didn't imagine I'd walk into a family wedding on my return, but here we are, celebrating Eugene's day and with you among us. How can that not be fun?"

Try as he might, Silas could not hide the bitterness from his words. He spooned the dessert into his dry mouth and pushed thoughts of Viola from his mind for the thousandth time that day.

Viola's throat burned and her head ached. She crept up the staircase, along the outside as always, and clung to the railing with one hand to dust the top of the *Sweet Clementine* frame with the other.

Looking into the eyes of her mother this way now came with fresh sorrow. She swallowed hard. More than a breakfast of Derry's thick slabs of brown bread, toasted and slathered with orange marmalade, she needed a deep mug of hot tea with honey.

In the kitchen, Derry measured beans into a large crock, and a box of onions and leeks stood on the table for whatever he planned to do with them.

"Tea?" he offered when she slid into her seat at the table.

She nodded. "The hotter the better. My throat is afire."

He filled a mug and pushed it to her. She reached for the honey pot. A delicious, thick Blue Gum honey. She hadn't finished licking the spoon when Cloda burst in.

"Glory!" She braced herself on the kitchen door and gobbled in a deep breath. A large basket on her arm overflowed with carrot tops. "I raced home as fast as I could."

Derry pushed a chair in her direction. "What's wrong, old woman. Who stole your lungs?"

She shook her head and smiled. "Nothing wrong. All good. Look!" She pulled a newspaper from her pocket and slapped it on the table. "It's you. On this list!"

<u>*Australia's First Christmas Postcard Contest*</u>

Judges have narrowed down their search and congratulate these shortlisted artists.

The winner will be announced next week.

Basile Constantine

Viola Buckley

Bill Ramsey

Matthew Thomas

Sophia James

Honors are bestowed on all finalists for their efforts.

Viola stood and read it again, not sure she'd taken it in properly while seated.

"Shortlisted?" She ran a trembling finger over the words.

"Says right there—"

"Says what?" Jasper appeared and peered over her shoulder.

"Our Viola's a finalist." Cloda tapped the paper, and her chest puffed with all the pride Jasper would never show.

He grabbed the paper and read it for himself. His dour appraisal snuck in with such force it nearly toppled Viola over. Silas would not have read the announcement with a frown like Jasper's. She knew the smile that would pucker his face.

"It's not a win." Viola tempered some of her enthusiasm. "It's just a list. And in no order, I expect." The order, in fact, bothered her as much as Jasper's displeasure. Second on this list, too. "Best not to get carried away. There will only be one winner, and the rest will be forgotten."

He shrugged and left the way he'd come.

"Don't mind old sourpuss. You just look at the grin on Derry," said Cloda.

"Honors bestowed." Derry reread the notice. "Honors for our Viola."

"And that may be all." She prepared them for the greater possibility.

"I'd have put you first," Derry said. "Lined you up in alphabetical order."

"Don't count your chickens," Viola countered. Even so, her heart hammered in ways it had not before.

The day after Eugene's wedding, Silas examined his books to assess the orders Swift Brothers would fill in the coming weeks. With Christmas only a few months away, spice cupboards and tea caddies, along with a rush on framed mirrors, would appear on their lists. He wanted them on the factory floor in various stages of construction as soon as possible.

On the other side of the desk, Patrick sat upright and rubbed his palms. The very desk Eugene had eased himself behind. Now Patrick circled there too.

Silas winced at the memory.

"She's crying, Silas."

"I hear her."

"Why don't you go to her?"

"She doesn't want me. Besides, Mary won't let me in. She says Honora needs her rest and that I vex her."

"Can't you ignore Mary?"

"I have to attend to this." Silas had tapped the overflowing stack of papers on his desk. Orders and invoices ruled his day then as they did now.

"Let me do some of this for you. I can." Patrick had jumped to his feet. *"I'm better at the books than I am on the tools. And you could go to Hon—"*

"I run this office, Patrick. Not you. Not Eugene. So sit."

Patrick had lowered himself back into the chair.

"But I could—"

The sound of Honora's crying reached them again. Not a soft, sad cry. Not one Patrick understood. But Silas did. This was the desperate sob that scuttled into all the childless corners of their home.

"You don't know us, Silas. You don't know what Eugene and I are capable of. All you know is what you think we need."

"You know more than me now?" Silas had wanted to pick him up and throw him out. But he'd let him talk until the steam in his brother had run dry. Anything not to hear Honora suffer.

"You're so scared something is going to happen to us and it will be your fault again that you won't let us grow up. You can't loom over us this way. And we don't want to sit in your shadow." Patrick had pressed clenched fists along the side of his legs.

They'd argued more, their voices raised and rising until Patrick had demanded his freedom and Silas had pushed a stack of papers onto the floor like a flock of dead birds. Severing himself into thirds was the only atonement that appeased Patrick. And Chester Sweeney had been the only one to smooth the way for that kind of transaction.

Now, two years later, the road before them had become a thorny, rocky, slippery alley, as treacherous as the unseen Shanghai trapdoors all over Portland he'd been warned to never stand upon.

Silas laid down his pen.

Patrick watched him, sweat on his nape, which he dabbed with a threadbare yellow handkerchief. Time had delivered them back to this very spot.

"You took a third of this business and abandoned us while we watched Honora die."

Patrick flushed. Silas hoped the shame went deep.

"Silas, I'm… so very sorry about Honora."

"We buried her without you, too."

Patrick sighed. "It was many months later that Eugene's letter reached me. By then, it was—"

"Too late." Silas shook his head. "Isn't it always?"

"I'm hoping it's not too late. For us. That somehow, we can make a way forward. For the sake of my child."

Silas leaned into the leather of his chair. Where was Mary when he needed her to soften their exchange?

"You haven't told me how you met Fern."

"I met Fern because you were right." Patrick leaned forward, elbows on his knees, hands together in a posture Silas himself often resorted to. "I put my foot wrong, like you always warned. And I ended up broke."

Silas pressed the words that came to him like hot bullets between his lips until he felt the clenching clear to his bones. But he did not take his eyes off his brother.

"What happened?"

"The day I left here I took a job on the *Shoo Fly* sternwheeler. I thought if I learned everything about transporting wheat on the riverways, I could launch my own vessel."

"What happened on the *Shoo Fly*?" Silas kept his voice low. But his temper flared.

"I met a man who promised we'd go into business together. He knew people I didn't. He had experience. I had money. He charmed me into believing him. We'd played cards once or twice, and yes… I remember you telling me to never sit at a card table, but it was not the cards that took my money, it was my partner. He disappeared with it, overnight. I never saw him again. He told someone he'd won it all in a poker game, but Silas, please believe me, I was swindled."

Swindled and broke. Silas swallowed hard, but still his breakfast churned.

"Why didn't you come home?"

"I knew you'd have a face like thunder, like now. I was ashamed and I joined the first logging crew that would take me as far from here as possible."

"And you learned how it feels to lose a sizable amount of money in the blink of an eye." Silas slammed the desk with his fist. If it would have helped, he might have punched it into the wall as well. Kicked a hole in the front door and shoved Patrick through it onto the street. "You lost it all? On a game of cards?"

"I lost some on a card game, the rest when a crook ran off with it." The humbling gravity of Patrick's foolishness crumpled in his face. His shoulders sank and he rubbed his hand as if the sting lodged in his palm. Maybe pain was all he had left.

"Fern's father is head cook for one of the logging teams down by Link River. I don't know how I got so lucky with Fern." Tears shot into his eyes. "No one was bothered by how I look. It wasn't disfigurement that held me back. It was the little I knew about life beyond this factory, and I was taken for a fool because in so many ways I was one."

Creases lined his face. Not the ones that came with weather or age. But the deep furrows that caved a man in when he'd made more blunders than he knew how to fix. And those raw creases ran right into Silas's heart. He'd always seen his own errors in the face of his brothers. He still saw them. People made mistakes. Costly ones. And some never stopped paying.

Patrick licked his lips again, and Silas felt the weight of what would come next. An expectant wife and life on logging gangs along Link River were no great match.

"I don't deserve to ask, but Silas, I need your forgiveness. And I need a second—"

The bell above the shop door rang. Taylor and a companion moved around the displays until they spied Silas in the office and waved. The other man looked familiar. Where had Silas seen him before? It didn't matter. It was Taylor he needed. And this visit could only be about the astrolabe. Patrick backed away but Silas called him back.

Why not let the man who'd crippled his business watch him piece it back together? If it was life lessons Patrick lacked, Silas had them in abundance.

31

"There's no room for bad news at a wedding feast. Yesterday was not the time, but I'm afraid my suspicions have been confirmed." Taylor's words bounced to the office floor like marbles, breaking through the bottom of a wet paper bag.

"Suspicions?"

"Your astrolabe is a forgery. I knew yesterday but wanted to be sure. In the light of day. It's…" He shook his head and handed it over like a fragile egg.

"Forgery?" Silas took the astrolabe. "All the scrollwork, the markings. The date, 1564. How can that—"

"It's the date that convinced me. Real astrolabes don't carry dates. Their uniqueness, the reliability of their provenance, is not found in any inscription but in the handiwork of the man who made it. That's the only signature needed."

"You're telling me this is a mere trinket?"

"Afraid so."

"All this time. All my energies, my boyhood fixation, all for nothing. A worthless duplicate."

"I'm sorry. I know it's a deep disappointment."

Silas stood and paced the hot room. Noose-like, his collar tightened.

"I chased a fake halfway around the world."

Awkward silence pooled in the room, and from the corner of his eye Silas saw Patrick lower his head.

"That's why I've brought my cousin Ruben with me. We're hoping he might soften the blow," Taylor continued.

Cousin Ruben. That's who he was, the chatty relative from the wedding.

Ruben Lockwood smiled. "I hope Swift Brothers can accommodate me. I can hear how busy you are in there." He cocked his head toward the lathe and saws and chisels of the workroom. "My wife insisted I speak with you first, before we leave town. She said now that we're practically family…"

Silas could not bear to listen to the man talk, without pause, about his wife or whatever present she desired. He wanted to storm outside. Let the wind buffet his skin and drill all the way to his numb core.

He couldn't attend to this man now, not with Chester Sweeney breathing down his back and ownership of this building at stake. The floor felt like a ship's deck. He swayed and grabbed the edge of the desk for balance.

"Patrick," he summoned his brother, "you remember how to show our customers around the shop floor, don't you? It's a little more organized now, but that's probably a good thing when you're looking for a gift."

Patrick rose, fast. "Of course. Gentlemen—"

"Oh, no." Ruben shook his head. "I'm not looking for a gift. I'm looking for a staircase. I'm going to need at least a dozen of the ordinary kind, and one grand staircase. For the grand entry."

"Grand entry?"

"We spoke of this last night. The new girls' boarding school, of which I am patron. Four levels, with staircase access to all classrooms and dormitories, but the front staircase must be a work of art."

"We don't make stairs for the public. We supply a builder of kit homes."

"You can expand the scope of your business, no? We'll need ordinary staircases too, but what I'm looking for is a design for a bespoke grand staircase, then perhaps we could make a deal for them all, the simple and the elaborate. I've asked two other craftsmen to submit their designs. I'll compare them with yours, if you take up the offer, and decide in the new year."

"You're not here to buy a spice cupboard?"

"Why would I want a spice cupboard?"

The men laughed. All except Silas.

"Perhaps you already have designs we could consider," Mr. Lockwood added.

Silas swallowed hard. Designs swirled around his head every day. Every night. They formed into patterns and scrollwork and embellishments like the one he'd left behind on a lonely Australian beach log.

But he could not afford to play. With his kind of debt, a man could not expand his business. And without the astrolabe, it would take everything to keep from losing the roof over their heads now, too.

"I am afraid I won't be able to make that happen." He winced to say it. "I have other business needs that I must concentrate on at present."

He turned to Patrick. If it weren't for him, perhaps this opportunity would not dangle beyond his reach. Perhaps Chester Sweeney would not be eyeing this building in payment.

Regretfully, the men made their way out of the office, but Patrick hung back.

"Please, Silas. Let me back in. I'll not cause any grief."

"Back into what? A sinking ship?"

"I'll work for whatever you think I'm worth. A day's wage for a day's work."

"You foolishly think you belong here?" Silas let out some of the hurt that he'd kept under his skin.

"I do. Let me help."

"And how would you do that?" Silas pushed his desk chair away with a frustrated kick. "How would you wipe away our crippling debt?"

Patrick stood his ground. "I'd sit in that chair for a start. I'd run the books twice as fast as you or Eugene. I didn't cut timber for long at Link River. That's what I wanted to tell you. Our crew lost their accountant to a ruptured appendix. And I stepped in until they could find a replacement. Ledgers and numbers are easier for me than most. You don't have to commit. It could be a trial period. And I have ideas. So many ideas on how we could make the business better."

Silas was in no mood for more forgeries. "Name one."

Patrick raised his chin. "We invite customers to trial furniture in their homes. See how it fits their rooms. It would make them more comfortable about paying the prices we charge, which are higher than some, but our quality is the best."

Silas ignored the *we*. It hadn't been *we* in years.

"If a piece doesn't suit, they bring it back. Think of it as a gesture of confidence. Fine furniture. Fine craftsmanship. The right price. And now, you'll be offering peace of mind."

"What if they run off with the furniture?"

The brothers looked at each other.

"There's nothing to gain without risk."

Silas was not so sure. Some risk delivered no reward. Only an empty pocket over an emptier heart.

Viola's bed covers felt like an acre of wet wool. They pinned her down and kept her there. She swallowed and her throat burned. Her ears throbbed, but only a little less than her head. She tried to sit up, but the dizziness pulled her back.

The hammering in her head intensified. *Thump, thump.* It sounded like a fist tried to push through her attic door. *Knock, knock.*

She heard it again. Only this time, a voice followed.

"Miss Buckley?"

Viola pulled herself from the bed. Cold from the floorboards swirled up her bare legs. She needed socks. A warm wrap. Powders for her head.

"Miss Buckley?" The voice of Helena Hall fell from all the other sensations into the memory of their appointment this morning.

"Oh no." With slow painful steps, she dragged herself to the door and cracked it open. "I'm so sorry, I…" She wanted to say *I forgot* or *I'm sick.* Whatever combination worked, but her tongue felt like sand. She swallowed, if you called that swallowing.

Gargling a rusty razor blade would feel better than this. She rested her head on the doorframe.

"Oh, you're ill!" Helena pushed the door open. "I can return another day, but here…" She helped Viola to her bed. "I'll find someone downstairs and let them know you need soup or something and…" She pressed the back of her hand against Viola's forehead. "And a cold flannel. You're burning up. That's what my mother would give. Oh, and today of all days."

"I will make it up to you. I…"

"It's not me I'm thinking of. It's you!" Helena's sweet face lit up. "I thought you'd be awake and celebrating."

Viola was awake enough to know this was no celebration. Her bones ached, and now humiliation burned from the shame of having slept right into Helena's portrait appointment. What celebration had she forgotten as well?

The girl pulled a newspaper from her pocket. "It's you!" She spread the pages over the bed.

WINNER!

Australia's First Christmas Postcard

Congratulations to: Miss Viola Buckley of Melbourne

For her entry:

A House by the Sea – An Australian Bush Vista

> *Miss Buckley's card depicts a beach, a white house in the background, a decorative border of eucalyptus leaves with a hint of pink galah in the sky.*
>
> *All cards to be sold from Forbes Booksellers, Collins Street.*

"I've won?" She sought Helena for confirmation. "I'm not dreaming this…?"

The girl laughed. "It's not a dream. You are the winner. Oh, I can't wait to see it, even more than my portrait, which is mostly an indulgence for Father. But this…"

She tapped the newspaper and brought her clenched fists to her mouth. Eyes wide, as Viola imagined her own watery ones appeared.

She had won.

Not first place, but the only place. Her hands shook and the newspaper shook along with her, as if everything she'd longed for came to life right there in the delivery of a regular newspaper by the beautiful Helena Hall.

"Now, you stay put. I'll find someone to tend to you. Whom

shall I ask for? Whom do you need?"

"Um, someone should be in the kitchen." Viola wasn't sure. What time was it? Would Cloda be here or at the markets?

Her eyes welled with tears. And the booming thump in her ears dissipated a little while Helena Hall's footsteps softened into the rooms beneath. In the silence, a fresh strength pulled Viola from her bed. Morning sun feathered in from the attic windows.

Her name. Right there on the page. No one else before hers. No one after, either.

She leaned on the wall beside the tracing she'd made of Silas's carving on their log.

Silas, I have won!

She let the newspaper flutter to the floor. Her breath hammered like something wild climbed out from behind her ribs.

Viola looked into the mirror. Hair in disarray, nightdress crumpled, but her eyes held happy tears, and the light from the window cast an eerie, familiar glow that reflected from her hair. Coppery, tinged with a spark she'd only seen like this once before. A radiance that had no way of being held. Not her fever. Not even the flush of winning. It was something more.

The elusive glow of *Sweet Clementine* now dazzled from all the reflective surfaces in the room. It was not only the light. It was what she knew from within.

It wasn't what. It was *who.*

Whom do you need?

She needed Silas. And in the silence of a tavern yet to awaken, her longing screamed with loss only she could hear. The win was all hers, as was the talent that secured it.

But the delight was something she wanted to share. With him. She pulled herself to the door and hobbled to *Sweet Clementine* to be sure she hadn't imagined any of this.

There shone the light in her mother's eyes. That light she'd hunted and never seen again until this moment because she had been looking in the wrong place. For that light, that kind of love had been extinguished in her mother when Mortimer died.

But now, she saw it for real and in her own eyes.

And more than anything a doctor could prescribe, anything the apothecary would dispense or Cloda might cook up, all she needed was Silas.

32

The days grew cold. The nights colder. In his bedroom, Silas scrunched up another dead-end paper strategy to feed his debt. No matter how he made the calculations, how many times he double-checked his accounts, re-counted their money, and factored in how much they'd need to keep the business turning, Silas failed to reconcile what he needed with the little he had.

If he was to build a staircase for a grand entry, he knew what he'd aim for. But that would demand extensive design and engineering. It would require a larger crew of workers on his factory floor.

ViolaViolaViola

Silas knew he had no way of delivering it. Still, his mind and heart worked together, and the pattern that emerged was no different to the one he'd left behind. A dream that never went away. Other craftsmen probably carved their own panels right now, too. Men with a team and resources to make it happen. Could he afford to spend his nights on a design that might go nowhere?

The sound of a carriage roused him from his deliberations, and he pushed the drape away from the window. Below, Eugene alighted and assisted his new bride from their conveyance. Olive dropped Eugene's hand the second her foot landed on the road beneath. Or was it Eugene who dropped hers?

Silas rested his head on the glass. He prayed this was the weariness that came from bumpy carriage rides, mixed with whatever tiff had taken root within. But the heat that fired in his chest like a warning shot reverberated into his head. Returning honeymooners rarely displayed this manner of coolness toward each other, no matter how many wayward springs poked out of carriage seats.

He listened for their entry.

Mary had been asleep for hours, bags packed for her journey home in the morning. Patrick and Fern had retired early, too. Before leaving for the day, Mrs. Knott had fussed over the room that would welcome the newlyweds, but they themselves uttered no happy conversation on their way up.

Doors opened. Traveling bags were dumped on the floor. Another door closed as if slapped shut.

Where was the cooing of their wedding day? The soft laughter? A giggle behind the closed door? He had little time to contemplate, little time to let the panic in his chest properly awaken before an angry knock sounded.

"Silas! Open up!"

He opened the door and braced himself. And for good reason. Eugene looked like a black typhoon, ready to erupt from his chest.

"You!" He pushed himself into the room. "You dog."

Silas held his brother back. "Wait—"

"You sat there. Not a word!"

"Wait. Tell me first what you're raging about."

But he knew. This was the flaming face of a husband betrayed. Even though Silas knew the betrayal had happened a year before Eugene had taken a wife.

"You mangy dog." He pushed Silas in the shoulder and knocked him off balance.

"Talk to me, Eugene. Pushing me around won't help."

"You." He nodded through his tears. "And Olive? My *wife!* Tell me she's lying. Tell me!" he roared.

Silas tried to shush him with two hands splayed in defense. "What did she tell you?"

"That I was sorry." Olive stood at the door, her clothes in creases. "That it was one sorrow-filled night and neither of us knew the other and it was an indiscretion I would take back in an instant if I could."

Eugene ignored her.

"You took advantage of her. And thought you'd take advantage of me, too. Well, your days of lording it over us are over. If you think I'd ever bring my wife to live under this roof with you, you've lost your mind," he bellowed.

"Eugene, please," Olive tried to calm him.

But Silas understood the rage that needed to be let loose. He, too, needed the unburdening.

"I'm so ashamed, Eugene. Of that night. Of not knowing how to confess it." There was so much more that needed saying, but he didn't know how to forgive himself, let alone ask someone else for it.

Olive and Eugene stood there, grim-faced, breathing hard, at war with him and with each other.

And Patrick now hovered somewhere behind, shock so chiseled into his face, Silas wondered if he too looked as stricken.

"What has Olive told you?" The only way to remedy something like this was to go back to where it inflicted the most pain.

Eugene rubbed the side of his mouth, but it did not hide his trembling lip. "She said I was a man above all men. That I was worth one thousand of my brother, Silas. And I wondered, why would she mention your name on our honeymoon?"

Silas dared a quick look at Olive, who wept into the knot of her fist.

"We'd taken our last meal at the hotel and perhaps one too many cups of wine." He shrugged. "When I looked at her, red and fumbling, I pressed her for more. Told her she could tell me anything, because I never imagined she would utter anything this loathsome." Spittle fell from his mouth, and tears welled in his eyes. Olive's tears fell freely.

"She told me the most sordid of tales, of the night when you suffered that mauling, and she happened to be there, with bandages and wounds of her own. She carried grief into a dark place and collided with you. For only a moment in time, she said. As if *time* was the problem and not the sneaky, low, feeble way in which you hid this from me."

He took a swing at Silas but missed. It didn't look like it was meant to land. It looked more like he wanted to push through the fog of what his mind would not hold.

Silas had no words to excuse that night. And Eugene did not need to hear about the easy way he'd duped himself into believing there was no other way to slacken the cold. The misery. The self-loathing.

"Eugene, when you introduced me to your fiancée, I dared not uncover what should have remained hidden. I offered my congratulations, and I meant them, but underneath I was as mortified as you are now. And the joy of your news, the purpose with which you held yourself, your work here… I saw a different man. One who'd found the happiness that has eluded me most of my life."

"Oh, please. You don't expect me to buy that."

"I do." Silas fought to keep his voice calm. "I would not have stolen your happiness from you, not then and not ever, if it were in my power. Everything I've done has been for you and Patrick. To secure your futures. To grow a business that would allow you a workplace and an income. The eve of your wedding was no time for me to drag up the sordid rags of regret. Your love for Olive and hers for you convinced me to say nothing."

"Well, you get to say anything you want now. Because she has."

"It's late," Silas said. "We'll talk more in the morning."

"In the morning," Eugene shoved him in the chest, "we will talk about how you will hand over my share of this business, as you did to Patrick, so I can take my wife as far from you as money allows."

"Eugene, you can't mean that."

"Why not? Why do you find my repulsion of you so hard to take? You've pushed me around for years. Only I never pushed back. I stayed behind and kept the factory going all on my own. But not this time. Starting this night, you will think of a way to split what's left of Swift Brothers because I can't stand to look at you. Make it happen the way you orchestrated every other mess."

He turned on his heel, pushed past Patrick, and stormed down the corridor with all the boiling rage of a wounded animal.

Silent and dismantled, Olive followed her husband into their room where, no doubt, anger would fester all night.

Patrick let out a long breath. "He'll simmer down by morning. But, Silas, did you…and Olive?"

"Yes." Silas could not look at him. "I was tricked by my own emptiness. I'd been at Honora's grave and was already in a bad way. That dog lunged at me, and she was there, and I wish I could take it all away."

Patrick knew about regrets and being tricked. Now Silas knew, too. Being tricked by one's own foolishness was the worst kind of swindling.

"Get some rest. We'll…" But even Patrick, with his many solutions, had none for this. He shut the door, and closed in by the revelations of that night, Silas sat on his bed and stared at the floor.

The astrolabe, now worthless, had become his obsession that

night when he'd visited Honora's grave.

"Find it. Sell it," Mr. Hinkle had said.

But that night, Silas had let his baser self intrude. Desolate, he'd found himself wanting. And in the moment and with little thought, had taken. Now, he was about to lose everything, all that he'd ever worked for. He would have to carve himself to the bone. Maybe beyond.

Because there was no other way to restore what he'd broken.

Not this time.

This would cost him everything.

By morning, Silas wished he could let the sorry lot of them keep sleeping, but Mary deserved a proper farewell. He dressed fast and made enough noise to let the household know he wasn't tiptoeing around anyone or anything.

"Wake up, Eugene." He banged on the door to Eugene's room but did not stop to listen for a reply. He did the same at Patrick's door and kept walking. "Mary's carriage will be here soon. Make sure you're downstairs to kiss her goodbye before she sets off."

He would not capitulate and wriggle around in his guilt. There would be plenty of time for that. In all their troubles, Mary was blameless and deserved the respect of her brothers.

They gathered in the street, bleary-eyed and crippled by the surly irritation that follows a man into the day when he's not slept well the night through. Eugene and Patrick stood side by side as they'd always been, sullen at the summons. Their wives did not make an appearance. Perhaps Fern had already bid Mary goodbye the night before.

"You didn't have to drag them out of bed, Silas." Mary fastened a cape at her neck by its ribbons.

"We've urgent business to discuss. It's best we start early," Eugene mumbled, and Silas could have clipped him over the head.

"You're here to bid your sister goodbye. Not grumble in her ear."

"I heard it all last night." Mary sighed. "You threw your voices around like you wanted the entire street to stop and listen."

"I'm sorry if we woke you," Eugene said.

Mary's traveling bag hung from one hand while in the other, she clutched a basket. "I'm going home to three boys just like you, but mine are all under five and better behaved."

"They don't wrestle grown men issues." Eugene crossed his arms over his chest. "But Silas is going to fix that today. He's going to give me my share of this business, the way he did for Patrick, and I'll be taking Olive away for a new start. Far from here. We appreciate you coming to our wedding, Mary. And, well… I'll write to you and let you know where we end up."

"End up?" Mary scoffed. "What a load of nonsense."

"It's not nonsense."

"Your share?"

"That's enough, sister." Silas tried to grab Mary's hand, but Mary refused to be corralled.

"You're mad at Silas for something that happened before you even knew Olive. He may have kept that from you for any number of reasons. You should be glad he protected you. It's your wife who made the confession."

She had a way of summarizing their lives like no other.

"If you're happy to leave here with Olive then there's something between you that's worth saving. I feel for you, Eugene, I really do, but asking Silas to carve up his business one more time is not the answer. He's already given Patrick what wasn't his. At great cost to himself. Please, think long and hard about asking for the same."

"What do you mean, *wasn't his*?" Patrick straightened.

A flare of warning spiked Silas in the chest. "Mary, I beg you."

"I won't let you do it, not twice, Silas. I wasn't here last time to say my part. But it's wrong. And there's no winners if you all go broke—"

"What does she mean, *wasn't his*?" Patrick asked again. "Silas?"

All eyes fell on him, but Silas petitioned his sister.

"Mary, I don't know what you think you're doing—"

"Honora told me on her deathbed." She paused until all three returned her gaze. "Patrick had gone, and Silas had taken out a huge loan for it to happen. This business our father left behind, all of it," she pointed to the building behind them, "belongs to Silas. None of it was Patrick's. Nor Eugene's. Father left it all to Silas and when you're fighting over it like alley cats, you're fighting over something that was never yours. It all belongs to Silas."

Silas felt some of the fight in him slip away. "Honora told you?"

"She did, and I kept my silence because Patrick was gone and there was nothing to be done about it. But now that you're all here, outraged over what you think is yours," she pointed to Eugene, "and sheepishly returning for another slice, like you," she pointed to Patrick, "well I won't stay quiet."

Patrick turned to him. "Is she telling the truth?"

Silas swallowed hard and wet his lips, but the words would not come, the ones he knew would hurt his brothers more than he ever had.

"Why does the shingle say *Swift Brothers – Fine Furniture Makers*?" asked Patrick.

Before Silas could answer, Mary's carriage rumbled down the street.

"Please sort this out with respect and brotherly love. I could not bear it, otherwise." She kissed their cheeks and left them to watch the conveyance disappear around a corner.

Patrick slumped onto the front step of Swift Brothers, legs buckled with his forehead atop his knees. "Silas, you have a lot to explain."

Silas joined him on the step, the energy that wrangled them all from their beds now gone.

Eugene remained standing, face grim, mouth a thin line. Whatever loathing he'd brought home last night now quadrupled in his horrified face.

"Well?" His hands trembled and he thrust them deep into his pockets. "Start talking."

Silas took a deep breath. It was here on these cobbles he'd made that dumb decision to run after Charlie Hinkle.

"Father's found treasure. Come and see. He says it's from ancient Persia and that sailors use it to find their way."

"When you boys were sick, we were terrified you wouldn't survive, but when you pulled through, Father was worried that, that in the future, you might be … impaired."

Neither brother replied.

"He studied you over the years. Eugene all quiet and timid. Patrick given to moods, easily angered, and he wanted to make sure you were both taken care of. He made a will. Left it all to me. Mother always said I had to look after you, but it was Father who secured it. From the grave. It's what I've done every day since you lay there, fevered and clinging to life. It's been my job to make sure you were safe, with some kind of future ahead."

"Why does it say *Swift Brothers*, then?" asked Patrick. "It was *Hal Swift, Fine Furniture* before he died."

"I chose the name. After the fire, when we rebuilt the factory. I figured if you felt a connection, you'd not want to leave."

"You took a loan to let me go?" Patrick's voice rang with disbelief.

"A loan that's too big for me to cover with ease. It would have been hard enough as it was, but then we lost the uninsured timbers and Honora died. That's why I went to Australia, hoping I'd return with the astrolabe that she made me throw away. Well, I did, but it's worth nothing. It's a fake, so..."

That last *so* hung in the morning mist and rattled around the empty street.

He stood and faced Eugene. What they had to work out was more important than any business or loan.

"Hinkle pressed me to hunt down the astrolabe *that night.* I was broken. Lonely. Grief stricken. In my misery, I thought I wanted to be comforted by someone. I was wrong. My pain was nothing anyone could fix. And now, I've landed the worst grief on you. I wish I could take that day and so many others and scrub them into the dirt. The day I brought home smallpox. When I brought home the astrolabe, thinking it an innocent amusement. The day I threw it away."

Eugene still wore a bleak face. Who could blame him? But his shoulders had softened a little. "So, I'm stuck here? Prisoner in this business?"

"You're no prisoner, Eugene. You're free to go."

Eugene considered this for the longest time, his breath visible in the cold morning air. His chest rose and collapsed in anger.

"Eugene," Silas tried again. "If I had the means to set you free like I did with Patrick, I would."

"Why did you do it?" Patrick raised his head. "Why not just tell us there was nothing in the will for us and let it be?"

"Because it wasn't fair. You should've had a share."

"But father didn't think so."

"He only wanted you to remain dependent on me because he didn't know you as well as I did."

"Know us?"

"Beneath the shyness, the brashness, I knew there was the making of good men. It's why I always pushed you to do what was right. Why I set you tasks and showed you how it was done. I wanted you to know you were capable."

"You've always bossed us around! Told us what not to do. Kept us from making our own decisions."

"Perhaps, when you were younger and I felt the weight of responsibility. But I let you walk," he said to Patrick. "And I left you in charge when I went to Australia," he said to Eugene.

"With severe warnings and a *don't-do* list as long as my arm."

"You can't run a business without smart measures," Silas replied. Weariness pulled at his legs, and the aroma of food wafted from inside. He stood and took a deep breath.

"I smell coffee. Let's eat and talk some more. If you want to leave, Eugene, maybe there's a way to make it happen. Patrick wants to return. Between us, we should be able to find a way. We're heading into a busy time with Christmas orders about to hit us, but if we put our heads together..."

They made their way back to the long table where Mrs. Knott set silverware down with a clang. Patrick walked beside him. Eugene followed, many paces behind.

Their father had been wrong. The twins had it in them to be fine men. One had found his long-lost spine after years of weak compliance. One had simmered down a little after running away to beat his chest. But there was much ahead of them.

And it was up to Silas to lead the way.

Along with his father, he had misjudged them, but Viola had shown him that admitting you'd misjudged someone was the only way through misunderstandings.

So he let them find their seats, and when they looked settled enough not to bolt or punch him in the head, he sat opposite them.

"I want to find a way out of this that will serve you both well, but it will take time, and I won't be able to offer a solution until after Christmas. To do something like what you need now, Eugene, would jeopardize us all."

His brothers said nothing.

"Chester Sweeney renegotiated the terms of my loan at a huge price. He's expecting a hefty installment at the end of the month, and time is running out. Now that the astrolabe is worthless, I have to find the money elsewhere or, per our agreement, he'll take ownership of this building."

Eugene's face darkened. "You didn't tell me you'd thrown in this building when you went on your wild goose chase."

"I didn't want you to worry."

"I took a wife, thinking I had a home to bring her to. You've kept me in the dark in more ways than one, Silas. What else is there you've negotiated on our behalf, other than risking our marriages with poverty?"

"Shut up, Eugene." Patrick threw him an angry look. "You're not helping." He turned back to Silas. "What about Ruben Lockwood's staircase project?"

Silas shook his head. "We either pay Sweeney or order supplies to continue our normal production. Adding something new is beyond us."

"Well done, Silas." Eugene stood and kicked the leg of the table.

"You've sent this business to the brink. And by the new year we'll be paying rent to Chester Sweeney. And who knows what that grub will do next?"

"I won't let that happen." Silas pressed his palms on the bench seat.

"What are you going to do? Get a genuine astrolabe from Hinkle this time? Or will you keep softening us to stay here with more fakery? More trickery?" Eugene scoffed. "*Swift Brothers, Fine Furniture Makers.*"

September 15, 1879

Helena Hall is a curious little thing. At first I thought she was shy, but I •iscovere• when a sitting has en•e•, nothing satisfies her more than a thorough poke aroun• my attic room.

She peers into my boxe• collection of seashells an• •igs her han• into a calico bag of feathers I have gathere• over the years. Of great fascination to her is one of Balthazar's. She returns to it each session an• for three weeks in a row now, I have foun• her, feather to cheek.

I tell her stories about that crazy bir•, an• she tells me she is a fan of exotic names like Balthazar an• Viola. She thinks her name is or•inary an• wishes her parents ha• chosen from so many others.

I •o not share with her the wis•om an• fortune in being name• for herself alone.

That my father •eliberately cast me in a role that •i• not fit. I •o not tell her because it thrills me to hear the story of a little girl secure in the cra•le of her parents' love. I •o not wish for her to know it is not always the way for other little girls.

Mr. Hall has refine• his commission. I am to paint a miniature portrait, a curio that will nest in the palm of his wife on her birthday.

I am touched by this gesture. I could not have painted a life-size portrait of Helena, like Sweet Clementine, *unpracticed as I am. But the delicate nature of this piece appeals to me.*

Helena's parents will hide this likeness in a reticule or drawer and pull it out, the way Clemmie did with Viola's dancing shoe. Perhaps one day Helena's children will pass it on to their own children, and the careful sketch and meticulous painting I render will take this little girl into the future. And a part of me with her.

I ask myself, could this be something I choose to do again?

Because for the first time since I allowed myself to look into the heart of Silas, I am glad to dabble in portraiture.

And each time I bid farewell to Helena, I close the door behind her and wonder if Silas ever stops to look at the sketch I made of him and wonder about me, the way I do about him.

33

The day bloomed with all the exuberance of spring. Brisk winds, sunshine, and the heady drift of wattle.

The sort of day that healed sore throats fast. Viola breathed deep draughts of air, thick with aromas and the allure of the Botanic Gardens that danced right to the front door of the Star and Garter, where she waited with Nasrin on the street corner.

Nasrin had arrived with her biggest and warmest embrace and plans for them to celebrate at the Botanic Gardens Tearooms. But Viola had sniffed through happy tears and the heaviest of colds and promised they would celebrate as soon as she'd put the finishing touches on Mr. Hall's commission of his daughter.

She was grateful for the opportunity and didn't want to disappoint him. Plus, her mornings with Helena had been fun, and at each sitting she'd discovered something new about the girl. She snorted a little when she laughed. She had a button collection that rivaled any of her friends. And in her pocket, she always carried peppermints, which she unwrapped and shared with Viola at the beginning of their sessions.

Today, Viola cradled the finished curio, secure in a white velvet pouch. "Oh, there he is. In the gray coat." A little more stooped than the last time she'd seen him, Jeremiah Hall walked with the assistance of a walking cane.

"I was expecting someone younger. He looks…" Nasrin peered at him.

"He runs a cheese importing business. Mr. Barnes said his wife is considerably younger, and he married her when she was recently widowed. A wealthy catch, he said. She already had two older sons, but Helena is their daughter."

They watched the slow, well-fed man cross the road.

"Here we are, Mr. Hall." Viola waved.

He lifted his head and stopped where he stood.

Nasrin sucked in her breath like someone who'd accidentally swallowed a fly.

"It can't be," she whispered.

"Miss Buckley." Mr. Hall came closer and nodded. "Good day to you."

"Mr. Hall, this is my dear friend, Madame Nasrin Karoly. And this is Mr. Hall."

"Mr. Hall, is it?" Nasrin's cheeks fired into red-hot blotches. "Or perhaps I remember you as someone else?"

Mr. Hall would not look her in the eye.

Nasrin let go of Viola and took a step closer. "This is not Jeremiah Hall." She pulled herself back a little, but it was as if she had no control of her body. It kept leaning in, staring, then pulling back in repulsion.

"I know you!" she gasped. "The last time I saw you, you were fleeing my theater with nothing more than your name. You left behind everything of value a man could dream of. Didn't you, Marshall?"

"Marshall?" Viola gasped. "What? You must be confused. This is…" She, too, peered at Jeremiah Hall.

If he were Marshall, would she not know it? Would not her broken heart have sounded the cry of her childhood? Her father had been lean. In frame and in spirit. This man was portly. Red-faced. Bent and bald.

Could time have altered him so completely? Surely Nasrin was wrong.

But fury vented from Nasrin's nostrils, and with each step she closed between them, she looked every inch a woman about to tear him limb from limb.

The eyes of Jeremiah Hall darted from Viola to Nasrin and back again.

"What do you want, Marshall? Haven't you taken enough from her? State your business or I swear, I'll scream for a constable."

A devilish howl mocked Viola from the darkest corner of her mind. A place where cobwebs held her down.

"I'm not here for any trouble," he implored. "I swear. I read about Clemmie's death in the newspaper. It said they kept her memory alive at the Star and Garter, so I came to see for myself. Viola," he turned to her, "every night, I hear how Clementine Buckley was a songbird like no other, and that woman in the painting they all adore was my creation. I haven't tasted praise like that in years."

His words stuck Viola like a blade to the chest.

"They praise Clemmie, not the man who deserted her." Nasrin tried to reach for Viola's hand. But Viola pulled away.

"You're… Marshall?" The words tasted like wormwood. "My father?"

"It is I." He bowed, and for the first time, she saw some of the theater in him. A showman. A charlatan. Even when faced with his own worst example of depravity, the broken child he abandoned, he had the nerve to bow as if he had just performed something wonderful.

"I don't understand. Why would you appear now, with another family to dangle under my nose?" Humiliation and bitterness twisted in her like twin serpents. One fought the other for superiority.

"I never expected to see you in the tavern, Viola. When you arrived that first day and everyone welcomed you in, I wanted to know more of what had become of you."

She could not speak, disbelief so jarring it crushed her breath.

"That's none of your concern." Nasrin tried to shove herself between them. "You walked away from the right to know anything. You left two bleeding souls on my doorstep. Did you ever think in the years since, while you reformed into an inflated importer, they scraped together a living and pulled themselves along with dignity that you'll never possess?"

He faced Viola. "That's why I commissioned the curio to begin with. And I have payment." He tapped his breast pocket. "But I haven't told my wife or Helena. They don't know me as Marshall. I met my wife in England, and well, by then I had become a different man. A few times over. They mustn't know. Please, Viola, can't we make amends?"

"Marsh…hall. Hall…" Viola pulled back and stared at him. Had the frailty of his eyes also robbed him of his judgment? "The last thing I remember of you is telling Clemmie I was useless. Do *you* remember that? You said you had no use for me, a mere child who had not turned out as you hoped. Well, how that has changed."

She thrust the curio at him. "How useful of me to paint your beautiful daughter into a token for you to give your wife." She cried now, sobs that would not be kept in. She didn't care if he saw them. She had a sister, a living, breathing, sweet sister.

"When you won that Christmas postcard competition, I wanted to tell all the men in the tavern you were my daughter. Mine and Clementine's."

"But you didn't."

"Well, no. My wife and Helena, they must never know. It is enough for me, though, to hear the accolades from your admirers, because in my own way, I am the reason Clemmie sang the way she did. And now, I'm a part of the talent you display."

A shiver ran down Viola's spine. "What is your part, exactly?"

He shrugged, as if it were already clear. "Strength is passed on from the father. Weakness is passed on by the mother. All I ever saw in you was deficiencies, but I see strength now. As do all the tavern patrons." A tiny, hopeful smile escaped his lips. The ugliest, most clueless smile Viola had ever seen.

"They already loved Clementine and were learning to accept me. But you, you had no time for us when we needed a roof over our heads. Food on the table. Medicine. Years and years and years of medicine that did next to nothing."

He wasn't listening. He rummaged in his coat pocket and pressed an envelope into her hands. "Do not fall into the hysterical patterns of your mother. Take this. It's payment for the portrait and something we shall call *extra*. The newspapers print wonderful things about you. Your star is about to rise, they say."

"Let go of my hand. If you need a newspaper to tell you my worth…" She shook her head, afraid to go on. Afraid she would find herself in the ventriloquist's trunk, along with Little Lazlo and her own vomit in her hair.

"It would not serve me well to admit to my dear wife I'm not who she thinks I am." He reddened a little. "It's a delicate matter."

"Of course." A soft, sad chuckle escaped her. "That's how I

remember you. A man who did what served *him* best. And even now, you're not sorry."

He raised his chin a little. "Remorse slows a man down. If I had let it get in my way, I'd not have the means to commission your work. Once this curio catches the eye of our friends, they will all want to know where to find you. I will do my best to send them—"

She threw the envelope back at him. "I don't want your money or your recommendations. Tell Helena it was a pleasure to paint that curio. She's a fine young lady. I give her poor mother the credit for that."

He picked up the envelope and smoothed it out.

"Please, Viola, won't you allow me to, at least…make some kind of recompense? How else can I secure your…" He may have wanted to say forgiveness, but something clogged his throat, and he cleared it as if a coward's feather lodged there.

"I know you need it. Mr. Barnes told me so when I offered a healthy sum for *Sweet Clementine.* He said he'd promised it to you, should your art ever provide the income. And well, you have earned it now. It's the best I can do for you without compromising myself and my family into scandal. Don't walk away from your dreams because your mother's bad temper still drives your antics."

Nasrin grabbed his payment. "What you owe her would never fit into a post office full of envelopes."

She hooked Viola by the elbow and took her back into the tavern where Clemmie oversaw them with her smile.

Viola did not look back although she had enough questions for the man called Jeremiah Hall. Marshall. Right on her doorstep. Wanting to buy back some measure of ownership. And only because she'd shown herself as capable.

Which was all she'd ever wanted to show him.

That she *was* useful. Well, she had. And now he knew.

September 27, 1879

Nasrin an• I or•ere• a pot of tea an• a plate of small cakes at the Botanic Gar•ens Tearooms. We took our seats like all the other well-•resse• people there, but we alone wore the rough cloak of shock an• sa•ness.

An• no tea or cream-lathere• sponge cake sweetens that kin• of bitterness.

For hours, we •eliberate• over how I coul• not have seen Marshall in Jeremiah Hall. Perhaps my eight-year-ol• self remembers a wolf that tore me to shre•s. An• now that wolf has tucke• his tail from view.

But a wolf lives there, nonetheless.

I thought if I ever saw him again, I woul• fire all the anger an• frustration an• bitterness back at him. Some of that rose in me to•ay.

But there was still a place in me that wante• to impress.

An• I ha•. Alrea•y.

For he sought me. For a piece of art he coul• a•• to his collection, if he has one. I imagine he collects all manner of things. Paintings. Ol• coins. Rare books kept behin• glass. Among them, rare volumes of Shakespeare. With Balthazars an• Violas an•... Helenas! Of course. Even Jeremiah counts among the Bar•'s characters.

An• my anger seethes even while I write here, while the sha•ows lengthen an• the can•le burns low. I have a sister, someone I alrea•y like. Someone he has let me meet an• paint an• turn into something he will cherish.

A cruel, cruel man. More refine• in his cruelty than I remember.

I have turne• over in my min•, a thousan• times, that Mar-

shall could sit for weeks and not reveal himself. That he would feast on the adoration of Clemmie and observe me from behind his mask.

Was there nothing of me on that first day, when I served tables in my weary, anxious way, that appealed? Something of me that he should gather up?

But no, it is now that he sees me.

And in his envelope, like a well-sprung-trap, is a bank note in my name, for more money than I have seen in one place in my lifetime. Enough to make an offer on the Sweet Clementine *and meet the stipulations of Mr. Barnes.*

Yes, I have earned this, but not for my art. It's blood money, but Mr. Barnes would never know. Generous payment given in exchange for the curio of Helena. I could knock on the office door right now and present Mr. Barnes with an offer. One he invited me to make when, if... I ever could. But can I exchange Marshall's guilt money for Sweet Clementine?

Can my silence be bought? Can the years of neglect be wiped away?

This day has only brought more unanswered questions. The worst of which is...

Am I, just below the surface, the very likeness of my shallow father?

34

Restlessness pushed Viola from her bed the next morning. Nervous energy that toyed with her all night in cruel dreams and fits of rude awakenings.

She slipped out of the tavern and turned into the streets of South Yarra, away from the Botanic Gardens. Today, confusion pulled her the other way. It was not the distraction of the gardens nor the soothing of nature that she needed. It was the sorting of hard facts.

Marshall was Jeremiah Hall. Helena, her half-sister. And somewhere, tucked away, a stepmother busied herself with whatever she did on a Sunday morning, unaware Viola roamed discarded and untethered to family.

She passed along affluent streets and corners, one much like the other. Bluestone buildings, others built of sandstone, with well apportioned homes and shopfronts.

What do you see of God's creation? How does it make you feel?

What do you hear and smell? How does it taste?

And the best question for you, mon Poupette, what story will it tell when you put it onto paper?

She mulled over questions formed to numb the childhood ache of neglect and abandonment. Nasrin had filled her with questions. With purpose. And each night, when she said her prayers, Viola had something in her pocket, her fist, or her heart for which to give thanks.

How she needed that today. How she needed to sift the road ahead for something. She kept her eyes on the ground. In the gutters. In the puddles and ditches. A rock would do. A curled leaf. Evidence of a Heavenly Father. That's how Nasrin had taught her of the Creator. Look for Him.

A bell tolled from a church tower. The good people of Melbourne gathered for services under roofs pitched in gothic splendor and in the glow of stained-glass windows.

But she didn't need a pew as much as she needed a moment to plead her case to God. To beg release from the spiral of fear. Was she more like Clemmie or like Marshall? Either held a condemnation she was not ready to accept.

She stopped at the bottom of flagstones that took parishioners up to the pretty double doors of a handsome church building.

Wilson Street Chapel. The well-dressed strode in to occupy their seats. And there, among a small group about to enter, stood Marshall. Or Jeremiah Hall. Him. Her father. And Helena, with a woman she figured was her mother.

Her stomach clenched to see them amassed like any other family.

Petite, like Helena, her father's wife was in most ways the opposite of Clemmie. Where her own mother had stood tall, this woman was short. And unlike Clemmie, her gaze remained fixed on her daughter.

Clemmie would have taken in her surroundings, looking for her place in this array of people. Marshall's wife already knew her place. She stood by her daughter.

Gray-haired, tidy and meek, Mrs. Hall walked with quiet dignity. She was not a lost soul like Clemmie. Nor was she a ball of sunshine or a woman who wore her clothes with the aim of being seen. Instead, she occupied her place in this family with quiet strength.

With no thought to what would come next, Viola stepped up and up until she, too, slipped into the cool church building, even more invisible than Mrs. Jeremiah Hall.

She didn't know what she hoped to see while she clung to the back row. Marshall turned and scanned the seats behind them, smiling at one or two acquaintances. Poise pushed into Viola's spine and she sat upright. Refusing to hide.

He did not see her.

Soon, the hymns of a traditional service washed over her.

Marshall sang like a man on stage. She guessed he still was, in his own way. His new life as Jeremiah Hall would always be an act. Chest up, hymnal high, his voice reached her, bouncing off the stone walls. His wife and daughter sang with less flourish, but they remained connected, somehow.

And the image skewered her like nothing else had, not since the day Marshall had left them. He could have been a decent father, had he chosen. That could have been her up there, between the reliable shoulders of two parents. A confident father and an undamaged mother.

The singing ended and Helena's mother smiled at her daughter when they took their seats. A casual but meaningful exchange. Marshall smiled over the two of them, binding the trio with a thread that he could so easily sever.

Did he rage behind closed doors? Did Mrs. Hall cower in bed or drink herself to sleep? Perhaps Helena nourished a peace between her parents in ways Viola herself had destroyed.

The preacher, an older man with a white walrus mustache and heavy gait, stepped into the pulpit, purpose-built into an upper corner. This church was not like the one Nasrin attended. There, they would gather in a simple hall, where the singing was lively and preaching was not a performance.

But here, in this ornate setting, with an orator's balcony, the preacher gathered his notes. This was Marshall's kind of stage. Elevated. The preacher may have been perched onto the pulpit like a wise old bird, but his voice carried over them like that of a younger man.

Viola hadn't expected that. He read the scriptures, and she closed her eyes and let the words paint a picture in her mind.

" 'I will restore the years that the locust has eaten,' " he read from the book of Joel, and an image popped into Viola's mind.

A barren field. A wasted crop. A sky darkened by the long shadow of thieving insects.

"Lost years can never be restored. Not literally," he began.

Viola's eyes snapped open.

"Time, once past, is gone forever. Who can call back the north wind or fill again the emptied rain cloud? Who among us bids the river which has hastened onward to the sea, bring back its rolling floods? Who dares imagine that years, once gone, can ever be restored to us?"

Like a tapestry that wove itself right before her eyes, his message came to life. He spoke of fruitless years. Of selfish years. Of rebellious years. Years characterized by Christ-less misdirection. But when he spoke of painful and loveless years, the steel in Viola's spine softened a little.

"You cannot have back your time, my friends. But there is a strange and wonderful way in which God returns the wasted blessings, the unripened fruits of years over which you mourned. The years lost to great sorrow, depression, and disappointment. God will grind sunlight for you out of your blackest nights, and in the oven of affliction, Divine Grace will prepare the bread of delight."

She hung on every word, desperate for more.

"Never was a fairytale more strange, yet here it stands in sober words. When we come into the region where the Lord works, we come at once into contact with miracles and walk in the midst of marvels."

Like Nasrin before him, this strange bird-looking man had intercepted her pain with a strategy. A promise. Divine. And it beat in the hollow of her miseries like Balthazar banging for freedom.

Restoration had never truly found Clemmie. Not how Viola had dreamed it for her. But now, with her father and his family listening on, Viola heard the words that whispered her own renewal.

"God can restore lost years by multiplying your fruitfulness. God can restore lost years by restoring loss into gain. Time is His to give. Over and over. First attempts may fail, but they are only first. Let's not forget how many second chances lead to victory. How may third attempts, and fourth, and fifth."

Only first.

Viola had never heard those words together like that, as if they carried but a little weight.

Only first.

"How ill to trade this life on what has been lost, when we have a promise here of golden restoration," the preacher continued, "of futures full of promise, because God himself intervenes and says so. Who are you to say or believe otherwise?"

Who was she indeed? Viola weighed his words in her heart until the people around her moved to stand during what must have been a final hymn. Still, she let the lesson take flight. A locust-stripped field turned into a lush, green, crop-yielding array of leaves, stems, flowers, fruits, and seeds.

If Nasrin were here she might ask, *What do you see?*

And there, in answer to Nasrin's question, Viola saw the charcoal eyes of Silas Swift. His reluctant smile. His piercing gaze. The way he rubbed the top of his eyebrow with his thumbnail. The way he carved a message of love onto a log.

Across the aisle, Helena waved to her. A finger-tip, happy-to-see-you wave. Would Helena expect them to talk? But no, her mother ushered her away, unaware and already deep in conversation with others. Behind them, Marshall closed the gap. His eyes flickered over Viola, and he nodded a cold greeting but did not stop.

And it did not hurt as much as it had when she had watched him walk in.

Outside, the church building dazzled in the bright sunshine. After a few polite greetings, she wandered the length of the huge stones that made up the chapel walls, touching, feeling the cool surface on her fingertips.

God restores the years the locusts have stolen. She let that sink in and prayed over the lost years. One stone for each year. Eight-year-old Viola. Abandoned. Ashamed.

She moved onto the next stone. Nine years old. Trying her best in lessons so Clemmie would notice her. Ten-year-old Viola. Learning to sketch. Peering at a desiccated leaf. Wondering how something so close to decay could also be so beautiful.

Eleven-year-old Viola. Twelve, thirteen, fourteen, all the way to now. The Viola who carried so many losses. Each year, relinquished. Behind her. As sure as a wall of church stones. Unlike the man in the pulpit who prayed with eyes closed and his hands in a reverent posture, she prayed with eyes open, her hands tracing the milestones of her life.

She stopped at the corner of the chapel, in front of a long wooden structure.

A sign read, *Hall for Rent.* She tried the door and it opened for her, so she stepped into a sunny room with long boards underfoot and high windows on either side that streamed with light.

The kind of light a painter's heart discovers when they need it most.

How does it make you feel?

What's the story you want on your page, mon Poupette?

Viola tucked her hands behind her back. She may not have found a leaf or feather.

But she'd scavenged something beautiful today.

35

"Viola, parcel for you," Jasper called from somewhere deep within the tavern.

She found him sitting on the stoop of the open tavern door and joined him, shoulder to shoulder. Something about him these last few days had softened. He was not as angry. Still subdued, but her friend nonetheless. One who leaned in to her when she sat beside him.

"Want my knife?"

"Yes, please." She slipped the blade between the wooden top of the box and the thick twine that held it all together. Under tissue sheets lay a thick stack of postcards with the words: *Christmas Greetings From Australia* printed in black across the top, within the scalloped, pink-feathered edge. Beach. Bush. House. And a boat. Along the bottom were the words, *A House by the Sea, Phillip Island.*

She held a dozen or more in her hand, like a deck of playing cards, but with so much more destiny than a game of chance.

Jasper also held a card. "Would you look at this?" He turned it over. "An original work by Miss V. Buckley."

A flush overtook her cheeks, and she fanned herself with the very artwork that stirred her delight. It settled onto her skin, like a vapor. Like a happy scent on the spring breeze that wafted past them now, loaded with jasmine that crept over stone walls and wrought-iron gates.

"It's quite something," Jasper admitted. "I'm glad this has come your way. I don't know anyone who works as hard as you. I don't mean the work alone. I mean, holding onto your dream. One day soon, I wouldn't be surprised if you could afford to buy the *Sweet Clementine*."

She smiled. "Do you think she belongs anywhere else?"

He stared at her. "Haven't you said exactly that all along?"

"Maybe I was wrong." She turned the postcard over. "Maybe it's not *Sweet Clementine* that will fly away. Maybe it's these." She flapped the card like a wing. "Far and wide, all over Australia."

"And into the world," he added. "A, tiny seed of our Viola Buckley, scattered as far as the post bags will take her. Imagine all the ships that will carry this card."

"Why Jasper, look at you enjoying my success, just a little." Her heart warmed to see it.

"I know I can't ever sway you from your course. This," he held the card to his cheek, "is way more to you than I will ever be, and you deserve to embrace what makes you happy."

"Oh, Jasper, thank you." She leaned into him and blinked through her tears. Happy, sad, regretful, mournful tears.

"Who's the lucky fellow who'll receive the first card?" He pretended to write by licking his fingertip and tapping the card. "Name and address?"

She looked at him. "Fellow?"

"Yes. Fellow. You didn't come back from Phillip Island the way you left us. And my heart knows the look. The way I catch you staring into nothing. So." he guzzled in a deep breath. "Who's the islander that's caught your eye?"

"There's no islander…" She stopped. Jasper was being a friend, someone who had learned to see her as an artist. Isn't that what she'd always wanted from him? She wondered how much it would hurt to hear about Silas, but a friend who was less than true was more hurtful than any truth.

"He's not from Phillip Island," she whispered. "Not even from Australia."

"He's not?" Jasper blinked. "I assumed you'd met someone on the island."

"I did. I met a visiting American named Silas Swift."

They looked at each other.

"American. That's quite far, don't you think?"

"Far?"

"Yes, for you to go."

"Probably," she smiled. "I've not been invited. So that's hardly a problem."

"What's the problem?"

She let the cards back into their box. Pristine. Freshly minted. They would fly, but regrets kept her buried. "He's been married before. Silas is a widower."

Jasper waited for more. "And?"

"And, well, I don't want to be someone's replacement or slip into a world where someone else was the wife. I've only ever wanted to be loved by someone as their first love."

"Well, you have that in me, but that's not enough, either. So maybe you're wrong about that too. Maybe you need to take what you get, Viola. I would, if I could. I'd marry you tomorrow and love you and no one else all the days of my life, but you don't want that."

Viola matched his long breath with one of her own. How true the words of her besotted friend. How heartbreakingly true.

"You want to be loved by this Silas fellow. Does he feel the same way?"

"He does. And I have pushed him away."

"Then bring him back." He wouldn't look at her to say it.

"How? It may be too late. His brother needs him, they've got debts about to dismantle their business, and he's made promises and the brothers, well one of them anyway, is waiting for Silas to sell the astrolabe I found in the staircase. And then, perhaps then—"

"I don't know what you're babbling about." Jasper sighed. "But here." He picked up one of her cards and turned it over to the blank side. "Start with Dearest Silas. The rest will follow."

She wondered how he'd grown up so fast. "And you, my dearest Jasper…?"

He pocketed the one card he'd taken. "I have my memento."

The wooden building that housed the Swift brothers had not hummed with the activity of women in years. Even when Silas had married Honora, she had joined them with barely a word on her breath.

She'll come around. She's in mourning. Rotten time to be a bride.

His mother had been a quiet one, too. Together, she and Honora had worked side by side, but the sudden death of Minnie Swift not long after Honora joined them had left his new bride to occupy the sole position that Fern and Olive found themselves in now, under the firm eye of Mrs. Knott.

Fern chattered and shared stories of life on Link River, and Olive nodded while they collected the luncheon dishes. It didn't escape Silas that poor Olive had married and entered this home with as much brokenness that had carried Honora over the threshold.

He would have liked to eat anywhere but at the table where Olive sat, eyes downcast, often tear-filled. He'd pondered asking Fern to make him a plate to take to the office, but if they were to rebuild as a family, he had to set the tone.

"Thank you, Fern. Olive." He pressed a smile into his gratitude for the meal and pushed away from the table.

Brown and Burrows had sent through five more staircase orders. His job this afternoon was to take stock of their Douglas Fir for treads and risers and all the posts they had in reserve for spindles. As for newel posts, counting the wood for those would be as difficult as eating lunch with angry Eugene and shame-filled Olive.

But he preferred to work with the carpenters on the factory floor away from Patrick, who scribbled at the desk, and Eugene, who pulled an entire bedframe into the window display.

A gust of cold air scurried into the building from the front door, and with it Chester Sweeney, wrapped in his best coat, hair slicked, smile a little greasier each time they met.

"Silas." Chester rubbed his hands together. "Bitter weather, isn't it?" He stepped onto the shop floor and ran his knuckles over a chess table.

"Chester." Luncheon food and dismay curdled in Silas's stomach, but he ushered him in. "Let's talk in my office, where it's warmer."

Instinct told him to toss Patrick out, but a sweet memory of Viola snuck in, as it did so often and at the worst times. Somewhere in the corner of his mind, she smiled.

Let me play.

He chewed his lip and pulled out a chair for Chester, who seated himself with a small groan and exaggerated smile.

Patrick stood.

"Sit down, Patrick. You don't need to vacate your chair." He hadn't expected it to feel so good to say it. A new accomplice of sorts—not as pretty, but certainly responsible for much of this predicament.

Patrick slid back onto the leather seat with a humble nod of thanks only Silas saw. Chester Sweeney was too busy pulling out a wad of papers from his breast pocket.

"Now, let's not mince words, Silas. Your renegotiated debt—"

"Wait. Eugene," he called to his brother, who pushed a set of drawers into the cavity of a chest. "Could you come here, please?"

Eugene crossed the floor. "What can I get you, Silas?" He frowned.

"I need you to join this meeting."

"Me?" His eyes softened.

Silas nodded and bid him enter. When Eugene had found his seat, Silas pulled the door shut and leaned against it. If Swift Brothers went down in flames, they would all be there this time.

"Chester, you know my brothers, Patrick and Eugene."

Chester threw the papers onto the desk. "Let's not waste anyone's time. Your re-negotiated contract states your installments were frozen for the duration of your journey to and from Australia, after which you were to resume monthly repayments, double our previous arrangement."

It sounded like he'd memorized the document. He probably salivated over it.

"And in the event you cannot meet these payments, you, Silas Swift, agree to incorporate me as owner of this building." He slapped his hands on his knees. "Because I have already lent you a third of what the business is worth, for Patrick to squander."

Patrick's fingers crushed the document, his head bent, cheeks poker-red. Eugene stared at Chester like a man plotting to assassinate him while he slept. And Silas prayed hard that somewhere on their desk was a column of money they'd not accounted for or a shipment of timber they could return, though he'd dug for that and pulled his hand out empty more times than he cared to remember.

"Am I correct, Patrick?" Chester had the arrogant habit of speaking in one direction while looking in the other. He looked at Eugene now, but waited for his answer from the other side of the room.

"I can't dispute what's written here," Patrick said. "But I think, if we were to negotiate once more—"

"I don't work like that, my friend. I offer high interest loans, the day they're requested. Your brother came to me once, to set you free. Who else would take on such foolishness?" He raised an eyebrow. "So, what's it to be, Silas? Do we draft new title documents on this building?"

If it would have helped, Silas might have unclenched his fists and collected Chester by the throat.

"I can't—"

"Let me see that." Eugene reached for the documents and carefully ran his fingers over the pages until he found whatever he looked for. He swallowed hard, read some more, and threw the papers back onto the desk, the way Chester had.

"We can pay this month's installment."

"You can?" Chester snorted. "I'm not sure that's what your brother meant to say. Shall we check with him before you run away with yourself, Eugene?"

Eugene pulled a wad of money from his breast pocket. "I'm not running anywhere. I'm about to pay what we owe this month so that we can all get back to work."

∽

After Chester Sweeney hastily pocketed his money, and only after Patrick reminded him he owed them a signed receipt, did the money lender slink away, placated for thirty days, proud feathers ruffled and wrinkled.

"What just happened here?" Patrick pulled Eugene around to face them from where he slammed the front door on Sweeney's rear.

"I bought us another month." Eugene returned to the window display.

"But—"

"How?"

Silas and Patrick had let Eugene take over in the office. Now they demanded answers.

"Where did all that money come from?"

"Have you had it in your pocket all this time? Good grief, man." Patrick shook his head. "I almost slipped off my chair when you handed it over, like you walk around with that kind of money every day."

Eugene, too, shook his head in wonderment.

"Where did you get it?" Silas asked.

"It's a down payment, from the Occidental Hotel in Seattle. I took an order while on my honeymoon for twenty desks and twenty chests of drawers. For their guest rooms."

He straightened the bedframe to sit square in the window.

Patrick loomed over him. "You've been home for days. Why keep this in your pocket until now?"

Eugene raised himself up, the kind of stance a man learns after he takes a beating a few times and knows the way up again. "I made that deal with the hotel people on our last day there. It felt so good. My new wife beside me, the Occidental owner shaking my hand." He sat on the display bed and Patrick joined him.

"I left my honeymoon hotel with a beautiful bride on my arm and a deal for us in my clutches." He let out a sigh. "On the train ride home, Olive praised me but crumbled under her own burdens. She said secrets may be hidden in furniture drawers, but never in a marriage. I think she banked on the euphoria of my bolstered spirits to carry a cruel admission. She was wrong, because that confession," he glanced at Silas, "stole everything, every shred of happiness."

"I understand." Patrick nodded for him to go on.

"With news of the fake astrolabe and all our debts, I thought we'd never fulfil the order. I was planning to return the money. Then Mary told us about the will. About Silas and Father and…" He shrugged. "I knew I had to step up if I could."

He turned to Silas. "I don't know where forgiveness lies in my heart. I expect something will crack and, like you, after a horrible loss, I'll find a way to carry on. But I don't want this business to fold or for Chester Sweeney to own us. If Olive can find a way to live here, I want to stay, too."

"Are you sure?" Silas knew his look was piercing, but he would not play games with Eugene any more than he'd willingly play with Chester.

"I am."

"I appreciate that." He tapped his brother on the back, but it was miserly in comparison to what he felt in gratitude. "How does a man talk business on his honeymoon, anyway?"

"I overheard a hotel guest argue with the manager about money stolen from his room. The next day, I told the manager I could make life easier for him, that Swift Brothers could make four different kinds of desks with hidden compartments in various places, and it might afford their guests a sweeter sleep.

I made a sketch and showed the manager where the secret drawers would go. He showed the owner, and by the time we left, I had the order."

"Just like that?" Patrick asked.

"Well, I had a pretty girl on my arm. When the owner discovered we were honeymooners, he was impressed with my ability to shift from vacation to business. He saw something admirable in that. I just saw a chance and grabbed it."

Silas let out a breath. How long had he held that in? Since Chester had arrived? "We've scraped through for this month, but now we have to recoup the hotel order money, keep our workers paid, and fill everything on the books by the end of next month."

"We can all work extra hours," Patrick offered. "I can work on the factory floor and do the office work at night."

"I can do the same," Eugene said. "Work out back on the hotel orders when there's no one in the shop."

Silas nodded. He was thankful, that was a given. He, too, would put in extra hours. This is why his father had insisted they all learn every aspect of this business. What his father hadn't told him, because he'd never known, was the strong men Patrick and Eugene would become.

36

If calendars could talk, the ones that hung on the back of doors, October 1879 would have whistled like a steam ship on course against stiff winds and loaded to the gills with cargo.

Laden with orders of their own, the Swift brothers and their team chiseled out a new day, which they awoke to relive, over and over.

Silas and Joe slid, measured, and cut the puzzle pieces of the simple staircases for Brown and Burrows. Together they turned spindles, rounded tops, and sawed and hammered newel posts. Side by side, they carried the largest portion of stock Swift Brothers took in and refashioned for sending out.

Silas tried not to think too much about where these newel posts would end up. If he let his mind wander, he always fell into the same place, with the same artist who'd sketched his face and found his heart.

On the other side of the factory, Eugene, Patrick, and the rest of the team cut and pieced side tables, a large sideboard, piecrust tables, and sugar chests. They also hammered and glued the writing desks for the Occidental Hotel.

The easy friction of metal on wood, the scrape of the chisel, and the *tap tap* of nails grabbing boards all melded together in a cacophony Silas and his brothers had been born to. In her seventh month, Fern cooked meals and took care of their basic needs. Now, Mrs. Knott only came in once a week to help with the laundry.

Which left Olive on the shop floor when needed and beside Fern for the rest of the day. Silas cast his eye over the small factory that strained against the urgency of time and profit. Sweat slicked back the hair on all who worked here. Chatter, for the most part, remained short and to the point. Everyone had their mission and less time to accomplish it than the clock offered.

By nightfall, he knew everyone under this roof would collapse to their beds, weary and aching.

"It's not called the grindstone for nothing." Joe carried an armful of finished spindles.

"We're going to need this burst of energy to last the entire month and then some." Silas rubbed the tightest spot on the back of his neck. How many months, nay, years would it take to be free of the debt he owed Sweeney? "I don't know how long we can sustain this pace."

"Got to work while you have it," Joe replied and pointed with his chin to the shop floor. "Customer."

Silas called for Eugene, who called for his wife. Together, the Swift brothers, their wives, and employees, pulled harder than ever.

By October's end, they had almost enough to cover their expenses and pay their installment to Chester Sweeney. But keeping afloat, their necks to the waterline, was not enough. Too tired to sleep, Silas lit his bedroom lamp and sat at his desk. From one of the secret drawers, he extracted a small drawstring bag.

Honora had sewn it after the fire. She'd chosen jet black for mourning. He pulled the bag open and let the contents fall into his palm.

One plain gold wedding band, the Ackerman ruby necklace salvaged from the fire, and one empty gold and emerald locket.

They'd not had time to collect more of the usual tokens that commemorated happy anniversaries and the birth of children. How she had mourned over that empty locket. Denied a tiny lock of hair from babies that had come too soon.

He dropped the ring and locket back into the pouch. They'd pay their way through October no matter how much it cost him.

"Can't sleep?" Patrick stood in the doorway.

"Just finishing up here." Silas hid the pouch under a stack of papers.

"I just read through today's orders." Patrick stepped inside. "Eugene and Olive know what they're doing. I tip my hat to them. Thanks to that festive table display in the window, we'll be turning eight Windsor chairs before Thanksgiving and two folding tables."

"I'll be glad to be awake by Thanksgiving." Silas yawned. "Food might not factor for me this year."

"Speak for yourself." Patrick stretched his arms to touch the top of the doorframe. "I could do with a day off. Don't fret, Silas, we're on track."

"Just." Silas knew how fast tracks buckled and melted when the weather fired up. "All we need is for one of us to get sick or break a bone..."

The brothers looked at each other. No matter how well you wrapped it, hanging by a thread dragged a soul beyond exhaustion.

"What are you working on?"

Silas turned to his papers. "It's nothing."

Patrick picked it up. "This is a full-blown design. What's it for?"

"For me. Give it back." Silas held his hand out for the scrap of paper, one of many he'd sketched and thrown away.

"Is this for Lockwood? It should be. This..." He skewered Silas with a look. "This is a staircase panel, isn't it, the one you said you'd not be able to make?"

"I'm still saying it. We could manage simple staircases for him, maybe. But not an elaborately carved grand staircase. We're barely holding it together now. Throw in something like this and..." He shook his head. "No chance."

"But Silas—"

"No, Patrick. I'd be carving for weeks just to have one *sample* panel. Even then, Lockwood could say it's not what he had in mind and engage a more impressive craftsman. None of us can afford to dither around with designs and grand wishes when there's Windsor chairs and trestles to make."

Patrick said nothing. And in the silence that closed in on the midnight hour, he didn't need to. Because Silas had already thought of everything.

Daisy Swift was born three weeks early on November 27. Unlike the food that had been prepared and the Thanksgiving table Olive had set for their festivities, Fern had not planned for a hasty delivery.

"And it's a good thing all you need is a willing set of arms for wrapping babies," Eugene said when beaming Patrick had shown the child to her uncles.

Baby Daisy was all pink, close-fisted, with a soft layer of dark hair and a little puckered mouth. Silas refused to think of the three children he and Honora had not held. Instead, he remembered little

Molly and the sweet face that had caught her lost breath in his arms when she'd fallen.

"She's beautiful, Patrick. You'd best take her back to her mama before she falls in love with Uncle Silas and Uncle Eugene."

Patrick did as he was told, and Eugene went to his own exhausted wife, who'd spent the long night behind the birthing room door where no man was ever allowed. Silas took his memories and slid into the office.

Their Thanksgiving meal could wait, but babies and bills never did. And neither would Chester Sweeney. Silas rifled through the papers. He didn't want to disturb Patrick's system, but there was never a time when he didn't want to know exactly what they worked on and when it would be ready. From what he surmised, many of the good women of Portland would receive new spice cupboards and tea caddies for Christmas this year.

The luckier ones, and there were three, would make room for silverware chests that stood almost as tall as the mistresses who would polish and fill them.

Silas leaned back in the chair. Looking over the quiet factory always felt good from here.

A tiny cry stole into the quiet. Baby Daisy would make herself known now. Even more reason to work hard.

He reached for a pencil and toppled the leather-bound wages ledger and a stack of other papers. Among them, he noticed a postcard. It bore the image of a familiar seaside vista and a salutation that made him freeze.

Christmas Greetings From Australia

Bewilderment ripped through him, splitting him open like a hardwood plank. He turned the card over.

Dearest Silas,

This pretty card captures some of our days in a house by the sea and who I became in our time there…with you.

It will take more than this card to convey what my heart needs to say. Someday, perhaps, you may wish to forgive my foolishness and hear it. But I shall begin with the most important, for, among my many affections, that is what I owe you first.

Thank you for feeding my dreams.

Faithfully Yours,
Viola Buckley

She'd taken the address. She'd written to him. But more! She'd entered the postcard competition, and this was her entry. The winning entry!

Hand trembling, he turned the card over. He knew that white house by the sea. That festooned boat. The sand, the seaweed. Balthazar's feathers. All the blues of a sky that fell into the sea, as sure as his heart had fallen for hers.

He read her words again. She offered thanks, and affections. And there, on the bottom of a postcard, was her name. And her vocation.

He wanted to whoop and cheer and raise the rafters off their beams. He shivered and laughed at the same time. All his problems were classified and categorized and annotated and filed in this room.

But all his deepest longings were here, Phillip Island. He ran his fingers along the scalloped top edge of the card. *Where did you end up, Balthazar? And where was Viola now? Where would he send his reply?*

His answer lay in the postcard's corner.

The Star and Garter Tavern.

Was Viola living under the watchful gaze of her mother's

portrait? His heart crashed a little to think of her huddled in the one place she knew neither she nor Clemmie belonged.

But… she needed him.

Her words said so. He tucked the card into his breast pocket and climbed the stairs, past the muffled sounds of his brothers and their wives. Up, into the emptiness of the room he once shared with Honora.

Would Viola care to join them here? Is that what this card meant? Was she that much changed since he'd seen her last? He pulled her shawl from the chest of drawers, held it to his face, and inhaled the aroma of roses. Some scents, along with some sentiments, refused to fade.

He ignored his breakfast and started yet another letter to Viola in his mind. How would he express his delight at her win? The longing for her that never left him? The heartache of the fake astrolabe?

But he didn't want to write it. He wanted to say it so she could hear him and he could watch her.

He stirred the sugar in the bowl as if the answers hid beneath and didn't notice his brothers sit opposite him until one kicked him in the shins.

Eugene and Patrick smiled, not the wide-eyed wonder of yesterday, when a baby came into their world. This was the brotherly ribbing they might have given each other. Only now, they focused on him.

"I glanced at the mail yesterday." Patrick grinned. "Dropped it fast when Olive called to say Fern had taken to her bed. This morning I remembered there was something for you of a personal nature, but when I looked for it, it was gone."

"You didn't glance. You read my mail."

"I'm sorry." Patrick's grin pushed into a smug nod.

"You don't look sorry."

"Viola. That's your artist friend, the one who sketched you like she owned a piece of your heart?" Patrick pretended to simper.

"Stop that. You don't know her. Next time, leave my mail alone."

"Now it's your turn to reply." Eugene followed Patrick's lead. His brothers performed a sterling double act of ignoring him and circling him at the same time. "And we think you should do more than write."

"Yeah, like what?" Silas cradled his coffee cup. The mention of her, spoken so casually at his table, made her appear alive in ways he'd fought for months.

"Go to her."

Three little words. He couldn't properly tell who'd spoken them, but they sat there like an explosive.

"Not that easy. Not the going. Nor the coming back."

"Do you wish she'd come back with you when you asked?" Eugene ventured.

"I didn't ask."

"What an imbecile."

"Silas! Did you know how she felt about you?"

Both talked at once. Silas closed his eyes. All grown up and one already a father, they were still such brats.

"Listen, when I left, her mother had died and she had commitments she could not abandon. As had I." His excuses ground past his teeth like bits of gravel.

For a moment, his brothers remained quiet.

"We want to help you, Silas," Eugene offered.

"You can. Get onto the factory floor soon as you've finished your breakfast. We have Chester Sweeney coming later today—"

"We mean with Miss *Viola Buckley*." Patrick almost sang her name.

"We have a plan." Eugene sat up straight, as if their proposal wired him with newfound height and purpose.

Patrick spread his hands over the table and took command. "I wrote to Fern's father. He's well paid, works hard, and hardly spends a cent. He's agreed to lend me the money you borrowed so I could run off. I'll have to pay him back, but his terms are not as steep as Chester Sweeney's. And if I wipe out what we owe Sweeney, perhaps you'd let me back into the business, this time as a proper partner?"

Silas let this sink in. "I don't know if Chester works like that. He's got us boxed in for monthly repayments for at least another decade."

Patrick shook his head. "I read the contract. There's an exit clause for lump sum clearance of all debt, an inclusion to sweeten people to sign with him, knowing there's hardly a soul who could procure the entire sum in one hit."

"You mean end it with Chester for good?"

Patrick nodded. "For good."

"And if you're happy with Patrick doing that," Eugene held his head high, his chest expanding, as if he'd found a way to breathe again, deep and fortifying, "you might agree with me securing my own loan. Then we can hire more workers, build a bigger crew, and repay you for all the years you carried us. This way, we all share the risks. If you'll let us partner with you properly."

In disbelief, Silas looked from one brother to the other. "Well, aren't you as smart as a couple of monkeys on a clothesline."

They puffed and nodded at their brilliance.

"It's what we want, if you'll have us," Patrick continued.

"And my Olive has become firm friends with Fern." Eugene looked him square in the eyes. "She's expecting a child too, and I guess the wives of twins enjoy their own bond." His voice carried a hope Silas had not heard in weeks.

Both brothers wanted to stay on their own merits and at their own risk. The ache he'd carried since the age of twelve, like a smallpox mark on his very soul, lost some of its grip. Was this what true relief felt like? Was this the first ray of atonement?

"Are you both sure?"

"We are," they said together.

"Mary should have told us years ago about the lopsided way Father left the business."

"And we've been trying to find a way for you to live the life you may have had if we weren't your burdens."

"You were never my burdens. Father was simply ignorant of your potential."

"Silas," Patrick dared, "what about you?"

"And your Australian artist. You *fed her dreams*," Eugene teased. "That postcard was an invitation."

Underneath the generous ribbing, his brother held his eye with determination.

The healing his family needed moved slowly into their midst, but would it roll in like beach waves, slipping in and out of their reach until time eroded pain and memory? Eugene and his wife had begun the mending needed between them. Now, Eugene offered some kind of fresh page.

But what of Viola? Would the ghost of Honora couple with the unexpected presence of Olive?

"I can't up and leave again. Not with..." He wanted to say, *all our crippling debt.*

"We can hire three more men while you work on a panel for Mr.

Lockwood. Didn't he say January for submissions? There's still time."

Patrick had thought it all through, his case so compelling Silas could only listen.

"You design it, and we'll present to Lockwood in January," Eugene said.

"Why? Where will I be?"

"You'll be on a ship by then. On your way to… *Miss Viola Buckley.*"

They said her name together, elongating each syllable. His heart thumped a crazy beat.

"You're both out of your minds. The fare alone—"

"Is a gift from us to you, including enough to bring Miss Viola back with you," Patrick said.

"And how can you afford a fare like that, almost twice over?"

Olive appeared in the doorway with Fern behind her cradling baby Daisy. Clearly, eavesdropping was as natural to his new family as reading another man's mail.

"I sold the astrolabe." Olive kept her voice calm, but excitement spilled from the way her eyes smiled.

Stunned, Silas blinked hard. Something unfamiliar whispered into his weariness. All four waited for him to respond, corded by growing expectancy. It grew around them, palpable, rising like a tide.

"Who bought it?"

"Father found a buyer." Olive slipped beside her husband. "Some folks collect them, real or not. A gentleman was happy to pay a fine sum for a rare trinket. Not the amount you expected, but enough for you to return to the treasure of your heart. We're all excited to meet her."

Eugene pulled her close.

His brothers beamed. As did their wives.

Bright stars that showed the way.

37

Saturday, February 21, 1880

Wilson Street Chapel, Melbourne

Viola shuffled her papers and slipped the most critical one under all the others. A splash of sun flittered through the windows of the Wilson Street Chapel hall and onto the small but happy group of young ladies.

"Miss Buckley?" Martha Sullivan sketched a rose she'd brought from her grandmother's garden. She'd also brought a bouquet for Viola. Grandmother Sullivan sent along a gift from her well-tended garden each week, a smoothing of the way, perhaps, for pulling her granddaughters away from Clemmie's piano lessons.

But now, here in this welcoming wooden building, Viola gathered the Sullivan girls and others back into her fold. Seated at three long trestle tables arranged in a C shape, Saturday students of the *Miss Viola Buckley Art Academy* worked on today's lesson.

"I don't know why this other petal looks wrong."

Viola took Martha's pencil. "Don't hold so close to the pencil tip. Further along will allow better flexibility, and your lines will look more natural, less forced."

She drew over Martha's attempt, adding a darker, bolder line.

"Rose petals are offset, like fish scales. Woven tightly in the bud, the other petals come undone with their individual shape and beauty, but they all sit just to the side of the one before, not directly behind."

Already the sketch looked closer to the specimen Martha studied.

"Miss Buckley?" Someone else raised her hand. "When will you announce the winners?"

Viola returned to the front of her classroom. "I am ready to announce them now." She knotted her fingers and looked over the room at her girls. Most were new to her classes this year, drawn in by the recommendation of mothers who'd brought their daughters in for experimental lessons she'd offered last year. A small test that already proved successful.

Now these girls had brought their friends. And together, they stared up at her with eager faces, keen to discover who'd impressed her enough to win this month's awards, of which there were three.

It still pained her to place them in this kind of order. To rank them, some better than others. Among them were one or two restless and unfocused students who might never win anything. Ever.

But eager parents had hinted at prizes, as had their daughters. And Viola herself knew judgment from her peers and other professionals would soon come for her, too.

"In third place, for her beautiful *Marigolds in a Pot*, Miss Elspeth Grey."

Elspeth blushed and received her third-place ribbon with much nodding and happy fists under her chin, while her fellow students applauded.

"In second place…" The words stuck in Viola's throat a little less each time, but she knew this particular winner would always go home with less shine in her eyes than the Elspeths. "For her eye-catching piece, *Purple Petunias*, Miss Flora Tucker."

Flora, much to Viola's surprise, leapt from her chair and ran straight to her. "Oh, Miss Buckley!" She pressed the second-place ribbon to her throat. "This is the first time I have ever won. My first win. The very first one." She curtsied as if they'd crowned her the overall winner.

Viola smiled. She was the teacher, but every week these girls taught their own valuable lessons.

"And in first place, with *A Basket of Forget-Me-Nots*, Miss Helena Hall."

Helena smiled and bit her bottom lip. Delight spilled from her mouth into her bright eyes and all over the room, as it had the other two times she'd come first. Entirely on her own merits.

"Thank you, Miss Buckley." She accepted her win with the same dignity Viola had observed in the girl's mother. The urge to stare into Helena's face for signs of her own eyes, mouth, or mannerisms had dissipated only a little. There were some, perhaps because Viola searched for them, but in most ways Helena was her own person.

As an artist, her emerging skills were not to be ignored, and that fired Viola like nothing else. She would do anything to grow that talent in all of them, but she held a secret fondness for Helena. How could she not?

"I only hope one day I will be as good as you." Helena voiced her aspirations, and the rest of the class echoed the same.

"You have made tremendous progress these last few months, and I am proud of you all."

Especially the one I cannot claim as my sister.

It was not Viola's responsibility to protect Marshall, and she did not do this for him, but she would not burden Helena with what she knew. It was enough for Viola, for now, to spend some time teaching the girl to draw.

Marshall's generosity saw a good number of Helena's friends here on his account. Viola did not object. And those girls brought along others who paid their own way.

All of this put extra coins in her purse and fortified the beginnings of her small business. She taught art. She mentored these girls. Her small income and savings allowed her to quit serving patrons at the Star and Garter, although Mr. Barnes insisted she live there until she was sure of where she would go next.

Every morning, she crossed off another day on the calendar that drove them into the new year, this new decade, which edged them closer to Melbourne's International Exhibition.

"Next week, I want each of you to find and bring in more gum leaves. Remember when we began with well-formed leaves? Well, now I want you to expand your skills and work on one that is incomplete. Find me the rattiest, most grub-eaten leaf. The more damage, the better. It will test your skills, and you will see something more beautiful in that one broken leaf than you will ever see in a perfect one."

"Why is that, Miss Buckley?" Martha Sullivan raised her hand. "I can walk past an almost decayed leaf and not see its beauty until I hold it up to the light. How does it delight me in here when it was only something the wind tore around in the garden?"

An ache tottered among Viola's fondest memories, like little Molly, tangled and stumbling among her skirt folds.

"Because," she ignored the rush of emotion that sprang into her nose and throat, "in this room, you are learning to pay attention to nature. To observe and consider the lifespan of something that held or still holds life. You are slowing yourself down. You're sinking in. You..."

The vision of Silas appeared, staring at her while she sketched him.

He'd not replied to her postcard. Perhaps that was wisdom on his part. She blinked hard. *Petals, Stamens, Pistils,* she reminded herself. *Stems. Buds. Leaves. Roots.*

Did she have that in the right order?

"The artist in you is awakening, and that is no ordinary thing. Lessons, and the hours you spend in practice, will open your eyes to… to…. so much more than you ever thought, right there, within your reach. Your challenge is to find what is looking back at you. What does it tell you? What will you say when you make your sketch? When you add shading? When you create strong lines," her voice cracked, "and… blurred edges…"

"Miss Buckley!" Flora gasped. "You're crying."

"Oh, so I am." Viola dabbed at her eyes. "A teacher's happy tears for the progress she sees in her students."

She calmed herself with a short laugh and urged them on. At the end of their lesson, they collected their kits and lap easels and helped her slide the trestles into the hall cupboard where they belonged.

When the last girl shut the door behind her, Viola let the real tears flow. The stranded pieces of her emotions that fell when the longing for Silas reminded her she had indeed seen more. Felt more. Wanted more. And she had watched him sail away.

Hot Melbourne sun streamed through the open damask hotel room curtains, accompanied by the gong of church bells. Silas pulled himself out of bed and shook the remnants of sleep like a man adrift. But he was no lost traveler; his course was set as sure as if a real astrolabe told him where to go. He looked over Melbourne Town from his second-story window. Was the Star and Garter Tavern among these chimneys and corrugated rooflines?

"Head south, right on the edge of the Botanic Gardens," the man at the hotel front desk had told him when he'd arrived the night before. "An easy walk from here."

Silas leaned both arms on the window frame and forced himself to slow down now, as he had done last night. It would do her no good to have him appear, full of all the force he held in check. He refused to think she might already be entangled with another man. That reality had no place in his heart.

Instead, he ate a hearty beef and Yorkshire pudding luncheon like a man who had all the time in the world. When he was done, he smoothed his hair, his clothes, his nerves, and set out for the Star and Garter.

It presided over a street corner. The white building needed a fresh coat of paint around the door and front stoop, but it looked like many other taverns he'd passed. He knocked on the door. Eventually, someone pulled it inwards.

The fair-haired young man yawned. "Closed on Sunday. Did you not see the sign?"

Silas knew when he'd annoyed someone. Enough years with his brothers had taught him to ignore it anyway.

"I'm not a patron. I'm looking for Miss Viola Buckley."

The young man squinted at Silas.

"And who are you?"

"Silas Swift. Portland, Oregon."

The young man swung the door open a little more. "Well, well." He appraised Silas. "Look at this now."

"You seem to be better prepared for me than I you."

"Sorry. I…" He let him into a narrow hallway adorned with the largest, most vibrant presence of Mrs. Buckley it stopped Silas in his tracks.

"*Sweet Clementine.*" He drank in the youthful face of a woman he'd only known in her final days, after the misery of years had worn her into a mere shadow.

"I'm Jasper Barnes, son of Fred. Proprietors."

Silas tore his gaze from the painting.

"But *she's* not here." Jasper folded his arms over his chest. "Viola, the woman you snared on Phillip Island, the one who won't so much as look at another man because whatever she saw in you," he shrugged, the tiniest lift of shoulders in defeat, "was enough for her. Anyway, she left earlier today. And now she's gone."

"Gone?" Silas throat thickened and he crushed a dry swallow.

Jasper nodded.

"Do you know where?"

"She takes off every few months. Normally leaves on a Sunday afternoon and doesn't come back until Wednesday."

"Where to?"

"Phillip Island. There's a log there she can't get enough of. Goes back to sit. Paint. Breathe, she says."

Clemmie smiled down at them.

Jasper rubbed a spot on the floor with his shoe heel and uttered a soft snigger. "I'm tempted to tell you she left here months ago with a new love and no one knows where to find her, only so I could have another try at winning her. But I'd never best whatever it is you've done."

"I would have come earlier but—"

"She's quite the sensation, you know. Used to work here nights, but she's pouring herself into a whole new life now. All her dreams are coming true. One by one on a solid foundation. Teaches her classes. Sells portraits."

Portraits? This was not the Viola he'd left behind.

Silas nodded, thanked him, and turned to leave. "Wednesday, then."

"Mr. Swift." Jasper called him back. "I can only hope, someday, to find a heart who'll yearn for me the way she has pined over you."

Silas returned to the street. She had pined for him. But building a *solid foundation* took determination and hard work. Would she abandon any of that? It was February now, many months until the exhibition in October. He hurried on, away from the tavern and to where he'd boarded the schooner to Phillip Island last time.

The smell of rotting fish hung over the docks. Two young boys sold thick sausages in bread from a cart with a *Vinegar Saveloys* sign.

Some who promenaded at this end took their time treading the wide boards, taking in their fill of Sunday sunshine and the cooling sea breeze.

Was there a vessel heading out there now? Tomorrow? There was not. The next schooner to Cowes was set to sail on Wednesday morning, probably the one that would return her to Melbourne. He paced the dock and found a smaller vessel, pulled up by a wrinkled old sea-dog that looked every inch the captain and crew.

"How much to Phillip Island tomorrow?"

"Can't do, fella. Not for hire on Mondays."

"Not even for double the fare?"

The old sailor looked up at him. "Double? Something on that island worth that much to you?"

Silas nodded. Worth every coin he'd ever carried.

"A woman, I'll bet. She get away from you and you need to hunt her down?"

"Something like that."

"Double it is, then. We push off at first light."

"Thank you!" Silas yelled back. "I won't be late."

"No, you won't," said the boatman. "But are you sure she'll be waiting for you?"

Silas shook his head. He wasn't sure of anything. Was besotted Jasper Barnes sending him on a fool's errand?

Confusion bobbed in his gut. Like the swaying of the streams beneath his feet. A seagull hopped onto the pier and dared to pick at a crust of bread right at his feet. It flew off with it in its beak.

But unlike Jasper, Silas was more than besotted. He was a man in pursuit of love.

38

Viola placed a tiny posy on the earth over her mother's grave. Some days she made one fresh from the flowers that grew in Finella's garden. Other times, she scavenged the bush and plucked something wild, like today's offering, the last of the wild rose that grew along Shadrach's fence line, mostly rosehips with a few flower heads still there, a reminder summer would end too soon and slip them into days she was not sure she cared to face.

Nasrin said the first year in which a loved one had passed on was often the worst. After that, the pain, which never really goes away, sinks like the very earth at her feet. Grief, Nasrin told her, did not always remain so raw.

"Clemmie, dear." She breathed in the crushed aromas of peppermint gum leaves. "The calendar holds much promise this October. The exhibition will be such a marvel." Even with the heat of an Australian bush cemetery pressing in on her, a shiver ran up her neck and into her hair.

"But there's all of April, May, and June, to live through first. The memory of us, here on this island. Those dreadful cold water mornings. Finella and sweet Molly. Shadrach's torment by that deer. Balthazar flying away..."

The days fluttered in the corner of her mind like shapes in the clouds. Shifting. Morphing. Wings bent against the wind.

"And Silas, him too." She spoke his name in a whisper, not because she feared anyone would overhear, but because the affection, like grief itself, needed carrying with care. She sank a little further, her knees more buckled than when she arrived.

"I can't think of those days without missing him. I can't think of any days without him, especially the ones coming, but I have to."

She pulled at a rogue weed. "Freddy Barnes is the best keeper of the *Sweet Clementine.* His allegiance to you meant he did not sell it when he could. I'm at peace leaving you there for now, but I know you'd want *me* to find a home. So I'm working hard on that dream."

The bush around her creaked. From up high, a magpie warbled, and from between the grass not too far from where she sat, blue wrens added their shiny chirps. A fitting resting place for a beloved songbird.

"Until next time, Sweet Clemmie." Viola rose, collected her gathering basket, and threw a kiss with her fingertips into the air. It was time to return to the house by the sea which had so beckoned her mother. Now it beckoned her.

She walked over red dirt roads shaped by years of wind and rain. Soon enough, her feet found the tracks that traced Shadrach's property.

How she loved this island. What better place for restoration than a wide seashore? Here, a soul revived in deep therapeutic breaths under open skies that swallowed you up and threw you around.

Viola had found love here, too. Like a spinning compass that found true north, she turned here, every few months, to fill her shoes with sand, soak her hem, and empty her loneliness onto the beautiful log with her name.

There were other places that reminded her of Silas. Up ahead she spied the fence, now mended, and the tree that hosted the rambling wild rose.

Rosehips. Jams. Kisses. She blinked into the light. Someone had stopped at the rose bush, perhaps to pick the hips, although she figured it was too early for that. Summer still lingered and swayed in the breeze.

Whoever it was had strung something up there.

Her feet hurried her along, her heart picking up an unsteady beat, sucking the air from her chest.

Purples fluttered like petals. Pinks and greens, then a much-loved pattern emerged. An arabesque flow of vines and leaves and thick white fringe.

Viola stood still as a stone in a dry creek bed. Rooted to the road. Searching the lonely bushland, the fence line. Someone had hung her shawl here for her to find. Her suzani. The one she had given to Silas.

She reached for it as if it were an apparition that might disappear in the wind, but it did not. The silken fringe fell between her fingers.

A twig snapped, and there, in a clearing, stood Silas. He made his way over the long grasses until he stood right there.

Right here.

His eyes sparked. Live coals in the wind.

He was here.

Tears filled her eyes, and she blinked them away.

"I hear you're painting portraits. Came to see for myself if it's true."

"Are you real?" she whispered and discovered her breath had been holding a sob that escaped with her words.

"I'm not a forgery." He stared right into her eyes. "But the astrolabe sure was."

"What? How?" Neither shortened the gulf between them. As if

they needed their words and assurances, delicate questions and answers, to first build some kind of stable bridge.

"Real astrolabes don't come with a date. If they do, they're fake."

"Oh, Silas, no." Her hopes plummeted for him. "It was worth nothing? Your debts…"

"Not altogether nothing, and the debts are being paid. By my brothers. Whom I left back home with their wives."

"Brothers? With wives?"

He nodded. "The astrolabe was sold for a small sum, for those who collect that kind of thing. Not enough to clear any debts, but enough to pay my fare back to you."

A swift, beautiful beat rang in her throat.

"Because I've been wondering, almost since the day I left," he continued. "What if Viola needs her shawl? What if she's found someone to spend the rest of her life with and regrets letting it go? Wouldn't it be wise to double check something like that?"

She stared at him.

"Will you be needing your shawl, Viola? I mean, summer's ending here soon, and you folks will be looking for another layer to keep you warm."

He came a little closer, and her breath hitched. Caught. So very caught.

"Or, if you'd rather, you could drape it over the end of my bed the way a bride might do. On her wedding night. That's what I'm praying for."

A riot charged within her. It raced and beat against her lungs. Into her throat. And she, who had stormed along fences and over rooftops, stood statue still. As if he'd stolen the muscle from her legs.

He'd stolen something, for sure. Her vision for one. She blinked away the teary mess.

His hands reached for hers. "You can think about it, but don't take forever, because I've come a long way, while my brothers rescue our business. But I …"

His words tripped. But he picked up full steam into all that had brought him back.

"I came here once, hoping to find a treasure. And I did. You. Only, I didn't hold you long enough. You are the first person I saved from a bullet. My first taste of rosehip jam. You're the first person I've ever decorated a boat for and my first thought every day. But I don't want you in my thoughts alone. I want you in my life, if there's a way for us."

Warmth from his fingers sank into her. He fired all her senses, and the embers shot right through her. Right there under the beat of her shawl in the wind, tied to the tree beside the fence where he'd sent her falling to begin with.

He gripped the side of her face as if he, too, needed to know she was real.

Then his lips found hers. And that was all she needed.

"I thought you were an apparition, but you're really here. You are truly standing here. You're real. You're here."

"As real and as true as all that brought me back to you."

"You have won me over, Mr. Swift."

"Too late, Miss Buckley. You won me over first, the moment I found you here, picking your way along the precarious edges of your glorious, wild life."

The wind carried the shawl up and into the tree, on a gust of celebration.

And that's what Viola saw last before Silas kissed her again.

What do you see, Poupette? How does it make you feel?

Now, Viola knew. She felt and heard and saw and knew. She was home.

39

February 23, 1880

I have learne• to travel with my Everlasting Journal. Wherever I go, I slip it in my artist's valise, for it is as constant as any part of my apparel.

This Everlasting carries all my heartaches an• now, my heartbeats, •esperate to be forme• into letters. Sometimes razor sharp. Always honest an• •eep. It is a mirror of wor•s set in scrolls of ink.

I •ip here now, while Silas an• Molly play with a set of woo•en spoons. I am back in my ol• room, where I have often come to capture what was lost. Now, the lost has returne• an• capture• me.

Silas is here. He tells me it was not enough for him to have love• me an• let me go. His brothers strive to a•• to their business in their unique ways, an• he has left them to execute one of his •eepest longings, so that he may fin• me again ~ his •eepest longing.

He has aske• me to become his wife an• make a home with him in a house he •reams of buil•ing for us in Portlan•. But no promise of bricks an• mortar, no promise of a far-off location, can beat what Silas has •one to recover what lay burie• between us.

Sifte• by Go• into a place of true contentment, I have become the prize that Silas sought. An• he is the fruit of my waiting.

I am love• by someone who walke• away from his •reams to

take me back into them.

No matter the crucibles of life, I shall do the same for him.

For if he has come this far to gather me in, at great cost, I know he is the one I want to carry me close.

The Melbourne Gazette

October 17, 1880

A curious turn of events occurred at the Melbourne International Exhibition this week.

Miss Viola Buckley, originally from Melbourne, has won second prize in the Local Artists category with her entry, *From Sea to Shore, The Beauty of Phillip Island*.

Miss Buckley, now Mrs. Silas Swift of Portland, Oregon, was not present to accept her award. She now resides with her husband in America, where she is making a name for herself as a portrait painter, and recently found acclaim for her study of Oregon's Cobra Lily.

Scholars who have studied at Miss Viola Buckley's Art Academy were at the Exhibition Building to cheer on her behalf, a high number of whom also achieved notable mentions in the amateur categories. Of curious interest, however, is this artist was also awarded a first prize, not for her customary botanical paintings or for one of her children's curio portraits, many of which adorn Melbourne homes, but for her ornithological study of a pink galah standing proud on the open door of an empty birdcage.

Suitably titled, *Freedom.*

Author Note

The story of *Carry Me Close* began as a tribute to the healing forces of the sea. I am among many who have walked the beach in prayer and sifted through my thoughts while the wind pummeled my back and pushed me on. Devoted historians may recognize the troubles islanders suffered when the Acclimatization Society introduced rabbits and deer to Phillip Island in the late 1800s. The deer no longer taunt us, but the bunnies remain in their burrows. Current islanders and visitors alike will know Swan Lake, where the local wildlife continues to enjoy freshwater and land dedicated to their protection.

Blue Wren House is inspired by **Glen Isla**, the heritage-listed property just outside Cowes. In the gardens there grows a tree that for many years stood unidentified. Botanical analysis has recently concluded it probably snuck on to the island as an acorn in the American kit home that became **Glen Isla House**. This little *solved mystery* caused me to ponder what else might have stowed away among the many planks of wood and building supplies. I chose a navigational piece of equipment because it meant I could draw on celestial wonders which would have appealed to a visiting American, searching for what he'd lost, among the treasures of another world.

In the Victorian era, seaside therapy was a prescribed remedy for those who required a quiet place to recover from surgery or recuperate from illness or injury. Sea air and saltwater bathing have always proved therapeutic for mind, body, and soul. Rest cure, on the other hand, treated ailments of the nervous system by isolating a patient to mind-numbing inactivity and a diet high in fatty foods. Prescribed mainly for women, some doctors believed rest cure would erase anxieties associated with reproductive complaints, hormonal irregularities, and other conditions too mysterious to diagnose and often cast in the 'female issues' category.

My research into Victorian era treatments led me to discover the terrifying cold water therapy employed to break the sufferer of *melancholia*, known to modern day readers as *depression*. While many Victorian era patients often become worse, and, in some cases, died from the 'cure,' the pendulum has swung and cold water bathing is now employed for sports recovery as well as a general therapeutic practice. Those who would like to know more of what Victorian era women were forced to suffer in the pursuit of physical and mental health may like to read Charlotte Perkins Steton's short story, *The Yellow Wallpaper*, as well as *Of Fat and Blood*, by S. Weir Mitchell, which I used to fashion Dr. Murdoch's restorative manual.

Viola's story is a seed I have carried since my teen years, after I witnessed the tragic drowning of a boy at my local high school. On the advice of their doctor, his parents conceived another child ~ a way for the grieving mother to shake her addiction to antidepressants. I often wondered if the replacement baby, a girl, met with her parents' expectations.

This led me to wonder ~ ***What if a child never fills the void for which it was born?***

And so, the story of Clemmie and Marshall and their two Violas came to life. I hung their dramas onto the theater world which sprang into great flight after the Australian goldrush of the 1850s. Leo and Nasrin Karoly are the embodiment of the many musicians and artists who sang their way to Australia from Europe and established

Melbourne's theater district. Melbourne's famous *Chloe* in the Young and Jackson Hotel was the loose inspiration for the *Sweet Clementine* painting, although I draped a diaphanous layer of modesty over my Clemmie. The preaching of Goliah Ashe and that of the unnamed wise owl in Melbourne is inspired by the sermons of British Victorian era pastor, C.H. Spurgeon.

Silas Swift brought to the page all the angst of being a firstborn as well as the accumulated burdens that come from a life of many wrong turns. Clementine Buckley brought the ache of being a mother who failed to get it right but desperately wished she'd done better. In an era where women were taught their propensity for failure was the direct outcome of the insufficiency of their brain weight, some women, like dear Clemmie, had no way of reaching for deliverance. Broken by heartache, addicted to opiates, condemned for her moral failings, no wonder she became stuck in the sinking spiral of her memories.

Viola Buckley added her own failings and regrets to a story I hope captures the desire we all hold to remain faithful to our values, and ... sometimes... even admit we've grown wiser, abandoning wonky beliefs for something sturdier. For many, this kind of outpouring of the heart often falls into the words of a journal. This is why I gave all three Blue Wren Shallows heroines their own Everlasting Journal, to examine their hidden thoughts, shared with you, dearest reader. Perhaps, you, too, have spilled your words onto a page and seen them in new light.

Viola's is a story of faith refined, of hope refashioned, and love reimagined.

My hope, as the author of *Carry Me Close*, is that somewhere in this story you have also brushed with faith, hope, and love.

About the Author

Australian author, Dorothy Adamek, writes Displacement Fiction ~ the stories of people upended by trauma and tragedy, and the struggle to belong in their new worlds. Couched in romance, her fiction is set in the late Victorian era. She lives at Crabapple House in Melbourne with her Beloved, twenty fruit trees and Gilbert the Cat. She loves black and white floors, collects blue and white china, and makes apricot jam every summer. Her favourite holiday destination is Phillip Island, the real life setting of the Blue Wren Shallows series ~ ***Carry Me Home***, ***Carry Me Away***, and ***Carry Me Close***.

Dear Reader, thank you for reading ***Carry Me Close***. Would you please consider writing a review? Authors love reviews because the more reviews a book receives, the greater its discoverability. Your reader feedback is the last step in this story-journey we've taken together… for which I am ever grateful.

For the latest updates and exclusive book release announcements please join my READER GROUP at dorothyadamek.com. I can't wait to meet you there.

Carry Me Home
Book 1 Blue Wren Shallows

Finella Mayfield hates two things: liars and thieves. And she's determined to marry a man who's neither. Chasing her dead father's dreams, the twenty-year-old English bride arrives in Australia in 1875 for an arranged marriage. Anticipating her future as village preacher's wife, she records her thoughts in her Everlasting journal.

But instead of her fiancé, Finella is met by Shadrach Jones, a poor farmer sent to collect her from the busy Melbourne pier.

This is not what her father planned. And it's only the beginning of the unraveling of Finella Mayfield - the bride with no groom.

All Shadrach Jones longs for is rows of mustard and chicory. He's busy growing a farm near the Phillip Island fishing village of Cowes, and caring for Molly, his simple sister. Far from the brutal life they remember with their ex-convict father, Shadrach's building something new.

But he's also made a promise to a dying friend. To collect and marry the English girl destined to never be a preacher's wife.

Can Shadrach convince Finella she has a future with a farmer? Can he convince himself, knowing his family secrets will haunt their future?

Carry Me Home - Book 1 in the Blue Wren Shallows series. An Australian historical romance set in the pioneering era of the 1870s, on Victoria's majestic Phillip Island.

Carry Me Away
Book 2 Blue Wren Shallows

When the Black Swallow sinks off the Australian coast in 1877, Australian midshipman Tom Darley rescues English passenger Ada Carmichael from the disaster that claims her entire family. News of the only two survivors enchants the world, but Ada needs to hide before secrets and old foes find her. Tom is chasing big dreams of a crumbling house he will convert into a small hotel ~ but the promising start he's acquired now sits at the bottom of the sea.

Inexplicably entangled, Ada and Tom lean upon each other to make sense of the tragedy that's displaced them. But when scheming journalists observe their affection they drag Tom into life-altering riches and a news-worthy romance he cannot resist. So he arranges for Ada's protection where only he might find her ~ the quiet Phillip Island farm of his friends Shadrach and Finella Jones.

And that's where real trouble finds them. When heroic promises fail to shelter, and love refuses to be silenced, only surrender will pluck Ada and Tom from where life has wrecked them.

Made in the USA
Middletown, DE
02 April 2022

63527496R00239